Tirade

Heven and Hell #3

By Cambria Hebert

Published by: Cambria Hebert

http://www.cambriahebert.com

Interior design and typesetting by Sharon Kay
Cover design by MAE I DESIGN
Edited by Amy Eye and Cassie McCown
Copyright 2012 by Cambria Hebert

Paperback ISBN: 978-1-938857-06-5

eBook ISBN: 978-1-938857-07-2

Dedication

I dedicate this book to my husband, Shawn. This book has always been special to me, but you made it more so by gracing the cover with your handsome face.

Acknowledgements

I can't believe I am wrapping up my third novel in this series. It seems like just yesterday I was getting to know Heven and trying to pry secrets out of Sam. Since I began writing *Tirade*, it has always been special to me. I am not really sure why. I think because I like where the characters go. I like watching them grow and change, I like the plot and poor Heven really has to overcome a lot in this book. Plus, there is Riley. I would like to acknowledge Riley. Riley Stone makes me smile, he makes me laugh and I love writing him. He kind of snuck up on me, but I am so glad he did. He's also an attention hoarder. He likes to try and steal the spotlight and he likes to bug me for things like motorcycles and tattoos. Still, I'm glad he's in my head.

I want to thank my husband Shawn—yes, I always thank him—but this time for different reasons. He gave a face to Riley, sat through several photo shoots, and paraded around in the yard with a red hood with fur on it—all for the sake of the cover. You may embarrass our daughter with your chest hair, but I think you make Riley look hot.

To my son Nathan, who keeps life interesting and reminds me to laugh when you wear socks in the shower, "forget" to wash your hair, and make me have *Beywheelz* races in the kitchen. To my daughter Kaydence, who paints my toes, wears my shoes and sets up shop to make me pumpkin bread and lattes. I can't wait to see you on the very next cover, and you are right… chest hair is gross (and so is armpit hair).

A shout out to my Street Team newly named "Cambria's Hellions." You all come by that name honestly, hahaha. You also make me laugh, cheer me on and encourage me to wear thongs on my head (or was that my idea?).

Big thanks to Jennifer Pringle for telling me I need a handler because I need someone to tell me to quit worrying and just believe a little more. You've brought a little Zen to my life and we all need a little Zen.

Speaking of Zen… I would like to thank Lipton tea makers for their Ginger Twist Tea. Every time I make a cup (several times a day!) I see the little messages on the tea packets like "Ginger Tea In; Stress Out" and I feel a little better.

I never thought I would actually enjoy having a stalker—but I do! Maghon Thomas, you are the only stalker that I have ever encouraged (I usually call the police!). Thank you for helping me get reviews, for hosting me endlessly on your blog, and for always being there with positive words and encouragement. You are always willing to help and you never ask for anything in return. Also, to Gladys Atwell, for believing in me and my series and telling me when I need to stab myself with a pencil (I often feel the need!) to make sure it's not mechanical but a solid #2.

Big acknowledgements to Cassie McCown and Amy Eye, the editors of this masterpiece (like I would call it junk!). Thank you both for helping me make this novel into everything it could be and spending hours working to make it great. Regina Wamba, your cover designs get better every time and I am so glad to work with you. I can hardly wait to see what you come up with next!

To my fellow writing buddies, Tish Thawer (*The Rose Trilogy*) and Heather Hildenbrand (*Dirty Blood Series*), thank you both for taking my emails, answering my questions, and helping me navigate the choppy waters of publishing. It's so wonderful to be surrounded by such talent. You make me work harder.

And finally, to my fans, thank you all so much for the emails, messages and posts! Keep reading!

Tirade

Chapter One

Sam

Seconds feel like hours, minutes feel like days and days... Days feel like eternity.

Being a prisoner of hell sucks. Endlessly.

All day long I pace inside this dark, tiny, cell... And I think. The thing about the dark is that it takes away distractions. Distractions that allowed me to ignore all the things I wanted to ignore. I liked myself better when I didn't have to think. How easy it is to act without thinking, to let your feelings guide you. I've done a lot of reacting to my situation—to Heven's situation. I've done a lot of things I would like to forget. But forgetting isn't an option when all you can do is think. Unfortunately, thinking changes things.

It changes you.

My reaction the first time I laid eyes on Heven was so strong—so all-encompassing that she was all I saw—all I wanted to see. But time's passed... And while I still love her like that first day, it's grown deeper and stronger. She's grown stronger. She doesn't need me to do the things I've done in the past because we can fight together.

Only we aren't together. I'm stuck in this hole and she's up there facing God knows what. I've never been helpless before. I've never needed a rescue. I'm not supposed to be weak. I'm the strong one. I always knew Heven was strong. I just never thought it was me she was going to have to be strong for.

Heven

On the outskirts of the orchard lies a long divot in the ground, a long, winding dent that swivels in the earth. If it wasn't dry, I would call it the perfect place for a curving stream. In this divot, a single apple tree grew, its twisting limbs stretching into the sky, reaching out like gnarled fingers trying to grasp its prey. The sky seemed to ignore the demands of the brittle branches while it turned a peachy pink in the early twilight hours.

It was beside this tree that I lay hidden.

But I was not afraid.

Pressing my ear to the earth, which felt cool and smooth against my skin, I concentrated with everything in me. My eyes narrowed, the only indication my tense, waiting body gave that I knew someone was headed this way.

It took them longer than I thought to find me.

I closed my eyes and did something that came as easily to me as breathing. I conjured a perfect image of Sam in my mind. He was so real and breathtaking sitting right there behind my eyes that, for a moment, he took my breath away. This was the real reason I was lying here. *He* was the reason for everything I did these days. Well, him *and* revenge for everything that's been done to everyone I love. Gripping the daggers in each palm, I waited, coiled and ready to face my opponents.

One, two, three…

I leapt out of the ground with all the force I possessed and caught the first attacker by surprise.

Exactly as I planned.

The muffled curse made my lips curve in a sadistic sort of smile as I launched myself, daggers extended, straight forward. My boot landed solid in my opponent's chest and we went down. Both my daggers tore into the earth on either side of my attacker's head, missing the skull by mere centimeters.

Our eyes met.

The person under me smiled.

I remained as I was. *Never let your guard down.* I reminded myself.

"Very good," Gemma said, motioning for me to let her up.

I did so without turning my back or relaxing my stance. She laughed as she got to her feet. But I knew it was a ruse, an attempt to get me to let down my guard.

I spun on my heel and threw a boot out, my foot connecting with something solid. He went down with a curse, but I didn't stop there. I brought my hand down in a chopping motion across the new assailant's back and heard a groan. Keeping with my momentum, I kicked out my other foot underneath his ribcage and sent him all the way to the grass. A steel dagger sank into the ground right beside his face.

"I win."

Cole rolled to his back. His face was red and streaked with dirt. "Damn, Heven."

I toed the thick padding he wore around his body to protect him from my attack. He laughed when I first suggested he wear it.

He wasn't laughing now.

"I told you," I said, pulling the dagger up and wiping off the dirt on my pants. "I'm not playing around."

"I see that," he said, getting to his feet.

"I'm ready," I stated and turned to Gemma. There was humor in her wide grey eyes.

"One perfect fight doesn't make you ready for war."

One perfect fight was all I needed. I pushed myself hard these last few days, further than I ever thought I could go. I wasn't about to let up now.

"I'm ready," I told her again, my body language dared her to defy me.

"It's your funeral," she stated, shrugging.

I ignored Cole's sharp indrawn breath and began walking back to the orchard.

As long as it wasn't Sam's funeral, I didn't care.

* * *

My arms shook and burned, yet I refused to stop. I refused to give up. When I hit my desired number, I wanted to collapse on the ground, but I didn't. Instead, I stood, shaking my arms out a little. Cole had followed me back to the orchard and stood over me with his arms crossed over his chest, staring at me in disapproving silence. In a strange way, his foul mood only made me more determined.

"How many was that?" he asked, disgruntled.

"I'm surprised you didn't count," I answered, mildly amused.

"Counting how many push-ups you can do is not what I call a good time."

Yet, he stood over me while I did them every day. I lifted a brow and he scowled. "Twenty-two," I said, then sighed. Tomorrow I would do twenty-five. I bent and scooped up the daggers I had been working with earlier and carried them over to Gemma and her never-ending bag of weapons.

I threw everything in the bag, stopping when I got to the last dagger. It was a little heavier than the others, but otherwise, it looked the same. It was fashioned out of solid steel and was tarnished and scuffed from repeated use. It wasn't as pretty as the enchanted dagger Gemma gave to Cole to carry when we were in Italy. The one that somehow housed the pure, bright light of heaven and saved our butts more than once. I should've known it was special the first time I saw it with its jeweled handle and rainbow-colored gemstone at its base. Yet, I hadn't realized what it was capable of until my photographic memory pulled up an image of it from an ancient drawing in the Catacomb of San Sebastiano when we were in Rome. Turns out when you stab the dagger into something and press the gem, a blinding white light is released, so powerful it destroys whatever is being stabbed from the inside out.

"What is it?" Gemma asked from beside me.

I looked back down at the plain dagger in my hand. It had been Sam's favorite. He chose it every time he trained with Gemma. I closed my eyes and called up a prefect image of it clasped in his hand. I used the memory to mirror how he held it. Knowing my hand was in exactly the same place that his had once been gave me comfort.

"Can I keep this one?" I asked Gemma, my voice turning hoarse. I cleared my throat and straightened my shoulders, sorry for my moment of weakness.

"Of course." She gave no indication she knew how my insides were churning.

"Thanks."

"Let's get some lunch," Cole said, coming up behind us.

"Can't," I told him. "I'm heading to the hospital to see my mom."

"Want me to come with?"

"No. You and Gemma stay here, go through the books. We have to find a way to retrieve a Lucent Marble and get through the portal to hell without a hellhound."

"I've been through those books a thousand times over the years," Gemma said, looking over at a large leather bag that contained three large leather-bound books.

"Then you aren't looking hard enough!" I snapped. Gemma's face didn't change, but instantly I felt guilty. "I'm sorry, I didn't mean that." I was yelling at one of the only people who had been working tirelessly to help me get Sam back. On day two of Sam being trapped in hell, Gemma offered up the books that are hundreds of years old. They contain knowledge I wouldn't be able to get anywhere else, including the internet (finally proof that Google does not know it all!). They contained fact after fact about heaven and hell, how they were created and all the information about what most people today would think are merely myths. From some of the stuff I've read, I've come to think it's better if most people do think of this stuff as myth. Otherwise, everyone would be afraid to come out of their houses.

Gemma was hoping there might be something in there we could use to help get Sam back. So far, we hadn't found anything but more proof of how hard it would be to go up against Beelzebub, AKA the Prince of Demons, and Hecate, the original witch of hell.

"I get it," Gemma said, brushing off my mood.

"No." I laid a hand on her arm. "You've been nothing but helpful and supportive. You didn't deserve that. I'm just so frustrated."

"It's not a big deal." Gemma shrugged off my arm and stepped back. She didn't know how to act when someone showed they cared for her. I had a feeling she spent a lot of years pushing people away and not getting close to anyone because of something in her past.

Cole glanced at me, then back at Gemma. "You go. I'll stay here and help Gemma look through the books one more time."

Gemma nodded. "I'll look again, even though I know there isn't an answer in that book. You need a hellhound or something else that is incapable of drowning and strong enough to swim to the bottom of all the sludge they call water."

I blew out a frustrated breath.

"Why don't we just free Sam and then let him get the marbles?" Cole said. It was an idea he kept on voicing.

And I kept on saying no. "We can't do that, Cole. He's been trapped down there for five days. Five! Before we killed the demon that had been living inside Logan, it sliced his arm with a dagger. He's exhausted and I'm pretty sure he has some broken ribs." I know because I can feel his pain through our Mindbond. "Not to mention, they are hardly feeding him and I will not risk his safety down there for one single second longer than I have to. I have to have those marbles because the second he's out of that cell, I'm busting them open and we're getting out of there."

"You may not have a choice," Cole said darkly.

"I have to go," I said tersely, not wanting to admit what Cole was saying might be true. "We'll meet up later?"

Gemma nodded and I left without a glance at Cole. I wouldn't fight with my brother. I had bigger battles to fight. Like ones down in hell.

Even still, I wondered if it would be enough.

* * *

I stopped outside his bedroom door, taking a deep breath and smoothing out my wrinkled T-shirt. Logan had been here, at Gran's, for five days, and in those five days, I spent time with him every single day, some days twice. Usually, if I wasn't training or with my mom at the hospital, I was here with Logan. But even with all the time I spent with him, there was still a wide valley between us. We weren't getting closer. I wondered if Logan would even accept my presence if I wasn't his link to Sam.

I tried to tell myself he seemed so distant because he was so weak and sick. He had been possessed by a powerful demon, a demon that made everyone, including me and Sam, believe Logan was a hellhound. Even Logan thought he was. No one could figure out why he didn't act like a normal one (if there is a normal for a such a beast), like why he didn't love the water, why shifting literally ripped his body apart every single time with intense pain and why he would black out and not remember anything.

I had been through a lot in my seventeen years, but Logan was only fourteen and I'd never been possessed by a demon. I figure that gave him reason to be distant—especially from me.

When the demon left his body—it literally left a dying boy with broken pieces we had to put back together like a puzzle. His bones, which had been broken and realigned several times, had never healed right. The angles of his joints were slightly off and therefore his skin looked lumpy in places where the bones stretched the skin. He wasn't as coordinated as he should've been, and when he walked, it was never in a straight line but always at an angle. His skin was pale, making me think that he lost too much blood when Sam was forced to stab him with a dagger. His body was so weak; he just couldn't produce more blood so he was left with nothing more than a ghostly pallor. Beyond that, he was too thin and could hardly eat, like his stomach had shrunk. The only thing he seemed to have an appetite for was candy—which we supplied in full force. After all he'd been through, I wanted him to have something that brought him some joy. Even if it was short-lived and not what he truly wanted.

I lifted my hand and knocked; the door swung open. Logan was on the bed, watching TV. I averted my gaze away from his bumpy knee caps and looked at his face. "Hey, Logan!" I said, walking the rest of the way in and plopping down on the corner of his bed.

"Have you talked to Sam today?" he asked, his eyes sliding away from the TV toward me, then back again.

"Sure have. He's still okay. Is there anything you want me to tell him?" I never wanted to sound too optimistic about where Sam was because he was hardly on vacation. He was trapped in hell and Logan knew everything wasn't good, but I never wanted to make it sound like Sam was suffering either. I had a feeling Logan blamed himself for Sam's entrapment. Well, himself *and* me.

"You're all dirty. Were you in the orchard?" Logan asked, still watching the TV.

"Yes, training with Gemma. I'm going to go visit my mom in a few minutes. Want to come?"

"No," he said quickly, shifting on the bed. He never wanted to come to the hospital with me. I never pushed it because I figured the place made him uncomfortable, but I always offered because he needed to know I wanted him around.

"Okay, then. Maybe we can go out for ice cream later? Or rent a movie?"

"You don't have to be nice to me," he said, looking at me and for the first time today, holding my gaze.

"I know that. I like you, Logan. I like hanging out with you."

"You just want to look good with Sam."

I let out a breath. "I don't see Sam around here, do you? If I didn't want to spend time with you, I wouldn't, and he wouldn't know anyway. This isn't about Sam. This is about me and you."

He nodded, his face losing the angry look. "I guess you aren't as bad as I thought."

"Of course I'm not." I flipped my hair backward with a grin. "I'm fabulous."

"You need a shower. You smell."

I let my mouth drop open in mock surprise and stepped away from the bed. Then I leaned close and I hugged him, rubbing my arms up, down, and all around him.

"Nasty!" Logan said, pushing me away.

"Just a little sisterly love for you." I laughed and pulled away. Logan was trying not to smile. "I gotta go. I'll be back later and we'll hang."

His eyes went back to the TV, but as I left the room, he called a thank you behind me.

* * *

My feet felt as though they were weighed down with bricks. I lifted my knees higher and forced my leg muscles to move. When the hospital came into view, I pushed myself harder, increasing my pace until my lungs burned and sweat blurred my vision. At the edge of the parking lot, I slowed until I was walking. I refused to let myself double over to gasp for breath. Instead, I concentrated on taking deep, controlled breaths. By the time I reached the large sliding doors at the entrance, my heart rate was down and breathing came easily. I glanced at my watch. Forty minutes. It was good, but I wanted to be better. Since day two of Sam being gone, I had been parking Gran's car several miles from the hospital every day and running the rest of the way. Every day my time got a little better.

The cool air of the hospital felt good against my heated skin as I entered and gave a small wave to the woman manning the information desk. She returned my wave, then went back to answering the phone. She knew I wouldn't stop to chat anyway. I never did. She also finally stopped gaping at my sweaty appearance every time I walked in. I didn't care either way.

I made my way up to my mother's floor and let myself into her room. The curtain around her bed was left open today and I was greeted with the same sight that I always saw: Mom lying in a bed of white in a coma. There was no change. I wondered if there ever would be. The doctors said the swelling in her brain, from the fall she took, was gone and there was nothing medically keeping her from waking up. They said she'd make a full recovery. But as the days passed and Mom never opened her eyes, I saw them standing over her frowning, searching through her chart for something they might have missed.

I couldn't tell them I knew the truth. I knew why she wasn't waking up.

Beelzebub wouldn't let her. I couldn't prove it, of course, but I just knew he was holding some kind of power over her and her well-being. Who only knew what he did to her during the time he was posing as her "boyfriend" Henry.

"Hi, Mom," I said, approaching the bed and adjusting the covers around her. It didn't need done, but it was better than doing nothing. "How are you feeling today? You look good. Are you ready to wake up yet?"

The only response I got was the beeping of her monitors. I sighed and headed into the bathroom. The cold water felt good as I splashed it over my face and hands. I reached into my backpack and pulled out my face wash, using it to cleanse the morning of training away. I grabbed the hand towel at the sink to dry my face and hands, then hung it back where it belonged. Next, I reached into my backpack and pulled out a change of clothes. The ones I wore were damp with sweat and were covered in streaks of dirt from my time spent in the orchard. After I pulled on the blue-jean shorts and white tee, I brushed my hair back into a ponytail. Most of my hair was damp with sweat and needed washed, but for now, a ponytail would do. After I finished, I threw everything back in my backpack and headed out to sit with Mom. I talked to her for a few minutes as I always did, but soon grew tired of talking to myself. I settled back in the chair with a bottle of water (also from my bag) and closed my eyes.

Sam.

Heven. I couldn't help but smile when his voice purred through my mind.

I'm at the hospital with Mom. No change.

I'm sorry.

At least she isn't worse. You doing okay?

I've been trying to break down this force field that's trapping me in here.

Any luck?

No. I felt the surge of his anger and disappointment as if they were my own. I also felt the echo of hunger pangs through my middle and the sting of a row of broken ribs at my side.

I swallowed back the despair that filled me. *We're still trying to find a way to get through the portal.*

I don't want you to come back here. I'll find a way out.

But he wouldn't. He knew it and I knew it. There was no way to break down the invisible barrier that Hecate used to trap him inside. He'd been trying for five days without any luck. I had an idea of how I could break down the force field—but I also had no idea if it would actually work. Even still, I didn't know how to get through the portal into hell. *How are your wounds?*

Healing. Don't worry about me. What about you?

I'm fine.

I feel the echo of soreness in your entire body. What's going on?

I started running. My muscles are sore.

Any demon trouble?

No. I prayed he didn't hear the lie in my voice. I felt guilty for lying, but telling him the truth would only make things worse for him.

Where's the scroll?

It's somewhere safe.

Dammit, Heven.

You know I can't tell you. If I tell you, he'll come get it. Then he'll have no reason to leave you alive.

He wants me alive because he knows you'll come back for me.

I felt the anger and the frustration in his words but didn't know how to expel any of his worry. He was right. Beelzebub wasn't keeping Sam alive for the scroll. He was keeping him alive for revenge.

Revenge against me.

Any sign of him yet?

No.

Right before Hecate imprisoned Sam, I tricked Beelzebub and pushed him into a scorching pit of flames. I thought that would be the end of him, but Hecate cackled and told me she couldn't wait to see what my punishment would be for doing that to him. Apparently, the Prince of Demons was immortal. And powerful. And he wanted me to rule in hell with him.

I shuddered.

How's Logan doing? Sam asked.

He seemed good this morning—better than usual.

Maybe he's turning the corner.

Maybe.

We sat in silence for a few moments while I pondered what it would do to Sam if Logan didn't recover from this.

Is it almost nighttime there yet?

My heart constricted as it always did when he asked me such questions. I can't imagine how he's been keeping sane these past days, shut up in a tiny cell without food, barely any water and no concept of time.

You keep me sane, he answered.

I wanted to kick myself for thinking such thoughts when he was close enough to my mind to hear them. I didn't want him to know how sick all of this made me. I didn't want him to worry about me at all.

It won't be nighttime for a few hours, I said apologetically. I lived for the night too. Somehow being driven apart strengthened our Mindbond even more, well, that and when he went into my mind to break the thread that Beelzebub put there to get into my dreams. Somehow, our connection strengthened. On day three we figured out that we could link our minds as we were drifting off to sleep and it almost felt as if he was lying next to me.

I felt his disappointment and thought about taking a nap just so we could be close. I opened my eyes and sat forward in my chair, looking at the curtain that was pulled back around Mom's bed. It concealed the other side of the room from view. I knew there was another bed there and I got up, telling myself that maybe a short nap wouldn't take up too much time. I pulled the curtain back and went toward the bed, taking the sheet and blanket in my hand to pull back.

It took everything I had not to scream loudly when I looked down. There was a demon lying in the bed beneath the covers. He was flat… like a pancake. It's the reason the covers hadn't looked lumpy. His skin was as white as the sheets, but his eyes were coal black and looked like big round saucers in his flat head. I jumped back as his body began to fill with air… He looked like a balloon being filled at a helium tank.

I stumbled backward, grabbing onto the curtain that separated the room and I tripped, pulling part of the curtain off the track as I fell backward onto the floor.

The demon, fully inflated now, sprung up off the bed and towered over me. It had fingernails that looked like claws and I was alarmed that its eyes didn't look any smaller now that its head was bigger. If anything, they looked wider and more empty than before.

He reached for me and I made a sound, yanking the curtain off the track even more and bringing it down over his head. He flailed around, making some grunting sounds as he tried to pull the sheet off. I looked around frantically for something to use as a weapon and saw something made of metal under the bed. I grabbed it as he flung the sheet away.

I sprang to my feet and swung, hitting him hard upside the head with the metal bedpan. The demon fell sideways onto the bed, and I took the opportunity to hit him again. He grabbed my arm when I tried to move away and pulled me closer. His nasty claws dug into my wrist, but I resisted the urge to cry out. The last thing I needed was to try to explain this to a nurse.

I yanked my arm, trying to get free, but it was no use. Looks like I was going to have to beat this guy's inflated butt with one hand.

I grabbed the rolling table beside my mother's bed and glided it across the floor, ramming it into the demon's middle. The force of the hit caused him to release my arm. I grabbed a fork from the untouched tray, shoved the cart aside and threw myself at the demon. I landed on top of him, pinning him to the bed. Before he could do anything, I shoved the fork into his chest.

He disintegrated beneath me and I was left on a pile of fine dust.

I looked at the fork still clutched in my hand. It made a pretty good weapon. I stuck it in my back pocket—a girl in my situation never knew when she might need a fork.

I glanced over my shoulder at my mother. The commotion failed to wake her. I climbed off the bed and did my best to spread the demon dust around the room. Hopefully, someone would just think the room needed a good cleaning. There wasn't much I could do about the curtain I ripped from the track in the ceiling, so I just folded it up and put it on the bed (which I remade).

What's happening? Sam asked.

I tripped and fell and pulled the curtain out of the ceiling. I'm wondering what the nurses are going to think.

You tripped and fell? He asked. I could hear the skepticism in his voice.

Well, it was a little more involved than that, but it's nothing to worry about.

Heven… Sam growled.

I thought about reassuring him that I was fine. But I don't think he would be happy to hear I was using a fork as a weapon. *I have to go before the nurse comes in here and wants to know what happened to her curtain.*

I'll be here if you want to talk.

Me too. I told him before spending a few more moments making sure the room was as close to the way it originally was, then kissed Mom's cheek and grabbed my bag. This hospital room was closing in on me and I was putting her in danger by being here. Down at the information desk, a security guard stood flirting with the lady behind the desk. It was funny because he was old enough to be her father. When he saw me step off the elevator, he straightened and smiled. I smiled back and together we walked out into the sunshine. His patrol car was at the curb. It was some generic model that looked a lot like a police car except the words HOSPITAL SECURITY were emblazoned on the sides.

"How's your mom doing, kid?" He always referred to me as 'kid' even though I told him my name several times. I thought this was funny, too, because the girl he was just flirting with was closer to my age than his. I bet he never called her kid.

"No change."

"Sorry to hear that." His words were genuine, as was his aura. It was a good color full of orange (which was uplifting and inspiring) and turquoise (energizing and dynamic). His name was Colin Sturgess and I met him on day two of Sam being gone.

I had come to visit Mom as I did today, parking miles (that day it was three) away from the hospital. When I got there, I was so sweaty and beet-red the woman at the information desk thought I was coming in to be seen at the emergency room. It would have been funny if it didn't speak volumes as to how out of shape I was and just how bad I looked after everything happened. I was trying to convince her that I didn't need medical attention and that the wound on my cheek was fine (it's still kind of raw, but its healing— AKA turning into a scar) when Colin walked by and stepped in to tell her that, clearly, I just needed some cold water and a seat. He was a friendly man whose skin crinkled around his eyes when he smiled and his hair was gray at the temples. He had broad shoulders and was tall, but his middle had gone soft probably years before.

The pair made me sit there at her desk until I drank half a bottle of water, explained to them that I was there to visit my mother and that I had decided to take up running because I thought it was a good use of time to do it on the way to the hospital.

The lady at the desk thought I was crazy.

Colin laughed and said he liked my style.

He walked me to my mother's room (partly because he didn't believe my story about her even being there), then asked me how I planned to get back to my car. I was completely dumbfounded. I hadn't even thought about getting back to my car and I wasn't up for another three-mile run in the afternoon sun. He saw the stricken look on my face and volunteered to drive me to my car.

He's been doing it ever since.

I gazed out the window at the passing greenery and thought about how very long ago that seemed. Yet, it had only been three days.

"Parked a little farther away today?" Colin asked when we passed the spot I had parked yesterday.

"Yeah, it's just ahead down here." I pointed.

"Are you training for a 10K or something?"

"I, uh, want to run track at school. I'm trying to get my run time down over the summer."

He nodded appreciatively. "That's a real good thing to be into. Keeps you out of trouble."

If he only knew. Gran's car came into view and I gathered up my backpack and fished the keys from my pocket. "Thank you for the ride."

"Sure thing, kid." He grinned and popped a piece of Trident in his mouth. "Gum?" He tilted the pack in my direction.

"No, thanks."

He tucked the pack back into the pocket of his shirt and saluted me. "See you tomorrow, kid."

"My name is Heven," I grumbled, climbing out of his cruiser.

"I know." He laughed. It was a merry sound and I found myself smiling.

He waited, as he always does, until I was in my car with the engine running before he pulled away. I did a U-turn and headed back the way I came. Hopefully, Cole and Gemma had found something in the books that we overlooked before.

The interior of the car was hot from sitting in the sun and I leaned forward to adjust the air-conditioning. When I straightened, I glanced in the rearview mirror and let out a scream.

A huge, black demon filled the back seat.

As I stared, he lifted his hand, revealing a gleaming row of razor-sharp claws.

Chapter Two

Sam

I have known pain. I have known longing. I have known death.

But this, I have never known this. To be confined… day after day, to hear silence so loud that I want to slap my hands over my ears and scream just for relief. To have my bones continuously knock against my skin because they are vibrating with the force of my anger.

I feel caged. Frustrated.

Damned.

I may be a hellhound, but this is the first time I've ever *felt* like an animal.

I paced the small "room," my hands clenched into fists, and considered my options for the millionth time. I wouldn't give up. But the truth… The truth of the matter was I really was trapped.

With a burst of overwhelming frustration, I hurled myself at the doorway again. I hit the solid, yet invisible, force field with a loud crack and I stumbled backward. A warm, metallic taste filled my mouth. I'd bitten my tongue. I vaguely wondered if blood was considered calories—for anyone other than a vampire. My stomach rumbled at the thought of food… I had never been this hungry before. I had never known this kind of gut-gnawing, consistent pain through my abdomen as my body searched for something… something other than what it was getting.

That thought cut off all thoughts of food. The last thing I wanted to do was think about what I had been eating in order to stay alive. I glanced back at the force field, angry at the way it taunted me. The cell I was trapped in didn't have a door like the other cells in the dungeon because I had destroyed it the first time Hecate flung me in here; so it appeared that there was nothing holding me in. It appeared that I could just walk right on out whenever I wanted. But the force field was there… silent but needing no words. Clear but needing no matter. It was virtually nothing, yet encompassed everything.

My body ached from throwing myself against the force field so many times and I sank down to the floor. I glanced down at the cut on my bicep, the result of the demon who had taken up residence inside my little brother. It wasn't healing like it should, but it didn't appear to be getting infected. The entire left side of my ribcage was broken, the result of being thrown into a large rock that jutted out of the nothingness here in hell. They weren't healing like they should, either. Of course, throwing myself into a force field constantly wasn't helping.

Right next to me, a large jug of water appeared out of nowhere. I snatched it up before it could disappear (that happened once—on day two), uncapped it, and took a long, greedy drink. The first swallow scraped the inside of my throat, but I didn't care. I needed this water. I didn't know how long it had been since my last "water allowance," but it had been too long. When half the jug was gone, I forced it from my lips and tucked it in my lap, keeping my hands around it. I should save some for later, in case the next one didn't come for a day or two.

I told myself it was a good thing Hecate (or someone) was making water appear for me. It meant they didn't want me dead. I leaned my head against the wall… No, they didn't want me dead. They wanted me for something else.

For bait.

To get to Heven.

I wondered constantly if she was okay. Yes, I could hear her voice when I wanted. I knew that she wasn't in immediate danger... but that stupid expression played through my head like a broken record. *All good things come to those who wait.*

Is that what was happening? Was Beelzebub waiting, planning... plotting?

I thought about Logan. My little brother who had been through far more than he should ever have to endure. His body was broken—he was weak and probably traumatized. Heven told me about him constantly. I knew she wasn't lying because I knew what bad shape he was in. If she was going to lie, she would have said he was doing better. I knew that once the demon left his body, he should've died. But he didn't. Because Gemma healed him. Sort of.

She closed the dagger wound in his body, she breathed air into his deflated lungs and gave his heart strength to beat, but not even Gemma and all her healing mojo could totally reverse what that demon did to him.

As honest as Heven was being with me about Logan and his physical state, I knew she wasn't telling me everything. She was only trying to protect me. Something I couldn't be mad about because it's all I had done for her since we'd met. I hadn't realized how suffocating being protected could feel.

I was beyond grateful that Logan was staying at Gran's farm. Gran thought Logan got sick and I went to our parent's house to try to talk some sense into them—to find a way to bridge the gap between them and my brother. Gran thought I was fighting to take my brother home where he belonged. But really, I was the one fighting to get home.

I knew Logan was being cared for. If anyone could take care of Logan the way he should be, it was Gran. Heven sat with him day after day, talking with him, relaying our conversation back and forth and trying to build a relationship with hopes they would be close.

It made me feel guilty.

Guilty because of everything Logan put her through, everything he did and said to her when I wasn't looking. Guilty because of her mother. Heven still had no idea Logan was the one who put her mother in the hospital. I couldn't bring myself to tell her. It wasn't because I thought she would refuse to watch over him while I couldn't, but because I knew that she would. She would do it for me just as I would do it for her. The fact was that her knowing would make it harder for her to do what she was doing.

I had to get out of here.

I looked back at the force field once more, wondering what its weakness was. There had to be a weakness. Even the strongest adversaries had weaknesses. I just had to figure out what it was and exploit it.

Heven

My foot hovered over the brake and I wanted so badly to press on it. But I didn't. Slamming on the brakes would jerk that gothic-looking freak even closer to me. I took a deep breath and willed myself to stay in control. *Don't let it know you're afraid.*

It reached for me and I floored the gas, throwing it backward into the seat. It hissed, making it sound inhuman (which, yeah, it was), and I prayed it wasn't one of those demons with a snake for a tongue. Afraid of keeping up the breakneck speed I was driving at, I took my foot off the gas. The car began to decelerate and the demon grinned. He grinned like he had caught me, and he leaned forward (did I mention his teeth were black like his skin?).

There was one good thing.

With his grin I could see that he didn't have a snake for a tongue.

But his teeth looked like pointy black daggers ready to rip the fragile flesh right off my bones.

I grabbed my reusable steel water bottle and slammed it into its face. He screamed and it was the kind of sound that would peel paint off walls. The car swerved into the oncoming lane. I heard the angry honking of another car and jerked the wheel back, just in time to avoid being in yet another car accident.

The demon launched itself at me, coming up into the front of the car, and grabbed the steering wheel, careening the car all around. The tires squealed and my head bounced off the driver's side window. For a second, black dots swam before my eyes and I let go of the wheel. The demon took advantage and seized control of the car, stomping his foot down over mine and driving like a bat out of hell.

Frankly, right now, I would prefer to be facing off against a bat.

He swerved around another oncoming car, narrowly avoiding sideswiping it. Though, I think he was disappointed in his poor aim because he began speeding again. He was going to crash this car, kill me and steal the scroll.

I would not die like this.

If I died, Sam would be trapped in hell forever, Logan would be all alone, and the rest of my family would be left unprotected.

I elbowed the demon and sent him sideways and took back the steering wheel. I guided the car to the side of the road as the demon grabbed my arm and dug in its filthy claws. Blood began to drip down my skin and I cried out, jerking the car to a halt. The sudden stop sent the demon into the dashboard and I reached into my pocket and pulled out the fork. There was no hesitation when I rammed it into its side.

He began screaming. I was so close that spittle from his mouth fell onto my arm as I opened the car door and all but fell out onto the shoulder of the road. I scrambled up and reached in, pulling the demon out into the dirt. He was clutching my bag and I tore it from its grasp and ran, wanting to put some distance between us.

The demon chased me, and as I turned to look over my shoulder, something whizzed by my cheek. It was the fork.

Clearly, it hadn't been strong enough this time.

And I couldn't outrun this one, either.

He slammed his body into mine and we both went down. Unfortunately for me, I broke his fall. He grabbed my bag, yanked it away and began riffling through it. I thought back to something I learned while in Italy and I took aim with my foot and kicked him hard… right in the man parts. He doubled over, thrusting the bag outward. I reached inside to pull out my dagger and I rammed it upward, right into his chest.

He made a grunting sound before he disintegrated. I stood there, breathing hard, as the wind carried away what was left of him.

Note to self: forks are not good weapons to use against all demons, but kicking them in their man parts works every time.

A burning pain in my arm caused me to look down. Along with the rips in my skin from his claws, I had burns from where the demon's spit got on me. It didn't help the wounds were also splattered with black demon blood. I used the hem of my T-shirt to wipe the blood away, but my arm continued to burn. I walked back to Gran's car to grab my water bottle from the floorboard of the backseat and used what was left to rinse off the area in case any poison was left on my skin. I didn't see any, but I wasn't going to leave it up to chance. I inspected the interior of the car for any demon blood or damage from his claws and was beyond thankful when everything appeared to be okay. No way did I want to explain to Gran how I messed up yet another one of her cars.

Weary, I climbed back into the driver's seat, my eyes automatically looking in the rearview mirror toward the backseat. I really hoped that had been the last demon for a while.

* * *

I resisted the urge to reach out to Sam the whole drive home. I wanted to hear his voice, to feel it caress my mind, but I was too afraid that he would know something was wrong.

I wouldn't want to tell him and then he would get frustrated just like before. It was better if I waited until I was a little calmer before reaching out to him again.

I could still feel an echo of pain through my ribs and arm and I wondered why Sam was still hurting. He should have been healed by now. Maybe his pain was distracting him.

I was relieved to see Cole sitting on the porch at Gran's when I pulled up, Gemma sitting close alongside him. One of the books was open in her lap, but they weren't looking at it. They were looking at each other and having an intense conversation.

"Did you find anything?" I asked before I was even completely out of the car.

"Nothing," Gemma replied, looking away from Cole.

I nodded. I had hoped for the best, but knew it was a slim shot. Gemma knew those books, and if she said what I was looking for wasn't in them, then it probably wasn't.

I nodded again. "Thank you for looking. I guess it's safe to say the books don't contain the information we need on how to get a Lucent Marble without a hellhound."

"They don't say anything about how to break the force field that keeps Sam in that dungeon either," Cole said.

"It doesn't need to. We can use the dagger—it will break the force field."

"No!" Gemma said, jumping up. The book fell from her lap. "You can't do that!"

"Why not?" I demanded, placing my hands on my hips.

"It's a force field! It deflects what you throw at it."

"I hadn't planned to throw the dagger at it. I planned to stab it."

Gemma shook her head. "If you stab it and press the jewel, that light will shine out from it and the force field will deflect it away and send it back onto you."

Cole whistled between his teeth.

"Are you sure about this?" I asked.

"Certain."

Could nothing go right today?

"Maybe it's time you tell us the rest of your plan," Cole said.

"I don't have a plan!" I yelled. "All I know is that I have to get Sam out of there and fast. The clock is ticking. As soon as Beelzebub comes back from what I did to him, he's going to take it all out on Sam."

Cole moved down the steps toward me.

"We need a way to get a Lucent Marble, we need a way to break the force field, we need a way into the stupid castle to get to the dungeon and we need a way to get the stupid demons off my back for five minutes so I can think!" I burst out.

"Were you attacked?" Gemma asked. I felt her gaze running over me for injury. Her eyes focused on the burns on my arm.

I sighed. "Since day three."

Cole made a sound and grabbed my arm. "Why didn't you say anything?"

I shrugged. Why bother? I was handling it.

"Were you attacked today?" he pressed.

"Twice."

He swore. "Maybe I should stay here for a few days."

"No. That isn't necessary." My stomach flipped and my vision blurred for a few moments.

"Are you feeling all right?" Gemma asked, eyes narrowed.

"I'm okay. I want a shower though."

"We'll wait here," Cole said, releasing my arm.

I nodded and went past them to the door. Before going inside, I turned back to Gemma. "Do you know anything about demon spit?"

Gemma's eyes widened. "It burns your skin."

I nodded and held up my arm. "So this will go away, right?"

She came forward and grasped my arm. "Did you kill the demon that did this to you?"

"Yeah."

"Did any of its blood get on you?"

"A little."

"What about that cut on your neck?"

"No, that's fine. A scratch."

She made a sound. "I'll get my salve. Go shower."

Cole appeared at my side. "I'll help you upstairs."

"I don't need help." I refused his hand.

"Yes, you do." I looked up at the sincere sorrow in his voice.

"What is it?"

"You're about to be very sick."

"What? Why?" Even as he said it, I knew.

"Remember all those bites I had in Italy?"

I nodded.

He opened the door and ushered me inside. "Their saliva made me sick."

"I barely got any on me, nothing like the bites you had."

"Yeah, but the blood got on you, on your open wound."

"So?"

"Their blood is like poison, Hev."

I let that sink in. "Just great," I muttered.

Upstairs, Cole leaned in the doorway as I gathered clean clothes for my shower. He watched silently, like he was ready for me to fall. Before going into the bathroom, I stopped and spoke. "I don't have time to get sick. I've already wasted five days training and trying to think of a way to get Sam out. I can't afford to lose any more time."

He came forward to lay a hand on my shoulder and squeezed. It was meant to be reassuring and comforting. It wasn't any of those things. I pulled away.

"Give me ten minutes. Then we have a plan to make."

By the time I got out of the shower, I was shivering and running a fever. My limbs felt weak and my stomach danced summersaults. Gemma was sitting on my bed. When I entered, she got up without a word and handed me a glass of orange juice.

"Drink it," she ordered. Then she grabbed my arm and began coating the burns in a rich salve. It was cool against my heated skin. I lifted the juice and took a long drink, but it tasted gross. I was about to spit it back in the glass when Gemma pinned me with a look. I swallowed.

"What is that stuff?" I half gagged.

Logan appeared in my bedroom door, teetering at the threshold. I could tell by his indecision that he wasn't sure if he would be welcomed or not.

"Hey, Logan," I said, taking my chance to set the offending drink down on the bedside table. I waived him in with the arm Gemma wasn't holding. "Come on in."

"Hey, man," Cole said from the chair he perched himself in as Logan walked farther into the room. "How's it going?"

"I'm good," he answered, then looked at me. "What's wrong with you?"

"I had a run in with a demon," I said, not bothering to sugarcoat it. I wanted his respect and I wouldn't get it by talking to him like he was five years old.

I watched him swallow. "A demon?"

"Yes, on my way home from visiting my mom. But don't worry, I killed it."

"You did?"

"Yeah, but some of its blood got on me and now I don't feel so hot."

"Does Sam know?" Logan asked, shuffling from foot to foot.

I patted the bed with my hand so he would sit down, ignoring the question. Gemma capped the salve and picked up my glass. "It will make you feel better; drink it."

"It works. Do what she says," Cole said from the desk chair.

Gemma smiled. "I had to force his down his throat. The big baby."

"I was ten times worse than she is!" Cole defended himself.

"I know." Gemma's eyes clouded over at the mention of how sick Cole had been after being attacked by a swarm of demons.

I grabbed the glass and downed the juice. Logan was watching so I avoided any kind of face, even though I wanted to make one because that stuff was horrible. I lay down on the bed, propping myself up on the pillows. "How long until that stuff works?"

"Depends on how much venom got in you."

"Not much," I said. "I should be fine soon."

Gemma didn't look convinced, but I was and that was all that mattered. I glanced back at Logan. "Mind if we take a rain check on the ice cream?"

He nodded. "Gran asked me if I wanted to go shopping with her."

"You should go. Stock up on more candy." I smiled.

He didn't return the smile. He just looked at me, frowning. "Sam doesn't know, does he?"

I sighed. I guess ignoring his earlier question hadn't worked. "No. I didn't tell him."

Logan thought about my words for a minute, but to my surprise, he just nodded and said, "You're going to be okay?"

There was genuine worry in his voice and it made me think that maybe all my effort with him was paying off. "Of course. Don't worry about me."

He got up from the bed, straightening his bad joints slowly, and went toward the door. Cole held up his hand for a high five, which Logan slapped him, but he glanced back at me before leaving. "Get me some candy too. Anything chocolate."

He smiled, then disappeared from sight. Out in the hall, he began to cough. It sounded like there was fluid in his lungs. I let my head fall back on the pillows and looked at Gemma. "That doesn't sound good."

"How long has he been coughing like that?"

"First time I heard him today. But it's been off and on."

"I don't know how much more I can do for him. Healing him only seems to help for a little while."

"I know." I sighed and shut my eyes. After a few moments I said, "I've been thinking. If I kill Hecate, would her magic die with her? You know, the spell that created the force field?"

"You can't kill Hecate." Gemma said.

"Maybe not alone but with the dagger…"

"You misunderstand. Hecate can't die. She's eternal."

"Eternal?" Cole asked.

"Immortal, whatever you want to call it. It's the reason she can be in hell without losing her soul."

"I thought that was because she was evil and had no soul." I snorted.

"That too," Gemma agreed. "But she isn't a demon."

I stared at the ceiling, trying to push back the frustration I felt. Every idea I had turned out to be useless. "Any ideas on how we break down the force field?"

"What about Kimber?" Cole said.

"What about her?" I opened my eyes and looked at my brother.

"She's a witch. She could cast a spell to weaken the barrier." I wondered if he noticed the way Gemma tensed at the mention of his ex-girlfriend. He didn't act like he noticed and I wasn't about to point it out. It wasn't important anyway.

"She's also trapped in hell and her soul separated from her body." I reminded him. I stopped thinking of Kimber as my best friend weeks ago, but I still felt beyond horrible for what was happening to her.

"What if we put her soul back in her body?"

"Can we even do that?" I asked, skeptically

"In my books, it says a soul can be convinced to return to the body it was separated from," Gemma answered.

"What do you mean convinced?" Cole asked.

Gemma nodded and turned to look at my brother. "Once a soul separates from a body, it usually just floats off into hell until it's corrupted and turns into something vile like one of those demons that keep showing up. The body it came from usually just dies."

"We saw Kimber. She isn't dead," Cole said.

Gemma's back muscles tightened slightly and I thought again about how talking about Kimber was making her feel. "I'm sure she didn't look like herself," she said tersely.

Cole seemed to sit up a little straighter at Gemma's short reply, but he kept his face impassive. "She looked like hell."

Gemma snorted.

I didn't have time for them to act like this, so I reached out and touched Gemma's arm. She turned back to me abruptly. "You have a fever!"

I waved off her worry. "I'm fine. Hecate put some spell on her cell to keep her alive and her soul from drifting away."

"How did she seem… mentally?" Gemma asked.

I thought back. Kimber had helped us get out of there—she gave us the Lucent Marble when we thought it was lost. "She definitely isn't the same, but I think there's still some of her left."

"That's a good sign." Gemma nodded.

"How is that a good sign?" Cole asked.

Gemma turned to look at him. "Usually, once a soul spends a lot of time out of a body down in hell, it turns completely evil."

"No. She won't." Cole shook his head spastically. "She's not evil. All we have to do is convince her soul to get back in her body."

"It won't be easy," Gemma warned. "Her soul has been free for a while now. It isn't going to want to be forced back inside her body, which has probably been deteriorating."

"But it's still her soul. Wouldn't it want to go home?" I asked, leaning back on the pillows.

Usually, her long dark hair was pulled up in a ponytail, but today it was down, waving around her face and it brushed against her cheek when she shook her head. "Souls are very fickle. They're easily influenced. They tend to take on characteristics of their environment. A soul that has been floating around in hell would not want to go back to being reined in."

"So we offer it something that it might not be able to have if it was left on its own," I said.

"Like what?" Gemma asked.

"I'll think of something," I muttered, feeling dizzy.

"Wouldn't it be kind of bad for Kimber if we forced her corrupted soul back into her body? Wouldn't it just corrupt her?" Cole asked, pulling his lip with his thumb and forefinger.

"She won't be the same person as before, but being in the same cell with her might be a good thing because it probably isn't completely corrupted." Gemma allowed.

"She changed the minute she made a deal with Hecate," I spat. "Besides, having a soul is better than not having one at all."

We all fell into silence. Gemma was probably wondering if Cole was still in love with Kimber. Cole was probably wondering what he said to make me yell, and I was lying there desperately trying not to vomit.

What a group we made.

"So that's what we'll do, then," I said, forcing the way I felt to the back of my mind. "When we get down there, we'll convince Kimber's soul to get back into her body and then she can cast some spell to make the force fields disappear."

Gemma cleared her throat. "Whatever magic your friend has, it's no match for Hecate's."

"She's not my friend, not anymore," I said quickly. "And you're probably right—but she should be strong enough to cast a spell to maybe weaken whatever spell Hecate cast, then Sam can break out."

"I thought you said he's weak from exhaustion and injured," Cole said and Gemma looked at him sharply.

"Then, I'll break it down," I said simply.

Cole looked like he might argue but I held up my hand, stopping him. "I don't want to hear it. I'm getting Sam out of there and that's all there is to it."

"You should get some sleep," Gemma said, getting up from the bed. "I'll come back later to see how you're feeling."

Suddenly, it was hard to keep my eyes open so I just nodded.

A few moments later, I was startled by the sound of Gemma asking Cole if he was coming. I thought they had already left.

"I don't want to leave her like this," he whispered.

"Yeah, okay," Gemma said. "I'll see you later."

"Cole." My throat felt like it was on fire and the word sounded hoarse and gruff.

He was at my side in an instant, his hands cool against my heated skin as he pushed a few strands of damp hair off my forehead. "What do you need?"

"Go… be with Gemma."

"I'm going to hang with you."

"I'm fine."

"I know what you're feeling right now."

"Not as bad as you were," I said as I started to shiver with cold.

I felt the heavy weight of a blanket settle over me. The weight was unpleasant, but the warmth outweighed my discomfort so I didn't protest. "Get some sleep," Cole said softly.

"Cole"—I reached for him and he put his hand in mine—"be with her while you have the chance. You never know when it might be gone."

My eyes were closed but I felt his aura shift, turn into anxiety and doubt. "Go," I told him. "I wanna be alone with Sam."

He hesitated only a minute before tucking the blanket around me farther and then stepping away from the bed. "We'll just be downstairs. If you need anything, yell."

"Thanks."

"Tell Sam I said to hang in there."

I didn't respond but sank farther into the covers and let my mind reach out to Sam. I wanted to be with him so desperately that I opened my mind too much, too fast and he was no doubt bombarded with what was going on with me. Almost as soon as I felt our connection, anxiety and fear flooded into me.

Heven? What's wrong?

Not feeling so great is all.

I feel a burning in my arm. What happened?

I didn't want to lie, and he was already freaked out, so I told him the truth. *I had a run in with a demon. His spit got on me, then some of his blood, and it burned me.*

A deep yearning and a desperate anger flowed through me and it actually eclipsed some of my own pain. I could feel him fighting the urge to launch himself at the force field again, but he and I both knew that he couldn't break out. After a few charged moments, he seemed to relax a bit.

What happened with the demon?

Nothing. I killed it.

You killed it? Fresh fear stabbed me anew, but I ignored it.

Yes, and it's just a small burn.

You're in pain.

We were all in some kind of pain. I was tired of thinking about it. *I was thinking of taking a nap.*

I wasn't worried about going to sleep. I fought sleep when I first came home from hell, in fear that Beelzebub (also known to me as the Dream Walker) would get into my head while I slept, but I can only not sleep for so long. Eventually, I fell asleep. And he never came.

Sleep would be good for you.

Want to link up?

I don't know if I can settle down enough.

Would you try?

Anything for you.

At first, I thought maybe he wasn't going to be able to relax, but I kept my mind completely open while sending out loving thoughts and waited. Eventually, I felt him soften and I hurried to picture him lying beside me on the bed. In my mind, he wasn't wearing a shirt and I ran my hand over his smooth, taut stomach muscles. His skin was warm to the touch and his chest rose and fell with every breath he took. A small groan echoed through my mind and I smiled. I wasn't really touching him, but we were linked so closely I knew he could almost feel my touch. And while it didn't seem like much, it was all we had and it was everything.

He laid his palm over my hand and lifted it to his lips, pressing a kiss to the inside of my wrist before settling my arm back around him and gathering me close. Suddenly, the too-heavy blanket felt perfect and I pretended it was really him wrapping his body around mine.

Gradually, the shaking of my muscles slowed and then subsided. I was left feeling completely exhausted.

Feeling better?

Yes.

Good. Get some sleep.

Want to stay like this with you.

I won't let go. I'll keep you here. I wasn't sure if he would be able to do that or not, but I was fading fast and I knew I wouldn't last much longer. Something niggled at the back of my brain and I roused myself enough to remember I wanted to ask him something.

Do you ever talk to your old roommates?

The question was random and momentarily startled him. I felt some of our link slip away so I made a small sound of protest and he came back, wrapping me in his mind. *Why would you ask me that?*

I thought maybe they could help.

They can't. Stay away from them. They're dangerous.

I didn't care how dangerous they were. They could get me a Lucent Marble. *You said they weren't as bad as China.*

No one was as bad as China. An image of Sam's old apartment slipped into my mind. It confused me because I hadn't been thinking of that place. Then an image of China and two guys sitting on a couch entered my mind. They were all arguing. All of their faces were screwed up in angry expressions. It was like I was sitting right next to them.

Then it hit me.

These weren't my thoughts. They were Sam's.

I was so closely linked with him that apparently I was seeing his thoughts. I hadn't known that was possible. I pushed away my surprise and I tried to get a good look at the two roommates, but it was hard because Sam wasn't looking at them or remembering them—he was looking at China. I tried turning his head to see the others, but it didn't work that way. These were memories and they didn't change.

Sam? I asked tentatively.

The memory faded but I was left with an idea. *Yeah?*

Do you know where your roommates went after you made them leave town?

It doesn't matter. Another memory of the last day he saw them flashed through his mind. It was right after he killed China and we were walking through the woods. Both hellhounds showed up and Sam expected a fight. I could feel the anxiety Sam felt as he was worried how he would protect me against them. I tried to pay attention to their appearance, but all I could really note was that they both had dark hair and dark eyes. Beyond that, Sam barely registered them. He was too busy thinking about defending me and sending them on their way.

But there was something else, too.

A sadness. He once liked these guys. But they were too volatile, and having them around me was a gamble Sam wasn't willing to take. So he forced them to leave.

The only people who truly understood what it was like to be a hellhound.

I barely noticed the tears that streaked my cheeks. He had given up so much for me. So much I hadn't even known about. And now he was trapped in hell.

You have no idea where they went? I pushed.

They can't help me, Heven. They wouldn't. I know you're only trying to help, but please just let it go. They're dangerous.

Okay.

Yeah? Sam asked. I could hear the partial disbelief in his voice that I would agree so easily.

Yeah. You won't let go of our link? I wiggled beneath the blanket, wanting closer to him, knowing it was impossible.

I promise.

I relaxed into him, concentrating on only him. If I really tried, I thought I could catch a hint of his deep scent.

Just the hint of his scent made me feel better than any nasty drink Gemma could concoct. I pushed back the guilt that crept into my mind. Guilt over the little peek I took into Sam's mind.

Without knowing it, Sam had given me exactly what I had been hoping for. Just to be sure, I called up the image one last time before falling asleep. It came easily and I smiled.

That information wasn't going anywhere. My photographic memory wouldn't forget what I saw.

Chapter Three

Sam

Water at night is an abyss. It's a never-ending blackness that one must push through, and though I'm the strongest swimmer possible, tonight I feel like my limbs cut through sand. Yes, I can see in this dark, murky water, but I don't want to. I want to close my eyes off to what I just did, because it was horrible and wrong.

Yet, I would do it again.

Before pushing off the bottom of the lake, I glance back once more. Long blond strands of hair float out around a shockingly pale face. A face that was once beautiful, a body that was once full of life is now sentenced here in this wet world of shadows. Her only crime was that she looked like the girl I love.

Heavy with guilt, but full of determination, I push away from the body. As I go, ripples in the water cause it to shift and move. One of her hands seems to float out away from her, reaching toward me, almost pleading. Don't leave me here. Don't I deserve better in death?

Yes, she does.

But it's too late for her.

I turn away.

My eyes opened and stared up at the black ceiling. So much darkness, so much shade. I could feel the tendrils of evil reach out to me. It was hard to concentrate, hard to *feel* when I was remembering the sinful things I'd done.

I sat up, brushing away those thoughts. The only way darkness would wrap itself around me was if I let it. I had too much to live for to let that happen.

But some of us weren't that lucky. Some of us hadn't survived. Like Andi. I kept thinking of her. I was being haunted, it seemed, by the things I'd done, the bad things. Whether it was the darkness's way of taunting me, showing me that I do belong here, or my conscience trying to tell me to make amends, I don't know. All I know was that it was increasingly harder to feel at peace with myself.

I felt unsettled. Guilty. Dirty.

There was a girl at the bottom of a lake because I dragged her there. Yes, China is the one who killed her, who defiled her body and took away her life. But how was I any better? I hadn't allowed her one dignity in death. I sentenced her to a watery grave. An eternity of solitude and unrest. And what of her family? The police tagged her as a runaway and said she'd be back. But her family didn't believe that. Her boyfriend didn't believe that. I used to pretend to not see the hollow look in his eyes and the forlorn faces of her friends in the hallway at school.

She wouldn't. They would whisper at school. *Andi wouldn't leave like that. She liked her life. She loved us.*

The last weeks of watching Logan suffer, the sleepless nights, the gut-gnawing worry over his wellbeing… is that what her family felt every single day since that night? Does her mother go into her room and sit, wondering what happened to her child, knowing in her heart it was something bad?

I pushed myself to my feet and began to pace the confines of the cell.

When I stumbled over the body in the woods at Kimber's party, grief like no other stole over me. I was blinded by rage, by despair, by denial. I thought Heven lay there broken and dead. I thought I failed her. Then, when I realized it wasn't my Heven, I was so relieved I wanted to do everything I could to keep something like that from actually happening to her. So I did it. I dragged the body into the lake.

I never thought about Andi. I never thought about her family and the fact they would never know a moment's peace. It was wrong. *I* was wrong.

When I got out of here, I was going to fix it.

Heven

Fresh sea air took over my senses and tore my hair out of the confines of the band that struggled to hold it back. I pushed at it impatiently and turned to watch the city of Portland get farther away. Peaks Island was only two miles away from Portland, which took fifteen minutes to travel by ferry. I got lucky and arrived just as a ferry was about to depart, so I didn't have to sit at the docks and wait.

I thought this was a good sign.

Considering how rough the earlier portion of my day had been, I felt relieved.

I looked out across the sea… The waving, dark water made me remember the slight panic I woke up in earlier. I think I had been dreaming about dark, choking water. And regret. But Sam had been there, our link holding strong, vanishing my might-have-been dream and moody feelings. It was hard to get out of bed. I would've liked to lay there and talk with him all evening and into the morning. But that wasn't an option. I had a lead. A lead that not even a slight fever would keep me from chasing.

Getting away from Cole and Gemma had proved harder than I thought. They were both still pretty concerned about me and didn't want to let me out of sight. It only got worse when I refused to tell them where I was headed.

But I was stubborn and wasn't about to be held back.

Gemma was the one who finally relented and talked Cole down from his overbearing, big brother mood. Although she never said, Gemma seemed to understand a lot of what I was going through. It made me wonder, and not for the first time, what was in her past. Whatever it was changed her, shaped her into the person she was today. What had she been like before? Had she been like me? Is that why she stuck around and offered to train Sam how to fight and share with us the wealth of knowledge she carried?

I shook my head, clearing my thoughts and turned my face toward the wind, imagining it blowing away all unnecessary thought. It didn't matter why Gemma was helping us, just that she was. And it didn't matter I was going to have to deal with Cole's anger when I saw him again.

Peaks Island was drawing very near and my pulse sped up. I tried to remind myself this might be a dead end, that I might not get what I wanted. But I couldn't seem to calm myself.

Then I remembered how I got here. Guilt weighed a lot and it brought me crashing down.

I stole the information right out of Sam's head. He hadn't even realized what was happening. And I hadn't told him. To be fair, I didn't really understand how I managed to see his thoughts—his memories. I only prayed he could forgive me when he found out.

The ferry docked and a few minutes went by before I could get off. I left Sam's truck back on the mainland, choosing to ride over and then travel on foot. When I stepped onto the wooden dock, I looked up and really noticed the island for the first time.

Peaks Island was part of Maine, one of the two hundred twenty-two islands that made up Casco Bay. It was one of the most populated islands along the coast and it was breathtakingly beautiful. From every angle the place looked like it belonged on a post card. It probably was.

Not far from the dock were charming cobblestone streets that paved the way toward lively summer attractions. It was nearing eight so there wouldn't be much daylight left, but I wasn't worried. I had a feeling what I was after preferred the dark.

Because it was summer, the streets were busier than I expected. I looked around, wondering where I should begin.

Museums, art galleries, various shops, boating and fishing rentals all lined the quaint streets. It was so utterly beautiful and charming here that I got swept up in the moment and closed my eyes, pretending Sam and I were here together with no other purpose but to have fun.

Then someone bumped into me from behind and I snapped out of it. I wandered along the streets for a while, stopping to browse in a few shops and store windows. All the while I scanned the crowd.

I wasn't even sure if I would know when I found what I wanted.

Soon, the sun set and it was dark. There was lighting on the streets, but not enough to completely illuminate everything, and for the first time, I began to doubt my plan. What if the memory I saw in Sam's mind was too old and no longer useful? I closed my eyes and called the image to my mind to study it.

Sam was standing in his old apartment, the one he shared with China and two other hellhounds. Except China was dead and his roommates had left town at his request. I was pretty sure this particular memory was from the day Sam and I went to clear out the place so he could move into his new efficiency. The bedroom around him was bare from when they cleared out all their stuff.

But they left something behind.

A hastily scrawled note.

Someone left it laying in the center of the bare mattress.

There was only one thing written on it. It was a place. Peaks Island.

When I asked Sam if he knew where they went, he said no, but this is the image that popped into his head. His roommates might have left, but they hadn't gone far and they had told Sam where they would be. Why had they told him? Why didn't Sam tell me?

Yes, Sam lied to me, but I didn't care. He was only trying to protect me. After all, I had lied to him for the same reasons. When I opened my eyes, the streets seemed a little more vacant than before and I wondered how long I had been standing there. I walked a little more, intently studying the faces of everyone who passed, to no avail.

There were no hellhounds here.

Feeling completely deflated, I turned to make my way back to the ferry, hoping I hadn't missed the last shuttle back to the main land. It never occurred to me to check the schedule. A large fishing boat had just docked for the day and I could hear the rowdy group of workers as they laughed and hauled the fresh oysters and lobsters onto the deck of the boat. I don't know why, but I walked past the ferry boat toward the fishing boat. I grabbed the strap of my bag and held it tightly as if it would anchor me.

The closeness of the sea was starting to get to me. I hated the water. The one time Sam tried to teach me to swim and be comfortable around water, it had ended in me being attacked by a red-eyed demon (who I later found out was Beelzebub) who broke into my head, leaving behind a thread so he could stalk me in my dreams.

I still wasn't sure that thread was gone. Well, the one Sam destroyed was gone, but then Beelzebub told us he left behind more than one. How many, I didn't know and since sending Beelzebub into a pit of churning flames wasn't enough to kill him, I was left wondering when he would reclaim his place inside my head and begin torturing me again.

A huge, wet mesh bag flung through the air and landed with a solid thud at my feet, startling me and I jumped back automatically, getting into a crouch, ready to pounce. I couldn't see what was in the bag because it was so dark here away from most of the streetlights, but from the smell, I would say it was probably a bag of seafood. More laughter sounded and one of the men on the boat leapt over the side, landing in front of me. The bag lay between us and I wondered about its weight and if I would be able to lift it and throw it at him.

"Look what we got here," he called.

I didn't relax my stance because that's what he wanted me to do. He thought he could intimidate me into dropping my guard. Little did he know that Beelzebub made him look like the tooth fairy.

"I was looking for someone, but it's clear he isn't here," I said loudly, confidently.

"I can be whoever you're looking for."

I started walking away, backward, keeping my eyes on the man. Then another jumped down behind me. If I went to either side, I'd go off the dock into the black water. That was *not* an option. I turned so my back was to the water and I could see both men.

Because it was dark, I couldn't make out much other than they were both big, smelled, and thought they were tough. Slowly, I slid my hand down the strap of my bag, allowing it to disappear inside.

"Why don't you come on up to the boat and we'll show you around." The man to my left said.

"No."

The man to my right was farthest away and he casually stepped over the bag of seafood. When he moved, so did the man to my left—lunging at me, trying to catch me by surprise. I pulled my hand out of my bag and plunged the dagger into the man's leg. He screamed and fell to his knees. I turned and hit him dead-on, which sent him spiraling into the sea.

I turned toward the remaining guy and held up the dagger, darkened with blood. The man stood in front of me, his eyes bouncing between me and the water to my right. Then he glanced at the dagger.

"What's a little girl like you doing carrying around such a thing?"

I sensed some movement behind me and wrapped both my arms across my chest just as two vice-like arms closed around me. Instantly, I threw both my arms down, loosening the hold the man had on me. He released me, trying not to get caught by the dagger's blade. I dropped onto the dock floor and crawled through the surprised man's legs. He grabbed hold of my foot and I turned, lashing out with the dagger. The man cried out and yanked his bloodied hand back.

"You're crazy!" the man yelled hysterically.

I jumped to my feet and watched as he backed away. The other man was helping his buddy out of the water while trying to keep an eye on me. He was stupid. I caught him off-guard and sent him into the water right next to his friend.

The entire crew on the boat was standing around, silently gazing down at the scene. Clearly, they'd come to the conclusion I wasn't as innocent as they thought. I backed away from them, keeping my body tense, the dagger visible until their images faded and I heard them scrambling to help their buddies back on the boat.

Only then did I let out a relieved breath of air. The ferry was loading passengers and I hurried on, checking behind me to make sure I wasn't followed. As I boarded, I held the dagger between myself and my bag so no one would wonder what I was doing with such a wicked-looking weapon. I could have put it away, but I wouldn't have felt safe. There were only a few passengers because it was getting late, so it wasn't hard to find a spot that was completely empty. I chose a seat away from the railing of the boat, placing my back to one of the walls that made up the little room where the captain steered the boat. The bench was hard beneath me, damp and cold. I pushed away the discomfort and looked again at the way I came, making sure no one followed.

Only after I was convinced I was alone did I slide the dagger back into my bag and slump against the wall. The burns on my arm were throbbing and my limbs were trembling. I couldn't wait to climb into Sam's truck, blast the heater and take a deep breath of the air that still smelled like him. With that, my eyes filled with tears. I failed. Again.

Not liking the direction my thoughts were going, I straightened and dashed the tears away. So I didn't have a plan to get Sam back. So what? I'd go with my back-up plan and just go down there and do what I had to do to break him out. If he had to be the one to get the Lucent Marble, then he had to be the one. Now, if only I could figure out when the next bus to hell was…

The ferry whistle blew, signaling it was ready to leave the dock. As we pulled away, I looked back at the island and the lights glowing in the cobblestone streets. It didn't seem near as beautiful as when I arrived. I didn't so much hear something but *felt* it and my body tensed anew. My eyes scanned the area, but there wasn't anything there. I heard a low thud and I jumped up, still searching the shadows for something, someone.

I stood for what seemed like forever, waiting for an attack, but none came. Just as I was about to sit back down, there was a flash of something at the railing. The dagger appeared in my hand before I even thought about grabbing it. There was another thud followed by something slowly rising over the railing. At first, I thought it was a demon, but the hands that gripped the sides were much too human-looking, as was the leg that came over the side next.

Before I knew it, there was a wet slap onto the floor of the boat and a man stood up from his crouch. He was dripping wet with dark hair hanging in his eyes. His black T-shirt was soaked and sticking to every one of his chest muscles. His cut-off jean shorts were soggy with ocean water.

He hadn't looked at me once, but he had to be aware of my presence.

I knew he was.

Because even in the dark, I could see that he had no aura.

I stopped breathing when he looked up. His eyes were as dark as his hair and I hadn't known until this moment that people were capable of having such dark eyes. Something cold slithered up my spine.

He silently stared at me for a long moment before completely disregarding me and shaking like a wet dog. Cold droplets of water sprayed my bare arms. When he was done, he looked up. His hair was no longer in his eyes but standing out wildly around his head.

He took a step forward.

I raised the dagger.

He laughed and the bottom of my stomach fell out. This was the first person (demon, creature, alien?) who had ever laughed when threatened with a sharp weapon.

"Why don't you put that thing away before you hurt yourself?"

"You just want me to put it away so I don't hurt *you*." I said, not lowering the blade.

He flashed a grin again, still not appearing threatened. I thought about stabbing him just to wipe that smirk off his face. But then he said something that got my attention. "You're more bold than I remembered."

"You know me?" I asked, suspicious. He just wanted me to forget he was threatening me.

"You don't know me?" As he spoke, he came forward and grabbed the dagger out of my hand. I made a motion to grab it back, but he clucked his tongue and slid it into the back pocket of his jeans.

Well, crap. It worked. Anger flared through me and I threw myself at him, trying to reach around and grab what was mine. He actually chuckled and grabbed my arms by each wrist.

I glared at him, my breathing heavy and annoyed. The front of me was wet from when I threw myself at him. The sea air was blowing and I felt the first hint of a chill. "Give it back."

"You can have it back *after* we talk."

I had an uneasy feeling, but it never even occurred to me to be afraid. I was alone, in the dark, and in the middle of the ocean with someone with no aura who just disarmed me and was clearly ten times stronger than I would ever be. Still, I wasn't afraid. I squinted up at him through the night, trying to figure out why.

He laughed again and released my wrists. "That's better." He seemed satisfied somehow that I was done attacking him. I wasn't yet sure if what he had decided was right. I was still pissed that he took my dagger, *Sam's* dagger.

"I want that back."

"You'll get it back," he responded mildly and moved away, actually putting his back to me before sitting where I had been moments before.

"I've killed demons, you know." I felt the need to point out I wasn't as harmless as he seemed to think.

Under the light of the nearby lamp, I could see much more of his face. When he looked up at me, I was taken aback by how beautiful he was. His olive-toned skin was flawless, his lips were full and dark, and those eyes... those dark, dark eyes were accentuated by a slash of thick, dark brows that knew no order. But there was something about him that wasn't beautiful... He was... dangerous.

He was dangerously beautiful.

"You're a tough girl, I know."

"How do you know?" I was suspicious instantly. He implied he knew me, but I was certain I'd never laid eyes upon him before. I would never have forgotten such dark beauty. At least, I don't think I would've forgotten.

He smiled, making his eyes crinkle at the corners. "I saw what you did to those fishermen back there."

"You were watching?"

"I was on the boat."

"You're a fisherman?"

"I was."

"But you're not now?"

"I have a feeling tonight was my last night." My stomach flipped at his lowered voice.

"Who are you?" I squinted through the dark and rubbed my arms against the cold air.

"You really don't recognize me?"

I shook my head slowly.

"The power of that guy still amazes me," he said almost to himself.

"Who?" I asked, suspicious.

"Sam."

"You know Sam?" I took a step closer, almost desperate for another link that would bring me closer to the man I loved.

He shook his head like he was sad, then stood. I looked at him warily, all my muscles tensing. His mouth tilted upward, noticing my discomfort, but he didn't back away.

He stepped closer.

Then he held out an enormous palm. "Name's Riley Stone."

"Riley," I murmured and slid my hand into his. His skin was warm and sent chills up my arm. I snatched my hand back and folded my arms across my chest as his name clicked into place. "I know you." I had come here for him.

He smirked. "That's right, sweetheart. Me and your precious Sam used to be roommates."

Chapter Four

Heven

"You're a hellhound," I said.

"Clever observation," he said sarcastically and returned to the bench. He was casual and nonchalant, but I was shaking like a leaf. It was windy out here on the water, and I was cold. That's all it was. Well, that and the fact some guy just swam out to the ferry, hoisted himself over the railing, and disarmed me while I stood there blithering like a total ass.

"You're one of the guys who attacked me back home?"

"If I had attacked you, you'd be dead," he said without any emotion in his tone.

Okay, maybe they didn't, but they wanted to. And who knows what he would've done if Sam hadn't intercepted them. I'd been walking toward a trashcan to discard our empty Bubble Maineia cups when two men grabbed me from the sides and began talking and jostling me. It didn't go any further because Sam intervened and I got in the truck. I watched in horror as they exchanged heated words until Sam threw a punch.

"Sam decked you."

He shook his head, bewildered. "No, that was Casey."

"Oh." I looked around, expecting this Casey to come out of the shadows.

"He isn't here."

"Where is he?"

"Gone."

"Weren't you friends?"

"I don't have friends. But we *knew* each other."

Ah, yes. I finally understood that note Sam found telling him where they would be. They were connected in a way that no one else would understand. They were hellhounds, part of an elite group.

"Why don't you tell me why you came looking for me?"

"Who said I was looking for you?" I asked, rubbing my arms. Yes, I *had* been looking for him and I was slightly embarrassed that I didn't even know it was him when I saw him. While I wasn't really afraid of him—I just didn't trust him, not yet, anyway.

Abruptly, he stood and my body went rigid, expecting an attack. He rolled his eyes. "I'm not going to hurt you." He motioned to the bench. "Sit down."

I don't know why, but I listened. Once I was sitting, he moved directly in front of me. The bench seat was still warm from his body heat and I realized he was blocking the wind from reaching me. A little bit of fight went out of me. Okay, *a lot* of fight went out of me.

"I need your help," I said.

He lifted a brow. "Go on."

"Sam is trapped in hell. I need another hellhound to get him out."

I was expecting some disbelief, maybe some denial. He stared at me without blinking and then he nodded. "I figured it must be bad."

I tried to look as unaffected by his words as he was by mine. "How?"

"Because he never would have let you come all this way alone." He reached into his back pocket and pulled out the dagger, handing it to me handle first. "And he never would have allowed you to carry this thing."

I rolled my eyes. "Sam doesn't *allow* me to do anything. I do what I want." I grabbed the dagger and wrapped both my palms around it, hugging it to my chest. Then in a lower voice I said, "You believe me?"

"Why wouldn't I?"

"You don't even know me."

"I know enough." He smiled a smile that didn't quite reach his eyes. I got a feeling Riley Stone knew a lot more than he let on.

I lifted a brow and tucked the dagger back into my bag.

"Sam risked a lot to be with you. He risked the wrath of that bitch and then he ordered me and Casey away. He wouldn't have done that unless he thought you were worth it."

Now I knew why I didn't remember Riley. The two times I saw him, Sam was with me. As gorgeous as Riley was, he paled in comparison to Sam.

"You liked him," I said.

He shrugged. "I *knew* him." He didn't want to admit that Sam got to him, maybe not as much as he did me, but he still got to him. That was fine. He didn't have to admit to liking Sam to help me.

"Will you help me?" The whistle blew, signaling the ferry had docked and we could disembark. Riley glanced over his shoulder toward the distant lights of Peaks Island. When he turned back, his eyes were guarded.

"Why don't you tell me what kind of trouble you guys are in."

My heart sank. He was going to refuse. Could I blame him? I stood rigidly and moved around toward the exit. I had wasted enough time on this. I had to move on to a new plan. But first, I needed to figure out what the new plan was.

"I didn't say no."

But he would. As soon as he heard what we were up against. I stopped and turned back. "We are up against people that have power... more power than you could possibly dream of."

He stepped up close. He was tall, towering over me. "I'll help you get Sam back."

"Really? I haven't told you what's going on yet..."

"I like a challenge." He shrugged. "I was getting bored on that island anyway."

I threw my arms around him and squeezed. "Thank you!"

He smelled a lot like Sam. Deep and slightly spicy. His body temperature was exactly like Sam's too, warm and welcoming. I think I hugged him a little longer than I should have. When I stepped back, I cleared my throat and avoided his unflinching gaze.

"Why don't you tell me about what I just agreed to get involved in.

I led the way to Sam's truck and climbed into the driver's seat. For the first time since Riley climbed over that railing, I was afraid. "It's almost unbelievable."

From the darkened passenger side, his voice came out of the night. "I'm pretty good at unbelievable."

I started up the truck and put it in drive. "That's good because I've got quite the story for you."

* * *

Sam's little efficiency apartment was hot. On day two of him being gone, I came over and turned off the small air unit. I walked over and turned back it on, then switched on the overhead light.

"I can find my own place to stay," Riley said, hovering in the doorway.

"Shut the door. I just turned the air on."

He did, but he didn't move away from the door. "So this is Sam's place?"

I turned from fluffing the pillows on the couch. "Yeah." I couldn't tell what he thought about the place but, really, it didn't matter.

"He deserved better than he had." He nodded like he approved.

"I know." And this still wasn't as good as he deserved, but it was a start.

"It smells like you in here," Riley said, finally pushing away from the door and coming into the room.

"The bathroom's right there." I motioned with my thumb. "The kitchen's there and the couch is here." I pointed in front of me, although it was completely obvious.

"The bedroom's there." He said, mimicking my movements, making me feel like a stewardess. (The exits are here and there and the beverage cart is here.)

"That's Sam's bed." I didn't mean for it to sound so territorial, but there it was.

He smirked. "Hands off?"

"I'm sorry. Of course you can sleep there." It was a small price to pay for what he was doing for us. After I told him the entire story about hell, the Treasure Map and Beelzebub, he still agreed to help. In fact, I think the impossibility of the situation appealed to him. He didn't even seem that shocked. I guess being a hellhound would make most anything plausible.

"No, it's all right. I get it."

I didn't think he did, but I didn't voice that opinion. "I'll go to the store tomorrow and get you some food."

"I can take care of myself."

I shut the fridge door and looked at him.

"It's enough that you're letting me stay here."

"Letting you stay here is nothing compared to what you're doing."

"I haven't done anything yet."

He came closer and my pulse quickened. "Your clothes are wet." I moved around him and went to Sam's dresser and pulled out a clean pair of shorts and a T-shirt. "Here. There isn't a washer or dryer here, but I can do your clothes for you at my Gran's house."

"I can take care of myself." He growled. He looked like an animal standing in a tiny cage.

I nodded and put the clothes on the back of the couch. "It's late. I'll go."

He watched me go to the door. Before I turned the handle to leave, I couldn't help but turn back. "I'll see you in the morning?" Part of me didn't want to let him out of my sight. He was the best shot I had at getting Sam out of hell. What if he disappeared?

He moved fast, coming to stand directly in front of me, and I stiffened. "I gave you my word," he said low, emotionless, and leaned down to stare into my eyes.

I gasped.

His eyes narrowed. "What?"

"Your eyes are blue."

He didn't move at my declaration. "So?"

"I thought they were black." They were such a dark navy they appeared black unless he was right up on you. They reminded me of the midnight sky above the ocean.

He smirked. "Don't go falling in love."

I rolled my eyes. "I'll... uh... pick you up tomorrow morning, then?"

"I'll come to you."

"But you don't know where I live."

He chuckled.

He did. Just how much did he know about me? I forced my face to look unimpressed that he seemed to know so much. "We start training early."

He saluted and reached around me to open the door. I stepped out into the dark. When I was halfway down the stairs, his voice stopped me.

"Heven." It was the first time he said my name. I didn't turn around and he didn't wait for me to; he kept on talking. "I gave you my word that I'd help Sam and I will."

"Thank you," I whispered, knowing full well that he could hear me. Then I hurried away without looking back.

* * *

I fought sleep the entire way home. When I finally got close to the farm, I had to park Sam's truck and walk to the house. If Gran saw Sam's truck in the morning, she'd assume he was home. But Sam wasn't home. Hence the reason I had to hide his truck. He was supposed to be driving it. I grumbled and stumbled a bit as I walked to the house in the dark while I cursed the fact I had to lie to Gran about everything. It was becoming increasingly more difficult to hide everything I needed to hide. Like where this new scar on my face had come from and where I was until all hours of the night.

Thankfully, Cole helped buffer some of the lies. I told Gran that I fell out of one of the apple trees while I was pruning in the orchard and landed on a broken branch that scraped my face. He also stayed and ate the dinner that Gran cooked tonight, lessening the fact that I wasn't here, though I'm sure I had some explaining to do next time I saw them both

I was as quiet as I could be when I let myself into the house and made my way to my bedroom. I was so exhausted I collapsed onto the bed fully clothed. Every muscle in my body ached and the burn on my arm hurt. At least I didn't have a fever anymore.

A noise in the doorway caught my attention and I looked up to see Logan hovering in the door. "Hey," I whispered. "Come on in."

"Where were you?" he asked, coming in and standing next to the bed. In his hand was a chocolate bar.

I sat up and leaned against the headboard. "I was making plans to get Sam out."

"Did you find a way?" He sat down on the side of the bed.

He seemed so vulnerable. I don't know if it was because I was exhausted or because I was feeling emotional about Sam, but seeing that candy bar in his hands and feeling like I somehow let him down was almost my undoing.

I cleared my throat. "Actually, I think I did."

His eyes lit up a little with hope.

"I found someone to help me get into hell."

"Who?"

"One of Sam's old roommates. You can meet him tomorrow."

He nodded. "I miss Sam."

"Me too. Is that chocolate for me?" I asked, holding out my hand.

"Yeah." He handed it to me and I took it. I unwrapped the bar, breaking it in half and holding out a piece for him. After he took it, we sat there eating the candy in silence.

"Cole was worried about you. He tried to hide it tonight, but I could tell." Logan shifted and stared at the floor, the chocolate in his hand forgotten.

"Hey," I said, sitting up. "I'm a lot tougher than I look. Nothing will happen to me and I'll get Sam out."

He nodded. "I'm sorry I've been so awful to you."

I took a chance and put an arm around his shoulder. "You haven't been awful. Annoying sometimes, but never awful."

He laughed, but it turned into a cough.

"How are you feeling?"

He shrugged. "I'm doing okay." He shoved the rest of the candy in his mouth to avoid saying any more.

After a few more minutes, I walked him back to his room and sat there for a while, watching TV with him. When his eyes started drooping, I covered him with an extra blanket and headed back to my room.

I was going to put my PJs on. I was going to put some more salve on my arm and wash my face. I was going to turn the covers on the bed down and reach out to Sam and hopefully, maybe, find some peace.

Instead, I fell on the bed. Face first. Sleep knocked me out and dragged me under.

Right into hell.

I felt the familiar vacuum pull on my chest and my stomach felt like it was up in my throat when I landed on the hard, unforgiving ground. I rose steadily to my feet, but an incredible pain seared through my head and I fell back down. I opened my eyes, but I couldn't see anything—the pain was blinding. I felt tears run down my cheeks, but I didn't bother to wipe them away. I couldn't. It was too hard to move.

It could have been minutes or hours that I lay there, but eventually, the pain ebbed away. My vision cleared and I wiped my face with the hem of my shirt. I felt like throwing up, but I resisted and pushed myself to my feet. Automatically, I reached for my dagger, but it wasn't here because I was dreaming.

Although, didn't I know this wasn't just a dream?

I had a very bad feeling about what this meant.

My surroundings were exactly the same as the last time I was here: dreary, gray and utterly lifeless. Everything looked like it was destroyed in a fire and the sky rolled with thick, dark clouds that resembled heavy smoke. I looked around warily, wondering what kind of evil was waiting to attack, but nothing was in sight.

I began running.

I was in hell. Sam was in hell.

I ran and ran until the rough, black granite castle came into view. The bridge was down, giving me access to the inside. Something niggled in the back of my mind, warning me. This was too easy. But I didn't care. Sam was here and I wanted nothing more than to see him. I raced through the castle and down into the dungeon. I didn't bother to be quiet because *he* probably already knew I was here.

The door to the dungeon was open and I skidded to a stop in front of it. Suddenly, I was very nervous. What if this was a trap? What if I rushed in there only to be killed? Then who would get Sam out? Another horrifying thought ripped through my mind and I tried to push it away, but another one of those headaches began at the base of my skull, pushing the thought firmly into my mind.

What if Sam was dead and this was my punishment— finding his body? A whimper escaped my throat. I jammed my fist against my lips and shook my head. Ignoring the throbbing pain in the base of my skull I stepped through the door to see what exactly it was *he* wanted me to see.

I walked quietly, almost silently because of my bare feet. There were some moans and a few shrill cries from some of the occupied cells as I walked by, but I didn't look in their direction. I kept my eyes focused on the cell I knew Sam was in. There was no door. A door wasn't needed to keep him in. I could see the edges of the force field shimmering as I drew closer. I realized how horrible it would be to sit in there day after day and stare at the open door and know that you couldn't just walk out.

As I drew closer, I felt the familiar feeling that I always felt when Sam was about to shift. He was shifting? But why? I peeked around the door and into the cell. A large hellhound was there, fully tensed and completely focused on something deeper inside. I couldn't see what it was. His large body blocked my view. I stood there watching, not wanting to distract him.

Sam threw out a paw and something slapped against the wall. I strained my eyes to see what it was that laid there unmoving… It was a rat. And thanks to Sam's hit, it was dead. Suddenly, Sam lunged and tore into the rat, eating it in two swallows. I made a sound and my hand flew to my mouth to muffle it.

The hellhound turned abruptly and saw me in the door. It made a low growl in its throat and shot into a darkened corner of the room. I could feel his embarrassment.

His shame.

He was ashamed that he had to eat rats to survive.

Mere seconds later, Sam came running out of the same corner, wearing nothing but a pair of jeans. He ran so fast, he was nothing but a golden blur, and when he smacked into the force field, it was with a sickening thud.

"Heven? Oh my God, Heven." Both his hands flattened against the invisible barrier and his eyes roamed every part of me.

"Sam," I cried, not even bothering to hide my tears. I threw my hands up against his and I marveled in the heat I felt radiating through the barrier. My eyes slid closed and I leaned my forehead between our hands. "It's you."

"What are you doing here?"

"I'm not sure. I was asleep and…"

I stumbled back when he slammed into the barrier. He ran at it again and again, trying to break through.

"Stop," I said sadly. "It's no use."

"God *damn* it," he yelled. "When I get out of here I am going to kill you, you bastard!" he screamed.

"Sam, calm down." I went back to the barrier without hesitation and laid my hands upon it again.

Breathing heavy, Sam did the same. "He's back in your head, then?" His eyes burned gold.

"I'm not sure, but it would explain how I got here."

"Has he talked to you?"

"No. Have you seen him?"

"No," he spat. "Let him come down here. I'll rip his head off."

"Sam!" I looked around. "Shhh…" It scared me he would threaten Beelzebub like this. What would happen to him?

"Shit," he swore. "I'm sorry. I didn't mean to scare you."

"I'm not afraid."

He looked me over, his eyes narrowing on the burns on my arm. "How are you doing?"

I was better than him. The dagger wound on his bicep was not healed, but swollen, and his ribcage was black and blue. "Why hasn't that healed?" I asked.

He shrugged. "I can't heal as good while I'm down here, I guess."

I glanced behind him. "You've been eating rats?"

He lowered his eyes and one of his hands fell away. I cried out, trying to grab it back, but my hand hit against the force field. "I don't have a choice."

"I know that. I don't care."

His eyes came back up to my face and I drank in every inch of him. He was so utterly breathtaking. Everything inside me warmed just looking at him. "I miss you so much," I whispered.

"Me too."

I pulled away from the doorway and looked around. "Hev?"

"I'm going to get you out of here." I ran to the cell over from his and peered in. "Kimber?"

She didn't respond at first and I yelled again. Then I heard this odd scrapping sound and she dragged herself over by the door. I gasped. Her hair was matted, blackened with dirt. Her cheeks were sunken in and her skin was gray and dead looking.

"Heven?" Her voice was a whisper of a sound.

I knelt down in front of the door. "You've got to convince your soul to get back into your body."

"No use," she said.

"Yes! I'm going to get you out of here.

"Why?"

"Because you don't belong here." I didn't consider Kimber my friend anymore, but no one deserved this. She didn't say anything so I continued. "Do you think you could weaken Hecate's spell long enough to break down the force field?"

"Her magic is too strong," Kimber said.

"Would you at least try?"

"No."

"No?"

"Heven," Sam called and I ran back to him. "It's no use, honey. She won't do anything without her soul to give her a reason to live."

"Then we make her soul get back in her body."

He was about to say something, but then he stiffened and his body began to shake; his eyes flashed gold and focused over my shoulder. "Run," he whispered.

I turned to see what would make him so upset. My eyes collided with someone I'd never seen before.

"Don't bother running, I would only catch you," he said. He was tall, blond and thin, but I could tell he possessed a good deal of muscle and power from the way he carried himself. He had blue eyes and wide cheekbones. Most people would probably call him handsome, but I thought he was creepy. Maybe it was because of where we were meeting.

"Who are you?" I asked.

Don't talk to him. Run the first chance you get, Sam warned.

"I came to check on the prisoners. Imagine my dismay to see someone trying to break one of them out." He made a tsking sound. "Such action deserves a punishment." He looked at Sam.

"No!" I cried. "He didn't do anything. Punish me instead."

"No!" Sam yelled. "Run, Heven." He began throwing himself against the force field again, trying desperately to get out.

I wasn't going to run. Whatever punishment this man was giving, I would do the taking. I felt my body begin to shake and I knew Sam was seconds from turning. Just as he was about to change forms, the man pulled something out of a box. An amulet. I looked back to see Sam twitching, sweat beading his face as his body struggled to shift but couldn't.

I ran at the man and he laughed, tossing the amulet at the barrier that Sam stood behind. To my amazement, it went right through and landed on the floor by his feet. Sam's body was still trying to shift, but thanks to his training with Gemma, it didn't hinder him as much as it could have, and he dove at the amulet. His hand closed around it and he threw it as hard as he could against the stone wall.

Nothing happened.

The man laughed. "You cannot destroy it. No matter how hard you try."

Abruptly, I spun and kicked my foot out, catching the man in the knee. He stumbled but did not go down. Anger stole over his face and he grabbed me, lifting me off my feet. I kicked him again in the abdomen and he cursed, throwing me to the ground. I tried to act like it didn't hurt because I didn't want Sam to see me in pain.

The man leaned over me, grabbing my hair and yanking my face up to meet his eyes. "I did exactly as you said. I punished you."

"No," I protested, struggling.

Sam was beyond himself, screaming and throwing things around inside the cell. I tried to look at him, to tell him I was okay, but the man wouldn't release my hair.

"Yes," the man growled. "I did *exactly* as you said. I punished *you* by throwing that amulet into his cell. Now he can't feed himself. Now he'll starve!"

I gasped.

The man laughed and released me, pushing me down onto the floor. "And that amulet will eventually weaken him to the point of exhaustion."

"Who are you?" I choked, holding back my tears. I'd never give him the satisfaction but inside I was breaking, splintering into a thousand pieces.

"Your worst nightmare," he said, grabbing me by the arm and yanking me up. I heard something in my shoulder pop but I ignored it.

He raised his fist to strike me and Sam roared… a sound that ripped right from his soul. It was so frightening that even the man holding me faltered. I took the opportunity and twisted out of his grasp, bouncing to my feet and falling into a crouch.

"Run, Heven, run!" Sam yelled.

But I couldn't. I was starting to feel disassociated with this place. I was fading and I knew I was waking up. I stumbled to the barrier and did what you never do to an attacker: I turned my back. I pressed myself as close to Sam as I could and pressed my fingers against his.

I'm coming back. I found a way to get you out.

Get out of here!

From behind, the man tried to grab me, but his hand went right through me. I held Sam's eyes until I faded completely away.

Chapter Five

Sam

When I was little, my mother used to say "hate" was a bad word. I wasn't supposed to say I hated anything. I never really understood why until recent months. It isn't really the word that is bad. It's the feelings that go along with it—the actions it inspires. I have acted upon hate. Actions I regret, actions that I'll never be able to take back.

Yet, still, I'm tempted.

Right now, I'm shaking with temptation.

It might actually be good I'm confined to this little dirty cell because, otherwise, the man standing in front of it might be dead. Scratch that. He *would* be dead.

Thank God Heven got out. For whatever reason, Beelzebub's hold on her dream was shattered. Seeing her had been a shock, but not unwelcome. It had been torture having her so close, yet so far away. And unfortunately, she was pulled here through her dreams, which meant Beelzebub was back.

"How did you do that?" The man outside the force field raged. "How did you break the hold?"

I growled, an unintentional sound but no less real. I wasn't sure who he was, but I knew he was just as depraved as Beelzebub himself.

"Answer me!" he roared, sinister darkness flashing in his eyes. Then he hit the force field in his rage. I stood there in shock when his fist came right through it instead of bouncing off. Every single time I touched the barrier, it stopped me. How was this man able to get the amulet through and now his hand?

It could only mean one thing.

"Beelzebub," I growled.

He yanked his hand back out and I watched as the barrier rippled and closed. "You figured it out, did you? A pity. I thought my new body would keep you confused a while longer."

"I would recognize your nasty stench anywhere," I spat, my body shaking with the need to attack him. But I couldn't shift. My body was being blocked from doing what came natural. As long as that amulet was inside this cell, I would remain in my human form. And I would weaken with every passing hour. How long could my body last fighting itself this way?

Then an idea began to form.

"You're lucky I want you alive right now." Beelzebub took a threatening step toward the barrier.

"You know, I don't think blond is your best look. You look like that guy from Scooby Doo, the one who always drove the Mystery Machine around. What a tool."

He stared at me blankly for a moment before scowling.

"Oh, that's right, you don't watch TV. Trust me, dude, that was *not* a compliment."

He took another step closer with clenched fists. "Shall I scar the other side of her face, then?"

I paused. What if my idea didn't work? Pissing him off wasn't a good idea when Heven was so defenseless. I shrugged. "Okay, keep the body."

I turned to walk away when his hand shot through the force field once more and grabbed my arm. I spun, throwing my weight backward, pulling him with me. He came through the barrier, stumbling. I yanked myself away and lunged at him, throwing out a fist and connecting with his new nose. Blood spurted across his face. I hit him again, enjoying the sound of crunching bone.

This is exactly why hate is so dangerous. It makes you forget all the reasons you shouldn't act stupid. But damn, hitting him felt so good.

He threw me off and jumped to his feet, wiping at the blood on his face. His chest was heaving with anger as I launched myself low, hooking him around the hips, and like a bulldozer, I pushed him back.

He grunted and fell right through the force field, taking me with him.

Heven

I jolted upright, gasping for air, clawing at the sheets on my bed. *"No, no, no."* It was me crying, but my voice sounded foreign to my ears.

"Heven, shit, calm down." Large warm hands grabbed my shoulders and I stilled. Through blurred eyes I made out Riley sitting on the edge of the bed. I hurled myself into his arms and sobbed.

His body was rigid, but his arms closed around me, holding me tightly against his chest. He didn't say anything and I was glad because the sound of his voice would remind me he wasn't Sam. I wanted Sam. After a while of crying, Riley pulled me back, but didn't let go and stared down at me.

"What's going on?"

I wiped my face with the back of my hand. "I'm so sorry. You didn't need to see that."

"No you don't," he growled when I tried to pull away. "Tell me."

"Remember how I told you about the Dream Walker?"

He nodded. "You mean Beetlejuice?"

I burst out laughing. Then I sucked in a breath, sorry for the moment of joy. Riley's usually icy gaze softened for an instant, and I looked away. "Beelzebub, Prince of Demons, Lord of Flies." I explained, then muttered, "He has like fifty titles."

"Yeah, I know who he is. Beetlejuice is just so much more fun to say."

"Stop."

"Stop?"

"Trying to cheer me up."

"Who says I'm trying to cheer you up?" He dropped his hands from my shoulders and let them fall to the mattress between us.

"You should've seen how bad he looked." I felt my lower lip quiver and I buried my face in my hands.

"Beelzebub?"

"No. Sam."

"You saw Sam?"

"I think the Dream Walker pulled me back into hell while I was sleeping."

"He's back?" Riley asked, getting up from the bed to prowl around the room.

"I didn't see him." I frowned. "But I wouldn't have been down there if he wasn't back."

"Tell me about Sam."

"He eats rats," I murmured.

"What?"

"He didn't want me to know…"

Riley leaned down in my face. "Make some sense already," he growled.

"How'd you get in here?" I asked abruptly.

"The window." He motioned his head toward the open window.

My stomach tightened. That's how Sam usually got in. "What time is it?"

"Six a.m."

"Crap." I stood. "I have to do the barn chores. I'm late."

"In a minute. You were telling me about Sam."

"It was so horrible," I whispered and launched into the tale of what happened and how I failed to get him out.

"Blaming yourself? What a martyr," he said sarcastically.

"I took away his only means of feeding himself. He can't turn and he can't eat rats as a human. He's going to starve."

"He's not and he could eat rats as a human if he really wanted to." Riley smirked.

I glared at him.

He sighed dramatically. "He's not going to starve."

"You're right. Since you're here, we can leave to get him." I stood up and wiped my eyes one last time. Then I grabbed a change of clothes out of my dresser. "I'll meet you in the orchard in an hour, no forty-five minutes. I have to feed the horses and do some stuff in the barn." Since Sam had been gone, I took over all his chores.

"I'll help you." Riley offered.

"I can handle it."

"The faster you get done, the faster you can train." He pointed out.

I nodded. "Yeah, okay."

He stood and went to the window.

"Riley?"

He turned.

"Thanks. And I'm sorry about earlier."

"Feel free to pay me back anytime."

I snorted. "I'll see you outside in five minutes."

I thought he might say something more, but he must have decided against it. Without another word, he left.

Sam

The amulet was still too close and I couldn't shift. My body shook so hard with need it hurt, but I ignored it. This was my one chance to be free. I lurched up off the floor and took off down the dungeon hallway.

But then I stopped.

And turned back.

I stopped in front of Kimber's cell and grabbed hold of the bars that confined her.

From the darkness, she whispered, "Just go; don't waste your time on me."

Behind me Beelzebub roared and jumped to his feet.

"I'll come back for you," I vowed and took off running again.

Beelzebub began raging and ripped down one of the torches that lined the black granite walls. He launched it at me and his aim was true. It hit me in the center of the back. I was fireproof so fire wasn't a good weapon to use against me. However, the sheer force of the hit made me stumble and singed what little clothing I was wearing.

I fell to one knee, my kneecap taking the brunt of my fall, and I twisted off it and got to my feet, favoring my uninjured leg. I would heal, but down here it wouldn't be fast enough.

"You run like a coward!" Beelzebub screamed.

I ignored the barb meant to enrage me. I was no coward, but I wasn't stupid either. I knew I was dehydrated, half-starved and exhausted from being so close to that damn amulet. And because I couldn't shift, running was my only option.

I made it to the dungeon door, flinging it open and starting up the stairs. That's when a heavy length of chain lashed out and wrapped around me, yanking me backward. I fell onto my back as he pulled me closer, dragging me across the uneven ground. I grabbed a fistful of the chain and yanked back, pulling Beelzebub off balance.

But it wasn't enough.

When I was closer, he let go of the chain, picked up the torch he hit me with earlier and raised it above his head. I rolled and shot to my feet as he swung. He didn't get me in the head like he planned—I was too fast, but he did hit me. Right in the ribs... The ones that were already broken.

Black dots swam before my eyes and I swayed a little on my feet. I heard his vile laugh and I knew I'd lost.

Seconds later, I was tossed right back into my cage.

Heven

I was grateful for Riley's help with the morning chores because I was pretty much useless. I couldn't concentrate. I was too worried about Sam and the man who was down in hell with Sam. I tried to tell myself that, for once, Sam being trapped behind that force field was a good thing. That man couldn't hurt Sam because he couldn't get to him. Still, my heart raced with anxiety and I kept feeling this sense of urgency. I was missing something. Something I shouldn't be. I did my best to calm myself, not wanting Sam to pick up on my feelings.

About halfway through the chores, Logan walked into the barn, stopping short when he saw Riley. Riley straightened rigidly and narrowed his eyes.

"Riley," I said, tossing down the bag of feed, "this is Logan, Sam's brother."

Before he could say anything, I turned toward Logan. "This is Riley, Sam's old roommate. I told you about him last night."

"Last night?" Riley asked while he and Logan stared at each other.

"Logan is staying here with me and Gran until Sam comes home."

"Hey, kid," Riley said with no real emotion in his voice.

"Are you strong enough to get my brother out of hell?" Logan said, not even reacting to the "kid" remark and keeping his voice flat.

"I think I can handle it."

Logan nodded. "Okay. Good. I might not look like much, but don't let that fool you. You pull anything and you will answer to me."

Riley's eyes flashed.

Not gold.

Silver.

"Logan, Riley is here to help. We can trust him."

"Sam didn't trust him. That's why he ran him out of town."

I glanced back at Riley as he took a menacing step forward. I moved toward Logan, who drew himself up to his full height and then stilled.

Riley's steps faltered and he looked around in disbelief. He held up his arms, straight out, and flattened his palms as if he were pressing against walls. Then his hands curled around something and he shook.

Like he was rattling the bars of a cage.

"Logan," I hissed. "Stop it!"

Logan didn't respond, just stood there watching Riley.

"We need him to help Sam. This is not the way to convince him."

Riley let out a growl and then Logan blinked and turned toward me. "Sorry."

"It's sweet you want to look out for Sam... for me. But no more of your false worlds, okay?"

Logan nodded. Sometimes I forgot about Logan's leftover power. Mostly because the demon that had possessed him had taken away so much from him. But it had left something behind. Logan still had the ability to look at a person and make their world, the room they were standing in, disappear. He could replace it with a new world, a false one, but one that completely fooled the person into believing they were exactly where he wanted them to be.

I knew exactly what it was like because I had been the victim of that ability more than once.

Riley didn't take it as well as I used to.

With his actual reality restored, he lunged forward and caught Logan by the throat. "You want to play games with me?"

Logan's eyes widened as his sneakers dangled above the barn floor.

"Riley!" I gasped and grabbed at his arms. "Stop it! Put him down."

It was like he couldn't (or wouldn't) hear me. "No one threatens me."

Darkness seemed to swirl right out of Riley while Logan clutched at the hand surrounding his neck, cutting off his air. Chills raced up my spine. Logan made a wheezing sound.

I pushed myself between Riley and Logan as much as I could and stood up on my tiptoes. "He can't breathe! Put him down right now! He's sick!"

Riley's eyes flashed down to mine and I gasped and stumbled back. He released Logan and we both went falling to the ground, with me trying not to land on top of him. I rolled and stood, leaning over Logan, putting my hands on his chest. "Deep breaths, Logan." He was gasping for air and struggling to get up. I pressed on his chest lightly. "Stay down, it's okay."

I spun toward Riley, whose eyes were glittering with sparks of silver. "If you ever touch him again…"

"You'll what?" Riley said coldly.

"I'm not as helpless as I look."

"I'm meaner than you think."

"That's obvious. He's just a boy." I turned away as Logan began coughing. I leaned over him, trying to calm him down, to help him breathe. Before his coughing subsided, blood leaked from his nose. I ran to get him a rag and held it out to him.

"I'm okay now," Logan said, getting up from the floor. "I'm sorry."

"Maybe you should sit down."

"What's wrong with him?" Riley said. There was more emotion in his voice than before.

I glanced over my shoulder. "He was possessed by a demon. It left him weak and…" My words trailed away because I didn't want to say what I was thinking.

"You got that power from a demon?"

Logan nodded. "I shouldn't have done that to you."

Riley shrugged. "Why not? I would've done it to you."

Logan wasn't sure what to say. Neither was I.

"I guess since Sam's gone, you're the man around here." Riley's eyes slid to me, then back to Logan. "I don't blame you for wanting to protect what's yours."

"Is that supposed to be an apology?" I said, turning back to Logan.

He seemed to be breathing normally and the nosebleed had stopped.

"It sounded like one to me," Riley said, back to his usual sarcastic self.

My back stiffened, but Logan said, "It's cool. I guess I deserved it."

I wasn't sure I agreed with that, but I wasn't going to rehash it all. "I have training."

"I'll come with you," Logan said, stuffing the rag in his pocket.

"Maybe you should go rest."

He rolled his eyes. "I can rest while I watch you kick Cole's butt."

I laughed. "Okay, come on." I turned back to Riley. "You coming?" I partially held my breath, wondering if Logan's stunt would chase him off.

"How could I miss you kicking someone's butt?" he said and motioned with his hand.

I breathed a sigh of relief as we all left the barn.

* * *

We beat Cole and Gemma to the orchard and were sitting beneath an apple tree when Cole appeared. His steps faltered just slightly when his gaze locked on Riley, but then he continued over, walking a little faster than before.

"Who's this?" Cole asked, stopping directly in front of Riley. His aura radiated suspicion and mistrust.

"Cole this is Riley. Riley, this is my brother Cole."

They assessed each other silently and it annoyed me. I stood up and put myself between them. "What do you have there?" I asked Cole.

"Your breakfast."

"For me?" I rubbed at my ribs. They were aching.

He rolled his eyes. "When's the last time you ate, Hev?"

A vivid image of Sam being hungry went through my brain and I shrugged. "I'm not hungry."

Cole frowned and shifted the coffees and paper sack into one hand, then used his free hand to feel my forehead. "Are you still sick?"

"No."

"Let me see your arm." He lifted it up, inspecting the marks, which thankfully were fading.

"I'm not five years old, you know," I snapped.

He must have been satisfied because he thrust a coffee and the bag at me. "Eat."

My stomach revolted and pain echoed through my knee. Maybe I was running too much lately.

Riley reached around and took the coffee and bag from my hands. Cole glared at him, but Riley ignored him and returned to his seat beneath the tree. I sat down next to him.

Riley reached into the bag and pulled out a huge blueberry muffin and took a bite. Cole's aura screamed.

"Thanks for the food, man," Riley said, shoving another giant bite into his mouth.

Cole took a threatening step forward and I panicked. They had to get along. At least until Sam was home. I reached over and plucked the muffin out of Riley's hands and took a bite.

"It's good," I said, forcing myself to chew and swallow. It tasted like sand.

Cole seemed to relax. Beside me, Riley took the lid off my coffee and smelled it. He wrinkled his nose, but then he took a sip.

"Who the hell is this guy?" Cole spat. He glanced at Logan, hoping for an answer.

"This is gross, Hev. Here, you drink it," Riley said, gaining all our attention once more.

I stared at the coffee warily. Cole glared at us and I didn't want to hurt his feelings; after all, he was sweet enough to bring me coffee. It was bad enough that Riley insulted it. I took the cup and took a sip. It was sweet and hot. I liked it. "This isn't gross," I declared.

"All the more reason you should drink it," Riley said smoothly.

It dawned on me what he had done. My eyes flew to his face. He smirked. He conned me into eating. I took another sip of the coffee. I felt the warmth slide down to my belly as I sat down in the grass next to Logan.

Heven, tell me you're okay, Sam's voice was urgent.

I'm okay. What about you? Suddenly, I realized that the pain in my ribs was his and probably so was the echo of pain in my knee. *What did that guy do to you?*

That guy is Beelzebub, Heven. He's definitely back.

I jerked like I had been slapped. I should have realized! The sense of urgency, the rapid heartbeat… those had been Sam's feelings, not mine. *What happened after I got pulled away?*

Something was gripping my arm, distracting me from Sam and I looked up. Riley was peering at me with a frown on his face.

"What's wrong?" he asked.

"Heven?" Logan asked anxiously. "Is Sam okay?"

Cole made a sound. "She's talking to Sam."

"She's *what?*" Riley asked.

"He's okay, Logan. We're just talking," I said to Logan quickly, as I waved Riley's hand away and focused back on Sam. I didn't mention that Sam and I shared a Mindbond. Cole could fill him in.

Be careful… I made him angry.

How?

He can reach through the force field; it yields for him. I tried to get out. But I didn't make it.

I reached down and felt my knee. *At least we know there's a way through the barrier now. This could help us. How bad are you hurt?*

I hit my knee and my ribs are still bothering me, but I will be fine. Listen to me, Heven. Trust no one you don't know. Just because he is in that body now doesn't mean he'll stay there.

Hang in there, okay? Get some rest.

Be careful. If anything happens to you…

Everything's going to be fine.

Six days… six very long days had passed, and though I just saw him, he felt farther away than ever.

"How's he doing, Hev?" Cole asked me quietly, sitting down next to me, drawing me out of thought.

"He's a strong guy," I answered, unwilling to voice my concerns because Logan was sitting right there. I looked at him and smiled before telling everyone, "Beelzebub is back.

We need to be careful. Right now he's in the body of a man with blond hair. But from this point on, we can't trust anyone we don't know."

I glanced at Riley to see if he grasped the situation—if he really understood how dangerous Beelzebub was, but he wasn't paying any attention to me. He was looking beyond Cole and me at an approaching figure.

Cole followed our eyes, and when he saw Gemma, he stood and met her a few rows of apple trees away. She smiled briefly at him, but then her gaze slid to us, or rather to Riley. Something around Gemma seemed to tighten even though her face was blank as she walked with ease. It might not have been noticeable, except Cole noticed it right away and his aura was bursting with anxiety over what might be upsetting her.

My brother was a lot of things, but stupid wasn't one of them. His eyes landed directly on Riley. Everything in me began to splinter. I knew something was about to challenge his presence. Could I go against Cole and Gemma if they didn't want Riley around?

I had to.

Riley was the strongest of us all. Even though Gemma was a warrior and a fallen angel with abilities that were amazing, Riley possessed a special set of skills that were absolutely necessary for going into hell.

Gemma and Cole stopped before us with Gemma looking more uncomfortable than I had ever seen her. I looked over at Riley, but he seemed completely unaffected by the cloud that settled over us.

I cleared my throat. "Gemma, this is Riley," I began, but she cut me off.

"No need for introductions," she said.

I looked between her and Riley. Cole looked at me for some sort of explanation and I shrugged. Gemma shifted uncomfortably and Riley smiled. I was pretty sure he was enjoying her reaction.

"Riley?" I asked. His gaze flitted to me and his smile faded.

Before Riley could say anything, Gemma said, "We've met."

"You know each other?" Cole burst out. His aura filled with muddy, faded colors. He was jealous and suspicious. If he liked Riley before, he sure didn't now.

Gemma nodded.

"How ya doing, Gems? Long time no see," Riley said, splaying his legs out in front of himself and crossing his feet at the ankles. He was so unaffected by everyone else's obvious distress, I wondered what it would take to upset him.

"What are you doing with him?" Gemma turned to me.

"He's going to help us get Sam out of hell."

Gemma shook her head. "Riley can't help you."

"Oh?" I asked, lifting my eyebrows. "So you can swim to the bottom of that sludge and get me a Lucent Marble?" Gemma's mouth opened, then closed, her lips settling into a frown.

"He isn't human?" Cole scowled.

Riley laughed again.

Gemma ignored Cole and Riley to stare at me levelly. "You shouldn't trust him."

"Why?" I asked.

"Because he's a killer."

Chapter Six

Heven

Gemma's declaration left me feeling cold. I glanced at Riley, and like always, he didn't seem the least bit offended Gemma had called him a killer. Did that mean it wasn't true? Or maybe his lack of emotion was a sign it was.

"Would someone please tell me what the hell is the deal with this guy?" Cole spat.

"He's a hellhound like Sam," I responded.

Cole made a face like his stomach hurt. "What is it with you and hellhounds?"

"Sam and Riley used to be roommates."

This bit of news seemed to surprise Gemma. Maybe she didn't know Riley as well as she declared. Cole made a rude noise, but I ignored him and turned back to Gemma. "How do you know Riley?"

"Don't you mean how do I know he's a killer?"

I nodded.

"I'm the one who trained him. I taught him everything he knows."

Riley laughed. "Don't flatter yourself."

"You trained Riley?"

"It was a long time ago," Gemma said softly, looking over at Cole.

Riley's white teeth flashed as he made a sound kind of like a laugh. "You and a human, huh?"

I kicked his foot, but he didn't take his eyes off Gemma. Couldn't he see he was causing trouble?

"I never thought I would see that," Riley mused.

Obviously he liked causing trouble.

Cole turned toward him. "What?"

"Gemma. Getting involved, making attachments."

"Shut up!" I spat and stepped in front of him, blocking him from my brother's view. Cole was standing there with clenched fists. "You need to explain," I told Gemma.

"You want me to explain?" She seemed surprised.

"Of course."

Gemma dared a look at Cole. He actually smiled. "You're not getting out of here that easy."

Gemma gave Cole a half smile and his aura, which had been crazy up until now, smoothed out and returned almost to normal. The deep magenta color that was unique to him bloomed out a little farther than usual and seemed to reach toward Gemma.

I looked over my shoulder at Riley, who was still lounging in the grass. I had a hard time picturing him as a killer. I mean, wouldn't I be afraid of a killer? Sure, at times he made me uneasy, but I'd never really been afraid… I glanced at Logan. Well, I guess that wasn't true because I had just been afraid of Riley when he went after Sam's little brother.

I looked back down at Riley, keeping my eyes on him when I spoke, gaging his reaction. "So, Gemma, why don't you tell us exactly how you know Riley?"

He looked up and his eyes flashed. Silver was a much colder color than gold.

"I'll start with why I fell from heaven."

I spun around in surprise and we all stood there, staring at Gemma… waiting for the information we've all wondered about but never dared to ask. She didn't seem nervous, just sad. Inside, I was screaming. I could hear the ticking of a clock inside my head, reminding me that Sam only had so much time, that *I* only had so much time.

I wanted to snap at her to hurry up, but I knew it wouldn't help so I forced myself to take a step back and sit down near Riley. I motioned to Logan and he came and lowered himself next to me. So far, he seemed pretty neutral about Gemma's declaration. Maybe he was waiting to hear the evidence like me.

"Heaven is… It's indescribable." Gemma began softly. "There is no other place like it. Light and peace and love fill everything. There are no feelings of anger or sadness. It truly is what everyone imagines it to be. I was an angel and my job was to occasionally come down from heaven to spread God's word. It was during one of those trips that I met Callum."

Beside Gemma, Cole stiffened, but she didn't notice because she was lost in the past.

"He was unlike anything I had ever seen. In heaven, everything is perfect, beautiful, symmetrical. Callum wasn't any of those things. He was flawed, striking and nothing about him was linear. Nothing was black or white; Callum existed in the gray area. I think that's why I was so taken with him. He was everything I thought was wrong with the world. But there wasn't one thing wrong with him."

"How did you meet?" I asked.

"I met him during one of my many trips here to Earth. We spoke only briefly, but those minutes stayed with me. I thought of him often, and then the next time I was here, I sought him out." She lowered her eyes as if that was something to be ashamed of. "I knew I shouldn't, but I did anyway. After that, we would meet in secret."

"Why in secret? Weren't you allowed to see him?" I asked.

"My contact with humans was to be on an as-needed basis only. As an angel, I was bound to God. My love was supposed to be only for him. It's considered sinful to love anyone but God."

"Doesn't God want you to love everyone?" Logan asked softly.

Gemma smiled at him. "Yes. Yes, he does. But you see, angels are held to a different standard. By nature we are caring and giving, but we are to only love God. That's why we are angels, his most loyal and devoted servants."

"So you fell in love with Callum? And you were punished?" I asked.

"Yes, I did love Callum. And he loved me." She glanced at Cole, who was stone-faced, so she continued. "I got into some trouble one time when I came down to Earth. I see now that it was because I was distracted, too involved with my own feelings to see what was going on around me. I was captured by some rogue fallen angels. Angels who should've been in hell, but were on Earth. Callum was there; he saw what happened. As a human, he was powerless against my kind. I begged him to go, to leave. And he did."

"He left you there?" Cole said, disgusted.

"Yes," Gemma said sadly. "He went and made a deal. A deal with Beelzebub. He sacrificed his humanity and the humanity of his family bloodline to become a hellhound so he would have enough strength to help me."

I gasped.

Riley yawned.

"He rescued me." Her voice faded away and she shook her head. "But he was foolish. He should've known making a deal with evil would only create more evil."

At this, Riley stiffened.

"So what happened?" Cole asked.

"Well, I was banished from heaven because I fell in love with a human… a human that basically made a deal with the devil… and despite his hellhound status, I loved him anyway."

She looked at me and I nodded. I knew exactly what it was like.

"But because my greatest crime was falling in love, I was sent to Earth instead of being sent to hell. I was stripped of my wings, but still able to keep some of my powers. I have dedicated my life to seeking and destroying evil."

"But what about Callum? Where is he?" Logan asked.

Gemma was silent a moment. "We were happy for a while. But after he changed… he was different. The goodness in him had fallen prey to the binds that held him to hell. I was trying to help him, to deny the darkness in him, but Beelzebub wouldn't allow it. He showed up one day with an amulet"—she fingered the pouch at her waist—"keeping Callum from shifting, from being able to defend himself and then he killed him."

Finished with her tale, Gemma looked up. Anguish stole over her features, and for the first time, I truly understood why she was so reluctant to let anybody in.

Cole cleared his throat. I wanted to reach out to him, but I didn't think he would let me and I didn't want to draw attention to the fact this story was breaking him. But then he did something beautiful. Instead of focusing on how crappy he felt (it was all over his aura), he reached out to Gemma and put a hand on her shoulder and squeezed. "I'm so sorry you had to go through that."

Gemma cleared her throat and then looked at him. "Thank you."

I didn't know what to say. She risked everything to be with the man she loved and then he was killed and she was left alone to walk the earth forever.

"Such a sad tale." Riley drawled, drawing all of our stares.

"How does this relate to Riley?" I asked.

"Callum was my grandfather," Riley replied.

My eyes widened in shock. Even Cole seemed taken aback.

Gemma nodded. "I had known Callum had a son, and after he was killed, I checked in on him from time to time. When Riley was born, I kept a close eye on the family because I knew the hellhound gene would surface in him."

"Because of the deal Callum made with Beelzebub," I said, looking at Riley with new eyes. What must it be like to know that his grandfather had made a deal that literally took away some of his humanity?

"Yes. I always watched them from afar, until the summer Riley turned ten."

Riley's mouth flattened.

"He had no idea what was going on with his body or how to control it. He was so much like Callum..." Gemma's voice faded away. Cole finally became restless and got to his feet and wandered off, but stayed close by.

Gemma watched him, no doubt wondering if she should go after him.

"Give him a minute to cool off," I said.

Gemma nodded. "It took a while, but I made friends with the family and I tried to spend as much time with Riley as I could. I taught him about what was happening and how to control his movements. I didn't want someone to use one of those amulets against him like they had Callum."

"And I turned into a killer. The end," Riley said, getting to his feet.

"Not a killer, not right away," Gemma said. She looked at me to explain. "Like Callum, Riley struggles internally... There's a part of him that's bound."

"We've heard enough," Riley growled, cutting off her words.

I began to worry that he was going to take off. Killer or not, I needed him. "I think you better talk to Cole," I told Gemma.

She nodded. Before she went after my brother, she grabbed my arm. "Be careful. You cannot trust him."

Riley made a sound and I shook off her arm. "Thank you for telling us this."

Gemma glanced toward Cole. "I never meant to hurt you or to keep this from you. I just never knew how to say it."

"It's okay," I said, meaning it.

When Gemma was out of earshot, I turned to Riley. "I don't care if you're a killer."

His dark eyes affixed on me. "Until I try and kill you."

"You wouldn't do that."

"Does Sam know you found me?"

I swallowed. "No."

"How come?" He took a step closer to me. I held my ground.

"I don't want to worry him."

"Because he would be worried if he knew that you were with me?"

"I'm not sure," I hedged.

"Yes, you are. He ran Casey and me out of town because he didn't want us anywhere near you. Why do you think that is?"

I didn't want to think about that.

Riley took another step closer, his warm breath brushing over my face. "Because Gemma is right. I am a killer." As if on cue, his eyes flashed silver.

"I'm not scared of you." My voice was strong.

He lifted a brow. "Don't ever think you know me because I'm a hellhound like your boy. Sam and I are nothing alike. I've done some very bad things."

"Is killing one of them?" I met his gaze straight-on.

"Why do you think I had to swim to catch up to the ferry last night? I stayed behind to take care of a few things."

I gasped. "You killed those men?"

"Not all of them. Just the two who threatened you."

"Why would you do that?" I searched for any indication he might be lying, but all I saw was truth.

"Better them than you." He shrugged. Did he have so little value for human life, then?

"I took care of them. Of myself."

"I thought the message you sent wasn't strong enough." He stared into my eyes, almost challenging me. Was he talking this way just to get a reaction? Was he trying to scare me away? Was I going to let him?

I stood there for a moment, not once looking away from his cold stare. Then, I shrugged. His eyes narrowed at the small movement.

"I don't care."

"You don't?"

"Nope. As far as I'm concerned, having a killer on my side will only help me get Sam back."

"Who says I'm on your side?" he said very quietly, almost a growl straight from his throat.

"If you weren't, you would've killed me already, instead of just threatening me, being that you're such a cold-blooded killer and all." I waved my hand in front of his face, wafting away his veiled threat and my fear.

He threw back his head and laughed. He had a good laugh. It wasn't the laugh of a killer.

"What do you say we get out of here? I have somewhere I need to be."

His eyes narrowed like he was trying to decide if I had an agenda. I picked up my coffee and took a sip. It was cold.

"Walk back to the house with me?" I said to Logan. We walked away without another glance in his direction. I suppressed a smile when he fell into step behind us.

"I don't trust him, but you're right. We need him to get Sam," Logan said quietly to me. Even though his voice was quiet, I knew without a doubt Riley was listening.

I smiled at Logan. For once, it felt like we were on the same team. Team Sam. "Thanks for the support."

Even though I was shaken about the things Gemma said about Riley and I was scared that I wouldn't be able to rescue Sam, I was still going to be strong. I wasn't going to let on how afraid I really was. Especially not in front of Logan.

I glanced over my shoulder at Riley and smirked, putting a hand on my hip. "Let's go. Where we're going… I'm going to need you to refrain from murder."

* * *

Training this morning had not gone as I planned and I was full of pent-up energy and anger. Probably because there was too much talking and not enough punching. My dream from the night before left me feeling a sick kind of dread in the pit of my stomach that I couldn't shake. I didn't ask Riley if he was up for a run because I knew he would be. He was a hellhound. He could outrun me with ease. He didn't say anything when I pulled off the main road and parked Gran's Toyota in the grass. He didn't say anything when I climbed out of the car and zipped the car keys into the little pocket in the leggings I was wearing. When I began stretching, his lips remained closed too.

I sighed. My little test to see how far he would go without asking any questions failed. "We're going to the hospital, to see my mother. I like to park a few miles from the hospital and run the distance there."

He nodded. "How far?"

"Today I parked seven miles away." I waited for him to scoff at the mileage.

"Sounds good." He pushed the hair off his forehead and glanced at me. "You ready?"

I hoped I didn't make a fool of myself by trying to run this far. Yesterday, I had only run five miles. "Yeah." I reached into the truck and pulled out my small backpack and strapped it onto my back. "Let's go."

We only made it a few yards when I stumbled. The next thing I knew I was hit with an overwhelming white light. I heard Riley calling my name and I tried to tell him everything was fine, but there wasn't time for that before I disappeared.

* * *

The InBetween looked the same as every other time I had been here: empty and white. Airis was standing in the center, dressed all in white (you think she would get tired of being colorless all the time). Her blond hair was long and hanging down her back. Her face seemed to be frozen in the same expression she always wore: serene and loving.

"Please excuse the interruption," she began smoothly. "I needed to speak with you."

"Has something happened? Is my dad all right?" I knew better than to ask to see him. After we had to leave Sam in hell, I went to Airis for help. She refused to help me, something I still hadn't forgotten. To her credit, and to soften the blow, she had gifted me a few precious moments with my father, who had died a few years ago.

"Your father is well."

"Has something happened to Sam?" I asked frantically.

"I can't see into hell, remember?"

I nodded. "What is it?"

"I wanted to speak with you about you. I'm concerned."

"About me?"

"Yes. I'm concerned you're veering from your path."

"My path?"

"As a Supernatural Treasure, you're protecting a Treasure Map. How's that going?"

"The map is safe."

"For how long?"

"Excuse me?"

"I'm concerned about the choices you've been making lately."

"My choices?" I echoed, confused.

Airis came forward and laid a hand upon my cheek; peace flowed through her into me. I pulled back. "Things are very confusing right now, I know. Do not lose sight of the path you are on by trusting the wrong people who could lead you astray."

Did she mean Riley?

"I haven't forgotten the path that I'm on and that I need to get the map to safety. And I will. But right now I have to get Sam out of hell."

"You would risk the map for him… a hellhound?"

Of course I would, but something held me back from saying that. "He isn't just a hellhound, and up until Sam disappeared, you seemed to think he was worthy and on the same path as I."

"He may not be the same if he comes back," Airis said, not unkindly.

"He's the same," I insisted. My anger was growing.

Airis bowed her head in what I hoped was agreement. "I just wanted to remind you of your path and to warn you of those who tempt you to turn from it."

"Are you worried that I might trade the scroll for Sam's release?"

"Would you?"

I was shocked that she would ask me so blatantly. While it had crossed my mind, I knew that it wasn't an option. It was why I was exhausting every other resource I had available to me, including Riley. Maybe that's what made Airis so nervous. "No. I wouldn't. I understand how important the scroll is."

"Do you understand how important you are to the scroll?"

"No." It was my turn to answer so directly. "I don't. Will you tell me?"

"Resist the devil and he will flee from you," Airis responded.

"What?"

"There's a thin line between heaven and hell. Remember which side you are on. Don't ever forget."

"I won't forget."

"Remember that God allows us the freedom of free will. Use yours wisely and beware of hidden evil."

"I don't understand."

"May God be with you." She lifted her hand and I knew she was going to send me away.

"Airis, wait…" But it was too late.

Everything went white.

Chapter Seven

Sam

Frustration. It was the kind of feeling that filled you up, made your skin feel tight, like it was stretching to the point of bursting.

I had been so close.

So close to escaping. To being free. So close, yet so very far away.

I lay on the dirty hard floor, ignoring the aching in my ribs and knee. At least my knee was healing enough that I could put weight on it. I would need to be mobile for the next time.

Because next time there would be no stopping me.

After being tossed back into this hole, Beelzebub stormed up the stairs and silence descended once more. But as I lay there berating myself, there came a noise. Muffled, but still I heard it. I glanced over at the doorway leading to the steps, realizing that whatever it was came from upstairs.

Beelzebub was still here.

A loud shatter sounded and there was a heavy thump on the floor above. Clearly, he wasn't alone. I moved toward the doorway of my cell, toward the sounds. My hearing was still good. Maybe I could find out what was going on.

"You dare challenge me!" Beelzebub roared. Well, it wasn't loud, but I heard it so clearly I knew he had to be yelling. Which, really, wasn't new for him. He had two tones: loud and extremely loud.

All the better to hear him.

Someone else spoke, but at a much lower tone, and I couldn't make out the words.

"Where is it?" Beelzebub demanded.

Again, I only heard the muffled voice in response. But judging from the sounds of shattering objects, I knew whatever was said did not make Beelzebub very happy.

"You *will* do as you are told. You have no choice," he demanded.

"I don't have it." I strained and was able to hear.

"You have twelve hours. Or the deal is off."

I wasn't surprised Beelzebub had a deal with someone. He probably had a million deals. There were so many desperate people out there that his power and false promises were probably very enticing. Still, I wondered what this deal was for.

"And if you betray me, you'll end up chained to the floor of hell to be fed on for all eternity!" He laughed like the idea thrilled him. Which, I'm sure it did.

Chained to the floor of hell? Fed on for all eternity? That was a new one. It made me realize we knew next to nothing about hell and the other dealings that went on down here. Maybe it was time we looked beyond the scope of the horror that plagued us.

I was ashamed to admit that I never thought anything could be worse.

It wasn't the first time I would be wrong.

My attention was caught once more by the muffled voice of another. I strained to hear through the thick granite walls.

"Go, now! The opportunity is now! The next time I see you, it better be done!"

More loud thumps and a few more shattering sounds echoed; then everything fell quiet once more.

I leaned back against the wall, and for once, I was grateful I was trapped in here. Maybe that was preferable to being chained to the floor of hell.

Heven

"Riley!" I yelled. "Riley!"

When I got back to the spot where I left Riley, he wasn't there. I ran to the car and peered in the windows, wondering where he went. Did he take my sudden disappearance as a chance to run off? Did he decide helping Sam wasn't worth his time? The interior of the car was clearly empty and I turned away, rushing to the line of trees. I ran right into something solid and warm. I would have fallen, but strong arms grabbed me by the shoulders and steadied me.

"Are you all right?" Riley asked. His face was smooth as usual, but his eyes betrayed him. There was a hint of that silver in them and his fingers bit into my arms a bit too much for me to believe he was unaffected by my disappearance.

"I'm fine. I didn't mean to worry you."

"I wasn't worried."

I didn't think calling an admitted killer a liar was smart, so I let that one go. I glanced down at his hands holding me and he let go, but he didn't move away.

"I was in the InBetween with Airis. I told you about her." He nodded and I continued. "She just wanted to talk to me."

"Does that happen a lot?"

"No. Usually, I call her."

"What did she want?"

"Nothing."

He lifted a thick brow. I wasn't about to get into it with him on the side of the road. Besides, I wasn't even sure what I thought of it yet.

"Are you ready?" I didn't wait for him to respond, but began jogging ahead. Now, more than ever, I needed to run. I wasn't worried I wouldn't make the seven miles anymore. I would. I had plenty of stress and anxiety to keep me going.

Riley fell into step with ease. "Relax your shoulders," he instructed. "You're too tense."

I wanted to laugh. Instead, I did what he suggested. He didn't say anything more and I was grateful. My mind was too distracted to hold a conversation. Had Airis been warning me about working with Riley? Out of the corner of my eye, I looked at him. There was a lot of evidence that said he wasn't to be trusted, that he was dangerous and unreliable.

But I didn't feel that way.

I trusted him.

What did she mean by turning from my path? She almost made it seem like I should turn my back on Sam and leave him there. That didn't seem very godly to me. How could she turn her back on someone who had risked everything for her cause?

I stumbled on a rock but righted myself and kept right on running. In fact, I pushed harder.

Airis talked a lot about those who would seek to turn me from my path. She warned me of people who weren't to be trusted.

What if one of those people was her?

* * *

When we hit the parking lot, I stopped running. My lungs burned and my legs felt like Jell-O, but I made it and that was all that mattered. I was still worried about my little visit with Airis and what it all meant, but the run drained the worst of my anxiety. For that, I was grateful.

Riley walked beside me and I had to strain to even hear him breathing. "Are you even winded? Was that not hard for you at all?"

He smiled. He had the kind of smile that was arrogant and self-assured. Stubble lined his jaw and I wondered how often he had to shave because his hair was so dark. I doubted he cared when he shaved and only did it when he felt like it. He didn't strike me as the kind of guy who cared what people thought. In fact, it probably amused him when people didn't approve. He noticed my stare and grinned wider. I dropped my eyes.

"You did better than I thought," he said. "You didn't collapse."

I rolled my eyes. "Gee, thanks."

"You going to collapse now?" he asked.

"No," I spat, offended.

When the entrance to the hospital was close, I cleared my throat. "I'll have to visit my mom by myself. They're only letting immediate family into her room."

"Okay."

"I didn't think about how boring it would be for you to sit around the hospital and wait for me," I said, suddenly sorry I'd invited him. It had been for selfish reasons, because I wanted to be sure he didn't just take off, but here I was leaving him alone.

"I'll manage."

"Usually, after I visit, I get a ride from the hospital security guard, Colin, back to my car."

He nodded. I bit my lip, looking down at Gran's car keys in my hand. "I guess it would be okay for you to go grab the car and meet me back here—in the parking lot—in like an hour?"

Riley smirked and snatched the keys from my hand. I scowled, already regretting my decision. "Listen, I've already trashed one of Gran's cars. If you trash this one, you'll be sorry."

"What are you gonna do, stab me with a fork?" he said with a smirk, looking at my pocket.

I looked down and saw the ends of my weapon sticking out of my pocket. The run must have jostled it upward. I narrowed my eyes. "It might not kill you, but I promise it would hurt."

"Fine," he said, exasperated, and held up his hands. "No funny business with Granny's car."

"It's Gran." I growled, irritated that he knew how to push all my buttons.

He nodded and shoved the keys in his pocket. "Better hide your fork," he said as we walked through the wide glass doors.

The information desk was empty and I didn't see Colin, but I was sure he was around somewhere. I pointed at the hospital directory on the wall and told Riley, "The cafeteria is around here somewhere, if you want to check it out."

"Don't worry about me," Riley said, ignoring the sign and looking at me. "I can take care of myself. Take your time. I'll meet you in the parking lot later."

"Don't make me regret giving you those keys." I warned.

He waved me away, already turning to size up a pretty, young candy striper. I sighed. Hopefully that girl was hiding a fork in her uniform.

At the nurse's station outside my mother's room, I learned there was still no change in her condition. The nurse looked at me with sympathy and I was beginning to see that no one thought she was going to wake up.

Even though there was no medical reason that she shouldn't.

"Hi, Mom," I said when I entered the room. I was relieved to see the curtain around her bed was completely open today. There was no chance a demon could be hiding on the other side of the room. For good measure, I went to the other bed and yanked back the sheets. I sighed in relief. There was no deflated demon in here today.

I dropped my bag in the chair and poured myself a cup of water from the pitcher next to the bed. It was fresh, cold water and I wondered why the nurses kept it filled when clearly they thought Mom wouldn't need it. Maybe they hadn't given up all hope like I'd thought.

After draining the cup, I went into the bathroom to splash cold water over my face, wash my hands and quickly clean myself up. It seemed superficial to care about what I was wearing when Sam was going hungry. I did take a minute to comb through my hair and pull it snugly back in a ponytail. I added a thin black headband to help keep back my side-swept bangs as I wondered why I bothered to cut it… At least when it was long I could pull it out of the way. What was the point of a cute haircut if I never styled it?

I left the bathroom and went back to Mom's side to spend a few moments brushing through her long hair. I paused when I noticed a small faded scar on the back of her neck. I leaned in closer to get a better look. It was an odd shape—circular—and it was very close to her hairline. I had never noticed it before, but she barely ever wore a ponytail and I never had to brush her hair like this, either. I shrugged, figuring it was nothing, and traded the brush for some lotion to smooth onto her face and hands.

The whole time I worked, I made a conscious effort to talk to her, telling her about mundane things like clothes and music and the weather. I told her about how her church group was praying for her and about the beautiful flowers they had sent yesterday. Finally, I sat down, pulling the chair close and taking her hand. I stared at her lying there, helpless and clueless, and I felt a pang of sorrow that I couldn't talk to her about what was really going on in my life.

My mother was a very religious woman and I wondered if she would agree with Airis about forgetting about Sam. I couldn't think that my mother would tell me to turn my back on someone I loved. I would like to think she'd tell me to follow my heart, that a heart as good as mine wouldn't lead me wrong.

Tired, I leaned back into the chair and curled my legs beneath me. I shut my eyes and thought of Sam. Of his golden locks and honey-colored eyes.

When you come home, what's the first thing you want to do?

Touch you.

What's the first thing you want to eat?

Your lips.

Where's the first place you want to go?

Anywhere with you.

Sam's responses rippled through my mind, the deep raspy quality of his voice sent goose bumps racing down my arms. *It's exactly what I was thinking,* I told him.

We're going to be just fine, Hev.

I know.

There was a light sound from beside me and my eyes sprung open. Mom's eyes were open, staring up at the ceiling.

I jumped up out of the chair. "Mom!" I grabbed her hand and she turned her head toward my voice. "Mom! Oh my God. You're awake." I turned to yell for the nurse, but she gripped my hand and I turned back. "We've been so worried about you."

She stared at me for a few long moments and I wondered if she understood anything. But then she said, "Where am I?"

"You're at the hospital, Mom. You fell and hit your head. But you're okay now. You're doing great."

"Heven."

"Yes." I reached out and filled a cup with water, grateful that the nurses never stopped filling it, and lifted it to her lips.

She took a sip and her eyes seemed to clear a little more. "I'm going to get the doctor. He'll be so happy you're awake!"

I ran out and alerted the nurses and went back into the room. I was half afraid that she wouldn't be awake anymore, but she was. When I entered, she turned her head and stared at me. I smiled. The nurses rushed in, followed closely by the doctor. They all hovered around her, checking the monitors, taking her vitals and asking her questions. I stood on the other side of the room a few feet from the foot of the bed and watched quietly as the doctor assessed her. She answered his questions without problem and her eyes returned to me again and again.

Her aura was a little dull and had a few clouds of gray and brown, but not predominately. I figured the presence of those colors were because she wasn't quite feeling as well as she should. After such a fall, who wouldn't have a muddy aura?

It seemed like the doctor spent hours checking her out, but finally he turned to me and smiled brilliantly. "Our patient seems to be in wonderful health. She'll need to stay here a few more days as a precaution, but I think that she's going to be just fine."

"That's great." I returned his smile.

"Well, I'm sure you two have a lot to catch up on," he said and ushered the nurses out of the room. "Press the call button if you need anything at all."

"Thank you," I said, noticing my mother was still watching me.

When the door shut behind them all, I let out a breath. "I thought they'd never leave!"

Mom didn't say anything. She just sat there, watching me.

"Are you feeling all right? I could call the doctor back to get you some medicine if you need it." I walked over toward the bed and her eyes widened.

"Don't come any closer."

I stopped, but I was confused by her words. "Mom?"

"What happened to your face?"

My hand slid up to the newly forming scar. A heavy feeling began forming in my belly. "I had an accident. It shouldn't be that bad once it heals."

"Do you know what happened this time?"

"Yes. I accidently fell out of one of the orchard trees when I was pruning."

"I knew it. Didn't I tell you?" I hadn't heard this tone of her voice in a while.

"I—I don't know what you mean." But I was afraid I did. I just didn't want to believe it.

"Evil wants you." Her voice dropped lower and she sounded horrified by the thought. "It's all my fault."

What was she talking about? "I thought we were past this. You said you didn't think I was evil."

She looked momentarily confused, like she couldn't understand why she would say such a thing. But I knew. She hadn't really meant any of those things she had said before I went to Italy. She hadn't really wanted to be close to me again. That was Beelzebub influencing her, making her act that way.

This is the way she really felt.

"Mom, I'm not evil."

"Don't call me that!" she yelled.

I jerked like she slapped me.

"You are not my daughter."

"Of course I am. Who else could I be?" I should have known that things weren't going to stay good between us. I should have seen this coming.

"You're the devil taking over my daughter's body!"

"I'm not evil," I ground out. I was very tired of telling her that.

"Leave my daughter be!" she yelled at me. "You can't have her!"

"Mom—really," I said, but she cut me off.

"You are not my daughter. My daughter is gone. You are just a shell of what she once was."

"You can't really believe that."

"I do."

"What about this summer? The good times we spent together?"

Her face stayed blank, like those times never even existed, like she didn't remember. "Leave."

"What?"

"Leave and don't ever come back. My daughter is dead and I will not stand by and watch her body be defiled."

"Mom." I ran to her side and grabbed her hand. "You don't mean that. It's me... Heven."

She began screaming and pulled away from my touch. "Get out! Get out! Get out!"

Her monitors began beeping because her pulse and heart rate were going crazy. I took a step back, helpless, not knowing what to do. A nurse came rushing in and took in the scene: me standing there in panic and Mom still screaming for me to get out.

"She just started screaming," I told her. "She doesn't want me here."

Pity flashed across the nurse's face before she hurried to silence the monitors. "Mrs. Montgomery, I need you to try to calm down."

"Get that thing out of here!" she wailed.

The nurse turned to look at me. I was already picking up my bag off the chair. I took a few backward steps toward the door, hoping Mom might calm down. She didn't.

"I'm sorry," I said, knowing that my words were lost in the noise.

She was still screaming when I rushed down the hall.

* * *

I didn't even think to look for Riley when I stepped off the elevator. My ears were still ringing from the harsh words Mom had said. Colin was at the information desk. When he saw me, his face fell with concern.

He hurried to my side to ask, "Is everything okay?"

"My mom woke up, but she's not doing so good," I told him numbly. "She's confused."

"Ah, kid. I'm sorry. That happens sometimes. Give her a few days; she'll straighten out." He put his arm around my shoulders and guided me toward the exit.

I made a sound of agreement, although I knew Mom wouldn't change her mind. My relationship with her was over. She wouldn't accept me ever again.

Outside, I squinted against the sun and looked around for Gran's car and Riley. Neither was anywhere to be seen. Figured. Colin was standing beside his cruiser, looking at me expectantly, and I figured the place to look for Riley was where I left the car. Maybe he was in it, taking a nap. I ignored the slight worry that maybe he took the car and left me here and he wasn't coming back.

The interior of the car felt stifling when I climbed in. A moment of panic hit me and I almost climbed back out, but Colin was already shutting my door and hurrying around the front of the car to the driver's side.

When he slid inside, I noticed that his aura didn't look as it usually did. The colors were faded and I actually had to look hard to see them and distinguish between them. The colors weren't different than usual, so maybe they just seemed faded because I felt so numb.

Colin didn't put the car into drive right away like usual, but turned to look at me. "Are you all right?"

"Yes. I'm just worried about my mother."

He leaned across the seat and placed his hand on my leg. My thigh actually. I was so shocked I barely heard him say, "People who suffer head injuries sometimes act a little different when they first wake up. Give her some time."

His words were kind and spoken with the thought of making me feel better, but I felt gross. The fact that it felt like he was groping me overshadowed his attempt at making me feel better. I shifted, trying to tell him that I was uncomfortable. He smiled and squeezed my leg before letting go and sitting back in his seat.

My fingers slid over to the door handle as he roared the engine to life and turned on the AC. When he looked over at me, I swear something dark and sinister slid behind his eyes. I blinked and he was smiling his usual friendly smile. "Ready, kid?"

"Sure," I said, not sure if I was.

As we drove out of the parking lot, a fly flew past my face and swarmed around Colin's head. He batted at it and cracked his window trying to shoo it out. "So how far did you run today?" he asked.

"Seven miles."

"You must be awfully tired." He turned his head just slightly to look at me and his aura blinked out. But within seconds it returned.

"Are you feeling all right today?" I asked.

"Right as rain." He glanced at me and smiled. I studied his eyes; there was nothing there. It was like I imagined it.

We rode in silence for a few minutes and I tried to calm my nerves. Something didn't seem right, and I had learned that if something didn't seem right, it wasn't. Another fly buzzed around his head and he craned his neck to see where it flew.

That's when I noticed the goose egg on the back of his head.

"Did you hit your head?" I asked.

He gave up on the fly and turned back to the road. "No."

"You have a huge bump on the back of your head. Doesn't it hurt?"

He looked at me, surprised, then felt the back of his head. When his fingers slid over the bump, he winced. "I don't remember hitting it on anything."

"What did you do yesterday after you got off work?"

His brow wrinkled as he thought. "Went home and cut the grass, worked in the garage. The sun made me tired and I went inside and took a long nap."

Warning bells went off in my head. "Did you hit your head in the garage?"

"Think I would remember something like that."

Unless the Prince of Demons erased it from your mind.

"Stop the car!" I yelled.

Colin slammed on the brakes and the car fishtailed before righting itself and coming to a halt in the center of the road. "What's the matter?"

"I think I'm going to walk the rest of the way," I said, reaching for the handle. I had to get out of this car. I had to get some space so I could think. Think about what to do about Colin. He had a demon living inside of him. I knew all the signs.

I'd seen it before. With Logan.

Only this time, I was afraid it might not be just any demon. This time it might be Beelzebub… the body switcher.

The flies.

The strange aura.

The darkness that lurked just beneath the exterior.

All these were signs that something was manipulating Colin. And trying to get to me.

But what convinced me the most was the fact that one minute, it seemed like Colin was a completely different person. One minute, he was a stranger, but the next, he was the same nice security guard that I always saw.

It was just like Logan.

I needed to get away, to think of a way I could save Colin. He didn't deserve what was happening to him. I pulled the handle, pushed open the door and reached down between my feet for my bag.

Colin launched himself across the seat and grabbed my shoulder. With a startled yell, I whipped my bag up and slammed him in the face. He gave a roar and released me. I scrambled out of the car, but he caught hold of my shirt and pulled. I ended up falling, half in the car, half out. The contents of my backpack spilled out onto the hot pavement. The sun glinted off the dagger.

I used my foot and kicked Colin in the face. He howled again while I climbed the rest of the way out of the car. Somehow, he managed to throw himself after me, his body rippling and contorting in unnatural ways. I shrieked and rolled, landing on my back to stare up at the cloudless blue sky.

It was too beautiful of a day to die.

Colin lunged, landing on top of me, and immediately I reacted. The minute he pressed his full weight onto me, I'd be as good as dead. My only chance of fighting someone who outweighed me by a good ninety pounds was to never let his advantage become my disadvantage. Before he even settled his weight to pin me, I brought up both my knees and kicked out, slamming him in the ribs and momentarily knocking the wind out of him. Using his shoulders as an anchor, I pushed myself upward, sliding out from under him and jumping to my feet. He reached for the dagger, but I was faster and palmed it first. I watched him warily as he got to his feet.

All traces of the demon fell away and I was left looking at a confused Colin. "Kid?"

"I'm gonna walk from here. Thanks for the ride."

He stared at the dagger I held in warning and he shrugged. "Yeah, okay."

He feigned turning back to the car, but his left foot didn't turn with his right. I practically watched the demon taking back over. His left foot stayed planted on the ground as his body pivoted around. There was a loud popping sound in his hip as he spun, but he didn't even wince. Then he was leaping at me, his eyes wild.

I stepped backward and onto my steel water bottle that had rolled from my bag. I fell back with a snarling Colin close behind. He landed on top of me.

Except I didn't take the impact of his fall.

My dagger did.

He made this weird gurgling sound and dark red blood ran out from between his lips.

I tried to push him off me, but I couldn't. He was too heavy. I was pinned. His blood ran down his chin and dripped on my face.

"I'm so sorry," I whispered.

Colin looked down at me, surprise making his eyes wide. "Why?" he asked before coughing. Blood splattered my cheeks. It made me sick but I couldn't look away.

I pushed at his shoulders until I managed to roll him off me. He stared up at the sky without blinking and I wondered if he thought it was too beautiful of a day to die too. I leaned over him. "Colin? Listen to me. I know you don't understand, but you had a demon living in you. He was controlling you. You tried to kill me. I was only trying to get away. I didn't want this."

I shut my eyes momentarily and whispered, "I didn't want this," again.

I wondered if it was me or Colin I was trying to convince.

He made a slight sound and I focused back on him. "I'm going to pull out the dagger and the demon will leave your body. You'll be okay then." At least that's what happened with Logan.

I gripped the dagger and pulled it out swiftly. Blood gushed out of the open wound, saturating his white shirt. I waited for the demon to rise out of him.

It never happened.

Then Colin's eyes rolled back in his head and he died.

I fell beside him on my knees. "No!" I put my fingers to his throat, feeling for a pulse. I couldn't find it, so I lay my head against his chest to listen. There was nothing to hear. Colin was dead.

I killed him.

Dark, evil laughter echoed through my head.

I looked up, thinking I would finally see the demon. No one was there. I pushed down the sob that threatened to escape and stood. The laughter was getting louder and there was a squeezing pain in the back of my skull.

"Well, this is a mess," came a voice from behind.

I twirled, raising the bloodied dagger and glimpsed Gran's car in the grass a short distance away. "Riley?"

"I leave you alone for an hour and this is what you do?"

I began to laugh hysterically, deep laughs that hurt my stomach. Riley just stood there staring at me, his face blank. But my laughs turned to sobs and Riley stepped forward. I threw up a hand to hold him off and it was completely red. Red with Colin's blood.

"I killed him."

"Yeah."

I looked up, waiting to see the disgust and horror on Riley's face. Except he wasn't disgusted. Sharp pain tore through the back of my skull and I cried out, dropping the dagger and gripping my head. Riley rushed forward, his arms shooting out to steady me. More laughter filled my head and the pain subsided. I wasn't sure which was worse: the laughing or the pain.

I looked up at Riley once more. "I killed him. I'm a killer."

"Welcome to the club," Riley answered.

Then I passed out.

Chapter Eight

Sam

"Do you remember that time we went and saw that really bad horror movie?" A voice spoke to me from across the dungeon.

I got up from where I was sitting and went to the door of my cell. "Kimber?"

"Why is it that all the girls with big boobs run up the stairs instead of out the door?"

I couldn't see her. She was in the shadows of her cell, but I knew it was her. It was the first thing she'd said since Heven appeared down here. I had begun to think she was dead. It was good to know she wasn't.

"Everyone knows the minute you run up the stairs, you're as good as dead," I said, going along with the question. Maybe it would relieve the anxiety I was feeling. Being caged was hell on a guy's emotions.

"I lied. I knew she liked you." Her voice was raspy and low, but I still heard her words and I knew exactly what she was talking about. "She pretended not to notice you but she did. When you were around, you were all she saw. I would've had to be blind not to see it."

"Then why did you go out with me?" I asked. I always knew when Kimber and I "dated" she was only doing it to hurt Cole. I'd considered that a bonus because I couldn't stand him and the way he made Heven smile. I wanted to be the one to make her smile. But she was too shy and insecure to let me close, so I had to be creative, and what better way to get closer to her than through her best friend? I never let on that I knew about Kimber's game, but I hadn't known that our "dating" had hurt Heven. I wouldn't have done it if I had. But clearly, Kimber knew and Heven's feelings hadn't mattered to her.

She made a sound, kind of like a laugh, then said, "I liked having something she wanted for a change. I always had the better clothes, the car, the boyfriend, but she never cared. Nothing I had ever seemed to measure up to her. Then, finally, there was something she wanted that I had. It was the perfect punishment for years of forcing me into her shadow."

I digested that for a moment, sickened by the role I played in her scheme.

"This must be my punishment for that," Kimber said quietly.

The regret in her voice was something I recognized. "We all do things we regret, Kimber."

"I never said I regretted it."

"If you didn't, you wouldn't assume you needed punished."

"Maybe."

I saw a movement in the shadow of her cell as she moved closer.

"Or maybe I'm just saying that to get you to take me with you when you get out."

"You know I won't leave you here." Hadn't I proved that when I turned back to try and free her? If I had run, I might have gotten away before Beelzebub could throw me back in here. "What happened to you? How did you get here?"

"It doesn't really matter how I got here because here I am."

"What did Hecate promise you to betray us?"

She made a sound. "Power, control, the ability to be noticed."

"You've never been unnoticed."

"You don't know what my life is like."

"Maybe not. But I know what it's like to be ignored by your parents. To be tossed out. To not feel like what you are is good enough. To think that no one would love you for who you are."

"We are nothing alike." Her voice had gone hoarse.

"Well, I really don't care about my hair and shoes, so you might be right," I joked.

She snorted and I smiled. "So how much magic do you have? How powerful are you?" I figured I would take advantage of the fact she was actually talking to me.

She gave a laugh. "Look at me. Do I look very strong to you?"

"I think if anyone else was in that cell, they'd be dead. So you look better than most."

She cackled. "Grunge is in this season. A trend I never understood."

Ahh, so Kimber was in there somewhere. "Can you break down this force field?"

"No."

"Will you try?"

"No."

"Kimber." My words were cut off by a mind-numbing break. It was kind of like something inside me was turned off... *Heven.* I leapt back from the doorway of the cell and dropped to my knees.

Something was wrong. Something terrible.

Heven!

No answer.

Heven!

Silence.

Heven, please answer me. Tell me what's happening

"Sam? What's wrong?" Kimber asked. Her voice seemed so far away.

"Heven," I said, my voice sounding hoarse. *Heven…*

Why wasn't she answering? I had never felt this before… I searched my mind, closing my eyes and trying to link myself as close as I could to her.

It was hard. Harder than ever before. But the link, it was still there. I told myself that was a good thing, but the fact that I couldn't quite grasp it worried me. Maybe she was asleep? But even in sleep, she would hear me call and answer me.

I called to her again and again, to no avail.

I was trapped here, powerless to know what was happening and tortured with the unknown.

"Sam," Kimber called, and I looked up. "I'll try. I'll try to break it down."

I watched as she lifted her hands to unleash her power.

Heven

When I opened my eyes, my vision was blurred and the room was dim. There was a dark figure next to me, but I knew I was safe. I could feel the heat radiating from him and I knew it meant only one thing.

"Sam," I murmured, reaching for him, curling into his chest and burying my face in his neck. My tears felt cold compared the heat of his skin and I pressed even closer. Only his arms didn't come around me. There was no faint peppermint scent.

This wasn't Sam.

I yanked back and rubbed at my swollen eyes. His eyes looked pained and for once, slightly vulnerable. "Riley?"

"Sorry I wasn't who you were expecting."

I fell back onto the bed, realizing I was in Sam's tiny rental. I smelled the metallic, bitter scent of blood and memories came flooding back. I shot up, yelling, "Colin!"

"He's dead," Riley said flatly.

"How did I get here? I just left him there!"

"I took care of it," he said quietly. It's a wonder I heard him speak at all through my panicking, but I did and I stilled.

"You took care of it?"

He sighed. "Yeah."

"What do you mean?"

"I couldn't very well let a dead hospital security guard lay on the side of the road with a dagger wound in his chest and his car abandoned. A car with your fingerprints all over it, just sitting out in the open."

"What did you do?" I asked, afraid.

"Don't worry. No one will trace it back to you." He went to the kitchen and pulled out some bottled water and brought me one. "Drink this."

I downed half the bottle greedily. Then I burped. Riley lifted a brow and sipped at his water politely. I think he did it on purpose to make me feel like a savage.

Like I didn't feel like one already.

"What did you do?"

"What did *you* do?" Riley countered.

"You saw." I lowered my gaze and my stomach rolled. I regretted drinking that water.

"Yeah, I did. You didn't have a choice."

I looked up at him. "Yeah, I did." I shook my head. "Wait. You saw me being attacked and you didn't help me?"

"I'm not a knight in shining armor like Sam. I wanted to see how you would do in the fight." He said it like he was bored.

"Are you kidding me? Someone died so you could *watch the show?*"

"Relax. I wasn't going to let anything happen to you."

He said it like that made everything okay. I took an unsteady breath, still in shock over what just happened. Riley took advantage of my silence to keep talking. "The guy attacked you, and from the way he was moving, I would say he wasn't human."

"He was," I said and looked down. My clothes were saturated in dried blood. I catapulted off the bed and ran into the bathroom and threw up in the toilet. I sat there and heaved endlessly until I heard Riley come into the bathroom behind me. I forced myself to get up so he wouldn't try to help me and I rinsed out my mouth at the sink.

"I need a shower." I pushed past him to rummage through Sam's dresser. The bottom drawer was filled with my stuff. Shorts, jeans, T-shirts and clean panties filled the drawer, along with a few toiletries. I grabbed what I wanted, then reached into one of Sam's drawers and pulled out his favorite T-shirt. I stalked into the bathroom, shut the door without a word to Riley and turned on the shower.

I scrubbed myself until my skin felt raw. I wanted every inch of what happened off me. It was a shame that I couldn't scrub my mind. Unfortunately, I had a photographic memory and the events of earlier today would haunt me forever.

Maybe my mother was right.

Maybe there was something horribly wrong with me. Maybe I attracted evil. Maybe there was something inside me that evil identified with. I shook my head and stuck it underneath the water that had long ago turned cold. I hadn't wanted to kill Colin. I tried to get away from him when I sensed something might be wrong. But he kept attacking me.

There had been a demon inside him.

At least I thought there was.

But I'd been wrong. I'd been tricked.

I thought I was doing him a favor by getting the demon out. But there wasn't a demon and Colin was dead. And he wasn't coming back. I killed an innocent man.

Beelzebub was back, and this was only the beginning of his tirade.

I should have realized he was messing with me, pushing me, trying to scare me. Colin hadn't been taken over by a demon. Beelzebub just made it look that way. He made me a killer.

He hadn't even been back for twenty-four hours and already he was tormenting me. First the dream and now this. Wasn't what he did to my mother enough? I guess not.

I shut off the water and stepped out, drying myself and pulling on my clothes. When I reached for Sam's shirt, I brought it to my nose. It still smelled like him. I buried my face in the soft cotton and groaned.

Heven, please, baby… answer me.

Sam?

Relief and fear slammed into me so hard that I nearly fell. I stepped back and sank down onto the toilet. *Sam? What's the matter?*

What's going on? What happened? Are you hurt? Are you okay?

I'm okay, I said, noticing even through my mind the tone of his words seemed strained.

I've called out to you so many times. You never answered. I thought…

Grief washed over me and took my breath. *I'm so sorry, Sam. I… I tried to think of a way to sugarcoat what happened, but there was no sugarcoating murder. Beelzebub tricked me and I did something horrible. I passed out and I must not have been able to hear you calling for me. I never meant to worry you.*

I thought I might go insane.

What?

You wouldn't answer and I couldn't grab that link we have. I couldn't feel you at all. It was worse than anything I've ever felt. It was like… I don't ever want to feel that way again.

I wanted to kill Beelzebub for what he was doing to Sam. *I'm still here, Sam. I promise I'm not going anywhere. I'm so sorry I scared you. I love you.*

The panic that welled deep inside me seemed to ebb away and I realized that Sam was calming down. Unfortunately, the panic was being replaced with a deep fatigue. He was completely exhausted.

Kimber tried to break me out. She isn't strong enough.

I said nothing for a moment, allowing that terrible news to sink in. It seemed the hope that lived inside of me grew smaller every day. But my determination was growing. *We'll find another way.*

You aren't hurt?

No.

Did you see Beelzebub?

No.

What happened?

Do you think I'm a bad person, Sam?

What? No. You're so far away from bad it's ridiculous.

Not anymore.

Heven? What's going on?

I killed someone today, Sam.

Then it must have been to protect yourself.

No. Yes. I'm so confused.

If Beelzebub was involved, then you didn't have a choice. What happened?

I gave him a brief account of the attack and it just reconfirmed what I felt before—I did have a choice and I chose wrong.

I can't imagine how terrified you must've been. You did what you had to. Beelzebub manipulated you and you reacted, but it still doesn't change the fact Colin would've killed you if you hadn't stopped him.

No. Beelzebub doesn't want me dead. He wants the scroll and he wants me to pay for what I did to him. He's only getting started.

He let out a choked scream that echoed through my already pounding head. *It's killing me that I can't be there to protect you from this!*

I knew he was probably ripping apart the cell and I didn't want that. He was already beyond exhausted.

Sam, calm down. Listen to me. I'm leaving tonight to come and get you.

Everything inside me stilled. *I told you not to come back here.*

And I asked you not to ask that of me.

Haven't you been through enough?

Haven't you? I countered. I wanted desperately to tell him about Riley, but I was afraid to. He was already angry and worried enough. Telling him I found Riley after he told me not to, after he told me he was dangerous, didn't seem like a smart idea right now.

I'm supposed to be protecting you, not placing you in greater danger.

When I get you out of there, you can protect me all you want.

Promise me you're really okay, that you're not hurt.

I'm just fine. I promise. Physically anyway. My mental health was another story.

Hev? Baby, you could kill ten thousand men and I would still love you more than anything. Please don't torture yourself over this. Beelzebub is going to pay for what he did to you.

I love you too, Sam. I can't wait to get you home.

Be careful, Heven. Don't risk yourself for me. If it looks bad, get out.

Okay. I winced, feeling lower than dirt. He still didn't know I contacted Riley. He didn't know Riley was here and that he'd been helping me. What would Sam say when he learned Riley had been here, in his house, protecting me from being caught for murder?

I wondered if he would still love me as much as he says when he realized I've been lying to him.

Try and get some rest, Sam. I'll be right here if you call. I promise.

Warmth spread through my chest and I knew it was his way of showing me his love. I slipped into Sam's shirt and ran a comb through my wet, tangled hair and gathered up my ruined clothes to shove into the trashcan.

Riley was sitting on the couch when I let myself out of the bathroom. His gaze flicked to me, then went back to the TV. I sat on the couch beside him, but not so close that we touched, and stared at the TV without really seeing it.

"What did you do with Colin's body?"

He clicked the remote to turn off the TV. "I put him in his cruiser and sent it down over the hill. Then I lit it on fire. It looks like he went off the road and the gas tank ruptured. They won't be able to tell he was stabbed to death."

I winced at that. "I was the last person seen with him."

"If the police come to you, just tell them he dropped you at your car and then said he was going back to the hospital. The car was going in the direction of the hospital when I ran it off the road. No one will be able to argue with you. Why would a seventeen-year-old kill an old man?"

"He wasn't that old," I murmured, feeling sick. I wondered how he could sit there and talk about covering up a murder and setting a car on fire. Did nothing bother him at all?

"It doesn't matter now. Forget about it."

How did you forget about something like this?

"How was your mom?" he asked, no doubt thinking he would change the subject to something better.

"She woke up," I said. This earned me a look from him.

"You don't seem too happy about that."

"She took one look at my face"—I gestured to my new pink scar—"and declared she was right all along and that I'm clearly evil. Then she said I wasn't her daughter anymore and she never wanted to see me again."

"You're a walking magnet for trouble," he said, unperturbed.

"Then I proved her right by going out and killing someone."

Riley turned his nearly black eyes to me. "Woe is me."

I sighed, got up and rummaged until I found a bottle of pain reliever and swallowed back three. "I have to go. I need to tell Gran what happened with Mom so she can go to the hospital and try to calm her down."

"I'll drive."

I began to shake my head but then changed my mind. Who really cared if I let him drive Gran's car? "Fine. But you'll have to get out before we get up to the house. I don't want to have to explain you to her. You can come in once she leaves for the hospital." I grabbed my bag, which was lying by the door, and wrinkled my nose. It was ruined with blood too. I really liked this bag.

"Thank you," I said sincerely, looking up at Riley.

"Whatever. I couldn't leave your crap all over the road. The police would be suspicious."

I didn't care why he did what he did, although I suspected his motives weren't just for covering up my crime. Riley might not want me to see it, but there was a heart inside him somewhere, and it was bigger than he wanted anyone to believe.

He brushed past me out the door and I caught his hand. He turned back. I hugged him, squeezing a little harder than I meant to. I pulled away quickly but didn't step away. "No, really. You didn't have to do any of that. You didn't have to bring me here. You could've let me get caught."

"It wasn't any big deal." He went down the steps, then turned to hold out his hand for the car keys. "Besides, if I don't keep your butt out of trouble, I'll have to deal with Sam."

I barely even blinked at the comment and I certainly didn't let on that Riley probably wasn't going to get a warm welcome from Sam.

Not only was I a killer now, but I was very good at lying.

* * *

It's strange how one man's life ended but everything in the world went right on turning. Life went on and I had no choice but to keep going with it. When I walked into the kitchen, Gran put down the dish she was drying and turned to look at me. I knew I looked like crap. I knew I couldn't hide the way I felt.

So I lied my way out of it.

Again.

Although, in my own defense, at least this lie was based on truth. Just not the whole truth.

"What happened?" Gran asked, taking in my damp, straggly hair, oversized shirt and bare feet.

Logan came in from the other room and stood, looking at me with worry on his face. I tried to smile to reassure him, but I don't think I did a very good job.

"I stopped at Sam's after I went to see Mom." I lowered myself into a chair at the table. My legs were wobbly and I felt like I might fall down. "I needed a little time alone."

"Was there a change in Madeline's condition?" Gran bustled about making what looked like hot tea for me. My stomach turned at the thought of drinking it.

"She woke up."

"She woke up!" Gran exclaimed. "How is she?"

Logan came a little farther into the room, his face brightening at the good news.

"The doctor said her vitals looked good and she has to stay for another day or two before being released."

"Well, that is wonderful news. Was she happy to see you?" Gran was upset; her aura was jittering with nervous energy. She could tell just by looking at me that things hadn't gone well.

"No, Gran. She saw the new mark on my face and declared that she was right before. She said I have evil inside of me and I'm no longer her daughter. She screamed so loud the nurse came in and I had to leave."

Gran forgot about my tea and dropped into the vacant chair next to me. "Honey, I'm so sorry. She doesn't really mean it. Her head... it isn't right from when she fell."

I appreciated her kindness and the way she tried to make me feel better, but I shook my head sadly. "She meant everything she said."

"Maybe she's just confused," Logan said, taking a seat at the table. Gran nodded.

Over on the stove, the teakettle whistled and steam filled the air. We all ignored it and stared at each other. "I'm very sorry she said those things to you. You know it isn't true, don't you?"

I nodded, not trusting myself to speak.

"Oh, honey." She leaned over and hugged me. She smelled good, like lemons and honey. "You will always have a place here. This is your home and I love you. I want you here."

I squeezed my eyes shut to prevent any tears. "I know, Gran. I love you too."

"Oh my! I forgot about the tea." She bustled over and poured me a mugful, adding honey.

She set the cup by my elbow and I asked, "I was hoping you could go see Mom. Make sure she's doing okay? I don't like to think of her there by herself and being confused."

"Well, I planned on going to see her this afternoon anyway," Gran said. "I'll just leave a little early."

She left me in the kitchen to go upstairs and change her clothes and grab her purse. I got up and dumped half the tea in my mug down the drain and sat back down at the table.

Logan pretended he didn't notice, which I appreciated. "So your mom is really going to be okay?"

"Yes, I think so."

"That's really great news. I felt really bad about what happened to her."

He looked so relieved that I smiled. "It wasn't your fault, Logan. In fact, if you hadn't been there to call for help, she might have been worse."

His face seemed to go a little pale as Gran came back in and offered to make me some more tea, which I declined.

"I'm not sure what time I'll be home. I have my monthly bridge night tonight, but I can stay home."

"No," I said, trying not to sound desperate to get her out of here. "I'll be fine. Cole is coming over and Logan is here. We can order pizza."

Concern clouded over Gran's aura and inwardly I groaned. "Cole's been spending a lot of time here lately."

"I thought you liked when Cole came over. He is your grandson and all."

"Of course I like to see Cole. I just meant that I haven't seen you with anyone else lately. Where's Kimber been?"

"We got in a fight. We aren't speaking." This was another example of a lie based on truth.

"Oh. Well, I'm sorry. Maybe you two could make up?"

"Maybe," I echoed.

"Have you talked to Sam lately?" Gran fished.

"This morning. He's coming home soon." Like tonight.

"Oh. Great. I was beginning to wonder about him."

"No need to worry, Gran. Things with Sam are good."

"Are you sure you don't mind being on your own tonight?"

I nodded and so did Logan. "Have a great time."

"I'll call you and let you know how your mother is doing." She squeezed my shoulder, then disappeared out the door. I listened to the Toyota start up and drive away. I got up and dumped my mug in the sink. I turned and gasped. Riley was standing behind me. I covered up my shock by scowling at him.

"Oh good, you're here." I grabbed my bag from beneath the table (glad Gran didn't notice the way it looked) and fished out my cell phone. "Can you be ready to go into hell tonight?"

"Sure," he said while he searched through all the cabinets and came out with a bag of Doritos. He tore open the bag and began shoving them into his mouth. "You have any soda?"

"It's in the fridge. I'd say make yourself at home… but you already have."

"I'm coming with you," Logan declared.

I dropped my bag and looked at him, but Riley pretended he hadn't heard a word as he popped the top on a Dr. Pepper. "Thanks, Hev."

Sometimes it really annoyed me when he called me that. It was like he thought we were best buddies. "I don't think that's a good idea, Logan. You might get hurt."

"Sam is my brother. I'm coming."

I sighed, not sure how to handle this. Logan wasn't strong enough to come with us. He might slow us down, and if he got hurt, what would I say to Sam?

"You're too weak to come. Do you want Sam to get hurt trying to protect you while he escapes?" Riley said bluntly.

He was a real poet.

"Fine." Logan relented. Then he looked at me. "I don't want to do anything to make it harder for Sam."

I nodded and went over to him. "Sam's going to be proud of you. Sit down. I'll make you a sandwich." I punched the button that dialed Cole and held the phone to my ear.

Riley sat down at the table and propped up his feet. "I don't like mayo."

I rolled my eyes and grabbed the mustard as Cole picked up the phone. "Can you be here in, like, an hour?" I said in way of greeting.

"Hey, sis, I'm great; thanks for asking! How are you?"

"Cole," I said, exasperated.

He made a sound. "Sure, I can be there."

"Bring Gemma."

There was an uncomfortable silence on the other end of the line. I sighed and slammed all the makings for sandwiches on the counter. "I do not care what is going on between you two. Fix it. Don't fix it. Whatever. But you will bring her. We need her. *Sam* needs her. And while you're at it, can you stop at the store and get me a few things?"

"What am I, your errand boy?"

When I didn't respond, he muttered, "Let me get a pen."

When he gave me the go ahead, I rattled off a list of what I needed and he promised to be here soon.

Before I hung up he called my name. "Yeah?" I asked.

"What's going on?"

"We're leaving tonight to get Sam."

Chapter Nine

Heven

Butterflies danced in my belly and fluttered close to my rapidly beating heart. Up until I spoke the words out loud, anxiety ate at my insides. Until now, flashes of crystal-clear memory of a dying Colin tortured me. But then something happened that pushed even the most awful events not away, but back, so I could breathe.

We were going to get Sam.

Sam was coming home.

I would soon sleep in his arms and know my first night of peace since he was trapped. Since we still had a bit until Cole and Gemma arrived, I left Riley and Logan with their food, fresh sodas and the remote to escape to my bedroom.

Once upstairs I washed my hair (yeah, I already showered but it looked bad), blew it out straight and even went over the ends and my bangs with my flat iron. Once my hair was glossy and smooth, I noticed just how bad my face really looked. It was blotchy red in some spots, my eyes were puffy with dark circles and the rest of my skin was pale. The paleness made the new scar on my left cheek stand out more than it probably would. With a sigh I reached into my makeup bag and pulled out all the products I hoped would make me look a little less… destroyed.

Once I had done all I could with my appearance, I grabbed a backpack from my closet and began to fill it with things I thought we might need. I wasn't sure if I should bring the Treasure Map because it would be putting it in danger and sort of adding another bull's-eye on all of our backs (if there was even room for more). I figured it would be best if I hid it here somewhere.

I pulled out my blood-stained bag and dumped out the contents on the bed and buried the ruined bag at the bottom of the trash. I grabbed up a few items right away to add to the backpack and reached for the scroll.

It wasn't there.

I stifled my moment of panic and sifted through the junk on the bed. It was here somewhere. I never let it out of my sight. Why did I have to carry so much crap around with me? I never used half of it. But soon my forced calm dissipated because I still couldn't find it. The scroll containing the Treasure Map was the biggest thing in my bag. It wouldn't be hard to see; it would stick out among sunglasses and lip gloss.

I felt a cold sweat break out on my forehead as I looked down at the floor, reaching under the bed and searching the corner where I had thrown the bloodied bag when I first got home. Then I searched the top of the bed once more, but I had to face the facts.

The scroll wasn't here.

It was gone.

I started pacing, my breathing coming in short gasps. This wasn't happening. I did *not* just lose the Treasure I was asked to keep safe. I did not just lose the Map that we've been protecting with our lives, the scroll that we had to go down in hell for, the reason Sam was trapped there still.

I wouldn't be that careless. I wouldn't.

Think! I told myself. I just needed to think. Where was the last place I saw it? I remember having it in my bag at the hospital when I went to see Mom. After that… everything was kind of a blur. She said awful things, Colin attacked me and I killed him… I gasped.

Colin! Everything fell out of my bag when he was attacking me. That had to have been when I lost it. *Oh, God. What have I done?*

I raced down the stairs and into the living room. Riley was standing in the doorway to the kitchen, staring at me with a cookie in his hand. Logan was on the couch, but he stood up when he saw my face.

"Sam?" he asked.

"I can't find the scroll." I rushed out. "Riley, please think. When you picked up my stuff off the ground after Colin, was it there?"

Riley's brow furrowed. "What did it look like?"

"It's a bronze tube, a cylinder. It's kind of heavy. The map was inside."

He shook his head. "I didn't see anything that looked like that."

I let out a whimper. "No."

Riley pushed out of the doorway and came closer. "You're sure you didn't put it somewhere and forget?"

"Forget where the one thing that is keeping Sam alive is?" I screamed.

His eyes flashed silver. "What are you talking about?"

"The only reason Beelzebub's keeping Sam alive is because he wants that scroll. If he gets his hands on it first, he will kill him just to make me suffer." Then he would come for me, but that seemed like the last of my worries at the moment.

"We have to get him out! We have to go now!" Logan began to cough. Deep coughs that shook his body and made his shoulders hunch. I went to his side and placed a hand on his back. He felt very warm, like he was running a fever. Again.

"Hey, calm down. Sam's fine, okay? I'm going to get him out. He'll be home very soon."

Logan kept coughing and I led him to the sofa and made him sit down. Finally, he stopped with a deep, ragged breath. When he looked up at me, his eyes were rimmed with red and had deep circles beneath them. His lips were pale, but his cheeks were flushed. "I want my brother."

"I know you do." I glanced up at Riley, who was watching us with no emotion on his face. "Will you grab a bottle of water out of the fridge?"

He disappeared and I brushed the hair off Logan's forehead. "You should've told me you were feeling bad again. I can call Gemma."

"No." He cut me off. "No more healing; it doesn't work anyway. Just let me heal on my own."

Riley came back in the room with Cole on his heels. "I laid the stuff you asked for on the counter," he said as he came in. Then he paused. "What's going on?"

"Logan's not feeling so hot right now." I took the water from Riley and twisted the cap off to give it to Logan. "I want you to relax the rest of the night, okay? Just chill. Everything is going to be fine."

"Promise?" Logan said, looking more like the little kid he was than he usually did.

"Yup. Sam will be here tomorrow, just wait and see."

He nodded and I handed him the remote to the TV before getting up and walking into the kitchen. Cole and Riley followed.

"Hev?" Cole asked as Gemma came through the back door.

"I lost the scroll."

The silence that followed my announcement was deafening. Then Cole spoke up. "Are you sure?"

"Yes, no… I don't know," I said as tears filled my eyes. "It might be in Gran's car. It could have fallen out, but she isn't here and I can't go look."

"Where is she? I can go check for you," Gemma said, the lines around her eyes looking grim.

"At the hospital with my mom."

"I'll just flash over there and look. I'll be right back." She disappeared out the door before I could thank her.

Then another thought occurred to me. "It could have fallen out in Colin's car." I looked at Riley. "Did you look in his car before… you know?" Before he sent it barreling over a hill and lit it on fire. I would laugh if this wasn't so horrible.

He shook his head, and for once he was showing emotion. He seemed so regretful. "I didn't. I was too focused on making sure everything was cleaned up."

"What are you talking about?" Cole wanted to know.

I shook my head. I didn't have the energy to go through the story of how I killed someone. "I'll fill you in later."

Gemma came through the door and we all turned to see her. She shook her head.

I let out a sob. "It had to have been in Colin's car… so that means it's destroyed. I destroyed the one thing I was charged by God to protect."

"I meant I didn't see anything. Gran's car wasn't at the hospital."

I paused. "She wasn't at the hospital? Then where is she?"

"Someone's coming up the drive," Riley said. I ran over to the window to see who it was.

"It's Gran," I murmured.

I looked at Riley and Gemma, unsure what to do. "We'll go upstairs," Gemma offered.

"Thanks. If you want, maybe you can go through my room again. Maybe you'll find the scroll."

My friends disappeared from the room and moments later Gran entered. Her aura almost knocked me over. Something was terribly wrong. She looked like she had been crying, and from the tissue clutched in her hand, I had a feeling more tears weren't far away. "Gran?"

She looked up and her eyes widened a little. "I didn't see you there."

"What's the matter?" Cole asked, going to her side.

"I... I don't know..." She looked up at me, tears filling her eyes. "I'm so sorry, honey, but your mother died this evening."

"What? No." My ears began ringing. "She was awake. She woke up."

"Yes. For a while. Then she slipped back in her coma. She died a few minutes before I got there."

I shook my head. "No."

Gran came forward and hugged me. I didn't hug her back. I couldn't. I stared straight ahead at nothing. "It's going to be okay."

She pulled back to look at me.

"How?"

"They're not sure. They did everything they could."

The room around me seemed to narrow and close in on me. My mother was dead. I was an orphan. Cole guided me into a nearby chair and sunk down beside me, his hands gripping mine.

"She's dead?" I whispered.

"We'll need to go to the funeral home in the morning to make arrangements."

"Arrangements?"

"Don't worry about that now. We'll deal with it in the morning."

I heard her moving around in the kitchen and I smelled brewing coffee, but I never really knew what was going on around me. I heard Cole's voice as he spoke to Gran, but I couldn't understand his words. I felt his hand in mine, but I didn't want him. I wanted Sam. I jumped to my feet, startling everyone in the room. "I..."

They were both staring at me with pity and sorrow and suddenly, I couldn't breathe. "I… just need a moment."

I ran outside and down the stairs into the falling night. I hoped it would swallow me whole. *Sam.*

What is it, Heven?

My mother is dead. She died, Sam.

Oh, baby. I'm so sorry. I don't know what to say…

I want you, Sam. I need you.

I'm here, baby. I'm here.

He's going to take you too.

What?

Beelzebub. He killed her. He finally got what he wanted. She was fine and he killed her. It was in that moment I knew for sure I had lost the scroll. Now everyone around me was going to start dying. I had no more leverage.

What do you mean? Are you sure?

I've never been so sure. And now… It finally happened. Tears started falling. *You have to get out of there, Sam. He's going to come for you. I can't let you die.*

I felt something ripple through me. It might be pain. I didn't know. I was numb. *Heven, listen to me. Listen, sweetheart.* When I didn't answer, he said, *Are you listening?*

Yes.

I'm not going anywhere. I promise. I'm going to be there soon. You've got to stay calm. Don't do anything crazy.

We were on our way to get you.

Don't come. Not tonight.

You don't understand; I have to come. The scroll is gone. I lost it.

There was a pause before he answered. *How?*

I think I lost it when Colin and I… when I killed him.

Don't think about that now. Don't worry about the scroll. We'll find a way to get it back.

How can you say that? Don't you see? He got what he wanted and now he's going to kill everyone I love.

I haven't seen him at all. He isn't here. I can take care of myself for another night.

I just need a moment. I can't breathe.

I'll be right here. I won't let go. I felt the frustration and the desperation behind his words. He wanted to be here and he couldn't be.

I sank down beneath an apple tree and stared up at the sky. I wondered if my mother was with my dad now, if she was at peace. I felt rather than saw something nearby and I turned in that direction to see Riley. I turned away, not wanting him to see my tears.

"You heard?" I asked.

"Yeah."

He didn't say he was sorry. He didn't offer his condolences, and somehow, it made it easier to breathe. He sat down next to me, his knee brushing mine, and still said nothing. For a long time, we just sat there listening to the evening bugs chatter.

"My mother said some awful things to me," I said, my voice sounding hoarse.

Riley didn't say anything.

"She meant them." Riley turned his head to look at me and I wiped a stray tear from my cheek. "But she was my mother and I loved her. Now she's dead."

Riley debated a moment, then reached out stiffly and pulled me into his side. I laid my head on his shoulder and closed my eyes. I sat there grieving all the while, thinking about the man who did this and wondering what else he was going to do. Beelzebub was on a tirade, hell-bent on making me pay, and he wasn't going to stop until I was dead inside.

Chapter Ten

Heven

"Gran's worried." Cole spoke from behind us. My eyes closed at the sound of his tight tone. He disapproved of me being out here with Riley.

I pushed myself to my feet. "I'll come in."

Cole nodded tersely, but his aura softened when I came to his side. He put his arm around my shoulders and leaned down to kiss my temple. "How's it going, sis?"

"You and Gran are the only family I have left now."

"Well, you're stuck with me," he said lightly.

"Sam doesn't want me to come tonight."

"He's right," Cole said and I stiffened beneath his touch. He tightened his grasp on me and sighed. "I know it's hard, Hev. But your mom just died. Your mind is in no state to fight with Beelzebub."

"We don't even know if he's down there."

"I thought you said he was back."

"He definitely is, but Sam said he hasn't seen him."

"That's a good thing."

The house came into view and I pulled away from Cole and turned back to Riley, who was a few feet behind us. "Are you leaving?" I tried not to sound upset at the idea.

"I'll be around," he said, sounding vague.

"I'll come by Sam's tomorrow after Gran and I go to the funeral home…" My voice dropped off. "We'll go get him then."

"It's too soon," Cole said. His aura was etched with worry and concern and I knew he was only looking out for me.

"It isn't. I'm going to be busy after tomorrow with the viewings and the funeral." I shivered a little and out of the corner of my eye I saw Riley take a step closer. "I need him home, Cole. Now more than ever."

"Yeah, all right."

"I'll see you tomorrow?" I asked Riley.

"Yeah."

I looked at him a little longer than I should have, but then he took off and the screen door banged behind us. I turned to see Gran standing on the porch peering out into the darkness, looking for us. "Heven? Cole?"

"We're here," Cole said and grabbed my arm to tow me toward the house. I didn't want to go with him. It was all too real inside. It pressed in on me and I couldn't take the sorrow on Gran's face.

"Is Gemma still in my room?" I whispered.

"No. I saw her when I came out to get you. She left."

"How are things with her going?" I asked.

"Fine," he said, but his aura said otherwise.

"I was worried," Gran said as we came up the steps. "You've been out here a while."

"Should I go to the hospital tonight?"

"No. I took care of it all when I was there. You're a minor so I signed all the documents and filled out the forms. We'll need to go to the funeral home in the morning and to your mother's house to pick out an outfit for her…" She trailed off, unable to say the rest.

I sat around the kitchen with Gran and Cole and tried to convince them as well as I could that I wasn't going to crumble into a million pieces. Thankfully, Logan had fallen asleep on the couch and was spared all the drama and I hoped he slept the night through. He wasn't looking too good.

I forced a cup of hot tea down to please Gran, but refused to eat and tried to discuss arrangements with Gran without crying. Soon, the night began wearing on me and I excused myself to go upstairs to bed. I felt Gran and Cole's nervous stares as I went from the room but had no energy left to try to make them feel better.

Upstairs, I stood in the center of my room for a while without moving. Regrets clouded my head as I thought of things I wished I had and hadn't said to my mother during the past few months. I would never get the chance to make any of it right. My last moments with her were horrible and that was all I had left.

I grabbed Sam's favorite T-shirt and changed my clothes, throwing my dirty ones on the floor and leaving them there, too tired to bother with them. The soft fabric brushed the tops of my bare knees. I went into the bathroom to remove the makeup I had applied with such care and anticipation. Tears threatened, but I blinked them back for the millionth time tonight. Crying wouldn't change anything. I was so incredibly tired, but sleep wasn't an option. Bad things happened when I went to sleep. I was terrified if I went to sleep tonight, Beelzebub would seize the opportunity to pull me back into hell. The thought of seeing Sam was tempting, but if I went down there, Beelzebub would show up and he would continue his revenge by doing something to Sam while I watched, helpless. At this moment, it seemed like the best thing I could do for Sam was to stay away.

I began tossing aside the fluffy throw pillows on the bed, thinking that even if I couldn't sleep I could lay there and talk to Sam, to feel him. I tossed the last pillow away and reached for the bedside lamp, clicking it on.

Then something clamped onto my foot and ankle.

I looked down and stifled a scream.

A gnarled, green hand was grabbing me. I kicked and stomped but whatever was under my bed was strong and it wasn't going anywhere. It started yanking, as if to drag me beneath the bed.

Every childhood nightmare I ever had came rushing back.

There were such things as monsters under the bed.

I threw myself forward, half lying across the bed, trying to unbalance my weight so I wouldn't be so easy to pull. I lifted my free leg up into the air, frightened another hand would reach for it.

This was the first time a demon had come into my house.

Into my room.

Turns out, lifting my leg didn't do anything because another terribly long arm shot out and grabbed my ankle and tugged me down. I fell backward, landing on my butt as the demon slowly dragged me under the bed. Frantically, I looked for something, anything to help me. I reached for the lamp, but it was too far away. I grappled for the cord hanging over the nightstand and managed to grasp it. The lamp came tumbling over the side and I caught it before it hit the ground and made a loud noise. It was still plugged in and the light was bright so I shoved it toward the darkness under the bed.

It was a sight I wished I never saw.

There was a swirling, black sort of tide pool thing that circled around the demon holding me. It didn't have any eyes, only a round white head with no hair and only two black holes for a nose. What was most disgusting was its mouth. It was a huge black hole that took up half its face and sharp, jagged teeth lined the mouth's circumference. In the center of the mouth, this pink thing came forward and released these long tentacle-like things. All of them waved in my direction, straining to reach me.

I gagged and kicked my legs harder.

The tentacle things weren't very long so they couldn't touch me. Yet. Thinking fast, I tore the lampshade from the top and smacked the bulb against the metal frame of the bed. I was left with jagged broken glass that was hot to the touch. The demon pulled me a little closer and I shot my arm out, aiming the makeshift knife at its hand. The glass cut into its green hand and it shrank back, releasing one of my feet. I brought it out and used it as leverage on the bed frame to push myself away from him. Surprisingly, it worked and I got free. I stood and backed away, pressing against the wall, hoping the thing would go away.

No such luck. I watched in horror as two green hands shot out and slowly pulled itself from beneath the bed.

It was blind—that much was obvious—so I figured I could use that to my advantage. But judging from the size of the two holes on each side of its head I guessed it relied heavily on hearing. As silently as I could, I tiptoed away from the wall to the other side of the room. It stopped, cocked its head and turned to face me. The next thing I knew, it shot across the room, its long snakelike body following behind it. I don't think it had any legs, just arms and a heinously long body. Which it proceeded to wrap around my body.

I bit down on my tongue to keep from screaming and tried to struggle. It was useless. This thing had me and I was dead. I watched as its head came closer and it sniffed me. Then it made a sound and the tentacle thing at the center of its gaping mouth extended and the things reached for me. I turned my head to the side and squeezed my eyes shut.

Wet, sticky things touched me, running along my cheek, and I whimpered. I waited for it to bite me, but it never happened. I heard this weird sound and then I was coated in wetness. Gross. Did this thing just barf on me?

"Sorry about that," Riley said from above.

I looked up to see him smiling. The demon's head dangled from his left hand and a dagger was in his right. I looked down at myself. I was covered in blood for the second time that day. "This is Sam's favorite shirt," I whined.

"Not anymore." Riley tossed the demon head to the floor, reached down to grab me by the elbow and yanked me up.

Then the burning started. I jumped up and ripped the shirt over my head, taking most of the blood with it. Thankfully, my tank top beneath seemed clean. I used the shirt to wipe away what was left on my cheeks and arms. "Damn demon blood is like fire to the skin." Oh well, at least there wasn't any spit this time and I wouldn't get sick.

The back of my head screamed in pain and I blinked my eyes at my blurred vision; then I looked up.

"Hey," Riley said, I could hear the concern in his voice. "Did that thing bite you?"

"No bites, just demon blood." I insisted. "Sorry, my head hurts."

"Did you hit it?" His fingers were gentle when he pushed them through my hair. I closed my eyes because, damn him, it felt good. The thought jolted my eyes open and I was glad to see my vision was clear. Riley's face was close to mine as he searched my head for bumps and I couldn't help but stare at his navy eyes. This close, I saw flecks of silver in the center.

His eyes shifted and he looked at me.

"I thought you went home," I whispered.

"Good thing for you I didn't." His fingers were still tangled in my hair and they flexed against my scalp.

"I'm not hurt."

"I know." He stayed where he was.

I cleared my throat and stepped back. "I need to shower and change."

He picked the head up off the floor and held it like a football. "I'll get rid of this thing."

I looked at the bed. "There was some sort of portal under the bed."

"It's gone. It died when this thing did."

I nodded. It's funny how I never questioned anything he said.

He tossed the head out of my bedroom window and then reached for the body.

"Umm, hell-O," I said as I got out some clean, demon blood-free clothes. "Don't you think Gran might notice body parts falling from the sky and into the yard?"

"Nah. It's dark and she's old. Good thing you don't have neighbors," Riley said. I swear he was trying not to smile.

I shook my head, trying not to be amused. "I don't understand why that thing showed up. If Beelzebub has the scroll, why keep sending demons?"

He looked back. "Maybe he doesn't."

"Maybe." I said the word, but I didn't believe it. "That's the first time one of them came into my bedroom."

"Are you sure?"

My eyes shot up to his. "What?"

"Maybe the scroll was here but a demon took it."

I hadn't thought of that. There were so many possibilities and all of them made sense. "I don't know anymore," I said, rubbing at my head.

The only thing I did know was that things were about to get a lot worse.

* * *

Riley was sitting on the floor with his back against the wall when I entered the room. I was carrying Sam's wet T-shirt that I scrubbed in the shower and then rung out. I draped it over the back of my desk chair to dry. I would throw it in the washing machine tomorrow. I still wasn't sure if it could be saved.

"I thought you left."

Riley shrugged. "Figured I would hang out a while in case any other demons came back."

"Did you get rid of the body parts?" I asked, looking at the window.

"No. I left them out there. What will Gran say?" He gasped, putting a hand to his chest.

"Whatever." I laughed. I was actually kind of glad he'd come back. I didn't want to admit it, but I was kind of scared.

"They're gone," he said. "I'm getting good at cleaning up bodies."

Everything inside me fell at the mention of Colin.

"Don't go getting all depressed now. It's over," Riley said, guessing the direction of my thoughts.

I went around the room, picking up, making sure there was no leftover blood from the demon, and we lapsed into a comfortable silence. Suddenly, I began to feel self-conscious at having a boy in my room who wasn't Sam.

"You know I love Sam, right?"

"I know who you belong to," Riley said, with nothing in his voice to tell me what he was thinking.

"Why did you agree to help Sam?" I sank down on the foot of my bed.

"I was bored." He shrugged.

"Liar."

He sighed. "I thought you didn't care as long as you got what you wanted."

"That's not true," I said. His words stung, especially when I decided he was right.

Riley chuckled. It was a warm, rich sound. "Want me to check under the bed for monsters?"

I shook my head even though I wanted to say yes.

His smile widened and he crawled forward to look. Dark hair fell onto his forehead when he leaned down. "All clear."

I let out a breath. "Look, I know that I've been kind of… focused on getting Sam out of there, but I do care about your reasons for helping. I care about you."

"Don't."

"Why?"

"I'm not like Sam," he said quietly.

"I know. No one is like Sam. But that doesn't mean we can't be friends."

"He wouldn't say that." Riley shook his head.

"Why is that?"

"He's seen me at my worst." I felt a pang in my heart for Sam, trying to fit into a group where he never belonged. "I made his life very hard."

"You're making up for it now."

He shrugged. "It's not always that easy. Things aren't just black and white. Sometimes the only choice you can make isn't the best one."

I stared at him as his words really sank into me. I finally understood why I liked him. He *got* it. He just put into words the feelings I had been struggling with lately. Sometimes the path you're on makes sudden turns. Should you turn with them or keep going straight because that's how you originally started? "Sometimes on the path to good, you have to be bad?" I mused.

"Or maybe sometimes you need to offset the bad you do with something good." Riley's smile was lightning fast and his teeth were a flash of light against the darkened room.

"Is that what Sam is for you? A chance to make up for the bad you've done?"

He sighed. "Something like that."

I could tell he was done talking. I'm actually surprised he said as much as he did. But still, I was certain I'd barely scratched the surface of Riley Stone. I yawned, long and loud.

"Get some sleep. I'll make sure no more monsters get you tonight."

"Sleep's not an option."

He raised an eyebrow. I got up and began cleaning up the broken light bulb beside the bed.

"Never?"

"You saw what happened the last time I went to sleep."

"Do you ever sleep?"

"Not much since Sam left."

"He kept the Dream Walker out of your head?"

"Yeah, he did. We thought he broke the thread Beelzebub left in here." I tapped my forehead. "But turns out there was more than one."

"How'd he keep him away?"

I paused. "He slept with me."

"It'll be rough, but I can take one for the team."

I laughed, but then I remembered that my mother had just died and I shouldn't laugh. "Not like that. Beelzebub couldn't get in my head when he was in the bed with me."

Riley got up and prowled over to the bed. He lifted the hem of his shirt and wagged his eyebrows. I shook my head and scowled. He shrugged and let go, leaving the shirt in place. I watched as he kicked off his shoes and lay down on the bed. "I hope you aren't a cover hog."

"We can't sleep together."

"Why?"

"It isn't right." I would feel like I was betraying Sam.

He rolled his eyes. "Come on. I'm not going to cop a feel. If I want some of *that* I'll go get some. The ladies love me." He made kissing sounds with his lips and rubbed his chest with his hands.

"I'll just bet they do," I muttered. "Poor things have no idea what's coming." I still stood awkwardly beside the bed, wondering what to do. I was so tired that the idea of getting just a couple hours of restful sleep was enticing. Yet, how could I sleep with someone who wasn't Sam?

"Heven." The tone in which he said my name called me out of my internal debate. For once, he was serious. "You don't really have a choice. You need some sleep. You look like shit and tomorrow isn't going to be easy."

I blinked back tears. He was right. If I wanted to be strong enough to spend a day making funeral arrangements for my mother and then go into hell, I needed to be clearheaded.

"Fine," I said, slinging back the covers. "But only because I have to." I climbed in and lay down on my side, putting my back to him.

He laughed.

I winced, thinking that those words didn't come out very nice. I rolled over to face him and he turned his head to look at me. "I didn't mean it like that. I…"

He smirked. "Go to sleep, Heven."

I closed my eyes but an image of Colin and then my mother flashed in my mind. I opened my eyes again. Riley was staring at me. There was knowledge in his eyes, and I felt again how much he understood. Without a word, he reached his hand over and placed it over mine. He didn't lace our fingers and I didn't try to hold his hand. He was simply offering some sort of comfort.

"I didn't say thank you for earlier," I whispered.

"You don't need to."

I was about to argue, but he sighed and rolled away, putting his back to me. "Go to sleep."

I rolled, putting my back to his as well and closed my eyes. *Sam...*

Hey, beautiful. His velvet voice filled the hollow spaces inside me.

I decided to listen to you this one time. I'm not coming until tomorrow.

When in doubt, listen to Sam.

I smiled. *I wish you were here.*

Can you feel me? he asked.

The force of his love reached out to me and I grabbed onto it and pushed myself closer. I imagined that we were together and he was holding me. *I've been waiting for this all day.*

Me too, sweetheart.

Can we stay like this?

All night.

Unfortunately, the night was too short.

Chapter Eleven

Sam

One minute, I was sitting in the cell, relaxed, keeping tight hold of the link I shared with Heven, and the next, he was walking right through the force field, once again acting as if it wasn't even there.

I eased away from my link with Heven as quickly as I could (so I didn't scare her) and watched with open violence as he paraded around. I wanted to kill the bastard for everything he had done but mostly for his most recent activities. The death of Heven's mother and the loss of the scroll.

I got slowly to my feet, acting as if I wasn't alarmed by his sudden appearance, as my fingernails curled into my palms.

Beelzebub smiled. "Well, well. What do we have here? Tell me how weak living with that amulet has made you?" He held his hands behind his back as he spoke.

I barely glanced at the amulet that I tossed into a shadowed corner and hadn't looked at since. Still, I knew it was there. My weakening limbs were proof. I was more tired than I wanted but brushed it off, determined not to look affected.

"I can't get into her head, you know," Beelzebub said, shaking out his arms, uncoiling a whip from around his wrist. "Do you know what that means?"

I didn't bother to answer. If Heven was somehow keeping Beelzebub out of her head, then more power to her.

"Word is you managed to get the scroll," I said, wanting to turn the topic away from Heven. And hey, maybe I'd find something out.

Rage flared in his eyes. "Don't play with me!" With a flick of his wrist he sent the whip smacking into the wall mere inches from my face.

Was that a yes or a no?

"You know full well I have that Map!"

Okay, a yes. "Good luck getting it open."

He threw back his head and laughed. "Is that why you pretend? Why you try to deceive me? I don't need luck, considering it was already open when it was delivered."

My breath caught. How in the hell had he managed to get it open? His face turned mean again. "Now tell me where the rest of it is!"

Ahhh, that's right. The bottom part of it was torn right before I was imprisoned here and right after Beelzebub took his fiery plunge. He had no idea he was getting an incomplete Map. What a shock that must have been… My lips curled with pleasure. "What do you mean?"

"Don't play stupid with me!" He roared and the lit torches out in the hall actually waivered.

"You've had me trapped down here all this time and you think I'll know the answers to your questions?"

"I know you talk to her! I know you know!" he screamed, spittle spraying from his mouth. "How am I supposed to torture you if she isn't around to see? I want answers!"

He lashed out with the whip, but I was faster and I caught it, leaving the long end to curl around my arm. Still, it stung. Beelzebub roared and yanked, causing me to lose my footing, but I managed to keep upright. The whip returned to him, curling around his feet like a venomous snake.

My body tried to shift but couldn't, and my insides screamed in frustration.

"Not so tough now, are we?" Beelzebub taunted. "Don't you wonder how she's managing to keep me away?"

Once again, I didn't answer, just watched his movements carefully.

"Maybe she found someone else to occupy her bed," Beelzebub mused. "I wonder what they're doing right now?" He lashed out once more with the whip; this time it curled around my waist and he pulled, towing me closer, then it was gone. "I bet he's touching her. Doing things to her body that you could only imagine."

I snapped, my patience and restraint only lasting so long, and I launched myself at him, but the whip shot out and slapped me, curling over my shoulder and striking down my back. The pain was sharp and stinging. I felt my flesh split and warm blood ooze out.

I didn't give him the satisfaction of screaming. And to his surprise, I kept coming. I knocked him off his feet and nailed him in the jaw before he recovered and got to his feet.

"But no matter! You have a link to her mind," he yelled. "I've felt it. She might not be able to see what's happening, but she's going to feel it. I hope she feels your pain for all eternity!"

And then he whipped me. Savagely, insistently and with fire in his eyes.

When my body would have sunk to the floor, he used his power to suspend me in the air. The pain was so intense I could barely breathe. The whip would lash against my skin and then draw away, leaving a searing pain stronger than I'd ever known, only to come back and do it again. The blood that poured down my back was warm and it felt like water to an open cut.

Throughout my beating, he tried to get the location of the remaining half of the scroll out of me, and every time I said nothing, he lashed me again. Still, I refused to give him the pleasure of sound. I bit my tongue until it bled. I might have to take this beating, but he wasn't going to get my pride or my pleading.

Beelzebub gave a frustrated cry and I was released, dropping to the floor, half unconscious. I prayed I would soon pass out. Kimber's screams filled my ears and I prayed she would shut up so she didn't draw attention to herself and have to endure his wrath too. Then I closed my eyes and had only one thought: *Heven.*

I prayed that she wasn't feeling this, I prayed that she was sleeping so soundly and whatever she was doing to keep him out of her head would prevent her from feeling anything. I prayed that she was safe and took comfort in the fact that since Beelzebub was here with me, it meant that he wasn't doing something heinous to her. I would do anything to keep something like this from happening to her.

Even die.

But dying would only deny me the satisfaction of exacting some revenge.

He crouched down, shoving his face close to mine. I opened my eyes and stared directly into his. "Lay there and bleed. Think about what you've suffered to protect her. You have the information I want. Give it to me and I'll set you free."

And by that he meant kill me. *Then he would chain your soul to the floor of hell to feed on for all eternity…* something whispered in the back of my mind. Freedom from him wasn't really free.

I spit in his face.

Fury burned in his eyes, but he only stood and walked away, right through the force field, which was far worse than the beating I just took.

"I know where the page you want is." A voice came from out in the hall. Beelzebub stopped and turned. Kimber was leaning against her cell door, her arms falling through the bars.

"You know where the piece of the map is?" he said quietly, deadly.

"Yes. I saw it all."

"Really?" Beelzebub glanced at me once more. I gave no indication I saw. "Well, isn't that interesting? What do you want in exchange for the information?"

"My freedom, of course. He might be willing to be a martyr, but I'm not."

"Tell me where it is and I will set you free."

"It was destroyed. Burned up right after you fell in that pit."

"What!" he screamed, slapping the whip across the floor.

"Hecate destroyed it because she was angry at Heven for ripping it."

"No! That stupid witch!" he wailed. "I need that paper! I need to know that name!"

So that's why he wanted the scroll. He wasn't interested in *all* the names. Just one. And apparently he knew it wasn't on the piece of Map he had.

"I kept up my end of the bargain. Let me out," Kimber said once he quieted.

Beelzebub laughed. "My end of the bargain, you say?" He wiggled his fingers and the door to her cell opened. Kimber rushed (as much as she could) to the door. Right before she stepped over the threshold, Beelzebub said, "A warning. The minute you step out of that cell, you will break the binding that holds your soul in there with you. It will be set free and you will be soulless and then you will die."

I watched her weigh his words.

"Well go on; you're free!" He spread his hands with flourish. "Just what you wanted, but your freedom will cost you your soul, and without it, you will die."

He turned his back on her as she crumbled to the floor. I actually felt bad for her. She wasn't a bad person... just selfish.

He came back toward my cell, stepping inside, and stood over my pain-wracked body. "She's coming for you, isn't she? Well, I say we give her something to find."

Heven

Pain lanced through my body, causing me to arch up off the bed. It burned. It burned so bad. I opened my eyes in panic, but not because of the pain. Strangely, I was getting used to pain.

"Sam," I called out, reaching for him, but he wasn't there. It was like the link we both held so tightly to during the night had been ripped away. Tears streamed down my face. Something was terribly wrong. I made a mistake waiting to go and get him.

Every muscle in my body ached and burned. Pain echoed through me and I struggled to push it away. Arms circled me from behind and pulled me back. "Easy," he whispered.

I shuddered. "Something's wrong. I can feel it. Sam…"

"I thought the Dream Walker couldn't get in your head with me here."

"He didn't. He can't. What if it made him mad and he's taking it out on Sam?" I pushed back to look at Riley. Horror ripped through me and I shoved at him. "Leave. I have to go to sleep. Then he'll stop whatever he's doing."

Riley's mouth flattened. "No."

"Yes!" I pushed against his chest, frantic to stop whatever was happening to Sam.

"Sam wouldn't want you tortured. He can take whatever Beelzebub dishes out."

"He could kill him!" I sobbed.

"Calm down. You're going to wake up the house."

"Don't you tell me to calm down," I growled, but it was in low tones.

"You don't even know what's happening."

"Please, Riley, I have to make it stop." Another tear slid down my face. Riley caught it with his thumb and I pulled away. "We have a Mindbond. Our feelings bleed to each other. Someone is hurting him. I can feel his pain. So much pain…"

"Have you tried to talk to him?"

My eyes widened. I was so frantic I didn't even think of that. *Sam. Sam what's happening? Are you hurt?*

He didn't answer. "He's not answering."

My body was shaking violently and my head was pounding, but I hardly noticed. *Sam. Please, Sam.*

I'm okay. Calm down.

I gasped and gripped the front of Riley's shirt. *Sam? What is he doing to you?*

Nothing. Please stop panicking.

I can feel your pain.

I can handle it. Don't come here.

He's mad at me, isn't he? He can't get in my head.

Whatever you're doing to keep him out, don't stop.

He's hurting you.

I'd rather him hurt me than you.

No.

I'm just going to rest for a minute, okay, sweetheart? I could feel his pain and his exhaustion.

I was afraid to stop talking. I was afraid if I let go it might be for good.

I promise I'm not going anywhere and nothing will take away our Mindbond.

I glanced at Riley. He was watching me without any expression on his face. "I think he's okay. But he's hurt. He says he wants to rest."

Sam, I love you.

I love you too. Oh and, Heven, Beelzebub does have the scroll and it's open. He's read it… His words faded as they came into my mind. I held back my shock because clearly there was something terribly wrong and he was fading.

Sam?

I'm just going to sleep. And then my mind was silent. I could still feel our connection, but Sam was far away. Fresh tears fell. I was here, in bed with Riley, and Sam was in hell being punished. This was a new low for me.

"We have to go now. To hell," I said, jumping off the bed and searching for some clothes.

"I thought you had to go to the funeral home."

I let out a frustrated sound. I did and there was no getting out of it. There was no way I could come up with a lie that would excuse me from planning my mother's funeral. Except the truth, and Gran would probably try to commit me if I told her the truth. "Yeah, okay. I'll go do that. Stay close because the minute I get home, we're leaving. I'm done waiting."

* * *

I spent some time on my appearance this morning because I felt that not looking like death warmed over while planning my mother's funeral was something she deserved. But I also felt stupid for caring about my appearance at a time like this. I did my hair and makeup, taking extra care to conceal the scar on my face. I didn't have the makeup I needed to make it disappear, but I was able to downplay its presence. As much as I hated to admit it, her final words bothered me. *You were marked for evil.*

I thought I put all that behind me, but I found the words haunted me still.

What if she was right?

Trying to put it out of my mind, I got dressed in black wide-leg pants and a snug black T-shirt. I grabbed a pair of oversized dark sunglasses and a dark-washed denim jacket and headed for the door to go downstairs with Gran.

Then everything went white.

* * *

Airis was standing before me when I opened my eyes. For once, she seemed different… Her eyes weren't as soft as they usually were and there was something brittle about the way she stood. There was an air around her that seemed… repulsed.

I watched her warily. I knew why I was here and this conversation wasn't going to go well.

"Hello, Airis."

"You did not heed my warning."

Something inside me shrank. "I'm not sure I know what you mean."

"I told you that you were going down the wrong path. I told you to resist the devil and he would flee from you. But you didn't."

"I'm so sorry about the Map. I don't know what happened."

"You allowed yourself to be distracted. You allowed evil to influence you. You murdered someone."

I sucked in a breath. "Beelzebub manipulated me. Colin attacked me."

Airis held up her hand. "I told you to be careful of whom you trust. You chose not to listen."

"I never meant for any of this to happen!" I protested.

"Your soul is compromised."

"It's not."

"We thought you had the strength to resist the temptation calling you."

"What are you talking about?"

"Since your conception, you've been marked. Two sides of one coin, marked by heaven but also by hell. Both places vie for you, yet you never seemed to understand the importance of your role."

"Please, help me understand."

"At first, we thought your unique position would be a strength, but now we see it may be a weakness. You were gifted with abilities and I've been here to guide you, but, alas, it seems that the hold *he* has on you is much stronger than we realized."

He who? Sam? Airis always knew how strongly I felt for Sam. She seemed to approve of that before; she seemed to think we were stronger together than apart. Had that changed in her eyes?

"This will be the last time you see me. I can help you no more."

My heart sank. "But what about the scroll? I can get it back." Knowing full well I couldn't.

"The scroll has been compromised. Higher beings have already been dispatched to make sure the people on that list are safe and remain so. The scroll is no longer your responsibility."

"All those people," I said almost to myself. They were in danger because of me. I felt like my world was being ripped away. Her coldness hurt me more than I thought it would.

"I'll give you one last warning. Heed me and all may not be lost."

I straightened and prepared to dissect whatever riddle she spoke.

"You still have the strength within you to prove that you fall on the side of heaven and not of hell. But you are in more danger than ever before. He thinks his claim on you is singular. He does not know you are two-sided. He does not know you have a claim on *him*. His ignorance is your only protection now. Your saving grace is the missing piece of that scroll. It must remain lost forever."

"Who is *he*?" At first I thought it was Sam, but it couldn't be. Sam knew I had good inside me.

"You will not see me again, but that does not mean that God has turned from you. He believes in you. But you must prove that you believe in him. That you are loyal." She lifted her hands as a ball of pure, white light formed.

"Airis, please! Wait, I have so many questions."

I barely noticed the flash of white that sent me back to my bedroom. I found myself standing in the middle of the room, staring at the busted lamp I used to protect myself from the demon. Then it dawned on me.

I knew who *he* was. What claim could I possibly have on him?

Chapter Twelve

Heven

It turns out it didn't matter how much effort I put into my appearance. My meeting with Airis totally ruined whatever I had managed to accomplish. I looked like I'd been through the ringer and hung out to dry. Thankfully, my oversized black sunglasses hid the worst and everyone at the funeral home, including Gran, assumed it was only grief for my mother that made me look this way.

And I was grieving for her. But maybe not in the way a loss of a parent deserved. There were so many things I was grieving over I could hardly focus on anything. Yet, I managed to make it through the morning. I thought it would be harder to choose a casket, pick flowers, music and decide who would be speaking, but all the choices were already made. Thankfully, Mom kept a last will and testament and everything she wanted had been outlined. It made things easy, and it went much faster than I expected.

When we arrived back at Gran's, Cole was sitting on the porch waiting. There were several glass bowls and dishes at his feet. Before I was out of the car, he was there opening the door and reaching in to grab me.

"You made it through the morning," he murmured in my ear as he slung an arm across my shoulders and led me toward the house.

"Beelzebub has started taking his anger out on Sam. We have to leave soon."

"What is all this?" Gran asked, pointing to the dishes.

"While you were gone, some people stopped by, most of them from Madeline's church. They wanted to pay their respects."

I never did understand why people felt the need to bring food to pay their respects. Sometimes, it seemed like the people who came by were only being nosy and wanted an excuse to come inside to view the grief of others.

"That was nice," Gran said, picking up the largest dish. Cole released me to help her carry the food inside and put them into the fridge. "We'll be able to put all this out after the funeral for the guests that come by."

I dreaded the funeral and the reception afterward. It was set for the day after tomorrow with two separate hour-long viewings at the funeral home tomorrow afternoon and evening.

"Gran, would you mind if I went upstairs to lie down for a while?"

"Of course not. It was a long morning. But before you go, I need to give you something." She pulled a white envelope out of her bag and handed it to me. "This was in your mother's room at the hospital. I forgot to give it to you last night with everything that had happened…"

"It's okay," I said, taking the envelope. My name was scrawled across the front in black ink. It was my mother's handwriting. "She left this for me?" I asked. "What is it?"

"I didn't look at it. I figured it was private."

After all the horrible things she said to me, I was shocked she left me anything at all. Part of me cringed at the note because it was probably filled with more words that would cut me like a knife. "I don't think I want to open it just yet."

"Of course, honey. Take your time," she said as she went to grab the tea kettle and fill it with water.

On my way out of the room, I stopped and turned back. "Oh, Gran? If it's okay, I planned to spend the night at Kimber's tonight."

Gran looked up from the tea kettle she was filling at the sink. "You two made up?"

I was aware of Cole staring at me, but I ignored him. "Yeah, after Mom… I figured whatever we were fighting about wasn't that important."

"I think that's wonderful. On the way home tomorrow, could you stop by your mom's and pick out that outfit?" My stomach knotted at the thought of choosing an outfit for her to be buried in.

"Sure. I'll take it over to the funeral home after."

Gran nodded and I left the room. Cole followed, telling Gran he wanted to make sure I was okay. In my bedroom, I flopped down face-first on the bed.

"How are you holding up?" Cole asked. The bed sank a little when he sat down on the corner.

I groaned. But then I propped myself up on my elbows. "What's the deal with you and Gemma?"

"Nothing."

"Come on, Cole, it isn't nothing."

"Actually, it is pretty much nothing. You know how hard Gemma is to talk to. She's a closed book; trying to talk to her is impossible."

I rolled over and stared up at the ceiling. Lately, I'd been letting my brother down. I'd been so focused on myself and Sam that I hadn't really cared or thought about what Cole might be going through.

I sighed and scooted back until I was sitting on the bed, leaning against the headboard. Cole was watching me and I patted the empty space next to me. When he was settled beside me, I rested my head against his shoulder. "I guess me showing up with Riley didn't make anything any easier."

"I don't trust him, Hev."

"Of course you don't." I smiled. "You're a Supernal Being, a regular angel on Earth, and he's a hellhound, a man twisted by sin."

"It's not just that," he began. "I mean, I've managed to accept Sam."

"I thought that might never happen."

"He's not so bad. He might even be good enough for my sister," he said with a smile in his voice.

"He's too good for me," I said, focusing on the pain that ran through my body. Sam's pain. Pain that I knew he wouldn't be in if it weren't for me.

Cole made a scoffing sound and was about to disagree when I interrupted him. "Have you and Gemma talked since Riley got here?"

A vision of Gemma flashed into my mind. She looked upset with tears in her eyes. I blinked and it was gone. Cole's aura was flaring with vibrant reds and oranges, colors that were not his usual greens and blues. Clearly, he talked to her and was at odds with whatever happened. Was that vision of Gemma from his mind? Was I mind-robbing his memories like I had done with Sam? Could I even *do* that? I thought the Mindbond I shared with Sam was the reason I was able to see his memories.

Maybe not.

I settled my head a little more soundly on Cole's shoulder and prepared to investigate. "Tell me what happened, Cole."

And just like that, I was transported. I may have been shocked if I hadn't been so engrossed by the scene that played out before me. It was as if I were at the movies with the best seat in the house. I don't have any idea how it happened. One minute, I was asking him a question, and the next, it's like I slipped inside his head to witness his answer firsthand.

They were standing in Cole's bedroom. At least I think it was his bedroom. I couldn't really be sure because I'd never been to his house. Our father left his mother for my mother, and I wasn't exactly welcome. I tried to check out the room from all angles but couldn't because I was seeing things from Cole's point of view. What I could see was nice. It was a large square room with a large window framed by navy curtains. Various football posters hung on the white walls. There was a dresser against one wall that was large and wooden. It was in front of this dresser that Gemma was standing. She was clearly upset, more upset than I'd ever seen her.

"Why didn't you tell me about your past?" Cole was asking her.

"Because my past doesn't matter."

I felt the words spear right through him. "So *I* don't matter?"

"My past has nothing to do with you."

"I'm beginning to think that nothing about you has anything to do with me," he muttered and he turned away.

Gemma caught his hand and drew him back. "That's not true, either."

"Then what's the truth?" His words were barely a whisper, but he stared right into her gray eyes. It was odd being in someone else's memories. I could feel what he felt and I could see what he saw. I wasn't sure I liked it. I was used to my brother from *my* point of view. To me, he was a rock. He was overprotective, sometimes bossy, and always stubborn, but I loved him. I didn't see him as unsure and vulnerable and I wasn't sure what I thought of Gemma for making him feel this way. Why couldn't she just love him too?

"I don't know." Gemma couldn't look at him and her eyes dropped, shielding whatever she felt from Cole's sight.

Cole laughed. It was bitter and incredulous. "You don't know?" He spun away from her. I felt his disgust. He couldn't stand to look at her. To look at the beautiful creature that he loved so much and have her dismiss everything he felt. Was he wrong, then? Did he imagine the way her gray eyes seemed to deepen when he was near? Did her heart not race whenever his hand brushed hers?

My brother was an open book, so he didn't understand someone who was buried beneath lock and key. I thought about pulling back. This scene was so personal and private; it felt wrong to watch it. But I couldn't; I was caught in his emotions and he desperately wanted to know how she felt. *I* desperately wanted to know too.

"What do you know?" he asked, keeping his back to her, staring at the bed. It was a large bed, queen sized, and it was far more inviting than any guy bed I had ever seen (which wasn't any other than Sam's) with its navy blue down comforter and neon yellow throw blanket.

Behind him, Gemma didn't say anything.

"I'll tell you what I know," he said quietly. Frustration welled inside him and he actually wished he didn't love her. Loving her was too hard. Abruptly he spun. Gemma's head snapped up and she stared at him. "You're miserable. You think you have to be alone because it's easier than caring. You act like you're forced to live the way you do, but you aren't. You act as if I'm nothing to you, and maybe I'm not, but you can't seem to walk away."

"Cole." A glimmer of tears shone in her eyes and turned her face soft. Everything about her seemed to soften from the way her flushed lips parted to the long strands of coffee-colored hair that fell over her shoulder and brushed her cheek.

Cole lunged forward and grabbed fistfuls of her hair, tangling his fingers deep into the silky mass and groaned. "What do you want? What?"

She didn't answer because he kissed her. Fiercely, bravely, deeply. His lips devoured hers in a way that staked a claim, yet pushed her away. Violent passion slammed through him and he groaned in his throat. I felt the sound rip right out of him. One part of him was so thrilled to be finally kissing her. Her lips were just what he thought they would be: soft, warm and giving. Why couldn't the rest of her be as giving as her lips? She tasted faintly of apples, sweet and tart. He smiled against her mouth. He like the comparison because it was exactly who she was.

He pushed his tongue past her lips, not caring if it offended her. This might be the only time that he would taste her and he wanted to satisfy his thirst. To his surprise, her lips parted under his assault and his tongue danced with hers as he tried to gentle himself. He actually began to recite football plays in his head, but they didn't make sense so he gave up and began kissing her with renewed force. When he was afraid he had pushed her too far, he pulled back, only to take her lower lip in his teeth and pull out, sucking it into his mouth and tasting her anew.

He was holding her so tightly his arms strained and he broke the kiss. His chest heaved as it pushed against hers. He could feel her shake against him, but all he could think about was doing it again. He wanted to kiss her until there was nothing between them but skin and then he wanted to kiss her some more.

She *had* to love him. She wouldn't have been able to kiss him like that, to make him feel like this if she didn't. He dropped his forehead onto hers and ran his fingers through the soft length of her hair. "Tell me," he said, his voice hoarse and low.

Somewhere in the house, a door slammed. Cole closed his eyes but tightened his grip on her. This wasn't over.

"Tell me," he demanded again.

"Cole?" his mother yelled from somewhere in the house.

Gemma began to pull away.

"Is it him?" Cole asked. "Is there something with Riley?"

She stopped on her way out the window. Her long hair fluttered from the breeze. "No, definitely not. But even if there had been something with Riley, you would have erased it from my soul with that kiss."

"Gemma." Cole half groaned.

The door handle turned and he watched as the door opened soundlessly and his mother peeked inside. "Didn't you hear me calling?"

Cole looked back at the window, knowing already that she was gone.

But he would see her again. And she *would* tell him.

I pulled out of his mind with a gasp and sat up, careful not to touch him, afraid that I would slip back in. That was intense. I had no idea that the feelings between my brother and Gemma burned so deeply. It almost matched what I had with Sam. It probably would if she didn't fight it so much.

"Heven?" Cole asked. He was staring at me warily.

"Sorry. What?"

"Did you hear anything I just said?"

"No." I stuck my tongue out, trying to moisten my dry lips.

"Are you okay?" He reached out and I flinched away.

"Don't touch me."

"Why?"

"Because of what I'll do to you."

"To me?"

I nodded. "I didn't hear everything you said because I *saw* it."

He looked at me like I was crazy. I probably was. "Explain."

So I did. I told him about how I accidently slid into Sam's mind and how I found out where Riley was. I told him that when I laid my head on his shoulder I saw everything that happened between him and Gemma. When I was done, I waited for him to yell at me. To tell me I was horrible for stealing his private moments and thoughts.

He didn't say anything like that.

"Do you think she loves me?" he asked instead.

I drew back in shock. "What?"

"You saw what happened. You felt what I felt. Do you think she loves me?"

"Aren't you mad?"

He shrugged. "No."

"Why?"

He seemed taken aback by this, like it never occurred to him to be mad. "Because you're my sister?"

I laughed. "You just want my opinion."

He shrugged. "I'm a good kisser, huh?"

"Ewww. You're my brother."

"Do you think she liked it?"

I remembered the insecurity and doubt that Gemma made him feel. I didn't like to think he felt that way. "Yes. I think she liked it. I think she loves you."

He grinned.

"But I'm not sure if she's going to admit it to herself."

His grin fell away. "Yeah."

"I wouldn't give up just yet, though." He lifted an eyebrow and I smiled. "Kiss her like that a few more times and then see."

He smiled smugly. "I'm the man."

I threw a pillow at his head, but he caught it and tucked it beneath his neck, leaning back and crossing his ankles over one another. When he closed his eyes, I let my face fall. Cole's happiness was important to me, but there were other things that took priority right now. I glanced at the clock. I couldn't wait another hour. I would just tell Gran I was having dinner at Kimber's as part of our 'make-up' sleepover. That would give me a few more hours to get Sam out of hell.

I picked up my cell and dialed Riley. He picked up on the first ring. "Can you be here now?" I asked without saying hello.

"On my way," he said, then abruptly hung up. I closed the phone and looked at Cole who was staring at me with his big blue eyes. I tossed him my phone and it landed in the center of his chest. "Can you get Gemma here?"

He dialed, spoke briefly, then hung up. "She's coming."

Seconds later, she was crawling through my window. Her eyes went first to Cole and lingered there for a second longer than they had to. He didn't change his position on the bed or even acknowledge her presence. But his aura did. It reached out to her and some of the magenta wrapped around her hand.

She looked at me. "Tonight, then?"

"Right now." I picked up my still-packed bag and tossed it on the bed.

"Riley's not coming?" Gemma asked, not looking at Cole when she talked.

"He's on his way. He doesn't travel at angel speed." It looked like everything I needed was in the bag and ready to go.

"Do you really trust him?" Gemma asked.

I stopped and turned to stare at her. "Yeah, I do. Can you give me a definite reason not to?"

She sighed. "I didn't tell," she began, but her words were interrupted when Logan came into the room.

"Logan, you're up. I glanced in your room earlier, but you were still sleeping. Are you feeling any better?"

He nodded, but in truth, he didn't really look any better. I glanced at Gemma who was frowning. "Well that's great!" I said, trying to add some pep in my voice.

"I heard you talking about Sam," Logan said.

"We are leaving for hell as soon as Riley gets here."

"Be careful, okay?"

"Of course. Sam will be here before you know it. He's going to be thrilled to see you."

He glanced at Cole and Gemma, then back at me and took a step closer. "I… uh… I appreciate everything you have done for me. Letting me stay here and stuff. I know I don't deserve it."

"Logan! Of course you do. You've been through so much. We've loved having you here."

His face was pale when he said, "I hope you still feel that way once Sam gets home."

"Of course I will. You're always welcome here."

He nodded. "I'm going to go back to my room now."

"Next time you see me, Sam will be with me."

He nodded and left the room. I looked at Cole and Gemma. "I'm worried about him."

"He'll be okay once Sam gets home," Cole said.

"I hope so," I said as Riley came through the window.

His dark hair was disheveled and he shoved it back, leaving it carelessly tasseled and perfect. His very dark eyes apprised me as he stood to his full height and leaned backward, cracking his lower back.

"Good, you're here. Let's go," I said, grabbing my bag.

"Should we go over the plan?" Cole asked, getting up from the bed.

I shook my head. "The plan is simple: get Sam and get out."

"My favorite type of plan," Riley said.

I ignored Gemma's frown. "Let's meet at the portal. I'm going to go say bye to Gran. Cole, come with me since she knows you're up here. You can offer to give me a ride to Kimber's."

Everyone sprang into action. Riley and Gemma went out the window and Cole and I went down the stairs. Butterflies danced in my ribcage. I was finally going to see Sam! I sobered a bit when I thought about what we were going to have to go through while we were down there. But it didn't matter.

I would do whatever it took to get Sam back, even if it meant stepping over that fine line between heaven and hell.

Chapter Thirteen

Heven

Riley led the way through the portal, and as soon as we hit the hard granite floor, we all began walking, with me leading the way. My photographic memory was the perfect map, showing me which way to go and never leading me wrong. As I turned and walked, the landscape around us remained the same: drab, depressing and colorless.

Riley fell into step beside. "How do you know where you're going?"

I tapped my forehead and immediately felt a wave of homesickness for Sam. The small act made me think of all the times he tapped my head to reassure me we were never far apart. "I have a photographic memory," I explained. "I've been this way before."

"Right," he said, his gaze sliding around as his steps slowed ever so slightly. Riley might not have an aura, but that didn't mean I hadn't gotten better at reading people without it. He seemed hesitant to be here, almost nervous.

"Is something wrong?"

His eyes shot to me. "No."

"If you're worried—"

"Please. Do I look like the kind of guy who gets worried?" His tone reflected his usual cocky self.

Well, he had. But I let it go because a flowing, black sludge-filled river came into view. "That's it," I said, fishing for some sort of reaction, wondering if his nerves would resurface.

"Looks refreshing," he said, his voice dry.

"You'll have to be careful because demons swim around in it."

"Yeah, I know," he replied, then cleared his throat. "I can handle it."

"How do you know? I thought you hadn't been here before."

"I haven't. You must have told me during one of the many times you never shut up."

His rudeness was supposed to distract me from the fact that what he was saying wasn't right. I hadn't told him about the demons in the water. I opened my mouth to retort, but I lost my thought because he stripped off his shirt and stuffed it into my hands. I tried not to look. Really, I did. But I couldn't *not* look. I don't think he had any body fat at all. Every muscle on him was defined and cut. His skin wasn't as tan as Sam's and looked smoother, cooler to the touch. He had a sprinkling of black hair on his solid chest that tapered down his navel to disappear into his jeans, which he started to unzip.

"What are you doing?" I asked, keeping my eyes above his waist.

He arched an eyebrow and silver danced in his eyes. His eyes were a good distraction from his body. "If I go in there dressed, I won't have anything to wear when I come out."

"Right," I said as his jeans hit me in the chest. His laugh echoed around me as he dove into the water, morphing into a sleek, black hellhound.

I stared after him for a long moment, hoping he would be okay, before I turned and dumped his clothes on the ground. Gemma and Cole were standing a few yards away, not even paying attention to us, but deep in conversation. They were in love and I wanted them to work things out, but not here. Not now.

"Hey, guys," I said, walking to stand in front of them.

"You can't trust Riley," Cole said abruptly.

I let out a long-suffering sigh. "Why are we still talking about this?"

"He's cursed," Cole blurted out, looking over my shoulder toward the black sludge.

"Wh—wait. What?" I said, wondering if I had heard right. "You think Riley is cursed?" That was ridiculous.

Cole motioned to Gemma, who nodded. "I tried to tell you. It was part of the deal that Callum made. He not only turned himself and future generations of the males in his family into hellhounds, but he also cursed them. All the hellhounds in Callum's line were cursed with servitude to Beelzebub. They are literally at his beck and call."

"That's ridiculous." I denied.

"It's the truth. It's why Callum seemed different after he changed. The curse was dark… It made it hard for the goodness in him to shine through. He had to fight against the darkness every day. And then Beelzebub came and wanted him to do something. It was a heinous crime and Callum resisted. It's why Beelzebub killed him."

"So you think Riley will betray us because he's bound to do Beelzebub's bidding?"

"I don't know," Gemma said. "I just think you need to be careful."

"It's kind of late, don't you think? Look around. We're in hell. He's in that nasty water doing us a favor. I trust him."

There was a loud sucking sound as Riley jumped out of the black sludge and shook, gobs of black ooze flying everywhere. He stared at me for a moment out of silver eyes that seemed to study me in such an intent way that I squirmed. Could he have possibly heard what we had been talking about? He walked over to where the three of us stood and unrolled his long tongue and three Lucent Marbles dropped into my palm.

"Thank you," I said as he padded away toward his clothes. I turned back to Cole and Gemma and held out the marbles and widened my eyes as if to say, "see?"

Cole sighed, took the marbles and began cleaning them off with his shirt. "Let's just focus on getting Sam. We'll deal with this later, okay?"

"Yeah, okay. Let's go," I said and started walking once more.

It didn't take long before the ominous black castle came into view. Once again, I noticed that Riley seemed to be getting nervous. I understood now that it was probably because this was the home of Beelzebub, the guy who cursed his family and seemed to have some kind of hold over him. I wanted to know more, to know how the curse worked, but I didn't think bringing it up right this moment was a good idea. It hit me then how much I was asking of Riley. I mean, this was a guy Sam practically ran out of town. He wasn't (or hadn't been) our friend when I found him and basically dumped a huge mess on him and asked for help. And now, I find out he's basically going against a man he's indebted to, a man that I'm sure Riley has avoided up until now. He had no reason to help us. He isn't getting anything in return. In fact, it seemed to me this was risky for him.

And yet he was here.

We came upon the castle and I stopped short. Something didn't feel right. "The draw bridge is down," I said in a hushed tone.

"Isn't that a good thing?" Cole asked.

"It's too easy."

"I did expect more of a fight," Gemma said.

"Maybe the fight is inside," said Cole.

Usually, the minute I dropped into hell, Beelzebub was in my head, squeezing my skull and racing to do something horrible. But now he was acting as if he didn't care I was here. "It's almost as if he wants me to come inside…" I said, then gasped. "Sam!"

I took off running. I charged through the heavy front door and made my way to a large set of stairs that seemed to plunge into a black abyss. I didn't hesitate. I didn't heed the warnings of my friends behind me. I was deaf and blind to all things not related to the dungeon.

There could only be one reason that Beelzebub would let me walk into his castle, around his land… It was because he wanted me to see something.

I prayed it wasn't a dead body.

As I raced through the dark, I told myself Sam wasn't dead. He was still alive. We talked just an hour ago… I would feel it if our Mindbond had been severed. I swung open the heavy door and rushed into the darkened dungeon. Burning torches lined the walls and I scrambled to the entrance of Sam's cell.

"Sam!" I screamed, not caring who heard. "Sam!"

There was no movement, no response as I skidded to a halt, practically bouncing right off the force field that kept him from me. I didn't see him. He wasn't answering. My eyes sought out the darkened corners, the places he could be sleeping… only there were none.

All the darkened corners were lit. In fact, the entire cell was lit up like the fourth of July.

Sam was not in that cell.

"Sam!" I screamed and raised my fist to beat on the force field, only my arm went right through. I was mere inches from throwing myself inside when Riley grabbed me and pulled me back.

"It might be a trap."

I didn't care. I wanted what I came here for.

"Sam!" I screamed, my throat ripping raw.

"He's gone," a voice said from behind.

We all turned. "Kimber," I said, "where is he?"

"I don't know. He took him. After…"

"After?"

Kimber didn't say anything else, but stared off into nothing.

"After what?" I cried.

Cole swore and I turned to see him staring into the cell, his eyes focused on something in the center of the room, something I hadn't noticed in my panic.

There was blood.

Sam

Underestimated. I have been underestimated many times in my life. Some don't like to be underestimated. They want people to know how strong or cunning they are. They want people to not want to mess with them. Me? I like it. Especially by people who should know better—by people who think so highly of themselves they forget to think of their opponent at all.

Being underestimated is an advantage.

I opened my eyes a crack to see Beelzebub had his back turned. He was staring out a massive window that overlooked the dull view of hell. His hands were clasped tightly behind his back and smoke practically poured from his ears, so I knew he was angry. I took a chance to look around at my surroundings. I was lying on—rather, had been dumped onto—a blood-red carpet. I seemed to be in an office of some sorts—if you could call a room with a desk and chains on the wall an office...

There was a sound behind me, and I slammed my eyes shut and tried to look natural in the unnatural and uncomfortable position I'd been dumped in. I was still very sore from the whipping I took, but I could already tell the wounds had at least closed, not healed by any means, but at least closed and were no longer bleeding. My knee injury from when I tried to escape was fine so I could walk—or run—when needed, and the pain in my ribs was manageable.

I don't know how long I had been out, but it couldn't have been long. Beelzebub was stupid for thinking that a beating would keep me down for any significant amount of time.

"How could you allow that piece of Map to be destroyed?" Beelzebub said and I felt rather than saw him turn from the window to face whoever made that noise behind me.

"I had meant to take it from her, but the flames were too close and it was destroyed," Hecate replied, her tone haughty.

"Excuses!" he roared. Then there was a pause and in a much more reasonable tone he said, "Do you know what you've cost me?"

Was he really attempting not to scream? That was like a pile of shit trying not to smell.

"I've lost just as much as you! I draw my power from hell just as you do. 'Course I'm not greedy about it." Her last words were said almost beneath her breath.

Interesting.

Something crashed against the far wall and I figured, instead of yelling, he decided to throw things.

"What is he doing here? Why did you take him out of his cell?" Hecate asked, and I tried not to react to the fact attention was being called to me.

"He isn't any of your concern!" Beelzebub snapped.

"Have you forgotten that everything in hell is of my concern?"

Charged silence reigned. I had a feeling as to why I wasn't in my cell and why he was suddenly trying not to be loud. He didn't want to give away where he was. *Heven, where are you?*

"So the name wasn't on the Map?" Hecate asked.

"Of course it's on the Map!" He demanded. "On the portion that you burned!"

Sam? Where are you? There's blood… blood everywhere.

"The girl. She looked at it before it burned. It was in her hands. I saw her look at the list."

"Are you saying that she knows the information that I seek?"

Oh, shit. I flinched at what this could mean and then stilled, praying they didn't see me move.

Sam?

Listen to me. Get out of the dungeon. Move quietly. Get outside. I'm in the castle. I'm going to meet you outside.

"It is entirely possible that she knows the name."

Beelzebub cackled. "Well, isn't it convenient that she just happened to walk right into this castle moments ago?" His footsteps drew near and I prepared myself. "And more convenient that I didn't kill her little boy toy when I had the chance. He'll make the perfect exchange for the information I seek."

In a fit of movement, I lunged low and caught Beelzebub around the knees, knocking him to the floor. He gave a shout and I sprang up with a growl and transformed in mere seconds. The hound in me screamed in freedom as I slammed into Hecate, sending her sailing through the air, and she hit the window that Beelzebub had been looking out only moments before. The glass shattered and she might have fallen through—I don't know. I didn't bother to stick around. I raced out the door and down the hall.

This time my freedom would not be taken away.

Heven

"It's not that much. He would have to lose way more blood than that to be…" Cole was saying. His voice sounded far away to my ears.

"Dead." I whimpered, staring at the red pool of blood that was in the center of the cell. I knew in my heart that Sam wasn't dead, but whatever had happened down here… it hadn't been good.

"Reach out to him," Gemma urged, grabbing hold of my arm and spinning me away from the sight. "Ask him where he is."

Visions of depraved acts filled my head, memories of the echo of Sam's pain… of his voice telling me he needed to rest. Oh, Sam. What have they done to you?

Heven, where are you? His voice alive and strong filled my head. It was such a welcome sound that my knees almost buckled. I reached out and grabbed on to Cole.

Sam? Where are you? There's blood… blood everywhere.

"He's okay," I told everyone. "He just spoke to me."

"Where is he?" Riley asked.

I waited for him to say more, to tell me he was all right, but he said no more. *Sam?* I asked warily.

It seemed I waited forever. All I wanted was another sound, another brush of his voice in my mind. And then it came.

Listen to me. Get out of the dungeon. Move quietly. Get outside. I'm in the castle. I'm going to meet you outside.

"He's upstairs. I think Beelzebub must be with him. He said we needed to get outside as quietly as we could. He said he would meet us out there…" I told everyone.

We all moved quickly to the stairs. I tried to go first, I tried to push past Cole and Riley, but they blocked me behind them. At least Gemma had the grace to walk alongside of me as we went up the stairs.

About halfway up the steep, dark stairway there was a loud shattering sound.

Then all hell broke loose.

Chapter Fourteen

Heven

We burst through the door in time to see a large black hellhound career through the room ahead, destroying everything in its path as it bounded toward the door, which was standing wide open from when I burst in only minutes before.

Beelzebub was screaming and hot on his heels. I watched in horror as he uncoiled a whip from his back and was about to lash out at Sam.

"No!" I screamed and lunged forward as Sam made it through the door to the safety of the outside.

Beelzebub stopped when I screamed and was now focused on me. "I've been expecting you."

Riley moved to put himself in front of me. As he went, he whispered, "Take advantage of this and get the hell out of this house."

I didn't understand what he meant until Beelzebub looked away from me toward Riley.

"You!" he screamed. "You dare betray me after everything I have done for you!"

"I just couldn't get enough of your pretty face," Riley said in a biting tone.

They knew each other?

Sam lunged back inside the door, his wild eyes locking with mine. I raced forward, Gemma and Cole close behind as Sam stood, lifting his considerable frame (had he gotten bigger?) onto his back legs and used his body as a shield as the three of us ran past.

We all made it outside and were running across the drawbridge when I heard a loud crash and I looked over my shoulder to see Riley, now in hellhound form, bound out the door.

Beelzebub was seconds behind, screaming as usual. "Stop them!"

Hecate appeared before us and lifted her hands and we all skidded to a halt.

Cole came up behind me, brushing his hand against mine. "In case we get separated," he said low as he deposited a Lucent Marble into my palm. I closed my fingers around it, not acknowledging what he had done.

Gemma gave a sudden cry and sent a dagger spiraling at an impossible speed at Beelzebub, who caught it. "I should have known you'd somehow be involved. I see you still haven't accepted the fact that you are *fallen*."

She didn't bother getting into a verbal debate with him, which I found impressive. Personally, I would have tried to get in the last word. Instead, she pulled out yet another dagger and fell into a fighting stance.

"Is that why you wanted the curse broken after all these years? Are you picking up where your grandfather left off?" he said to Riley.

Cole wasn't as good at ignoring Beelzebub's taunts. He gave a shout and threw his own dagger at Beelzebub, which he dodged with ease.

"Ahhh, so it's that way, is it?" Beelzebub said with amusement, then sent the dagger in his hand hurling through the air toward Cole. He wasn't fast enough and it lodged itself in his belly.

He made a weird gurgling sound and went to pull it out.

"No!" Gemma and I cried at the same time. Pulling it out would only make him bleed faster.

Cole looked from the wound up to me and then Gemma. "Well, shit."

"Cole," I whispered, staring at my brother, the only family I had left besides Gran. I looked at Gemma. "You've got to get him out of here, now."

Gemma nodded. I threw down the Lucent Marble that I was holding and a swirling portal to home appeared. "Go!" I yelled.

"Come with us," Cole urged.

I looked over my shoulder at Sam and Riley who were circling Beelzebub like they had found a tasty snack.

"I'll be right behind you," I yelled and Cole handed me the last two Lucent Marbles he had before Gemma pulled him through the portal and disappeared.

Sam and Riley had backed Beelzebub up to the moat and were about to pounce when two demons, coated in black sludge, rose behind him and reached out, yanking Sam and Riley down into the nasty water.

They struggled to break free as Beelzebub grabbed my arm and yanked me off my feet. "Give me the name!" he demanded as I struggled to stand.

"What name?"

"Don't play with me. I know you saw it!"

"I don't know what you're talking about!"

Hecate appeared at my other side and stared at me with empty eyes.

"The name of the Soul Reaper. *Tell me!*" Beelzebub demanded again.

The Soul Reaper? I must have not answered fast enough because Beelzebub stamped down hard on my ankle and foot and I screamed as the bones gave way.

"This is only the beginning if you don't tell me what I want to know."

"But I don't know," I cried, as my ankle burned.

I heard Sam snarling and knew he would be here in seconds. Beelzebub seemed to realize he wouldn't be able to torture me much longer because he pushed me toward Hecate. I stumbled, as my ankle wouldn't support my weight, and I fell to my knees. Both Lucent Marbles fell from my hand and rolled away.

"I want her to know what it's like to feel true evil inside her. I want her to come begging me to make the pain go away. I want the only peace she will know to be here, in the place she hates most. In hell." Beelzebub ordered. And then he turned his evil face toward me. "Let's see if this loosens your tongue."

The witch started chanting. I didn't understand a word she said, but I knew whatever she was doing would not be good. I tried to get up, to get away, but her words held me frozen, helpless to what she was doing. Sam and Riley also seemed to be held back by whatever spell Hecate was casting. My skin crawled when she muttered the word *beast* and *cage* and I flinched when a strong wind picked up and a dark cloud seemed to wrap around my body, then dissolve. I felt as if my skin was being ripped open. It hurt so much that I couldn't even cry out.

And then it stopped.

Beelzebub looked down at me with satisfaction as Sam attacked him from behind. Beelzebub gave a startled yelp and looked to Hecate, who smiled a brittle smile, then disappeared—leaving him to be attacked. Yes, Beelzebub was powerful, but he was no match for the angry teeth and claws that ambushed him. It seemed Sam had finally gotten the upper hand.

He probably would've been able to fight off Sam if he had seen him coming, and if Sam's teeth weren't already buried in his neck. But they were. He made one feeble attempt to fight and then he didn't move at all. I turned away from the carnage. Not because I was sorry Beelzebub's latest body was ruined, but because it was gross.

I struggled to stand. Riley noticed and came to my side so I could use his body to lean on. But Sam beat him to me, sliding his bulky, furry frame beneath me.

The wind picked up and The Devourer swooped out of the sky. He landed right next to Beelzebub's remains, sniffed, then drew back as a white cloud seemed to lift out of the body and float up into the sky. It didn't really have a shape, but I knew it was Beelzebub's immortal soul and it would be searching for a new "host" body.

I wasn't sure what power he held without a body, and I watched warily for what he might do. But he did nothing, just floated into the air and disappeared. I let out the breath I was holding and then turned back to Sam, opening the backpack still strapped to my back, pulling out some clothes and dropping them on the ground.

Both Sam and Riley morphed and pulled them on. Then, finally, blissfully, Sam was there reaching for me. He wrapped his arms around me and I buried my face in his neck.

I was finally home.

"What did he do to you?" Sam murmured, running his hands down my back.

"I'm fine," I said, tightening my arms around his neck. "You're free."

Sam pressed a kiss to my forehead and I wanted to weep at the familiar feel.

Behind us, Riley cleared his throat.

Sam released me and turned toward Riley, narrowing his eyes. I moved to step forward, but stumbled and grabbed Sam's hand. "My ankle is broken," I told him.

He growled and swept me up into his arms. "The marbles!" I gasped. I had no idea what happened to them during the commotion.

"I'll get another one," Riley offered.

"What the hell are you doing here?" Sam asked.

A large growl came behind us and Sam turned. The Devourer was still sitting there, staring at us.

"What the hell is that thing?" Riley asked.

"That's The Devourer," I said, reaching for the bag Sam held. I reached inside and pulled out a Snickers bar. The dragon took a step closer and Sam stepped back. "He wants a snack." He was probably hanging around because he didn't get to suck up a soul like he usually did, or maybe he figured death followed us everywhere, so there was bound to be another body turn up.

"Let me down," I asked Sam. He did what I asked and I quickly unwrapped a Snickers bar and tossed it to the waiting dragon. Then I tossed him two more.

Even after the dragon ate his snack, he still stood there as if waiting for something. I thought after his chocolate fix (a dragon with a chocolate addiction is so unreal it can only happen in my life), he would fly away.

"We need to go," Sam said, and I nodded.

We turned and the dragon made a horrible sound. I peeked back over Sam's shoulder and it was coming at us, doing its best to move its massive body in a nonthreatening way.

"No more," I told it. "Chocolate should be eaten in moderation, even for big guys like you." It stared at me for long moments, then dropped down and offered me its back. I glanced at Sam. He was frowning at the dragon.

"No," Sam said flat.

My reaction went along the line of Sam's, but then I told myself to think past my overwhelming need to just go home and be with Sam. I thought past the throbbing in my ankle and the questions that simmered at the surface of my mind. There was a reason The Devourer was still here. There was a reason he was offering his back. Ignoring that reason, though I wanted to, probably wasn't a very good idea. Besides, how often did a girl get to ride a dragon?

"I think we should go with it," I said.

Sam frowned, but Riley was all for it. "Cool. Let's go."

He stepped toward the dragon. It made a hissing sound and raised some of the sharp spiky things on its back. Riley took a step back and I thought maybe I was wrong in thinking The Devourer wanted to take us somewhere.

In experiment, I took a hobbled step toward him, cautiously. The dragon lowered himself to the ground. I turned toward Sam, who stepped up next to me, and held out my hand. The Devourer didn't seem to mind.

Sam turned to Riley. "He doesn't like you." That fact seemed to please Sam.

"Clearly."

I thought it was odd and it reminded me of something Beelzebub said earlier. "Beelzebub acted like he knew you. He said you betrayed him after everything he had done for you."

Riley shifted uncomfortably. "How am I supposed to know what he was talking about? That guy makes no sense at all."

"He did seem to recognize you," Sam said thoughtfully.

"He also was screaming at Heven for some name. Did *you* know what he was talking about?"

"Well, no," I admitted. "You can't trust anything he says."

"Exactly. And since Dragon Breath here doesn't want me around, I will leave you two for your joy ride."

"Riley," Sam said in a serious tone, "don't disappear. Clearly, we have things to discuss."

Riley saluted, then headed toward the black sludge to get a Lucent Marble. I looked at Sam. "I know I have a lot of explaining to do too."

Sam's eyes softened and he held out his hand. "Later. How's your soul?"

"It's fine."

"Then let's go for a dragon ride." He stepped toward the dragon, who watched him warily, but didn't make a sound when Sam found a place on its back that was not lined with sharp quills. He sat me between his thighs and wrapped his arms around my waist. My ankle was throbbing and my head was pounding, but I was determined to see where the dragon would take us.

"Maybe we should make sure Riley gets a marble," I said, glancing at the black sludge Riley dove into moments before.

"Riley can take care of himself," Sam said.

Before I could protest, the dragon spread its great wings and took off.

* * *

I wish I could say flying on the back of the soul-eating dragon known as The Devourer was thrilling and exciting, but I couldn't. It was terrifying and extremely uncomfortable. The speed at which he flew jostled us around and sent pain shooting up my leg. Although, I was relieved that those insanely sharp quills and spikes on his back didn't feel sharp at all against my skin (for reasons I couldn't explain. I mean, those things looked brutal). I felt dizzy and weak and the insane chanting that Hecate had done while standing over me kept replaying through my mind. I didn't understand much of it, but a few words stuck out and they made fear churn in my belly. The Devourer swooped down abruptly and I jerked, trying to stay on, trying not to make Sam support all of my weight.

"I've got you," Sam murmured into my ear. That deep raspy voice brushed over my skin and I almost groaned. It was so, *so* good to be with him again. Desperate to look at him, I turned and another wave of dizziness came over me, making my stomach turn. Sam frowned. "We need to get you home." He reached up and brushed away the hair that was sticking to my damp forehead.

I closed my eyes, thrilled at his touch, and let myself sink a little bit deeper into him.

"You're positive this dragon doesn't plan to make a Heven and Sam shish kebab?" Sam said into my ear.

I opened my eyes and looked up.

It absolutely couldn't be missed.

It was a huge wall of fire. It burned with awe-inspiring intensity, rolling in colors of red and gold mixed with orange. I looked down, pushing away my fear and dizziness to note that it stretched as far as I could see. There was no getting by it. If we went through it, we would indeed be a Heven and Sam shish kebab.

Well, really, it would only be a Heven shish kebab.

Hellhounds were fireproof and I had a feeling The Devourer was too.

"It's the gate of hell," Sam murmured.

"This is the entrance to hell?" I asked, yelling a little over the roar of flames.

Sam gathered me closer and I felt his words echo through his chest and tickle my back. "Yes. I know it instinctively. Originally, hellhounds were charged with guarding this gate and helping souls cross over."

"Why are we here?" I asked, fear sliding into my belly. I was so tired of being afraid.

"How good of a friend did you say this dragon was?"

"I didn't." I pointed out, wondering if maybe I had been wrong about the connection I seemed to have with The Devourer.

Just as I thought the words, The Devourer made a shrieking sound and turned to fly directly at the wall of flames.

Chapter Fifteen

Heven

Sam's body was tense and his breathing was labored. He gathered me as close as possible and wrapped every part of his body around me while still keeping balance on the dragon's back. My ankle screamed in pain and my muscles ached at being held this tightly, but I kept my mouth shut. This pain was way better than being burned to death.

We neared the wall of fire, so close the intense heat stole my breath. Brilliant flames reached out to me until red was all I saw. Then the dragon turned. Actually, it felt like he fell from the sky. My stomach threatened to empty itself, but I swallowed it back and reached out to steady myself. Just when I was sure we were going to die, the dragon threw its wings out and took a wide arc away from the flames, dropping down in the gray sky. I opened my eyes and looked back.

"That was close," Sam said, gentling his hold on me.

I looked down and gasped. We were flying over what looked like an ocean. An ocean filled with black sludge. But that wasn't the surprise. It was what was sitting in the center or the ocean.

An island.

One side of it was gray and desolate. There was a huge mound of rock in the center that I realized was actually the entrance to a great cave. Small fires burned around it, giving off a heavy smoke, but there was nothing else. It was depressing and sad.

But then came the other side.

It was a shock to the eyes. It was an unexpected twist among the dead.

It was *life*

"Oh my," I said to myself, my eyes straining to see more of the beauty.

It was completely covered in brilliant green. An expanse of grass that promised to be soft under the feet and gentle on the skin. There was also a stream, a *real* stream with *real* water. It looked fresh and cool and it made me realize how thirsty I felt. There was a great tree with abundant reaching limbs that twisted into the sky and bloomed with more brilliant green.

These things were spectacular, but they weren't the most wonderful thing I could see.

In the center of the all the green was a house. A house made of white stone with a thatched roof. It was large but quaint. Old school, but new. And it was beautiful.

"Isn't it wonderful?" I asked Sam.

"It's amazing," Sam agreed.

The dragon made a rather smooth landing on the depressing side of the island. Sam was the first to climb off and then he reached up to help me. My heart began to pound as we all stood there next to a dragon's lair. No, he didn't make us into shish kebab, but maybe he liked sushi… as in raw meat.

"Now what?" I asked Sam, gazing over to the side of the island that looked so beautiful. For some reason I saw no way to actually get there.

The Devourer gave a roar, then lumbered inside the mouth of the cave, turning back to stare at us.

"I think he wants us to follow him."

"In there?" I asked dubiously, looking at the black hole of the cave.

"We've come this far," Sam said.

"Why not?" I said. "No one likes sushi anyway," I mumbled.

"What?" Sam said, gazing at me.

"Nothing, let's go."

And then we walked right into dark mouth of the cave.

* * *

"I certainly hope following the most feared creature in hell into its dark and scary lair isn't a horrible mistake," I said as Sam practically carried me as I hobbled through the dark.

"Eh, he's only ten times the size of me, covered in prickly scales and razor sharp spikes. Just because he has more teeth than a shark, could swallow us whole and eats the dead souls of demons doesn't mean he's going to kill us," Sam said nonchalantly.

Oh, how I missed him. I giggled. "Well if all else fails, we can feed him a Snickers."

"How's your soul?" Sam asked, his voice turning serious.

Actually, my chest was beginning to feel a little odd… but I hadn't been feeling well anyway so how was I supposed to know the difference? "I think it's okay for a bit longer." I hedged, when in truth I had no idea how much longer I had.

"Maybe this wasn't a good idea," Sam said.

Suddenly, pure, bright light filled the inside of the cave. The Devourer was no longer leading the way. He had stepped through another doorway, an exit to the back of the cave and his massive body was no longer there to block the light. Sam and I looked at each other and he moved in front of me, keeping a hand behind him and firmly on my waist. "If I tell you to run, go as fast as you can on that ankle, back into the cave and find somewhere to hide. I'll come and get you."

I didn't bother to argue because I didn't have to. Sam stepped through the opening and I heard his intake of breath.

I wasn't about to wait for his permission so I stepped through, coming up behind Sam, and forgot to breathe.

It was stunning.

It was incredible.

It was the most perfect place I had ever seen.

And it was in hell.

Irony at its best.

"Holy cow," I whispered, so in awe I could barely speak.

"If I didn't know better, I would think we were in heaven," Sam said, wrapping his arm around my waist and drawing me against him.

We were welcomed by the greenest of grass, not mowed short by the brutality of lawn mowers, but left to flourish. It didn't take over, almost as if it knew exactly how long to grow so it invited your toes to wiggle into its depths. Swaying ever so slightly in the cool breeze that caressed your skin, it promised a luxurious respite from anything and everything that ailed you.

The sky, the most dazzling shade of azure, had no blemish in sight and the trees grew in abundance, their branches knowing no bounds and growing with a joyous, twisting freedom.

The stone cottage that I saw from the back of The Devourer was sitting not so far away and it looked warm and welcoming.

"Where did The Devourer go?" Sam asked, and we both turned and gasped.

The Devourer wasn't there, but there was a giant… bird? Creature? Animal? Standing there staring at us. It was covered in feathers, brilliant feathers of blue, red and yellow. It spread its wings to reveal more jewel-tone hues of orange and green. It had a large body, but somehow it seemed graceful, never clumsy. It had a wide face and the top of its head was covered in a yellow Mohawk, while the feathers around its eyes were green. But there was something familiar about this creature.

It's eyes… I gasped.

This was The Devourer. Somehow, remarkably, its ugly exterior was transformed in this place to a thing of great beauty. "It's The Devourer," I whispered to Sam, who nodded, not taking his eyes off the dragon.

"I've been waiting for you," a woman said from behind and Sam spun around quickly. I turned too, just not quite as fast.

She was just as striking as everything else. Her beauty rivaled that of Airis, except there wasn't an untouchable vibe. She wasn't as austere as Airis. She was more natural, but nature had given her its every gift. She had long hair the color of sun-kissed wheat and her wide-set eyes were as green as the grass beneath our feet. She wasn't very big. In fact, I was taller than she and I guessed her height wasn't more than five feet. She moved with an elegance and grace that I would never master, even if I practiced for a hundred years. Her skin was smooth and creamy with pink undertones, making her appear very young. But none of these things were her most beautiful feature.

Her most beautiful feature was her aura.

I had never before seen such pure, unfiltered color. There was a bright yellow and a crisp orange that weaved with emerald and blue. But the most abundant color of all was magenta—the unique blend of purple and pink that I had only ever seen one other person wear. My brother. Except this woman had about three times the amount of that color and, instead of circling only her head, it encompassed her entire body.

We shook ourselves from staring as Sam asked, "Who are you?"

She smiled. "My name is Aniano."

"Once again?" I asked.

"An-yah-no," she pronounced more slowly.

"I think we'll just call you Ana." Sam replied ruefully.

"If you wish." She smiled back, her green eyes amused.

"What is this place?" I asked her.

"My home," she said simply. "Come, I will show you around.

Forgetting my ankle was broken, I moved to follow. I stumbled, but Sam was there to catch me.

"You are injured. I can help." She didn't wait for us but walked toward the cottage. Sam picked me up and hurried after her. There was a large set of French doors, open to the breeze, where I thought she would go, but instead, she passed the open doors and walked across a small clearing on the other side of the house.

"Heven is human. Her soul…" Sam began to say, obviously concerned that we were wasting time.

Ana lifted a hand. "Her soul is not in danger here. It will remain in her body." Then she stopped and looked down with unfiltered joy on her face. Sam made it to her side and stopped, placing me on my feet (well, my one good foot) and we both looked down to see what she seemed so awed by.

It was a flower.

It was growing alone among the softest patch of green grass. The breeze played lightly with the petals. It was golden and seemed to be lit from within; its edges were glittering and magnificent. The creamy yellow petals were open, inviting the warmth of the sun and the gaze of our eyes.

"You brought us out here to look at a flower?" Sam asked, trying to sound polite.

"It isn't just any flower," Ana said kindly. "It's a piece of the sun."

"A what?" Sam asked.

"This flower grows from a drop of the sun. It is the purest form of life."

"Then what's it doing in hell?" Sam asked, curious.

"Proof," I murmured.

Ana turned toward me and smiled.

"Proof that God created hell, not Satan. If Satan created it, then this place wouldn't exist."

"That's right," Ana said.

"I guess no one would think to look for it here." Sam allowed.

Ana turned her smile on him.

"Come," she said, bending down to pick a petal off the flower. I gasped at destroying such beauty, but the petal grew back immediately.

This time she led us through the French doors and into the house. I took in everything as we stepped inside. It was awfully large for a cottage and the inside had an old-world look with modern conveniences. The floors were dark, scuffed up wood that looked uneven yet charming. The walls were all white, but looked bumpy and when I peered closer, I saw it was because they were made of stone. The ceiling was vaulted and made of the same dark wood that covered the floors, and there was a large fireplace filled with crackling logs. The mantle was a huge piece of wood and the only thing on it was a bulky white vase filled with wildflowers. We walked across a multi-colored braided rug that was old and in some spots worn, but was otherwise extremely soft underfoot.

We walked past overstuffed aqua-colored couches and into the kitchen, which was open to the living room. It was a large room that had stone countertops and stainless steel appliances. There were more braided rugs of every color on the floor and peeling white-painted stools beneath the island.

"Please, sit," Ana invited as she grabbed a teakettle off the stove and filled it with water and set it to boil. Then she opened up a cabinet filled with white porcelain mugs. She wasn't tall enough to reach them, so she climbed on the counter to get what she wanted. Her hop back onto the floor was soundless. Then she set the cup by the stove and placed the flower petal at the bottom.

Sam pulled out two stools for us to sit on. While I was fascinated with her movements and what exactly she was doing, I found myself growing dizzy again. I was sweating and shaking and I wanted to go to sleep. Sam seemed to pick up on my crappy feeling and rubbed slow circles over my back with his hand.

The kettle began to boil and Ana poured the water over the petal. The cup seemed to glow the minute it was filled and the steam that came off the top danced with golden glitter. "Drink this," she said, sitting the cup on the island in front of me.

Sam looked at her like she just grew three heads.

I leaned down and inhaled some of the steam dancing above the liquid. Warmth filled me and I felt a light surge of energy. Before Sam could protest, I lifted the cup and drank. The water was scalding hot and I felt the burn all the way down my throat. My eyes watered at the temperature, but I took another smaller sip.

Sam stared at me, poised and waiting for something horrible to happen. But nothing did. Instead, warmth spread throughout my body, different from anything else I had ever felt before. It was as if I were being lit from within and for a moment, all the horrible things that happened to me melted away. Then a tingling feeling began to spread, starting at my toes and traveling up until my fingertips and head felt as if tiny people were dancing upon them. When I looked down at my hands, they were shimmering with golden flecks. My whole body was shimmering.

I had never felt so relaxed or alive.

"Drink," Ana insisted, and I lifted the cup again. Suddenly, my broken ankle no longer hurt and the swelling and bruises faded away.

Sam stared at me in wonder as I healed; then he looked up at Ana with a new appreciation in his eyes. The mistrust was gone, replaced with genuine gratitude, and it completely transformed his face into something so beautiful I was struck breathless.

But then I got a vision of all the blood on the floor of his cell. I hadn't even checked him for injuries. I choked a little on the liquid and Sam stood abruptly, his arms coming out on either side of my body as if he expected me to collapse.

I looked down into the cup at the shimmering water and noted there wasn't much left. I already felt better than I had felt in so long and it seemed selfish to drink the rest, especially after everything he had endured. I smiled to let him know I was fine and lifted the cup toward him. "Your turn."

He began to shake his head and I glanced down toward the dagger wound still festering in his bicep, but it was partially covered. I lifted the sleeve of his shirt and examined the wound. It was swollen and red around the edges. Carefully, I lowered the shirt and looked back into his eyes. Without taking my eyes away, I lifted the delicate cup up to his lips and tilted until the liquid met his mouth.

His honey-colored eyes watched me as his lips parted and the drink slid down his throat. I watched as he swallowed and prayed there was enough left to heal him. He took on the same glittering glow and I felt the transformation in his body the minute it took place. He was healed.

Satisfied, I turned to Ana and handed her the cup. "Thank you."

The effects of the tea were still flowing through me and I felt overly warm, but more wonderful than I had in a very long time. "Why did The Devourer bring us here?" I asked Ana.

"I told you, I have been waiting for you. He recognized you right away. There has been no one before you to trust such a beast."

"About that," I said, straightening on the stool. "He looked so… different on this side of the island."

Ana smiled. "That's because here, on the island, you see The Devourer for who he is on the inside, not as he appears in hell and to those who only know how to hate."

"But he appeared ugly and scary when we were in hell."

"Yes, because that's what you expected to see. But you knew there was more to him, didn't you?" Ana asked, placing my cup in the sink and walking out of the kitchen. She sank into one of the cloud-like couches.

I guess I had always sensed something good within The Devourer.

"She feeds it candy," Sam said, his voice laced with amusement.

Ana laughed. "What kind?"

"Snickers." A small smile played on my lips as Sam and I sat on the couch opposite her.

"I'm afraid I have never had this candy that you speak of," Ana said.

I drew back in shock and fished through my bag to pull out the one remaining candy bar that wasn't melted. I slid it across the wooden coffee table between the sofas. Ana picked it up and tore the corner off the wrapper. She stared at the chocolate bar for several seconds before she bit into it and chewed slowly. Her eyes closed and then she looked up. "This is magical!" She laughed.

"I actually prefer a Milky Way," I told her.

She wrinkled her forehead.

"We'll bring one of those next time," Sam said and Ana nodded around another bite of candy.

"Do you live here alone?" Sam asked.

Ana nodded. "Yes. I am the only one who knows of this place, other than God… and now you. I am the keeper of life here in hell. It is my job to hold up the glamour and protect the flower."

"Glamour?" I asked.

"The island is hidden behind a heavy glamour. No one would be able to see it even if they knew what they were looking for. All that can be seen here is the dragon's lair, which most try to stay away from."

"But, we could see it," I said.

"That's because you were meant to. Normally a person would have to come through the cave and step onto the island itself before they were able to see through the glamour. Once they see it, they will always be able to. But you, you were able to see it because you have a purpose here, a purpose I can help you with."

"What is our purpose?" I asked Ana.

"I'm not entirely sure, only that I will assist you. In time, I am sure you will know."

I hated answers like that. "So why did The Devourer bring us here if none of us know why?"

"You needed healed and you needed to know I am here to help you. There will come a time when you might need me. My door—or island—is always open."

"If I came back would you still be here?"

"Oh, yes. I will always be here." Ana smiled.

"We should be going," Sam said, standing from the couch.

"Of course." Ana stood, her green eyes meeting mine.

"Thank you for sharing the flower with us. I'll never forget it," I said, rushing to Ana and hugging her hard. She returned my hug with a strength that surprised me.

Before going out the cottage door, Ana stopped us. "Please remember that this place must be kept secret at all costs. If anyone found out about the flower… Well, I guess you know how badly things could go."

We nodded. "We understand."

"No one must know of this location. When you leave here, you must act as if there is nothing here at all. If someone is given a hint of my location and they stumble through the glamour…" Her voice trailed away.

"Of course." Sam assured her. "Your secret is safe with us."

"I believe you," Ana said. "I look forward to seeing you again."

"You seem so confident that we'll be back."

"When the truth of your journey settles within you, you will be back."

"Why does everyone always talk in riddle to us?" Sam wondered. "Why can't you just tell us whatever it is straight out?"

Ana lifted her hand in a wave. "Because sometimes in order to believe you have to come into the truth on your own."

Ana didn't follow us outside, and when the cottage door closed behind us, we walked away from the green side of the island toward the entrance to The Devourer's cave. We walked through the dragon's lair (though I was beginning to think he lived on the island and this cave was just for looks) and came out into the depressing side of hell. I sighed.

"Guess I will fetch a Lucent Marble," Sam said, looking at the black sludge with distaste.

Then the wind began to blow. Dust and ash swirled off the ground around us and made me cough. When it died down, a robed figure stepped into view.

Hecate.

"What have we here?" she asked, stepping closer.

I refused to cower and stood my ground. "The Devourer brought us here and now we're trapped on the island."

Her eyes narrowed, sensing my lie. Yet she had no proof. "Tell me why you are really here."

"We're about to become dragon shish kebab. Maybe you'd like to join us?" Sam asked sweetly.

"I could just torture you into telling me the truth." Hecate mused and raised her hands. Lightning seemed to spark from her palms.

Behind us, the ground vibrated as The Devourer lumbered out of his lair. I looked over my shoulder and tried not to gape when I realized I still saw him in his brightly colored, feathered state—his true form. I hurried a glance to see if Hecate saw him as I did, but clearly she didn't because she took a step back in fear. He shrieked loudly, then bent low, offering us his back.

Sam and I hurried to climb on. The witch was yelling as we lifted off the ground and she raised her palms like she might do something, but then the dragon soared through the air and out of her reach.

"What are we going to do?" I yelled. The inside of my chest began vibrating. I couldn't be down here much longer.

"I think The Devourer has his own ideas," Sam said, looking straight ahead.

I gasped. We were flying right at the wall of fire, the gate to hell. Even if I made it through the flames without being burned alive, would we even be able to get out that way?

It seemed we had no choice.

Sam must have come to the same conclusion because he turned me to face him, shoving my face into his neck and tucking my hands against his chest. *Whatever you do, do not move.*

He wrapped his body around mine as I tried to make myself as small as possible. I didn't have time to be afraid because The Devourer wasn't slowing down and we flew right into the blazing wall of flames.

Chapter Sixteen

Heven

The heat was the most intense thing I have ever experienced. It was how I imagined the core of the earth to be, boiling and unforgiving. The heat was so intense I actually felt myself go numb as if the pain was so bad my body refused to feel it. My bones ached with the pressure of Sam crushing me into his body. His legs felt like steel vices closing in on me and his arms were like thick cables that held me tight. The fear of being burned alive was so great I thought my heart might stop beating.

I couldn't see anything because I was tucked against Sam so closely, but I could still hear and feel. Sam swore when the worst of the heat hit us, when I knew we were actually inside the flames. His whole body spasmed, but he didn't let go, and I wondered how bad the heat was and if it was hurting him. I knew he couldn't be burned, but did that mean it didn't hurt?

Thankfully, the moment passed quickly. The wall of flames couldn't have been very thick; it didn't need to be. I felt the dragon slowing and the drop in my stomach told me we were lowering from the sky.

I made it. I wasn't dead. I tried to lift my head, but Sam wouldn't let me. I could hear the frantic beating of his heart as my ear was pressed against his chest. I didn't know a heart could beat that fast.

I'm not hurt, Sam. We made it.

He didn't let go of me, but after a few minutes the beating of his heart slowed. The Devourer hit the ground with a jolt, his wings fell out to the sides and he sat still, patiently waiting for us to dismount.

"Sam?" My voice was muffled against his shirt.

Reluctantly, he pulled me back, gripping my shoulders and staring down at me. There were tears in his eyes.

"Are you hurt?" I asked frantically, looking over his face.

"I thought you were going to be burned alive."

"Oh, Sam." I wrapped my arms around his neck and pressed as close to him as I could. I brushed my lips against his neck and was amazed at how hot his skin felt. "We made it." I sat back and pulled my arms away. "Besides, you should know by now, I have lives like a cat. No wall of fire is going to stop me."

He smiled as his shirt fell down between us and I frowned, lifting up the fabric. It had all been burned away except for the piece that was between us. I looked down at his shorts, which amazingly were still on, but there were several holes burned in the sides. I, however, was still clothed. Sam managed to completely conceal me from the flames.

The Devourer made a noise and shifted. My bag was still intact as well, with just the strap being burned away. I pulled it out of my lap and we climbed off the dragon. He was watching us, puffing smoke from his nostrils. Sam gasped and I turned to him. He was looking down so I followed his eyes. He was staring at my shoe.

My shoe that was completely burned away. I wiggled my toes, watching them move with ease. My sock was gone too. What was left of my shoe hung around my ankle, a few pieces of rubber and half a shoelace.

"I didn't cover your foot," Sam said, dazed.

"That's not possible," I said, even though we were both staring at the irrefutable evidence. Obviously, the fire hit my foot because my shoe was gone. But my skin was unburned; there wasn't a mark on it at all.

Sam stared up at me, a puzzled look on his face. "Did you feel it?"

I shook my head. "No."

We stared at each other, confused, for long moments. Then the dragon made a sound and I turned. He was staring at me, waiting. "Thanks for the ride, buddy." I reached out to pat his oversized muzzle covered in bright feathers. *I don't think I'll ever get used to seeing him this way.* He pulled back and looked at me suspiciously. I reached into the bag and pulled out a few of the ruined candy bars. They were still a melted mess. Completely inedible. "Sorry, big guy." I went to shove them back into my bag and he made a sound.

I paused, then shrugged and tossed him the candy, wrappers and all. He ate them without chewing. "You're gross." I told him. "But pretty."

"I would think melted candy tastes better than demon souls." Sam snorted.

"For real. You would think he would find something tastier to eat."

"We need to go," Sam said, taking my hand.

I looked up at our surroundings for the first time. The wall of fire wasn't far behind us and I assumed its close proximity was why I was still feeling so hot. We were standing on a patch of land, of dirt really, with the fire behind us and a body of water about a mile wide in front of us. Beyond the water all I could see was white.

"What is this?" I asked. The Devourer noticed my lack of attention and flew away, disappearing back through the wall of fire.

"It's the entrance to hell. In order for a soul to pass into hell it must first pass through a body of water and a wall of fire."

"That's why hellhounds were made, to help the souls do this?"

"Yep," Sam said, looking out over the water. He seemed tense and worried.

"What's beyond the water?"

"I don't know. I think it might be the InBetween."

My heart sank. Even if we made it to the InBetween, how would we get out? Airis already made it clear that she would not help my compromised soul.

Sam looked at me. "Let's go."

"Where?"

"I'm going to swim across the water with you."

Nerves cramped my stomach. I hated the water. It was my worst fear. The one time Sam convinced me to get in was the one time Beelzebub (AKA: the Dream Walker) got into my head.

"We don't have a choice here, Hev. I promise I won't let anything happen to you." He came forward and took my hands. "I want to go home. I want to really see you,"

I wanted that too, more than anything, certainly enough to go through an ocean. Even though Sam was free and I was with him, it wasn't exactly the homecoming I was hoping for. This trip to hell had been even more disastrous than I anticipated.

"Let's go," I said.

Sam was already shifting, changing into a hellhound. He approached me slowly, warily, as if afraid to frighten me. I wanted to laugh. Of all the things I had seen, this was the least scary. I reached out and stroked his ears. They were bigger than a panther's and a little floppy, but they felt like velvet to the touch. *You're beautiful,* I told him.

He blinked his golden eyes and crouched down low and I climbed onto his back, securing my bag in my lap. He was an excellent swimmer. I was expecting to be low in the water, holding my chin up so I didn't go under. But that didn't happen. The water only reached to my chest. Sam was so powerful that he could keep his body upright enough so I wasn't completely submerged.

I wondered how he swam through the gross sludge as it was. It was so thick and it clung to everything it touched, greedy for contact. I tried to ignore the way it stuck to my skin and I focused on the white ahead. A few demons tried to grab at us, but Sam would snap his jaws and make some intimidating sounds and the demons fell away.

It didn't take as long as I thought for him to swim the mile and soon the water ended abruptly, with no ground for support, and we began falling into an endless pit of white.

* * *

One minute we were falling and the next we were standing in the InBetween. Our clothes were completely clean of the black sludge and Sam was back in his human form, wearing a white T-shirt with his burned up shorts. I stared at him curiously and he just shrugged.

"Airis!" Sam called, thinking she would send us home.

I cleared my throat. "She isn't coming,"

His golden stare turned to me and my heart sank. How did I tell this beautiful, perfect person that I let him down? That good had turned its back on me because I'm not good.

"She said my soul was compromised and she wouldn't help us anymore. She said I would never see her again."

"She was too snooty for me anyway, with all her rules and riddles. We'll find another way out."

I let out a sigh. I knew Sam wouldn't be angry with me, but I still hadn't wanted to disappoint him, either. I looked around, hoping for some clue as to how to get out, but it was just endless white, endless nothing. But then something caught my vision and I turned toward the movement. In a cloud of white, a figure appeared, stumbled really.

He stood up and dusted off his light-colored pants. "Harder than it looks," he grumbled.

"Dad!" I cried and ran toward him, hurling myself in his embrace.

"Heven!" He hugged me tight.

"What are you doing here? I thought you couldn't get into the InBetween?"

He shrugged. "Something had to be done. I don't like the way Airis treated you."

"She doesn't know you're here?"

He glanced over his shoulder. "Not yet. We don't have much time."

"Are you going to get into trouble for this?"

"Don't you worry about me. You've been through enough." He held me out and looked me over. "Are you okay?"

I nodded. "I got Sam back." I pulled away and took Sam by the hand, pulling him forward. "Dad, this is Sam."

Dad stared at him for a few long seconds and then his face broke out into a smile. "I had my doubts about you, kid. But I was wrong. You've taken care of my little girl."

Sam offered his hand and smiled when they shook. "It's a pleasure to meet you."

When he released Sam's hand, he looked at me. "I'm going to send you home."

"Now?" I felt a little disappointed.

"We don't have much time." Again, he glanced over his shoulder. "I haven't done this before so I'm not really sure if you'll end up where I try to send you." He looked a little sheepish.

"I don't care where we end up as long as it's earth," I said.

Dad smiled sadly and touched my cheek. "I never realized what was in store for you. If I hadn't died, things might have been different..."

"I've done some bad things, Daddy.

"You've made the only choices you could have, given your situation."

"You really think so?"

He nodded and leaned forward and hugged me. "Follow your heart," he whispered. "It won't lead you wrong."

"I love you, Dad."

"I love you too." He straightened. "Now stand back. You need to go."

I didn't want to go. I wanted to stand here with my dad and just be with him. To see him and to talk to him. I just wanted his presence to fill me up.

"Thank you, sir," Sam said, taking my hand.

"Watch out for my girl," Dad said while a ball of light formed in his palm.

"Dad? Have you seen Mom?" I needed to know she was happy before I went home.

His eyes widened. "Why would I have seen your mother?"

My heart stopped. "She died…"

"What?" The light in his palm dimmed considerably. "She died?"

"Yes. Yesterday. You haven't seen her?" He should have seen her. Her soul should be in heaven, at peace.

"I haven't. I didn't know…," he murmured, not really looking at anything.

"Dad!" I cried, trying to capture his attention. "What's happening? Why haven't you seen Mom?"

He looked up at me, sadness in his eyes. Then he flinched and looked behind him. "You have to go. Remember what I told you."

"Wait!" I cried.

But he didn't listen. He threw the ball of light at us and everything went white.

***

I'm not sure where Dad was trying to send us, but we appeared a few blocks from Sam's little efficiency. It was good enough for me. It was dark out and I wasn't sure how much time had elapsed since I first went into hell. It seemed as if we were down there endlessly, but I knew it had been much shorter than that. When we rounded the corner there was a large clock outside a bank that told us it was only nine p.m. I glanced at Sam and he was looking around at everything, drinking in his first time in civilization for eight days. It suddenly hit me then that we made it. He was free and we were finally together and we were alone. He glanced at me, no doubt picking up on my thoughts and feelings as something shifted in the air between us. Both of us looked away and began walking.

The whole way back to his apartment, we didn't touch. We hardly looked at each other again, except to steal glances out of the corner of our eyes when the other was trying not to look. All the muscles and nerves in my entire body were shaking, but not from what just happened. As terrible as it had been in hell, I didn't think about it. All I could think about was Sam finally being here. I ached to touch him, but didn't dare. Of all the days he was gone, I never once worried that things would be awkward between us. I never once thought that maybe things wouldn't be the same.

Even now, I didn't worry about that.

This was Sam. *My Sam*. The only boy I'd ever love. I went to hell and back with him and I could honestly say I would do it all over again.

But in small ways he *was* different. I wasn't sure of all the ways yet, only sensing he wasn't quite the same. I didn't worry about that either because nothing would change things between us. Of this I was sure.

I focused on the next street over, the street where Sam's apartment was. I clenched my hands at my sides and counted the breaths I took, all the while staring at Sam out of the corner of my eye. I knew he was fighting the same fight that I was and I knew he was just trying to get there. I picked up my pace to a full run. He seemed a little surprised, but he matched my pace with ease, not even breathing hard. Finally, the front door of the apartment came into view. Sam ran ahead and up the steps to the door, but then he stopped, his back going stiff.

I don't have the key.

I came up the steps behind him. *I do.* I reached around him and held out the key. It seemed important that he let himself into his own place.

He took the key without even brushing his fingers against mine and quickly opened the door and went inside. I followed him, closing the door behind me and leaning against it. The room was dim because all the shades were drawn and it was cool because I turned the air unit on the last time I was here.

Sam turned around, his whiskey eyes deepening and focusing on me in such a singular way that the breath caught in my throat. *It smells like you in here.* His chest rose and fell with his deep breath.

I nodded while I pressed my palms flat against the door behind me. He stared at me for a few long, charged moments and then exactly what I knew would happen did. Exactly the reason we avoided touching each other until we were completely alone rushed to the surface.

We were like a pair of strong magnets, resisting was useless.

Sam rushed forward, his wide hands splaying against my ribs and lifting me off the ground. His touch seared me, set every cell in me on fire and turned my brain to mush. I wrapped my arms around his neck, my legs around his waist and hugged him hard, never intending to let go. I wasn't ever letting go.

His hands found my face and he grasped it, held it firm as his lowered. The minute his lips touched mine I started to cry silent, fat tears that fell quietly from beneath closed lids. The relief of being where I belonged was so great I thought I might turn into a puddle. After spending so much time fighting, being strong and pushing away my emotions, it was overwhelming to finally be somewhere I could fall.

I don't know how long he kissed me. Endlessly, blissfully, urgently.

Then he pulled back. Not away, but just enough to look at me. His image was a little blurry at first, but then it cleared and I could see all the emotions play on his face. My heart turned over.

He brushed the pad of his thumb over my cheek, then he frowned. *I got you dirty.*

I don't care.

I need a shower.

My fingers dug into his back, twisting his T-shirt. I couldn't let him go.

He carried me into the bathroom and turned on the shower and kicked the door shut. He didn't put me down, but began kissing me again. There, in the center of the tiny bathroom, he stood, holding me in his arms and kissing me while the room filled with warm steam.

I'll be fast. He promised before reluctantly sitting me beside the shower.

I didn't shy away when he began stripping off his ripped, ruined shorts and white T-shirt. I stared down at them while he showered and imagined all the things he went through that I would probably never know about. He wouldn't tell me. I wouldn't ask. I would never ask him to relive that nightmare twice.

The shower shut off and his dripping, strong hand reached out from behind the curtain and grabbed the towel I hung there just for him. It occurred to me then that I should probably clean myself up too. I went to the sink and washed my hands and face and rinsed my mouth out with the mouthwash in the medicine cabinet. I was about to do something with my wild mass of hair when the shower curtain slid open. I turned and my heart began hammering in my chest.

I had suspected, but now I knew.

He was bigger. He was always built well, with strong corded muscles, but now he was just big. His bare shoulders seemed to fill the tiny room. His hair had grown longer and the wet strands curled around his neck and fell over his forehead. Even his feet seemed larger as he stepped onto the tile floor.

He was wearing only a towel, slung low around his hips.

I swallowed. *I should shower too.*

He shook his head, slowly approaching me, and I held out a hand, laying it on his chest. His skin was warm and moist, causing a burst of butterflies to dance in my belly.

How long do we have? he asked.

I told Gran I was staying at Kimber's. I wasn't leaving here tonight. If I got caught in my lie, I'd just take the punishment.

All night?

I nodded.

My hand vibrated with whatever sound moved through his chest. He led me from the bathroom and the air out here was so much cooler against my skin that gooseflesh rose along my arms. He barely glanced around the room but went toward the bed with single-minded precision. When he stopped and turned, his eyes were heavy lidded and I wondered if he knew how badly my knees were shaking.

His palms cupped my face and tilted it upward. *I dreamed of you.*

I nodded. I dreamed of him too.

His kiss was as intoxicating as ever, melting my bones until he had to support me against his chest or else I would slip to the floor. I did notice something new, however. He had stubble on his jaw and chin. As he kissed me, it tickled and prickled against my skin. It was rough and sweet at the same time. His body seemed to tower over mine, wrapping around me until I was completely lost inside him, hoping I never found my way out. I knew then what else seemed different… I could no longer think of him as the *boy* I loved because he wasn't a boy. He was a man. The changes I sensed in him weren't external (besides his size); they were internal. And as he kissed me, I thought his size *was* larger, but it seemed even more so because of the way he carried himself.

I liked it.

I *really* liked it.

He pulled our lips apart and rested his forehead to mine. His chest rose and fell heavily as I reached up, threading my fingers through his hair. The slightly damp ends curled around my fingers, inviting me to stay. I sighed.

I felt his gaze and turned my eyes upward. I knew exactly what question he was asking me, though he never spoke a word. Slowly, I nodded. I dreamed of this moment so many times and I was sure this is what I wanted, but I was still nervous. I still felt awkward and unsure of myself.

Golden lightning streaked his eyes before he shut them. It reassured me that I could feel his hands shake as he held me. *He's nervous too.* When he opened his eyes, the gold was gone, replaced by the liquid honey that I knew so well. He watched me as his fingers slowly found the hem of my shirt and slipped beneath to touch skin.

Heven…

Sam…

They were the last words we spoke for a long time.

* * *

Loud growling woke me. My eyes opened and for a moment I was unsure where I was. Then I remembered. Sam was back. I was in his bed, wrapped tightly in his arms. His stomach was growling like he hadn't eaten in days.

Of course he hadn't.

I did my best to slide from beneath his arms without waking him, but it was useless. He was up, gripping my arm like I was trying to escape. "I'm getting you some food," I whispered, stroking his hand.

His grip lightened instantly as his hand slid down into mine. Butterflies danced beneath my ribcage. I wondered what it would be like *after*. If I would be different, *feel* different. I wondered if Sam would be different. Shyly, I looked over my shoulder at him. A stray blond strand fell over my eye and I was partially glad for the extra concealment. Sam smiled and leaned up onto one elbow and brushed the hair away. The way he stared at me made my cheeks grow warm and I glanced away, down at our clasped hands.

"I love you," he said, his voice sounding foreign to my ears since he'd spoken to me with his mind up until now.

Some of the butterflies settled down but didn't go away. "I love you too."

He stared at me for a few more short moments before his stomach growled again and he grinned. I got up to pull on one of his shirts, smiling when the fabric reached my knees and turned toward the kitchen. Behind me, Sam pulled on some shorts then caught my hand so we went together over to the fridge.

"I put a pizza in here," I said, reaching in and pulling out a large cardboard box. The room was completely dark. I had no clue what time it was, and the light from the fridge made me blink. I was about to offer to heat it when he opened the lid, took out a huge slice and stuffed half of it in his mouth. I giggled and pulled away from him to place the pizza on the counter and get some napkins.

"Come back here," he said around a mouthful of cheese and pepperoni then wrapped his arm around my waist, towing me into his side. A slice appeared before me and I opened my mouth to take a bite. We stood together in the darkened kitchen, eating cold pizza together, and laughing.

Is this all? I asked myself. Was our *after* to be exactly as before? But it wasn't really exactly as before. I felt a little unsure of myself, unsure of how he felt.

Sam pulled away, opened the fridge and leaned in, palming two sodas. I gasped. He spun swiftly one of the sodas falling to the floor and rolling away. "What?" His eyes roamed all the shadows of the room.

"Your back," I started. "It's… What happened?"

He grimaced and bent to pick up the lost soda. "Nothing."

It wasn't nothing. There were puckered scars crisscrossing his back. Images of blood flashed into my mind. Sam's blood and the way it looked on the floor of his cell. So this is where it came from. It looked like he had been whipped.

"Sam." I rushed forward. How had I not noticed until now? I walked around him to see his back and opened the fridge door for the light. "Oh, Sam." I sighed, taking in the wide scars.

"I'm all right," he said, spinning and closing the door. His arms wound around my waist and he pressed my cheek to his chest. "That tea of Ana's completely healed them."

"I'm so sorry." I remembered when I woke up with the pain echoing through my body, positive something was happening to him. Seeing the scars, the reminders of that pain… It was horrible.

"Don't be sorry. Not tonight."

I lifted my face to stare up at him. "I'm not sorry about *that*."

The corner of his mouth turned up. "No?"

"No. Are you?" Dread settled in my chest; it was heavy. Was I not what he thought I'd be?

"I could never be sorry," he whispered, his lips brushing over mine.

"Come on," I said, drawing him along behind me to pick up the pizza and walk toward the bed. "You need to eat."

After he had eaten the entire pizza (he shared) and we were settled back beneath the covers, he spoke so quietly I hardly heard him. "Tell me how you found Riley."

I knew this question was coming. I tried to convince myself Sam wouldn't be upset that I went and found Riley. I told myself he wouldn't care. Not only had I been lying to everyone else, I had also been lying to myself.

I saw the way Sam looked at Riley when we were in hell. Sam didn't want Riley here, for reasons that I didn't completely understand. And after seeing Sam's back and the blood in his cell… I felt worse than ever. If Riley hadn't been here, if he hadn't spent the night with me, Sam might not have to carry those scars for the rest of his life.

Sam sat up and looked down at me. "I can feel your hesitation."

"Because when you find out everything I've done…"

He laughed. "There's nothing you could have done that's that terrible."

I robbed your mind, I said, unable to get the words past my lips.

He frowned. "What?"

I sat up, throwing my legs over the bed and letting my feet dangle off the side. "I didn't realize what was happening at first. I still don't get how I do it, but whenever I touch someone and I want to know something, I somehow go into their mind and see their memories."

"When did this happen?"

"One night when we were closely linked and we were talking. I asked you if you knew where your roommates were and just like that, I saw your memories. I saw the note that was in the center of the bed. Peaks Island."

His eyes rounded a bit, realizing there was no other way I would know this. He got up from the bed and began pacing the room. It stung a little that he didn't sit next to me, but then I decided maybe it was better this way. "What else did you see?"

I shrugged. "Nothing. It freaked me out and I felt guilty for doing that to you so I pulled out."

"Have you done this to anyone else?"

I bit my lip and nodded. "To Cole, I looked down at my feet. I really needed to paint my toenails. Some cheerful color. "We were talking about him and Gemma, then his voice just went away and I could see and feel everything from his point of view. It was weird."

"Wow. Does he know?"

"Yeah. He wasn't even mad." It still shocked me.

"Why would he be mad?"

"Aren't you?"

The corner of his mouth lifted into a lopsided smile. "Sweetheart, you're in my mind every single day. I love it."

His words sent a rush of warmth through me. "Yeah, but this time was different."

"Guess I'll have to be more selective with my thoughts when you're touching me. Wouldn't want you to discover my deep dark secrets." He winked as he crouched down in front of me, slowly reached out and grasped my foot in his palm.

"What deep dark secrets?" I narrowed my eyes and smiled.

He smiled, then released me and stood. "So you found Riley from that note you saw in my memory?"

The mention of Riley made my stomach dip. "Actually, he kind of found me. I went to Peaks Island to look for him, but I had no idea who I was looking for. I know I'd seen them—your roommates—before, but I never paid attention to them. I had no idea what they looked like."

"Bet Riley really loved that," he said smugly.

"He did seem annoyed."

Sam flashed his perfectly straight, white teeth.

"Anyway," I said, reminding myself not to get distracted. "I ran into some trouble on the docks."

"What kind of trouble?" The words rumbled from his chest and I swear he seemed to swell in front of me. How had he grown so much in the past eight days?

"There were these fishermen. They were just playing around. Nothing happened," I hurried out.

He didn't seem to believe me. "Just tell me."

"They made some advances and I fended them off. I ran onto the ferry and that was it." He nodded and I kept talking. "Riley climbed onto the boat after it moved away from the docks. He said he saw me looking for him and he wanted to know where you were. I told him what was going on and he agreed to come here and help."

"He agreed, just like that?" He seemed surprised.

"Yes. I don't understand why you and Gemma don't trust him."

"Gemma doesn't trust him, either?"

I explained about Gemma's past and her connection to Riley and how she trained him. He nodded thoughtfully as I talked, settling next to me on the bed. When I was finished, he said, "I didn't put it together, but the moves she taught me… I've seen him do them before."

"She says he's a killer."

"He is," Sam said matter-of-factly.

"So you don't like Riley because he's a killer?" I asked, a hard knot forming in my belly.

He sighed. "That would be a little hypocritical, don't you think?"

"I don't understand, then."

"It's not that he kills. It's *how* he kills."

It was my turn to not understand.

"He likes it, Hev. Sometimes he kills because he has to, but mostly he does it because he enjoys it. There's something about him that's twisted… He's violent."

The image of him at the cemetery this afternoon flashed into my mind. He had the upper hand. He could have just punched through that demon's chest, but he didn't. He cut off its head and then threw the body away like it was nothing. "The curse," I said to myself.

"The curse?" Sam echoed.

"Right before we got you back, Gemma told me that Riley's family line is cursed with servitude to Beelzebub. She thinks the reason he's so mean is because of the curse." I explained to Sam in detail about Riley's grandfather and the deal he made with Beelzebub all those years ago.

"So Riley works for Beelzebub?" Sam said thoughtfully when I finished talking. He went to the fridge and pulled out a water.

"I don't think it's like that," I said, feeling like I was betraying Sam with my feelings. I *liked* Riley. I went to grab a water too, but Sam handed me his before I could open the fridge door.

His whiskey-colored eyes were intense as he looked down. "This is exactly why I didn't want him around," he whispered. God, the deep, smoky tone of his voice was wonderful. He cupped my face in his palms. "Riley is twisted. He would backstab his own mother and now we find out he's cursed, but yet… he's likable." His fingers flexed against my jaw.

"He helped me. He helped you." I protested, trying to prove he wasn't all bad. I didn't want to believe he was.

"Yeah." He dropped his hands and walked across the room. "And now I owe him."

"No." I protested. "It isn't like that."

"With Riley, it's always like that." He turned to stare at me with hardened eyes. "Don't let his charm fool you, Hev. You can like him, but remember he'll turn on you if he's offered something better. There's a reason he's back. He wasn't helping you out of the goodness of his heart. He wants something."

I didn't want to believe that. But I could feel Sam thought he was telling me the truth and Sam had good instincts. The best. Which made what I had to admit next even worse.

"There's something else," I whispered.

His whole body tensed as if preparing for a blow. I took a breath and the words rushed out. "He spent the night with me."

There was a charged moment of silence before Sam erupted. His body began to shake and swell, and for a moment I thought he might turn.

He was in your room? In your bed? Sam demanded, the words slapping into my brain with force. His eyes were flashing gold and I wondered if maybe I made a mistake. But if I hadn't told him I would feel like a liar forever. I didn't want to feel like I was hiding things from him. It made me feel dirty.

"It was nothing! He stayed to keep the Dream Walker out of my mind." I wanted to retch when he turned away.

Tears welled in my eyes. "Those scars…" I pushed away a tear that dropped from my lashes. "You got those because Beelzebub was mad he couldn't get into my mind. Because Riley was there." I spent the night with another man and Sam was beaten for it. "I'm so sorry."

"I don't care about the damn scars!" he yelled.

"I was only trying to get some peace," I said wearily. "I was so tired and the demon, it was the worst yet."

"What demon?"

I closed my eyes. I hadn't meant to say that out loud. "It was under the bed. It tried to pull me into some kind of vortex or something. I fought it off, but it managed to get the upper hand. Riley showed up and killed it."

He protected you.

This hurt him worse than anything, I think. There wasn't anything I could say.

Did he touch you?

No! It wasn't like that. I got up and went to face him so he could see the truth in my eyes. *We were fully dressed.*

He didn't say anything, but stood there with his jaw clenched and looking over my head. After a few minutes I turned away, going back to the bed and climbing in. I should have just taken my chances with the Dream Walker, anything to spare Sam. He didn't speak and I was afraid if I did, it would only make it worse. Besides, offering excuses for what I did was wrong.

Behind me, the bed dipped with his weight as he lay down, wrapping an arm around me and pulling me against him. "I'm sorry I yelled at you," he rasped against my ear.

I wanted to laugh. "You have a right to be angry." If Sam spent the night with some girl, I'd probably claw out her eyes.

"I'm glad he was there to keep that psycho out of your head. I just wish it was me, not him."

"It is you," I whispered. "It's always you."

A purr vibrated in his chest and I rolled in his arms to face him. "Can you forgive me?"

"On one condition."

"What is it?" I would do anything.

"Kiss me." He smiled.

Chapter Seventeen

Sam

I jolted awake, not sure what caused the disturbance, but my senses were instantly alert and listening. It took a moment to remember where I was as I lay there in the dark, but the feeling of something soft and warm pressed against me was all the reminder I needed.

I smiled slowly. I was at home. In bed. With Heven.

Memories of what we had done washed over me and I forgot about waking suddenly, instead just reliving a few of those moments. Everything I went through down there—the feelings of hate, anger and regret—I would experience them all a thousand times over just to end up exactly where I was now.

Slowly, I moved, wrapping my arm a little tighter around her and pressing a kiss to the soft hair on her head. God, how I missed her.

Whatever caused me to awaken seemed to disturb me once more. I lay there and listened to everything around us, looking for something, but finding nothing—we were alone. I sensed no threat lurking. I heard no sounds other than the occasional car passing by and the low hum of the air-conditioner.

My stomach growled, hungry even after I ate that pizza. I was probably going to be hungry for days. I thought about getting up, seeing if there was anything else in the fridge, but I didn't want to move. I'd waited so long for this that giving it up wasn't going to happen.

I relaxed back onto the bed and drifted back into a light sleep, part of me still alert just in case. I don't know how long I lay there—it could have been minutes or an hour—but

Heven began to stir. She just shifted in sleep a few times, but then she began to shake and curl in on herself before straightening back out again. After a few moments, she slid out from my embrace, wrapped a blanket around her shoulders and tiptoed quietly away from the bed. I opened my eyes and watched her as she rushed into the bathroom. She didn't bother to turn on the light and several moments later she began to retch.

I jumped up from the bed and went into the bathroom, flipping on the light and crouching beside her. "Hey, not feeling so hot, huh?"

"I just started feeling… strange," she said, reaching out to close the toilet lid. I helped her up and the blanket around her fell off her shoulder. I caught my breath.

"What the hell is that?" I demanded, looking at the welts across her back. I had just seen every inch of her and those marks had not been there. I reached out to touch one and she shrank back, a sound of pain escaping her lips.

It's like she was scratched from the inside out, I thought to myself, staring in horror at the wounds. They looked angry and red, puffed up underneath her once-smooth skin. The skin over the wound was bubbled and stretched thin, looking like it might break open at any moment.

I think I was. She answered my thought.

"Heven…"

Help me to the bed?

As carefully as I could, I lifted her, taking her to the bed and sitting her down with great care. I sat down next to her, glancing once more at the marks on her back, and then pushed the hair behind her shoulder. "Hecate did this to you, didn't she?"

"I think so."

"What the hell did she do?" The words came out as more of a snarl than I intended and I tried to control my anger.

Heven didn't answer; she seemed to not hear me. She was looking a little green again, and I grabbed her hand. "Heven, are you feeling sick again?"

"What?" she said, looking up at me, focusing. "No, I'm okay."

"You should have left me there," I muttered, feeling responsible for this.

"No!" She gasped, grabbing my wrist and staring into my eyes. "This isn't your fault. It's mine. He wanted answers I don't have. He would have found a way to do this whether I was in hell or not."

"What did they do to you?" I groaned.

"I'm not really sure. I want to see."

"No, you don't." I protested, but she was already up and walking into the bathroom, turning on the light. I watched as she blinked against the brightness, then turned to stare at the claw marks on her back.

"Beast," she murmured, her face going pale.

"What?" I asked.

"Hecate said the word beast. I look like I was clawed from the inside…"

Realization and horror dawned. "No," I said, hoarse. "They wouldn't." But they would. They had. Is *this* what had caused me to wake? Is *this* what I sensed?

Beelzebub might be immortal, but that would only give me the pleasure of killing him a thousand times over.

"Sam?" Heven said, her voice low, as she stared in the mirror at her back.

I clicked off the light and ushered her out of the bathroom. "Tell me everything that happened."

Maybe it wasn't what I was thinking. Maybe I was wrong and it wasn't as bad as I thought it was. She sighed and turned to face me. "I don't want to talk about it. Not tonight. This is our night. You're finally home. Beelzebub took so much away from us and I refuse to let him have tonight."

She was standing in front of the bed, blond hair falling into her eyes and the blanket falling off her shoulder. She held out her hand and stood there in silent invitation. I wanted to go to her. I wanted to forget all about what just happened.

So I did. I pushed it all away, for her. For me. For us. Until she fell asleep in my arms.

It was then, as I was lying in the dark, that I couldn't deny what I saw and what she said. I couldn't deny what the hound in me was saying.

Hecate trapped a beast inside Heven, inside my love, and I hadn't the slightest clue how to get it out.

For the rest of the night, I would awaken, sensing that thing inside of her every time it stirred. I would lie there and worry that I wouldn't be able to get it out. I wondered about everything I didn't know the answer to and everything that I did. I lay there and imagined ramming my fist into Riley's jaw. Yeah, I guess I was glad he'd been here to fight off that demon in Heven's room, but he was bad news.. And he wanted something.

It was eight a.m. when Heven woke up. I knew she was awake before she even opened her eyes. I enjoyed the way she settled farther against me and tucked her hand between my side and the mattress, like she had no intention of ever getting up.

"How are you feeling?" I asked, keeping my voice to a whisper.

She stretched like a cat before answering. "I'm good."

I smiled up at the ceiling. "You're sure?"

"Yeah." She sat up and looked over her shoulder. "How does it look?"

I looked at her back; it did look better. The skin no longer seemed stretched to the point of breaking. The welts didn't seem as swollen and they weren't as red. It seemed whatever was inside her was calm. For the moment. "Looks better."

"It doesn't hurt." She lied.

"Heven," I growled.

"Fine." She sighed. "It's a little sore, but nothing like last night."

I brushed my fingertip over the end of one of the longer marks and sighed. "Did you understand at all what Hecate was saying when she did this to you? I only heard the very end."

She turned to face me, tucking her legs under her and pulling the sheet up to cover her bare skin. "I did hear the word 'beast' once or twice. Beelzebub told her he wanted me to know what it's like to feel true evil inside me and to only be at peace in the place I hate most. Which is hell."

"Hecate trapped a beast inside you," I said, voicing what we both were thinking.

She swallowed. "I guess so. By the looks of the claw marks on my back, I would say it wants out."

"We need to get it out. Right now." I jumped out of bed and went to the dresser to find some shorts and a T-shirt.

"I don't have time right now."

I dropped my shirt. "You don't have time?" I said incredulously. What could be more important that getting that thing out of her?

"I have the viewings for my mom and the funeral tomorrow."

Her mother. It still hadn't sunk in yet that she was dead. My parents cast me out, turned me away, so in many ways

Hev and I were both orphans now. With the exception that my parents were still alive. I guess in the back of my mind there was always that very remote chance I would see them again. That they might apologize for what they did to me. But Heven… Heven didn't have that. Her mother was yet another victim of Beelzebub and the crap that I brought into her life.

A victim of my brother.

I looked at her sitting there with a sheet wrapped around her thin frame. She had lost so much, yet she was still strong. What would it do to her when she found out my brother was responsible for her mother's head injury?

I sank down on the edge of the bed next to her. She reached out and wrapped her hand around my bicep. "I'm sorry about your mom, Heven. I wish I had been here."

"I know." She cleared her throat. "She woke up before she died."

My eyes widened. "She did?"

Heven nodded. "She said horrible things to me, Sam. Those weeks of her accepting us… accepting me… that was Beelzebub controlling her. She said I wasn't her daughter anymore."

"Oh, babe." I pulled her close. "She was wrong."

Heven pulled away after a few seconds. "I have to go to her house today and take an outfit to the funeral home. There is a viewing this afternoon and this evening that I have to attend. I'm sure Gran is expecting me soon." She glanced over at the clock and groaned.

"We'll get it all done and I'll be there with you through it all." I promised. I brushed the hair back from her face and kissed her long and slow. "I missed kissing you whenever I wanted," I told her when I pulled away. "You feel warm."

She shrugged. "I've felt that way since I drank that tea Ana gave me."

I pressed a palm to her head and studied her face. "Would you tell me if you were feeling bad?"

"Yes." She climbed out of the bed, taking the sheet with her, and went into the tiny kitchen. "I'm not sure what's in here, but I'm sure I can make you something to eat."

The front door burst open and sunlight streamed inside the tiny space. I growled and moved to get in front of Heven when a familiar voice caught me off guard.

"Sam!" Logan cried, rushing into the room. "Sam! You're back!"

My little brother launched himself at me and I caught him in a hug. "Hey, bud! It's great to see you!" I couldn't help but notice how thin he felt as I hugged him. He pulled back, and I got to really look at him.

I knew he was bad, but this was worse than I thought.

I held up my hand for a high-five, which he gave as he bounced around on wobbly legs. "We brought you some breakfast!"

"We?" I asked as Riley strolled in, kicking the door shut behind him. The thought of my baby brother hanging out with someone like Riley made my skin crawl. Why did this guy think he could carve himself a place in my life?

He was carrying a large, flat donut box with a paper sack on top and a drink holder with three large coffee cups. I thought about tackling him to the floor. But he was holding all the food.

"You should have knocked," I said tightly.

"I have a key." Riley smirked and I wondered what my odds were of kicking his ass without harming the food.

I looked at Heven for an explanation as to why this guy would have a key to my apartment. She glanced at the floor. "I let him stay here when he got to town."

Well, I guess that was better than at her house every night.

I was surprised when Logan came to her defense. "Heven went and found him so he could help get you back. She's been working so hard to bring you home."

Heven shifted, pulling the sheet tighter around her body.

"Clearly, you've been very busy," Riley drawled, his eyes sweeping Heven as she moved.

"Get out," I snapped moving to block Heven from view.

"No," Heven said quietly. "I was just going to take a shower and Logan and Riley brought food." She glared at Riley before moving toward the bathroom. Riley grinned and popped one of the lids of a coffee and took a sip.

"Don't you want your coffee? It's hot," he called as Heven moved away.

She did want it. I could tell by her slight hesitation so I went and grabbed it. "Wrong one," Riley said, amused.

I took a deep breath and set the coffee down and grabbed the last one. I told myself not to give him an opening. I told myself to keep my mouth shut. I said it anyway. "You know how she drinks her coffee?"

"We've had a few mornings together," Riley quipped.

And there it was.

My invitation to nail him.

I barely managed to set the coffee down before leaping across the counter and taking Riley down. He knew I wouldn't want him here. He knew I wouldn't want him as much as fifty feet near Heven or my brother. Riley wasn't here to help. He had an agenda.

I got in a few good hits and I enjoyed the way his head bounced when I punched him.

"Sam, stop," someone behind me said, but I ignored them and went for another hit.

"Heven!" Logan cried and Riley and I both stopped and turned. Heven was bracing herself against the back of the couch. Her face was pale and her breathing was shallow. The sheet had slipped off one shoulder to reveal a new red welt.

Logan looked at me with a helpless look on his face as I went to her side. "No more fighting," she said. "It... it excites it."

"Heven?" Logan said. "What's wrong?"

I swore, feeling like a complete ass.

"What's going on?" Riley asked.

Heven straightened and banked all the pain out of her eyes to look at my brother. "It's nothing. I'm fine." Then she turned her attention to Riley. "You owe Sam an apology," she snapped. "You were way out of line."

I blinked. "Calm down. Don't get all worked up."

"That's not how you treat your friends." She continued, pinning Riley with a stare.

"I don't have friends," Riley said without heat.

"Then what the hell are you doing here?" she yelled. "You brought us coffee and breakfast because you hate us? Get real."

"Calm down, Hev," I told her again, pulling the sheet up to cover her newest mark. She winced in pain.

"I'm going to take a shower," she said and went to the bathroom. I followed, afraid she might collapse. In the doorway, she turned to look at Riley. "Thanks for bringing Logan and breakfast by. You can leave. Now."

Then she slammed the bathroom door.

When she looked at me, I straightened and pushed a hand through my hair. "I shouldn't have let him get under my skin."

"I get it," she said and clutched at the sheet, like she was uncomfortable with my presence.

"I just... It makes me crazy knowing he was here with you."

"He wasn't *with* me." She sighed. "And I'm sorry I never told you he was here."

She reached around me to turn on the shower and I grabbed her before she could move away, wrapping my arms around her.

I think whatever is inside me liked when you were fighting. It wanted out so it could fight too.

I'm so sorry

I know you are. She leaned up and pressed a kiss to my lips. Then, she laid the sheet on my arms and stepped beneath the spray of warm water, pulling the curtain closed.

Out in the living room, Riley was making himself at home, eating a donut and drinking his coffee. Logan was watching TV.

"What the hell are you really doing here?" I growled low at Riley.

"You heard. Heven asked me for help."

"Since when are you the helpful kind?"

Riley turned his flashing eyes to me. He didn't say a word, just sipped his coffee.

"How long have you been here?"

"Couple days."

"You might as well tell me what you want so I can send you on your way."

"Who says I want something?"

"You don't do anything for free."

He actually looked offended. Then he recovered to say, "Who's to say I haven't gotten it already?"

"If you had, you'd be gone." I glanced at Logan to see him watching us and I decided to let the subject drop for the time being. I grabbed one of the coffees and went to sit next to him. As he told me about his stay with Gran, I kept half an ear out for Heven in case she needed me.

"The funeral is tomorrow," Logan said, drawing my complete attention.

"Yeah, she told me."

"This is all my fault, Sam." The despair in his voice was so deep.

I looked him in the eye and held his stare. "This was not your fault. This was Beelzebub's fault. He did this. Not you."

"She's been so nice to me. I didn't deserve it."

"Of course you deserve it," I said, grabbing his shoulder and squeezing. He started coughing and I drew back. "Logan?"

"I'm okay," he said after a few minutes. "I haven't been feeling too well."

By the looks of him, that was an understatement. That demon had completely wrecked his body. I tried to remind myself he had only had eight days to recover, that he would, it would just take a while.

"I have to tell her, Sam," Logan said, and I noticed Riley was listening.

"Yeah, okay. But let's wait until after the funeral."

Logan nodded, looking relieved that he would soon be free of his lie.

I glanced back at Riley, who was pretending not to listen to my conversation. I had a feeling that very soon a lot of truths were going to come out.

Chapter Eighteen

Heven

Dark clouds rolled overhead and thunder rumbled so closely the saturated ground vibrated beneath my feet. As the priest spoke, lightning cracked and lit up the sky, making it look violet.

I was dressed all in black with a black fedora soundly perched on my head. Dark sunglasses covered my red-rimmed eyes and I clutched several tissues in my hand. I stood beneath a sizable black umbrella that Sam held over me while Gran and I huddled close for necessity and comfort. Rain splattered around us, falling in heavy sheets. The priest had said that heaven was weeping at the sudden loss of life.

Despite the miserable weather, the crowd was substantial. My mother and I may have had our problems, but she was well loved. Especially by the congregation at her church, who all stood nearby silently praying as they stared at the simple coffin about to be lowered into the ground. Also in attendance were many of my father's old co-workers, who were all decked out in their finest police uniforms, adding a bit of polish to this otherwise dull day.

Underneath the umbrella next to ours stood Logan and Cole, also dressed in all black. His injuries from our trip into hell were gone, courtesy of Gemma's healing powers. His mother hadn't come, but she did send along her condolences, and his father stood at the edge of the crowd with sincere sorrow on his face. It made me respect the man who raised Cole even more. It made me think of my own father and the things he said when I saw him.

I had so many questions and so few answers. But it seemed wrong somehow to think about that now, here, so I turned back to the crowd and the coffin.

There were people here from school too. I felt their gazes on me even as they tried not to look. Even though I had made strides in reclaiming my once-popular status last year, I knew those strides no longer mattered.

I was back to being a freak. An unknown, a person of mystery and suspicion. No one could keep themselves from staring at the new scar that was gracing the left side of my face. Granted, it wasn't like the old one. It wasn't disfiguring, but it was there. Worse, I hadn't offered a word of explanation. I could almost hear the rumors flying through the crowd now. And to top it off, my mother was dead. Befallen by some freak accident and no one really knew what happened. She suffered a head injury, should have woken up, but died instead.

I lifted my chin and brushed them all off. After having my head invaded by a Dream Walker, who also happens to be the Prince of Demons in hell, being hexed by an all-powerful witch and taking a terrifying ride on the back of a dragon through a wall of fire, a bunch of rumors from some high school students was a day at the park. I searched the crowd, my eyes going to the back to find Gemma standing alone, holding her own umbrella, and dressed in black with her hair down framing her face. Even in sorrow she was beautiful and her eyes never once left my brother.

The priest said his final words, then invited Gran and I to toss a single red rose down into the seemingly endless hole that the casket was being lowered into. I held the rose out, suspended above the hole, and looked down, saying a short prayer of my own before letting go and watching the flower fall gracefully down. Sam wrapped his arm around my waist and pulled me gently into his side while tilting the umbrella and blocking me from curious onlookers. It was here that I said my final good-byes. Here, I said all things I never got to say. I hoped she heard them and I hoped she finally understood me. If even a little.

Sam ushered me back so that a few others could come forward and toss a rose, paying their final respects. I couldn't watch them. Instead I looked out over the cemetery at all the other marked graves and spots of color from the flowers decorating them. It was then that I noticed the movement. He was a shock of black amongst a sea of gray headstones.

Riley was standing without an umbrella as the rain pelted him from every angle. His already black hair was like midnight and plastered to his forehead. Water dripped off his face and fell onto his already soaked clothing. He saw me looking and gave a brief, almost imperceptible nod. Then, shockingly, he clasped his hands and looked down.

It was the most respectful thing I'd ever witnessed him do, and the nicest. He did think of us as friends and he just proved it. Otherwise, he wouldn't stand in the pouring rain to pay respects to a woman who would have hated him.

People started to leave, a few of them coming to me to offer one more condolence. Most, however, hurried to their cars to get out of the storm. When just a few people were left, I looked back at Riley, not really knowing why, but sensing I should.

He was no longer alone.

But he didn't know it.

He was being ambushed from behind.

Most likely, it was a demon, but I couldn't be sure because it was covered in a long, black trench coat and had an oversized hat on its head. The biggest indicator was its lack of aura. I tried to ignore the way the beast inside me seemed to take notice of its 'friend.' It was running low with its arms extended, ready to take him out from behind.

I made a sound in the back of my throat, but it was too late.

The demon was on him.

Riley wasn't startled and he didn't jerk in surprise. Almost as if it were a reflex, he kicked out behind himself and caught the demon at the waist. Then, seemingly not in a hurry, he turned to kick it in the face, this time sending it to the ground. Instead of just punching his hand through its chest, a dagger appeared in his hand, and in one swift motion he cut off its head. He tossed the body behind a nearby oversized tombstone and walked away through the pouring rain, the head dangling from his hand as he moved. He didn't once look back. I stood, shaken, cold to the bone, as I watched morbidly as the rain washed the blood away.

Like it never even happened.

I even blinked, trying to decide if it had. Unfortunately, it must have because the beast inside me was awakened by the violence that I just witnessed. It felt like he charged at full speed but hit the wall of my body, causing him to crash backward, which made me stumble back. Sam was there to steady me, but unfortunately, the thing wasn't done. It charged again, throwing me forward, and I fell to my knees. Gran was there, fretting, helping me up, and the priest was looking at me with pity.

"I'm sorry," I managed as I got to my feet. "It's very muddy and I'm not used to wearing heels." It was a lame excuse, but I could do no better. Logan, who seemed very subdued during the entire funeral, reached out and took my arm to help me toward the car. I smiled at him and he lowered his eyes.

"We should go," Gran said. "It's cold and we have guests coming to the house."

"Of course," I said, feeling a searing pain across my stomach. I wanted to lurch forward, but I didn't want to draw more attention to myself so I leaned into Sam for support.

What set it off? Sam asked as he led Gran and I away.

There was a demon across the cemetery. Riley killed it.

His mouth flattened into a thin line as his eyes searched the immediate area. I prayed there were no more. I climbed into the backseat of Gran's Toyota, trying to ignore the pain in my stomach, not needing to look to know I would find a fresh set of marks.

On the way home I tried to remember some good times that my mother and I shared over the years. But it was hard. I kept hearing the words she said to me last. *You're evil; you're not my daughter anymore.* Visions of hell clouded behind my eyes and called out to me. I saw the charred, desolate landscape and the sunless, smoky sky.

Nothing terrible or too frightening yet, but the images shook me to my core.

Not because they were unsightly and depressing, but because they *weren't*.

No, what was scariest of all was that these images of hell actually looked inviting.

* * *

I felt restless and edgy. I prowled the dimly lit room because I couldn't sit down. I'd already changed out of my funeral clothes and threw them into the back of my closet where hopefully, I would never see them again. I didn't understand this energy I was feeling. I was uncomfortable in my own skin and I wanted a distraction, anything to take my mind off how I was feeling. I glanced at the clock for the tenth time and sighed.

I missed Sam. He left about twenty minutes ago, kissing me gently and giving my hands a squeeze. I closed my eyes and tried to feel that touch now, but my hands were cold. His touch was never cold. I pictured his retreating back as he walked to his truck and turned back. His devastating golden beauty made it difficult to stand in the door. But then Gran had called to me and he drove away. I knew he would be back as soon as possible, just as I knew he had to actually leave so he could sneak back through my bedroom window.

Logan was still here, still in the guest room. It was most likely going to be his last night. Now that Sam was home, Logan was going to go back to Sam's apartment and I was going to have to come up with some sort of lie about why Logan wasn't going home to his parents. It would be hard to explain why those eight days Sam spent "visiting his parents" and working things out so Logan could go home weren't successful. Sam wouldn't be able to sleep here when Logan went home. He would need to stay with his brother at their apartment.

Sometimes I hated being seventeen. I was too young to live the way I wanted and governed by rules that were so unfair. I had already lived through more than most people could even dream of. Some days I felt so old.

I heard a sound behind me and I tensed, but before I could react, Sam's arms were wrapping around me, drawing me back into the heat of his body. I sighed. Finally, I was where I wanted to be. *You were gone too long.*

He nuzzled the back of my neck and I forgot my words. I turned and laid my head on his chest, bringing my hands up between us and curling into him as much as I could. I fit so well against him. It was like he was made just for this. That I was made for this. When he hunched himself around me, some of the edginess I felt disappeared.

You did good today, he said.

Burying my mother isn't something I want to be good at.

He rubbed slow circles over my back and I enjoyed hearing a long, slow breath fill his lungs.

I feel guilty because I'm just glad it's over. I admitted.

There's nothing wrong with wanting some of the pain to go away.

I wasn't sure the pain of losing a parent ever went away. My dad died a few years ago and the pain wasn't gone; it had just changed. It was more of a yearning, a deep feeling of loss for things that would never be and things that we could never share. Of unspoken words and questions that sometimes haunted me, like: *What would he think of me now?*

Even though I have talked to him (a blessing, I know), those feelings hadn't left

Losing my mother was different, though. Our relationship was more complicated. In the end, I don't think she even liked me. She definitely didn't know me. I wondered if it would make mourning for her harder or easier. I couldn't tell because I was so regretful about never getting to make things right with her.

That's when I remembered the envelope.

The one that Gran found at the hospital. The one that had my name written across the front.

I pulled away from Sam, going over to my dresser and opening the drawer, staring down at the envelope. Slowly, I reached in and pulled it out, holding it in front of me, wondering what was inside—if I was ready to know.

"Hev?" Sam said, coming to my side. "What do you have there?"

I held the envelope out for him to see. "Gran found this in the hospital room after Mom died. She brought it home and I put it in here because I wasn't ready to read it."

"But you are now."

I wasn't sure if I would ever be ready. I was terrified she put into writing all the horrible things she said to me. Hadn't it been enough that I had to hear them echo through my head without reading them on paper as well? I sighed and went over to the bed and sat down on the edge, ripping the envelope open and pulling out a single piece of white paper, folded in half.

I unfolded the letter and began to read:

Heven,

I know I have hurt you. The things I have said to you—about you—are not things a mother should say to a daughter. I made mistakes in my life. Mistakes that I have lived with for a very long time. I tried to repent, to change. But I have learned that some mistakes cannot be erased no matter how hard one prays. When I could no longer deny that you were being punished for my mistakes, I tried to push you away. I thought that distance from me would protect you, but it only made things worse. It hurt you. Don't ever think that I don't love you. I do, more than anything. It is why I am doing this. I should have done it long ago. I will not allow you to suffer for my mistakes a moment longer. Please accept my apology and live your life in the light. I must go... He's waiting. I love you.
Mom

I stared down at the words long after I read them. The tears in my eyes made the letters blur together until they were a giant ball of ink. What did it mean? Who was waiting? And what mistakes had she made that I was being punished for?

Heven? Sam spoke quietly in my mind, not wanting to disturb me, but no doubt curious.

I looked up at him, blinking back the tears. Without a word, I handed him the letter and stared off at nothing while he read. When he finished he sat beside me, the paper between his fingers. *What do you think it means?*

I sat there for a long time just thinking, staring down at the floor and shying away from the answer that just wouldn't let me push it away. Finally, I looked up at Sam. *I think the 'he' is Beelzebub. He killed her, Sam. He killed my mother.*

He didn't say anything for a moment and then he nodded. *I think you're right.*

I took a deep breath. *I think there's a reason that my father didn't know my mother had died. I don't think she went to heaven, Sam. I think Beelzebub did something with her…*

Suddenly, Beelzebub's words echoed through my head. *Soul Reaper.* I reached out and grabbed Sam's wrist. "He took her soul."

Beelzebub dragged my mother's soul to hell.

What's worse? She let him.

* * *

I dreamed of chanting witches, of Kimber laughing and of a beast roaring. I dreamed of pain, searing pain against my skin and a feeling of longing so intense that I wanted to weep. I wanted to go home. I wanted to rejoin my family.

I opened my eyes. The room was dark. *It was only a dream. You're home,* I told myself. I tried to calm the racing of my heart and to ignore the burning in my shoulder. I rolled, trying to get comfortable—I felt so hot—and thought about my mother. Where was she? Was my theory right? Had Beelzebub really killed her and taken her soul down into hell?

The letter made it sound as if she agreed with whatever happened, that she thought it would make things right. "Oh,

Mom." I sighed into dark. Making deals with Beelzebub was never going to make things right.

I reminded myself I was only thinking up theories, that perhaps I was wrong. Maybe that letter was a result of whatever happened to her brain when she fell and hit her head. Maybe she hadn't known what she was saying.

I didn't believe that. But maybe it was true.

Something inside me shifted, pushed forward, and Sam's head snapped back. His eyes sprang open and they were pure, glittering gold. The hellhound in him was being disturbed by whatever Hecate trapped in my body. Sam squeezed his eyes shut and I waited for him to move from the bed. He didn't move and I saw him struggling, so I began to back away. His eyes snapped open again and he pulled me back in.

No. Stay.

It's hard for you. I'll move away for a few minutes.

I've spent enough time wanting to hold you. The hound in me will have to deal. I don't care if the devil himself takes up residence inside you. He gathered me close and I laid my head in the crook of his neck. *I'm not letting go,* he said, directed more toward the hellhound inside him instead of me.

He fell back asleep almost immediately and I marveled at the control he seemed to have over his own body. He seemed to grow stronger with each passing day. But me... I lay there haunted. Haunted by everything that was happening, haunted by whatever lived inside me and haunted by something that Sam had just said.

Exactly where was the devil and how come he never put Beelzebub in his place?

I pushed the disturbing thought away. The last thing any of us needed was to catch the attention of the devil himself. If Beelzebub was second in command to Satan and had this much power and hate inside him, I could only imagine what Satan himself must be like.

When I finally began to drift asleep, a vision of my mother swam before my closed eyes. It was from when she

had been happy… from before life started spiraling out of control. I wondered if she would ever know happiness again.

Chapter Nineteen

Heven

Sam ate and ate and ate. He ate so much that Logan, Gran and I (who had long since abandoned our own plates) sat and watched, astonished.

"Didn't your mother feed you?" Gran asked, watching him polish of his third stack of pancakes. "She must have. You look bigger."

So it *wasn't* just me that noticed.

Logan winced and Sam paused in chewing. "Yes, ma'am. But your cooking is so much better."

Gran put another stack in front of him, which he attacked with equal vigor. Before the pancakes, he had eaten two plates of eggs, heaping piles of bacon, toast and a huge bowl of fruit.

"Should I make more?" she asked, rising from the table.

"No," he said between bites. "But thank you. This was the best meal I've had in a long time."

I resisted the urge to shudder. Anything would beat rats.

"I'll get a roast in the oven for dinner. You'll stay, Sam?"

"Yes, ma'am. Thank you."

"What about the leftovers in the fridge?" I asked, thinking of all the funeral food. My stomach turned uncomfortably.

Gran waved a hand. "That's just sandwiches and light food. Clearly, he's starved." She motioned at Sam who was still consuming pancakes. "Invite Cole for lunch and he can help eat up those leftovers."

"Great idea," I said, lifting my coffee to my lips, but then sitting it back down. That plate of food I ate for breakfast wasn't settling well.

Gran nodded. "Call Kimber if you want, as well. Since you two made up from your fight, I haven't seen her at all."

Sam glanced at me and I shot him a look. "Thanks, Gran. I will give her a call. But I know she planned on doing some major shopping this week with school starting soon and all…" I hated lying. I hated more that I was getting very good at it.

Gran chuckled. "That girl and the shopping mall." Thankfully, she let it go to say, "I'll be gone this afternoon. I have some errands to run and a meeting with your mother's lawyer."

"Her lawyer?"

"It's just estate planning. I was the executor of her will. There's no need for you to be there today. But the next meeting, you'll need to come."

"I will?" I never thought about her will and everything she left behind.

"Of course, honey. Everything is going to you."

"To me?"

"You're underage so the money will go into trust until you're eighteen this fall, and we'll need to decide about her house."

"Do I have to move?" I asked, alarmed. I didn't care about the money or the house.

Sam dropped his fork and pushed his plate away.

"Of course not. I'm the only family left." She seemed lost on this thought for a moment before looking back up. "I'm your legal guardian now."

I let out the breath I had been holding. "That's good."

"I know it's a lot," Gran said softly. "We can take it slow. We don't need to make any decisions right now about her estate, but we will have to sign papers and get everything in order so when you do decide what you want, we can do it."

I got up and hugged Gran. "Thank you. I don't know what I would do without you."

"I love you," she said and hugged me back. "Now help me get this roast ready."

* * *

I wasn't feeling that well. My head was throbbing and my back hurt. The claw marks on my stomach from yesterday were burning and it annoyed me to have to wear a shirt. Every time the fabric touched them, more pain shot through my body. Why hadn't they healed like the other ones? I had a feeling I might be running a low-grade fever and I was still regretting the big breakfast I ate. The food was laying in my stomach like lead. Even though I had no energy and wanted to lie down, I still felt restless.

I watched as Cole pulled up next to the house and cut the engine to his truck.

"Hey, sis," he said, coming around the hood of his truck and towing me in for a hug. I held back a wince when discomfort tinged through my body. "I feel like I haven't seen you at all these past few days," he said into my ear.

I pulled back, though not completely away. "I know. I've thought about you too. It's just with the funeral and all…"

"Yeah, I know. You doing okay?" His eyes flashed with concern and he studied my face.

I nodded. "I wanted to apologize about what happened to you in hell. I'm so thankful you're okay." He looked good, and I was sure it was all thanks to the healing powers of Gemma.

He shook his head. "There wasn't anything you could do. He's one powerful, evil man. I hated leaving you there like that."

"He tried to run back," Gemma said, practically appearing out of thin air beside us. "I had to heal the wound he got from that too."

I frowned at Cole and he rolled his eyes, then moved away from me toward Sam, who was sitting on the porch swing with Logan. "I know I've seen you since you came home, but I haven't got to tell you how damn glad I am you're back, man." He held out his fist, which Sam bumped with his own.

"Thanks for keeping an eye on Heven," Sam told him. I rolled my eyes and turned back to Gemma.

"Thanks for coming over. I have something I want to talk to you about."

"What is it?" Gemma asked.

"Some stuff happened in hell and then I read this letter from my mom…"

"Where's Riley?" Gemma asked, like she automatically assumed he was responsible for whatever I was about to say.

"I didn't call him," I said. "Sam isn't too happy he's here."

I thought back to the last time we saw him, before the funeral when he acted like a jerk and got into a fight with Sam…

The beast, or whatever was trapped inside me, seemed to like (or dislike) my memory of the fight. I suddenly felt like it was throwing itself around in a tantrum, trying to escape, trying to get out.

I stumbled forward, bending at the waist. I felt like all the organs inside me were being pushed around and I gagged.

"Heven," Gemma said from above, reaching down to help me up. Fresh searing pain ripped through my chest and I cried out.

"Don't touch me," I said, hoarse.

Then Sam was there, lifting me up and walking through the house with me as the beast fought against my skin, trying to rip its way free. I couldn't understand why it hadn't managed to get out already.

Behind us, Cole was making a fuss, demanding to know what was wrong with me. Sam laid me on the couch and hurried to grab the blanket draped across the top, but I shook my head.

"I can't stand to have it touch me, please."

"Did it scratch you?" Sam said, the blanket falling to the floor as he kneeled beside the couch.

"I think so." I pointed to my chest. I was wearing a simple pink T-shirt with a rhinestone pocket off to the side, and Sam grabbed the shirt to rip it open.

"I like this shirt." I growled.

He let go and I sat up and lifted the shirt over my head and threw it aside, leaving me wearing only a pink bra with my white cotton shorts. The air brushed over my skin and I felt instantly better. The fabric of the shirt felt so heavy against my skin. I sighed and closed my eyes.

"Heven," Sam said, exasperated.

My eyes shot open and Cole stormed into the room. "What the hell is going on?" He roared. He looked at me and his eyes widened. Then he looked at Sam and his eyes narrowed.

"I couldn't take it anymore. It was driving me crazy." I lay back against the pillows and everything around me fell silent.

"Can you heal her?" Sam asked Gemma quietly.

Gemma leaned over the couch and looked down at my chest. "What the hell is that?"

I looked down, trying to see. Fresh claw marks blistered beneath my skin, puffing up the edges like giant bubbles filled with blood. The skin around them appeared to be bruised. I glanced briefly at the claw marks on my stomach. They weren't healed, but they looked good compared to this new mark.

"Beelzebub had Hecate trap some kind of demon or beast or something inside her. It's been trying to get out." Sam explained, his voice strained. Then he looked up at Cole. "Will you get her some ice?"

He rushed from the room.

"I can try, but I'm not sure I can heal this." Gemma came around the couch and sat in front of me. She held her hands palm down above my chest and closed her eyes. My skin warmed and tingled, but the pain didn't stop.

"It's not working," I said.

"Try." Sam insisted. The look on his face was enough to get me to close my eyes and focus on the warmth that Gemma was creating. But I didn't think it would work. Slowly, the pain ebbed and I was able to relax against the couch. Gemma fell back, looking drained. Cole was at her side, helping her into a nearby chair, momentarily forgetting the ice bag in his hand.

"Are you okay?" I asked Gemma.

"I'm sorry. Whatever they did to you, I can't undo."

"I feel better, though." I insisted. Well, sort of. My claw marks didn't hurt, but otherwise, I still felt the same, which wasn't good.

"They're still there," Sam said, staring at the marks.

"Sorry," I muttered, feeling like it was somehow my fault.

The front door opened and Riley waltzed through, whistling a tune. We all stopped and stared as he came into the room. When he noticed us all staring, he stopped. "No one called to invite me to the meeting?"

"What the hell are you doing here?" Sam demanded.

Riley smirked. "Can't a guy visit his friends?"

"What do you want, Riley?" Sam said, barely holding onto his patience.

He shrugged. "Just curious as to what the Mickey Mouse Club is up to today." Then he glanced at me. "Love the pink."

Sam moved in front of me and looked down. "You need a shirt," he said softly.

I didn't want to put on a shirt. The thought of the fabric pressing in on me was horrible. But I couldn't lay there in my bra either. Sam went up the stairs and then reappeared moments later with a black tank top dangling from his fingers. I took it and carefully pulled it on. It wasn't too bad because the neck was low enough that the marks on my chest weren't covered. I settled back against the pillow after I was decent and Sam sat on the floor in front of me, leaning back against the sofa.

"Are you going to tell us what's going on?" Cole asked, tossing Sam the ice pack and sitting on the arm of the chair that Gemma was sitting in. Across from them, Riley dropped into a chair and propped his feet on the coffee table, making himself at home.

Sam handed me the ice pack and I grimaced, setting it beside me and not placing it on the newest claw marks.

"I thought you said they didn't hurt." Sam worried.

"They don't, when you don't touch them." I looked at Gemma. "Is there a way I can get this thing out of me?"

"What is it?" she asked.

"I don't know. All I heard was the word 'beast' when Hecate was chanting over me."

Gemma shook her head. "Hecate's magic is very powerful. Usually she alone is the only one who can undo the spells she creates."

Well, that was positive news. Not.

From behind the couch, Logan spoke up. Until now, I forgot he was there. "Can't you stab her with the dagger like you did me? It got the demon out…"

Sam stiffened, no doubt replaying the horrible memory of when he stabbed his brother to protect me. I looked over the back of the couch at him. "That's definitely an idea, Logan." I patted the end of the couch where I was lying and he came around to sit down.

Look at what that did to him, Heven. He's weak… he's… I'm not going to stab you with a dagger.

It might be our only choice, but I didn't think it was a good time to point that out. I shifted my weight on the couch to make room for Logan. I was still feeling dizzy and my stomach was turning.

Sam twisted so his side was leaning against the couch and his arm was across my waist, consciously avoiding the claw marks on my belly. His fingers were warm and reassuring, folded around mine, and I gave him a small smile.

"I'm sorry, Heven. I wish I had an answer… I'll see what I can find," Gemma said.

I nodded. With no solution in sight for that problem, I turned to the next one. "Gemma, do you know if Beelzebub takes people's souls?"

Gemma sat up a little straighter in her chair. "Of course he does. All of the princes of hell collect souls."

"There is more than one prince of hell?" Logan asked.

"There are seven. One for each of the seven deadly sins."

"How come we've only ever seen Beelzebub?"

Gemma shrugged. "I would assume because he seems to have an interest in the scroll."

I cleared my throat. "He has it. He got it open and read it."

Gemma and Cole gasped. "How could he get it open? I thought you were the only one that could open it?" Gemma asked.

"I really don't know how he stole it, or how he got it open." I reached up to finger the key necklace around my neck when I remembered I took it off and placed it in my jewelry box when I realized I no longer had to protect it. No one would come for it now. "Airis has turned her back on me, on us. She said my soul has been compromised and she will no longer help me on my journey."

"Did she tell you what that was?" Cole asked.

I shook my head sadly. "Her and Ana both said I had to figure that out on my own."

"Who's Ana?" Gemma asked.

"Aniano," Sam said, pronouncing her full name (and pronouncing it correctly!). "We met her in hell. After I destroyed the body that Beelzebub was in, The Devourer took us for a ride… to an island."

Gemma gasped and sat forward, excitement danced in her eyes. "Then it's true? There really is life in hell?"

"You know what we are talking about?" I asked, leaning up and forward toward Gemma. I ignored the pull on my chest and the protest in my stomach. My vision blurred, but only for a second before refocusing.

"Of course I have heard of the Island of Life in hell… The angels used to gossip about that place all the time. But we all thought it was just gossip and not true."

"The Devourer took you to an island?" Riley asked skeptically.

Sam shot him a look. "Yeah, and I find it a little odd that The Devourer didn't want you along for the ride. Why is that, Riley?"

"You want me to tell you what a dragon thinks?" Riley asked dubiously. But I saw something move behind his eyes.

"Tell us about the island, Sam." Logan urged. I smiled at the eagerness in his voice.

"Actually, we aren't really supposed to tell anyone. We were sworn to secrecy." Sam said, lowering his voice to match the secret.

This seemed to entice Logan even more. "We won't tell anyone!"

Sam laughed. Everyone was watching him, waiting, hoping he would spill the beans. He glanced at me and I smiled. "As long as they all swear not to tell." I said, loudly.

Everyone agreed immediately. Except of course, for Riley.

All eyes turned toward him. He sighed dramatically. "Fine. I won't say anything."

Logan grinned.

I collapsed back against the pillow, thankful Sam could explain about the island. I was exhausted and I closed my eyes. Visions of hell flashed in my head and I went with them, looking at the depressing wasteland. It didn't scare me like before. It was almost welcoming.

Sam's deep voice soothed me as he told everyone about the island that no one could see and about the woman who lived there. He was a good story teller.

I wasn't prepared for what happened next. I made the mistake of dropping my guard and I slipped right into sleep. The visions of hell solidified around me and I knew I was there now. I shook my head. I had a headache, but that was pretty much a permanent thing now… Had Beelzebub pulled me down here? How had he managed with Sam right next to me?

I pushed myself up off the ground and began walking. I had no idea where I was going, only feeling like I was being pulled in a certain direction. I walked for what seemed like hours and my feet were sore, but then I came upon what looked like freestanding mountains in the middle of nowhere. Maybe a more apt description of this place would be massive mounds of dirt and rock that had been carved out into caves just sitting in the middle of burnt up landscape. The land was barren and the atmosphere was even more so. In fact, I struggled to breathe. I began to feel anxious, a real feeling like I might climb out of my skin at any second. Something inside me began to shake and a guttural sound ripped from my throat. I hurried to slap my hand over my mouth, trying to silence myself.

I was losing control. This… this… *thing* inside me was beginning to take over. If it couldn't get out, then it would take over. It would own me.

I took a step backward and then another, rushing, tripping over my feet and falling down onto the hard, ashy ground. But the beast wouldn't have it. It wanted to be here and it began knocking against my insides, trying to push me forward. I fought against it until I felt strained and exhausted. Finally, I gave in and crawled toward the caves. The entrances were dark and carnivorous and I knew something heinous lurked inside. At least now that the beast thought I was complying, it seemed to have calmed. I could still feel my insides rattling and my back hurt, but at least it wasn't fighting me.

A few feet from the entrance to the largest cave, I stopped. I wasn't going any farther. The beast pushed against me and I fell onto my knees. Another inhuman sound ripped from my throat.

Something inside the cave took notice. I heard a scuffle and an answering noise that matched the one I made. Had the beast been calling it? I began to shake as heavy breathing drew near. I didn't bother to get up. I was frozen with fear and the thing inside me wanted me to stay here. There wasn't much I could do.

Then I saw movement from just inside and a huge, hulking figure stepped out.

It could have been a hellhound, a hellhound that had been hexed and cursed with vile deformations. It walked on four paws like a hound. It had a long tail like a hound, large wide-set eyes and an over-exaggerated long snout. But that's where the similarities ended.

Its eyes were the color of blood.

Its gums and teeth were coated with what looked like flesh, and I was pretty sure tiny maggots crawled along at the base of its overcrowded rows of razor sharp teeth.

It had a huge humpback and walked like it favored its left side over its right. One ear was larger than the other. The ear that was biggest (the right) was covered in hair, but the deformed one was just black skin. Most of its body was covered in hair, hair that was the color of the gray ash that covered the ground. Actually, I think it was black (like a hellhound), but only looked gray because it lay on the ground and got dirty.

It walked over, controlling its awkward, massive weight with ease, and stood over me. I scrambled back, trying to move away, but the thing inside me let out another one of those sounds. The beast staring at me cocked its head to the side and let out a deafening roar. Within seconds, I was surrounded by identical beasts who came pouring out from the other caves.

Were they going to eat me?

One stepped forward and sniffed at me. I flinched and it snarled. It began to drool, or rather its mouth began to ooze with some sort of light red substance. The thing in me let out another wail and all of them sniffed at the air.

That's when it hit me.

This beast inside me was trying to get out. It belonged here. This was its home. It brought me here because it wanted these things to kill me. The minute my body was torn apart, it would be free.

And I would be dead.

Chapter Twenty

Heven

A massive paw reached for me, its claws extending until they looked like sharp daggers. I threw myself to the side and the paw swiped into the ground, slashing the shale and rock where I had been.

Another massive wail left my throat and I screamed. "Stop it!"

Of course, no one listened.

The original beast that found me lunged and pounced on my back. Suddenly, I had a flash from the attack that left me disfigured. Of a heavy, dark beast throwing itself on me and clawing me within an inch of my life.

"No," I cried as the claws dug into my flesh and seared me with pain.

A sharp slap rocked the head on my shoulders and I blinked open my eyes. Automatically, my hands came up to defend my face.

"What the hell is wrong with you?" someone roared. "You don't hit her. Ever!"

I opened my eyes, confused. I was back in the living room on the couch at home. I woke up.

"Someone had to do something to wake her up." Riley spat. "Whispering sweet nothings in her ear wasn't working."

Sam threw a punch and hit Riley square in the mouth. His lip split and blood ran down his chin.

"Stop it!" I yelled.

Everyone turned to look at me.

"Heven." Sam came back, leaning over me, looking in my eyes. His chest was heaving, but his face was pale.

"I fell asleep," I stated.

"You started struggling and making these sounds…"

"This thing inside me pulled me into hell. It took me to its lair." It sounded sinister, but that's what it was. "There were others…"

"What did they look like?"

"Like a hellhound, only deformed and disgusting. Evil." I shivered and my stomach lurched. I got up and ran into the bathroom and retched over the toilet. When I was done, I rinsed my mouth out and splashed cold water over my face.

Sam was standing in the door, watching me, and he looked ashamed and disgusted at the same time.

"Oh, Sam. I didn't mean it like that. I think you're beautiful as a hellhound."

"I know that." He pulled me close. "I hate that this is happening to you. I don't know how to get it out."

"We'll figure it out." I tried to sound optimistic as I pulled away and went back to the living room. I prayed he didn't feel my worry. If we didn't get this thing out of me, it would find a way to get out on its own, and judging by what just happened, it wouldn't care whether I lived or died in the process.

"Where's Gemma?" I asked.

Cole was standing by the window and he turned. "She'll be right back." His eyes drifted to the claw marks on my chest. I turned away, toward Riley. At least he didn't look at me with pity or even concern. I wondered if he really cared at all what was happening.

"You look like hell," he told me.

I actually smiled, glad for once someone wasn't trying to sugarcoat things. "Close your eyes, then," I shot back and went over to the couch to lie back down. I still felt beyond dizzy and I knew if I fell over, Sam would probably go crazy. There was a frosty, fresh water bottle on the table right next to the couch. I glanced over my shoulder at Riley and he shrugged.

"You're probably dehydrated. That thing is probably stealing your water and food intake. If you pass out again and I have to hit you, then Sam will hit me, and I am done taking all the hits for free." He looked over at Sam. "Next time I'll hit back."

Sam didn't seem bothered by this and he turned his back on Riley to sit down next to me. I gave Riley a dirty look before focusing on the water, which I began drinking in small sips. It felt cool and really good going down.

Gemma appeared and in her hands were three big leather-bound books. Wordlessly, she sat them on the coffee table and began flipping through one. When she found what she wanted, she turned the book toward me. "Is this what you saw?"

I leaned forward to look down at the image. It was a drawing of the beasts in the caves and it was precisely accurate. "Yeah."

Sam leaned forward to see and everything in his body tightened. "This thing is inside you? Is that what you're saying?"

"I'm not sure." I frowned. "I got that feeling. It led me to the caves and it recognized the others there. I assumed that's where it lived."

He swore low, a very creative and colorful slew of words. Riley laughed. Gemma tossed the book at him. He grunted when it hit him in the chest. He took it and looked at the image and grimaced. "It was nice knowing ya, Heven." He tossed the book back onto the coffee table.

"What is it? How do we get it out?" Sam asked Gemma.

"In essence, it's a hellhound," Gemma said. "It's just an unnatural one. They weren't born like you and Riley. They were sired by evil. Because pure evil made them, they were tainted and ended up deformed and much less controllable than even the wildest hellhound."

"Weren't original hellhounds created?" I asked. Did they all look like this in the beginning?

"Yes, but not like these," Gemma said, tapping the photo. "Two animals that already lived in hell were both given abilities and then they were mated. A hellhound was born from them, housing both parents' abilities times two."

"And the one inside of me?"

"It wasn't born from two parents. It was created by the princes of hell—basically, they were an experiment gone bad."

"How do we get it out?" Sam asked, grim.

"It doesn't say anything about that here." Gemma frowned. "My guess would be Hecate would have to remove it because she put it there."

Sam stood, knocking into the table and sending the burning candle over on its side. Melted wax went everywhere. I hadn't noticed the candle had been lit in the first place.

"Oh, no!" I said, jumping up.

"Leave it," he said. "When it cools I'll peel it up."

I stared at him for a moment, wondering how to get him to calm down, but I knew it was useless. He felt helpless and I understood. I spent eight days like that. I grabbed his hand and pulled him down onto the couch with me and curled into his side. His body was rigid, but his arm was gentle when he wrapped it around me.

"Who wants pizza?" I said.

Everyone looked at me like I was crazy. Except for Riley, who said, "With beer?"

"You want to eat?" Cole asked, incredulous.

Well, no. I didn't, but sitting around here while they all watched me struggle with this thing inside me—*this rabid, deformed hellhound*—was getting old and only making Sam miserable. I shrugged. "What else are we going to do? We have to eat the leftover funeral food too or Gran might get upset."

No one had any better suggestions so Cole called and ordered the pizza.

"I'll go get it because no one else here is old enough to get beer," Riley said, standing.

"Are you old enough?" I asked dubiously. He grinned a very wide, toothy grin. I took that as a no.

Sam pulled out his truck keys and tossed them at Riley, who caught them and threw them back. "I have a ride."

"You have a car?" I asked.

"Yep."

"Where'd you get a car?" Gemma asked suspiciously.

"Where else? I stole it." With that, he walked out the door.

* * *

I couldn't eat. It was all I could do to sit there and smell the food, watching everyone else eat. I didn't so much feel sick anymore, but I had a feeling it was because my body was so exhausted. And maybe it was, because the beast was calmed down after seeing its family.

Please eat something, Sam said.

Maybe later.

You've lost weight.

How come you didn't lose any? You're actually bigger.

I'm worried about you.

"Gemma?" I said. "We kind of got off track before, when we were talking about the souls."

Gemma sat down her slice of pizza and looked up. "All seven princes of hell steal souls and take them to hell. It's how they get their power."

"What do you mean?"

"The seven princes of hell all originally fell from heaven. They were very powerful angels until they turned against God. When they fell, they took some of their powers with them, but not many and they were weak. They are power hungry, greedy and want to rule hell without anyone being a match for them. So they began stealing souls and dragging them to hell. The souls are somehow trapped in hell and that's where their power comes from—where hell's power comes from. They feed off the souls."

I got a very sick feeling in my stomach.

"Chained to the floor of hell and fed off for all eternity," Sam said softly... realization in his voice.

"What did you say?" Riley said, narrowing his eyes on Sam.

"Sam?" I asked, reaching out and resting my hand on his arm.

"When I was trapped down there, I heard Beelzebub. He was talking to someone... He threatened them. He told them he would chain them to the floor of hell and feed off them for all eternity."

"Who was he talking to?" Cole asked. Out of the corner of my eye, Riley shifted, and I could sense how closely he was listening to Sam.

"I don't know. I couldn't hear anything they were saying."

"It's okay," I told Sam.

"I always wondered where and how they kept the souls. They must chain them to the floor of hell. It makes sense because then hell could feed off the soul's energy and the prince's could draw it from the ground when they needed."

"If they draw it from the ground, wouldn't all the demons do that too?" Logan asked, no doubt remembering the demon inside him.

"Not if they don't know they can," Gemma said. "The princes probably haven't told anyone where they keep the souls. They probably haven't told anyone what they're doing."

"But wouldn't the soul die?" Cole asked. "Wouldn't they be drained of whatever the prince's take?"

"Possibly." Gemma allowed. "I don't know how it works. My guess is the better the soul, the longer it will live. Hope takes a long time to die, and if a soul is hopeful it will be set free, it might hang on. I would think once a soul is drained the princes just release it and it twists into a demon and joins their army."

"What about a soul from a very powerful person?" I asked, noting the tension from across the room. I didn't acknowledge that I felt it, though.

"I would think that soul would be very valuable and be a great source of long-lasting power."

"But what about the really powerful demons? How do they get so powerful?" Logan asked.

I glanced at him and smiled. He turned away, almost like he was guilty of something.

"I would think the demon was given powers from one of the princes to make him stronger so he could do whatever bidding they required. In your case, I would think Beelzebub gave the demon inside you powers so he could control you."

Logan got up and ran from the room, up the stairs, and then I heard the slam of his bedroom door. Sam stood up, a bleak look on his face. He didn't look at anyone when he said, "He's never going to get any better, is he?"

I turned toward Gemma and we shared a look. It was what we both had been thinking, but never really voiced out loud.

I stood up and wrapped an arm around Sam. "I certainly hope so."

He kissed my forehead. "I'll be back."

I nodded and watched him go up the stairs after his brother.

"I wish I could do more for him," Gemma whispered. "That demon destroyed Logan's body and it's like it took away all the strength Logan had to repair himself."

"You've done everything you could," Cole told her, reaching out and taking her hand. "We're all grateful you've been here to help."

I nodded.

Riley sat forward in his chair. "You've spent over a decade roaming around alone, refusing to care about anything, and then I find you here with another hellhound of all people and you're helping them."

"You're helping us too," I pointed out.

Riley pretended I wasn't even there and kept his midnight eyes intent on Gemma. There was a mean streak in them and I began to worry. He pursed his lips momentarily, making his already chiseled cheekbones stand out even more. "Were you looking for someone to replace my grandfather? When you figured out Sam"—he tossed his head in my direction—"was in too deep with someone else, you decided to take up with a *human*. Tell me Gem's." Riley's voice dropped low. "Does he remind you of Callum?"

Cole leaped out of his chair and threw himself at Riley. Both of them fell back, tipping the chair over. Riley was faster and stronger than Cole so he tossed him up into the air and against the wall with ease.

"Stop it!" I cried.

Gemma was already across the room, pulling them apart, when Cole lunged at him again.

Riley smiled, but it looked like a snarl. "Do you have any pride left at all, man? Your girlfriend could kick your ass in her sleep."

Cole lunged anew and Riley decked him, snapping his head back. I ran forward at Riley, shoving against his chest. "Stop it! Stop it right now!"

Riley grabbed my arm and yanked me closer. His eyes looked like silver fire and his chest was heaving.

"Don't you dare touch him again." I warned.

Riley's eyes narrowed. "Or what?"

His fingers dug into my arm, but I didn't say a word. Sam appeared at my side and pinned him with a glare. "Let go." He looked at my arm.

Riley gave me a little jerk. Sam grabbed my free arm and kicked out with his leg, catching Riley in the gut. Riley flew backward, hitting the coatrack and scattering jackets everywhere. Sam thrust me behind him as Riley came flying back across the room. The two went at it, fists flying and legs kicking.

Sam sent Riley across the room again and before getting up, he picked up a piece of wood from the coatrack and held it like a club. He stepped forward, menacing and wild.

"Riley, don't you dare," I said.

He didn't even look at me. His focus was all on Sam, on hurting him. I closed my eyes. Anger was sweeping over me. He attacked Gemma, then my brother, and now he was threatening Sam with a broken piece of wood. I wished I were strong enough to stop him… I wished…

A scream snapped my eyes open. The wood had burst into flames and was burning toward Riley's hands.

"Throw it in the fireplace!" I yelled. Riley whipped the burning wood into the fireplace and the whole stack of timber inside went up in flames. It cracked and hissed with intensity.

"What the hell was that?" Riley asked.

"What is your problem?" I yelled, trying to race at him, but Sam intercepted me, placing his body in the way. "You just attacked everyone in this room."

"I was bored," he said mildly.

"You're a drunk idiot," I snapped. "If you wanna know why Gemma walked away from you, that's why."

Riley's eyes narrowed.

"Go upstairs and sleep it off." I ordered.

He smirked. "I don't take orders from you."

"Fine! Drive off and kill yourself. That'll make things better."

"Whatever," he muttered and stomped up the stairs.

The room fell quiet. "Look at this mess," I said and went over to pick up the broken coatrack and coats.

When no one else moved, I straightened and looked up. "What?"

"Did you set that on fire?" Cole whispered.

"What? No." Was he crazy?

They all looked at the fire, then back at me. I focused on Sam. He would know that I couldn't do that. But he didn't seem as sure as I would have thought.

"I didn't do that," I said, my voice a little too unsure for my liking.

Sam glanced at the fire. It was dying down. I shrugged. "I'm going to go talk to Logan. I tried earlier, but Riley decided to be an ass."

I nodded.

"I'm going to go," Cole said, drawing my attention. "Today has been… yeah. I'll just see you later."

He went into the kitchen before anyone could say anything. I glanced at Gemma. "Aren't you going to follow him?"

She shook her head.

"Then you're a fool." I spat and ran after my brother.

He was on the porch when I caught up with him. "Cole, wait."

"I can't stay right now, Hev."

"Yeah, I get it. I just…" I wasn't sure what to say. "Riley is an ass."

"Yeah, but what he said probably wasn't a lie."

"I still think she loves you," I said, coming to his side.

"I'm not so sure."

"Want me to talk to her?" I offered.

He swiveled around to look at me. "I want you to touch her."

"You what?" I said, confused, but it didn't take long to know what he meant. "You want me to mind rob her?"

"Yeah." He didn't seem proud to ask, but he wasn't unsure.

"But why?"

"I can't do this anymore," he said tiredly. "Do you have any idea what it's like to love something so much it hurts?"

"Yeah."

He laughed bitterly. "I think my situation is a little different."

He was right.

"It physically hurts me, Heven. To be that close, but so far away. It's the worst kind of lonely. I can't do it anymore. I'd rather never see her again than see her and know she's out of reach. I have to know. If she loves me, then I can handle it, the distance. I'll know she's going to come around. But if he's right…" He looked back at the house where Riley was and shook his head.

"I'll do it."

"You will?"

I nodded. "I'll call you after."

He hugged me swiftly, then got in his truck and drove away. I watched until he was out of sight.

Gemma came out the back door seconds later. "He's gone?"

I nodded, my gaze sweeping over her. She was dressed, as usual, in dark jeans and brown knee-high leather boots. Her navy blue T-shirt was half tucked in, half out. Her hair was up in a high ponytail and the glossy strands fell down behind her. There was a dagger strapped to her leg and probably a smaller knife in her boot.

As she came down the stairs, Gemma told me, "I'll see you later."

"Wait, can we talk?"

"About what?"

I lifted a brow. "Really? You have to ask?"

She sighed and dropped down on the middle step. I took a seat beside her. "I know I haven't been the best listener lately, but I'm here now."

"You think I'm going to talk to you about your brother?"

"Why not?"

She didn't seem to have a comeback for that so we sat quietly for a minute. She surprised me by starting the conversation. "I thought I was ready."

"Ready for what?"

"For him. I didn't think he would matter this much."

"But he does?"

"I don't want this. I didn't come here for this."

"Then why did you?"

"What Riley said isn't true, you know?"

"No?"

"Well, not all of it. Back then, when I first met Riley… he was so much like Callum. I did try and make him into who I thought Callum was and that was wrong. But, you can't make someone into something they aren't. And then there's the curse. It changed him… made him cold."

"So you left."

"I thought it would be easier for everyone."

Instead, he felt abandoned and unworthy of even her friendship. My heart went out to Riley.

"You should apologize."

She looked up, surprised.

"Maybe if you explained, he would understand."

"I don't think so."

I wasn't sure he would either so I let it go. "What about Cole?"

"He's different than anyone I've ever known."

"You're hurting him."

She bowed her head again and I made my move. I reached out and laid a hand on her shoulder, a gesture in comfort and friendship. I guess now it was also a gesture in deceit.

I felt myself slipping into her mind and I wondered what I was going to see.

"Has he told you that he loves you yet?" I asked.

"Once," Gemma answered. "It didn't go that well."

Just like that, I was in. It was time to find out the truth once and for all. Did Gemma really love my brother? If she didn't, would I have enough guts to actually tell him and break his heart?

Chapter Twenty-One

Sam

I wrapped my knuckles against the door and heard a muffled "Come in," and I smiled as I let myself into the room my brother had been living in for the past ten days. I glanced around as I entered and was surprised to see the room looked like it belonged to him.

There was a navy blue comforter on the bed with pillows in red and gold. The curtains were striped with the same colors and there were posters on the walls of his favorite comic book heroes. There was a TV on top the dresser across from the bed, a stack of comic books on the nightstand and empty candy wrappers sticking out of the half-closed drawer. He had a plastic clothes hamper in the corner and it was filled with jeans and shirts. If I closed my eyes, I could picture Gran bustling around in here to collect the laundry and looking for loose socks.

Heven and her Grandmother had really taken care of him while I was gone and I actually had to pause to swallow past the lump in my throat that I suddenly felt. Words couldn't express how grateful I was that he had been taken care of, that these two women had taken him into their home—a boy who was sick and essentially homeless. They cared for him—for everyone around them—in a way that left me awed and breathless.

"Hey, bud." Logan was sitting in the center of his sloppily made bed, staring at the TV, but I don't think he would be able to tell me a thing about what he was watching. One of his socks was loose on his foot and he had a hole in the toe of the other. I grinned and sat down on the edge of the bed. "All that talk about demons and stuff brought up some memories, huh?"

He nodded and glanced at me. "I didn't mean to act like a baby."

"No one thinks you're a baby. We all think you're awesome for everything you went through."

Logan sat there a minute, then said, "I did some bad things. Things I wish I could make up for."

"So have I."

He glanced at me. "Like what?"

Up until this point I tried to shelter him from everything I had gone through, everything in my past that I thought would color the way he looked at me. I thought I had to be strong. I had to show that I could handle anything and be the perfect brother. But that isn't what Logan needed.

He needed me to be there. To show him that everyone makes mistakes, everyone has hardship, but it's how you deal with it that makes you who you are.

"Well, for starters, I used to be friends with the hellhound that disfigured Heven."

Logan narrowed his eyes. "China?"

I nodded. "Yeah, I used to be roommates with her and she would kill people, lots of them, and then I would help her cover up her crimes."

I had his full attention now.

"I thought I was supposed to be that way because I'm a hellhound. I thought I was supposed to be bad. But I never liked the way I felt when I was around China. It always felt wrong to cover up her crimes.

"So what happened?"

"I killed her."

His eyes widened. "You killed China?"

I nodded. "She kept trying to kill Heven. She *had* killed Heven and Airis—the angel?" I asked and he nodded— "brought her back to life. Then China tried to kill Heven again and I killed her."

"She deserved it."

"Maybe. But it wasn't really for me to decide and I didn't feel good after I did it. I have to live with the fact that I killed her every day, forever."

"I have to live with what I did to Heven's mom and all the other things I did when that Demon was inside me."

I nodded. "You're right. You do have to live with those things. But you can tell yourself you didn't really want those things to happen. You aren't defined by them. Learn from them and try and make the rest of your life better— something you can be proud of."

"I don't deserve how good they've been to me," he said quietly, looking away.

"There are a lot of things I don't know, like why you keep wearing those fugly socks with holes in them." I made a face and he laughed. "But I do know that you deserve everything good they ever gave you. They love you, Logan. That much I can see. Gran loves having you here. She told me herself just the other morning at breakfast."

"Really?"

I nodded then made a mock concerned face. "Although, I think they feed you too much candy."

He smiled. "I like it here. It's like it was before you changed, before Mom and Dad started fighting all the time."

"You know none of that was your fault, right? If you want to go home, I'll take you. I'll explain everything and they'll let you stay."

"You would go back there?"

"Not to live, but yes, to visit. And if you stayed, I'd come see you on the weekends. I'll always be a part of your life, Logan. I promise."

"What if I want to stay here, with you?"

I smiled. "I think Gran would fight me for you. She was hinting around about you living here this school year with her and Hev."

His eyes widened. "Can I?"

"If that's what you want."

"It is. My home is with you now… and with Heven."

"She's not so bad after all?"

"She's cool. She worked really hard when you were gone. Demons were attacking her, she got sick from one's blood and she's been dealing with Riley." He rolled his eyes.

I forced a laugh. Hearing everything Heven had gone through made me sick.

"I want to make it up to her, everything I've done."

I didn't think he needed to, but sometimes it was the best way to get past something. To admit and apologize. "You know, I have something I need to make a mends for too," I said, my thoughts turning a bit dark.

"What is it?"

"You think I'm going to share all my secrets with you in one night? Get real!"

"Do you have time for a beat down on the Xbox before you go?"

"A beat down? Them's fighting words, bro."

He laughed and pulled out the controllers and hurried to turn on the game. When it started, he began coughing, deep, hacking coughs that made my throat ache. He grabbed a tissue by the TV and wiped his nose and the tissue came away red. He quickly tucked the red part under and glanced to see if I saw. I said nothing, pretending to watch the game.

"You okay?" I asked causally.

"Sure, I just cough sometimes."

He began playing again and I let him, but in the back of my mind I was worrying.

Heven

What if I wasn't enough? The thought pounded through Gemma's mind, through her body, like blood pumping through veins. She was scared, more scared than I thought a warrior like her could ever be.

Her feelings were so strong and so overwhelming that I almost pulled back. Gemma was clearly a woman who felt things with great intensity. It was something I never would have believed about her, but I couldn't refute it now because it was taking over me. Wasn't doing this to her a betrayal? She went to great lengths to conceal her true feeling to us all and I was completely disregarding whatever her reasons for doing so.

But then Gemma looked at him.

Still and pale, lifeless and cold.

He was lying in the bed and the only light in the room was from the full moon, which shone brightly through the open windows. Even in the dim lighting I could make out everything. Gemma's eyesight must be like a cat's. Clearly, I was seeing the night Gemma pulled Cole out of hell, the night Beelzebub hurt him just to make me watch.

I'm not going to be enough. He's going to die and I'm going to lose him. Gemma stood over my brother's injured body and I felt the cool tear slide down her cheek. He was shirtless with a white sheet pulled to his waist. The dagger that had been buried in his stomach was gone and the wound was closed. It was raised and red, but it wasn't gaping and bleeding like I imagined. There were angry bite marks along his arms and shoulders and I could see the edge of one that wrapped around the back of his neck. His ribs were purple and swollen as well and I struggled to think of how that injury might have happened. But my thoughts were fleeting as Gemma's took over.

She kneeled beside the bed and lifted her hands to hover over his body. She took a deep, steadying breath and tried to gather as much energy as she could and will it through her arms and into her palms. *Please be enough,* she thought. I felt the warmth flow through her body, her strength push outward toward my brother. The feeling was incredible. It was like a whirlpool inside me that flowed out through my hands and wrapped around Cole's body. The heat was intense, but it wasn't burning. It was healing and soft.

Gemma's energy began to fade away and her hands began to shake, but still she gave. She reached down into herself and found the last of her energy and sent it out over him. Finally, her hands fell to the mattress and she lifted her head to see if what she had done worked.

This hadn't been the first time tonight she had healed him. The first had been when she pulled him through the portal. Then he had gone running back to the fountain, trying to get to me, and broke his ribs.

Gemma inspected his body where the injuries were and she was satisfied to see the dagger wound even smaller and less red than before. The bite marks on his arms were still there, but they no longer oozed and looked painful. The bruises on his ribs were gone and his skin was smooth and pale once again. She frowned. He was still too pale and he was still unconscious.

She stood and went to her bag, which lay on the floor near the window, to pull out a jar of salve. She sat it next to a bowl of steaming water on the nightstand and picked up the already dampened rag. Once it was rung out, she used it to wipe his brow and face. Slowly, gently she moved down to his arms and neck, paying close attention to his wounds. When she was finished she replaced the rag and began smoothing the salve over the demon bites. She knew the healings had worked and he wouldn't be in pain, but this eased her ache. It was something she could do while waiting for the turmoil inside her chest to release the death grip it had on her heart.

She'd almost lost him tonight. He was angry with her for pulling him out of hell like that. He had screamed at her when they were free. In his fit of anger, he'd asked her why she bothered to pull him out. Why not just let him die so they would both be free?

The thought of him dying was like a knife to her heart. She loved him. She loved him more than she had ever loved anyone, including Callum. And that was what was so scary. She had given up everything for Callum—her home, her friends, her purpose in life… her beautiful white wings. And now she had nothing left to give.

Callum had taken it all and then died… died because he made a deal he couldn't get out of.

What did she have left to offer Cole?

She knew he was hurting and she was the cause. What choice did she have? If she told him how she really felt then she would be taking everything from him too. At first, she was relieved he was a Supernal Being. It meant he had an advantage over being just a human. It meant maybe they had a chance at real, lasting love, that even after he died they could still be together. For one perfect moment she actually felt happy.

But then she remembered.

If she were to become involved with Cole, she would be putting his soul in danger. She would be gambling with his eternal life.

As a Supernal Being, he would keep his body forever, even after he died, but he would live in heaven. A place she was no longer welcome. Cole could be punished, stripped of his status—*of his body*—when he went to heaven. As a fallen angel, she was tainted… and Cole loving someone who was tossed out of heaven would taint him too.

She should have left before it got this far, but she couldn't do that either. Before she met Cole, she gave her word to me and Sam. I reminded her so much of herself, of who she used to be. I was so in love and didn't care about what it cost me. I was a strong girl. Even when I thought I was weak, I wasn't. My path had been set, but I veered and instead of accepting that I might be compromised, I changed my direction. I made up my mind to change what I could from the place I was in.

In Gemma's mind, that was true goodness.

And Sam… she smiled softly. He might be a hellhound, but there isn't one evil place lurking inside him. From the minute she sold him that bracelet, she knew he was inherently good. She'd never met another hellhound who could so easily turn his back on the bad qualities of a hellhound yet still use its powers to his advantage. Not even Callum had done that. She had hoped Riley would be that way… but the curse tainted him, made it harder for him to accept goodness.

How could she leave me and Sam in this mess without helping? She had knowledge and skill that we needed. Sam was a ferocious fighter and determined man, but he needed training so she offered. It was the first time in over a decade she had stayed in the same place for more than a week.

Cole made a soft sound and her focus went to him. His chest was rising and falling with ease and she laid her palm against his bare skin. His heart beat steadily against her palm and she closed her eyes. So few times she allowed herself to touch him, to really feel him. Sometimes at night she lay awake and thought of the way his lips had felt against hers… His kiss had been devastating.

If she hadn't already lost her wings, then she would have given them up for another chance to kiss him like that.

Her hand began to travel over his skin. It was warming and the color was beginning to return. Her fingers went gently over his abs that were taunt and defined. He'd always been muscular, but all the training had made him more so. He had a sprinkling of black hair across his chest and her fingers teased the strands. Next, her hand went to his shoulder and slid lightly down his arm and over his corded bicep. When her fingers reached his palm, his hand tightened around hers for the briefest of seconds before going lax against the mattress.

She pulled her hand away quickly, thinking she'd been caught in her perusal of his body. But he was still out, his dark eyelashes casting shadows over his face. Unable to resist, she let her fingers trace the strong brow above his eyes and trail slowly over his cheek to rest at his soft, full lips. She yearned to kiss him again, but she was afraid if she did what was left of her strength would be lost.

She didn't have anything to lose, but he did. She couldn't ask him to give it all up for her. They might share something wonderful for many years while he was alive, but once he died he would lose his body and his status and she would be alone once more.

She should walk away now. She turned to look at the open window, the curtains floating in the breeze. *You could go right now and never come back. They would forget you.*

She turned back and lowered her forehead to the mattress. Should she go? She could watch from afar just to be sure they would all be okay and then leave. Cole would heal and Sam and I were strong enough now to take care of ourselves. And Riley… She'd burned that bridge a long time ago. Fresh tears gathered in her eyes and she let them stain the sheets. Something brushed against the top of her head and she lifted it to look at Cole.

His eyes were open. She'd never seen anything that blue except in heaven. He cupped her cheek with his callused palm and before she could stop herself she pushed herself closer.

"You healed me," Cole whispered.

"I was afraid it wouldn't be enough."

"It's exhausted you." He brushed the pad of his thumb beneath her eyes where there were probably dark circles.

"Are you in pain?"

He shook his head. "But you are. Tell me why."

"I should go." She pulled away, gently, remorsefully, and felt bereft from his touch.

He moved so fast she hadn't seen it coming. Her exhaustion made her slow and the thought of leaving made her careless. He grabbed her around the waist and pulled her backward, the two of them landing on the bed with his body breaking the fall.

She tried to get up, but his arms clamped around her like vices and she didn't have the strength to pull away. She didn't want to.

"You gave up too much of yourself to heal me," he whispered. "Let me give you something in return."

"I can't." She was embarrassed that her voice broke.

He rolled them over. His body was heavy, pressing her into the mattress. He didn't try and support his weight on his arms. He knew she could take his weight and she loved the fact that he gave it to her. Before she could say another word, his lips were on hers and what little restraint she had melted away.

He kissed her softly at first, his mouth meeting hers in the briefest kiss before pulling back to look into her eyes. Then he did it again, testing her will. She had none left and she buried her hands in the dark softness at the back of his head. He groaned and kissed her deeper, his teeth grazing her bottom lip before smoothing his tongue over the same spot.

His body moved against hers and she relished the feeling. His hand traveled down her side and back up, his fingers splaying out over her neck as he kissed her with an intensity that she never felt before. Everything inside her urged her to get closer, that it wasn't enough. When he found the hem of her T-shirt and tried to drag it over her head, she gasped.

He paused in kissing her to look into her eyes.

"You're thinking too much," he murmured and pressed kisses to each of her eyelids.

But she had to think. Someone had to. If she loved him as much as she knew she did, then she couldn't let him do this. If they slept together right now, then all would be lost and she would never be able to walk away.

She put her hands on his shoulders and made like she was going to pull him closer, but then she pushed him away and slid out of the bed.

"Gemma," Cole said. Hurt and desire laced his voice.

"You need food. Something hot that will replenish your body."

"I'm not hungry for food," he growled, reaching for her.

"I'll go get you some and be back. You need to rest." She rushed to the window as her body screamed to get back in the bed.

"Why are you doing this to me?" She heard him whisper as she went out into the night.

When she hit the ground, she stood there for a moment with her eyes closed and body trembling. "I don't know what else to do," she whispered into the night. Then she forced herself away from the house and denied herself the pleasure of looking back.

I gasped and fell backward, the railing of the steps stopping my fall. Gemma's eyes narrowed as she watched.

"What did you just do?" She demanded.

I took a deep breath, struggling to push away her strong feelings. "You really love him."

She jerked like I slapped her and folded her arms across her chest. "You were in my head?"

I nodded and gave her a very brief explanation of what I could do. I made sure to leave out the part about Cole asking me to do this.

"Those were my private thoughts." Her face actually flushed. "You had no right."

"I had to know if you loved him." I pushed away from the railing and stood tall. "He's my brother. I can't stand to watch him hurt."

Her shoulders slumped. "You can't tell him."

"Why not?"

"Because he'll throw it all away to be with me. He can't do that. He has no grasp on what eternity really means, of how long it is."

I shrugged, pretending it didn't bother me. "If that's his choice…" I let my words fall away.

"You would let him give it up, then?" Gemma asked not unkindly.

I sighed. "I don't know." Gemma looked triumphant so I added, "But I think he should get a say in how he spends eternity."

"I could leave right now and never come back." Gemma warned.

The idea hurt me. She cared about us all. I hadn't understood just how much until I felt it—heard it—in her own words. Cole wouldn't be the only one to miss her. I would too. Sam would.

"We all feel the same, me especially," I said.

"What?"

"The way you feel about us, we feel the same about you. You're family."

She didn't seem to know how to react to that.

"You could go, but we'd still feel the same way."

"He would be better off."

I shrugged. "Maybe. What about you?"

"I don't matter," she said quickly.

"I think you do," I said, stepping closer. "You deserve to be happy too. I think you belong here just as much as the rest of us."

Gemma just stared at me with her wide, unblinking gray eyes.

"Look, I don't know what's going to happen between you and Cole. That's for you two to work out. He isn't the only reason I want you here. My mother's soul is trapped in hell. I'm going to need all the help I can get to set her free— to set all of them free."

As I spoke, an idea, a purpose, filled me. "If we could find and set all the souls free, we would diminish hell's power; we would diminish Beelzebub's power."

Gemma nodded. "And all those poor tortured souls would be free."

I grabbed her wrist. "Oh my God, Gemma. I think I just realized what I have been meant to do all along."

Gemma smiled. "I don't want to, but I like you, Heven."

"I like you too." I smiled

Gemma shook her head and started to walk by me, assuming the conversation was over. It wasn't.

"You keep saying you have nothing," I said softly, but she heard because she stopped in her tracks. "But that is so far from the truth. You have everything. My brother loves you. I've never seen him this way about anyone before. And you have me… me and Sam, who consider you family. Please don't take that away from Sam. His parents turned him out; they pushed him away. Please don't take away the family that he's finally found. Even Riley cares about you." Gemma snorted and I held up my hand. "You know as well as I do that Riley is meanest to those he cares about most. He's afraid to get hurt."

"I'll think about it," Gemma said and went to the door. I knew I won her over when she looked over her shoulder and said, "I can't promise anything about Cole. There's too much at stake and I love him too much to take away his eternity."

"Tell him that. You owe him at least that much."

She didn't seem convinced, but I let her go. I was tired and dropped down onto the step for a moment of rest. I had found the answer my brother was looking for, but I was very afraid it wasn't going to be the answer he wanted.

I had also found my purpose.

Chapter Twenty-Two

Heven

"Oomph." Riley jerked from his sound sleep when I hit him with a pillow.

"Get up," I ordered. Part of me was even surprised he hadn't left. According to everyone, Riley only cared about himself. Riley was cursed; he had a mean and angry streak inside him. Sam was convinced he was only here because he wanted something, because being here would somehow get him what he wanted.

I hadn't believed any of them.

But I was starting to.

Ever since I saw Riley's reaction to the things Gemma was saying and how he seemed to enjoy killing the demons, I began to doubt him. And then he picked a fight with my brother. I never denied Riley had a mean streak, that he had done some very bad things and not shown an ounce of remorse. But I never really thought he was bad—evil. I caught glimpses (as fleeting as they might be) of another side to him. A softer side—a nicer side.

Two sides of the same coin. The words Airis spoke the last time I saw her floated through my mind. They jolted me. And just like that, I understood why I liked Riley, why I never wanted to believe the worst in him.

Because he was just like me.

We were both one person, a whole body, but there were two sides to us. The side that was connected to darkness and the side that fought that darkness. I was better at fighting that darkness—maybe because I wasn't entirely sure how I was connected to it. But Riley, he knew. He was cursed. He was a hellhound and he was indebted, thanks to his grandfather, to someone who would ask him to do heinous acts. But there was that good side to Riley—that light. But I think he sometimes forgot it was there.

"What are you staring at?" Riley demanded, his eyes narrowing.

I shook myself, not wanting to give away what I was about to do. "Sorry, I'm still not feeling that well." That, at least, wasn't a lie. It was getting harder and harder to calm that beast living inside me. It was only a matter of time until it shredded my insides. I needed a way to get it out.

But first I wanted answers.

"Where is Sam?" Riley asked.

"He had somewhere he had to be."

"While the cat's away the mice will play?" Riley took a prowling step toward me. I did not back up. "Hmmmm?"

"Something like that," I said as he stepped closer. "I wanted to talk without Sam around for you to fight with."

Riley shrugged. "You can't blame the guy for being jealous."

"You are so arrogant." I rolled my eyes and smiled.

"You like it." Riley leaned forward.

I shrugged. "Maybe."

Riley's eyes narrowed. "I know damn well you didn't suddenly decide to ditch the love of your life. Tell me what you want to talk about."

It was now or never. I reached out and grabbed onto his wrist. "I want to know what you're hiding," I asked, my eyes locking on his, which flared silver before widening with guilt.

And that's when I saw his answer.

Sam

I stripped off my shirt and dropped it on the ground. It was soon joined by my shorts, shoes and socks. I stood there, at the edge of the woods in the deepest cover of night, staring out over the inky dark lake. There was a breeze that moved the water; it rushed toward me, lapping at the bank, almost calling to me, begging me to come in.

I wasn't scared. Very few things scared me anymore. At the top of the list was death. But not my death. Death of those I loved. I could pretty much take anything as long as I knew the people I loved more than myself would still be there.

Which is one of the reasons I was here, at this lakeside at night. I had someone to set free. There was a group of loved ones who mourned because they didn't know if the person they loved was safe.

I tossed my boxers with the rest of my clothes and then I dove into the water. Icy liquid rushed over my skin, but I wasn't cold. My eyes blinked, adjusting to the darkness, and a line of bubbles floated from my mouth. I wouldn't need to breathe down here. I began pushing my arms and legs through the heavy water, remembering exactly where I needed to go.

I wouldn't ever forget this place. The place where I hid a body.

It didn't take long to find her. Or rather, what was left of her.

Andi. It seemed important to remember her name, to give her that respect of identity, because to my shock, there really wasn't any physical identity left to her.

I will help you. I told her as I treaded water just over where she lay.

She wasn't in good shape. I hadn't given much thought to what she would look like. I'd been so focused on setting her free. But now reality was sinking in. It was probably good that I didn't need to breathe right now, because I probably wouldn't have been able to anyway. Being sentenced to a dark, watery grave hadn't been kind.

When I first left her here, I had wrapped the vegetation growing from the lake floor around her ankle, securing her body to the bottom. But those plants were not what held her here anymore. No, she was basically reduced to a pile of bones that lay partially concealed by the plants and matter of the lake bottom. Her skin was no longer covering her bones, but I did note there were some patches here and there. Those patches were being slowly eaten away by hungry fish.

Her clothes were nowhere in sight and most likely had been carried away by the current. I realized there was really nothing left to identify her by… except her teeth.

It was a gruesome sight. I thought of all the movies and shows on TV that portrayed dying and death as something that wasn't ugly and scary—but it was. It was horrible and stomach turning.

I wanted to shut my eyes, but I didn't. I needed to see what I had done. This girl, once full of life and beauty, was a girl still missed and loved by many. She had done nothing wrong, but I punished her by trapping her down here, essentially making me no better than Beelzebub.

I hadn't chained up her soul, but I had chained her body to the floor of the lake.

I wanted to make it right. I shook my head. There was no making this right, but I could at least, hopefully, bring some peace to the people involved.

I swam closer to her remains and reached out to take her hand, to lift her body up, but her hand was gone. The bones from the wrist down were missing. I looked at her other arm and that hand was still intact.

I realized then that I couldn't just grab her body and pull her to shore. There wasn't much left holding the bones together. Her body would break apart and pieces of her would be lost.

God forgive me.

It seemed like an even worse crime to disturb her further. It seemed disrespectful somehow to break apart her body, to drag her to shore, all because I wanted to feel better about what I had done. There was no feeling better. There was no way to make this go away. Yes, I wanted her family to know peace, but dragging her bones to shore suddenly felt like it would only make things worse.

I didn't know what to do.

Slowly, I sank back into the depths of the lake and swam away, leaving her body where it lay. Once back on shore, I dried and dressed, still pondering what I should do. I needed to do something. I pulled out the disposable cell phone that I bought on the way here and I dialed.

"9-1-1. What's your emergency?"

"I-I've found a body in the lake," I said, using my palm to cover up the end of the phone.

"Where is your location?"

I quickly gave the location and then I hung up the phone and wiped my fingerprints away with my towel. It was easy to crush it in my grip. Then I opened the towel and let the many pieces fall into the water and slowly sink from sight.

I didn't know what the police would say when Andi was found or even if they would find her. I only hoped they would and that it brought some peace to her family. China and her stupid quest for that scroll. The scroll that I had foolishly helped look for.

I made my way through the forest toward where I parked. It was a long walk because I didn't want my truck to be too close to where I would be. As I walked, I remembered, I thought…

I realized.

Riley once practically admitted that he knew what China was looking for. He once practically told me he wanted it too. Heven told him that she had it when she found him… *That* was the reason he had come back.

Pain seared through my middle, causing me to double over and gag into the grass. The hound in me began to fight and I gave in, changing right there on the forest floor. *Heven.* That thing inside her was riled up. Something was setting it off.

I had a feeling I knew exactly who it was.

Heven

I was sucked into his memory—his confession—hard and fast. I almost jerked back because of the brutality of it, but I held strong. This would be the only shot I had to get into Riley's head. I shied away from thinking about what Riley would do to me when he realized what I had done.

I blinked, focusing, not on what I saw, but what he did. Because I asked him what I wanted to know, the answer—the thoughts—were in his mind for me to see.

He was standing outside, on a dock. The ocean was rough that night and the moon was the color of blood and it reflected right off the water, giving everything the shade of death. He was angry, beyond anger… to the point of shaking. He wanted to shift, to morph into the strong hellhound that he was and rip *him* from limb to limb.

But he couldn't.

He wasn't sure what was worse… his body unable to shift because of some stupid amulet or the knowledge that even if he could, he wouldn't be able to kill him.

The invisible bonds of a curse, a curse he was born with, were heavy. He felt them every single day. They might be concealed to everyone around him, but to him, some days they were all he could see. Even when he tried to ignore them, he felt their pressure; he felt them squeeze. It was as if they wanted to wring out every last drop of humanity he had so he would become an empty shell—a robot. A controllable being.

But Riley would never allow himself to be controlled.

So he turned himself hard—cold. He learned how to turn off his emotion so he didn't have to feel and he did things… just enough to keep the evil at bay… to keep *him* satisfied.

But this time *he* wanted more.

He watched the dark surf turned red from the moon. He watched as it lapped against the dock, coming in rougher and rougher with each passing moment. And then there was the wave… It crested high, it rolled closer with a threatening roar and just when he thought it was going to crash overhead, it split in two and out stepped his controller… his puppeteer.

Beelzebub.

He stepped onto the dock and the wave dissolved and the ocean went back to what it was before, erasing all evidence of his dramatic entrance.

"You've been hiding from me," he intoned.

"If I had been hiding, you wouldn't have found me."

"Don't talk to me that way!" he screamed. It was basically his natural tone.

Riley resisted the urge to laugh. He wouldn't kill him. Not today anyway. He wanted something. As long as Riley was useful, he would remain alive.

"What do you want?" he asked, like he was bored.

"I want the Treasure Map," Beelzebub snarled. "Something you failed to deliver the last time I sent you looking."

"That's because you put a woman in charge. She was too busy killing people and trying to prove herself to you to actually do what you wanted."

"Then you should've killed her!" he roared.

"Didn't have to." For once, someone else did the dirty work.

"You underestimated that boy… the young one. He's the one who has my Map!"

Riley tried not to react. But this was an interesting turn of events. "Who?"

"You know who! The young hellhound, the one with the girl. The girl who is mine!"

So he staked a claim on the girl and Sam had the Map? That kid was as good as dead.

So why don't you take it from him?"

"I have contained him. But the girl… she's been a problem. She hides it and she wears a key that only she can use to open the scroll."

Riley wasn't sure what it meant that Sam had been "contained," but he didn't bother to ask. "What does this have to do with me?"

"Go there. Entrust yourself to the girl. Steal the scroll."

"No.

"What did you say to me?!" he screeched.

He didn't bother to repeat the word; he heard just fine.

"Need I remind you that you are bound to do my bidding?"

Anger and rage swirled inside Riley. He was tired of doing his bidding. Before he was even born, his grandfather bargained away his life for a woman.

"Maybe you need a reminder of my power? A vision of what could befall you?"

Riley yawned.

He heard a struggle behind him and he turned. Casey was being brought across the dock, two demons practically dragging him as he fought. He could see the sweat upon his forehead and the tremor in his muscles. He looked at Riley, confusion clear in his eyes. He couldn't change and didn't know why. His body was weakened by a force he couldn't see and he was scared.

Part of Riley felt bad for him, but the other part was already detaching from the unfolding scene.

"Riley," Casey called, relief in his voice. Until he looked past me at Beelzebub.

"Agree to my terms," Beelzebub said, spreading his hands wide like he was offering me a deal.

"No."

Just like that, Casey was tossed into the sea. Riley saw the fins circling, stalking. Then he heard his screams as the sharks began to bite. Before they could make him their dinner, Casey's body was lifted out of the water, his blood dripping, drop by drop, and mixing with the blood moon's rays.

He looked at Riley, half unconscious, and mouthed the words "help me."

He looked away.

Then out of the sea, a swarm of flies rose, like a swarming army of death, and they covered Casey's body, every single inch of him until Riley could no longer see his stare.

He screamed.

And screamed.

And screamed.

Then the flies carried him into the ocean, where the water once again buried the secret of his death.

"Get me that scroll, or this awaits you, only your death will linger…"

Riley stared at Beelzebub, Lord of Flies, Prince of Demons, and knew true hate. He wasn't really sure if he hated him or himself. Beelzebub's eyes narrowed and his lips curved, and Riley turned away.

"If you get me the scroll, I will release you from the curse."

Riley turned back.

He smiled a toothy smile of perfectly straight, white teeth. "No more visits like this, no more chores, no more killing, no more bidding. You will be free."

Riley knew he shouldn't make a deal with him. It's how his grandfather died; it's how he was born cursed. But even just the thought of freedom…

He made the deal.

I felt my body slam up against the wall and my head snapped back. My eyes struggled to focus and I looked up at blazing silver.

"What the hell did you just do to me?"

"It was you." I gasped. "You took the scroll."

"Were you in my head?" Riley asked, his voice low and mean.

"I trusted you."

"What did you see?"

Images of flies and sharks swam before my eyes. "I saw Casey."

Riley's eyes actually lost some heat at the mention of his dead roommate. Maybe he felt bad about that, after all. But then I remembered how he just looked away when Casey asked for help.

"How?" I asked, straightening from the wall. "How did you get the scroll?"

"It doesn't matter."

"Yes, it does," I said, determined, and stepped toward him with my hand out. He slapped it away like it was a live wire.

"Don't touch me."

"What else are you hiding?"

"Deep, dark secrets," he intoned.

"Tell me right now, you bastard."

"Ooohhh, now she's really getting angry."

I caught him off guard when I slapped him across the face. He was shocked I would dare try to touch him so soon after he told me not to. I was pleased to see a red handprint blossom across his cheek. He growled and lifted his clenched fist like he might strike me, but then he stopped.

"It was that day… the day I killed Colin, wasn't it? Everything in my bag spilled and you took it when I passed out."

"Bravo."

"You took advantage of me."

"I cleaned up your mess. If it wasn't for me, you'd be in jail."

That didn't make what he did okay. "How did you get it open? How?"

He smirked. "You wore that stupid key around your neck." He shook his head at my stupidity. "While you were sprawled on the ground, with Colin's blood soaking your clothes, I wrapped your hand around the key and inserted it in the top of the scroll. And just like that, it opened."

He hadn't touched me, yet I felt like I had been slapped in the face. How stupid and silly I had been. I knew wearing that key was a bad idea. Sam told me again and again not to keep the scroll and the key together. And I hadn't. But then Sam was trapped and I wanted a piece of him with me. He gave me that key. It was supposed to be a symbol of his love for me. Had Airis been right? Had I been so blind to everything around me that I saw nothing at all?

"Do you realize what you've done? Do you realize what you cost me, everyone that I love and every single name on that list?"

Riley shrugged.

"I trusted you. I *liked* you. Everyone told me not to and I stood up for you. My mother is dead because I no longer have something that Beelzebub wanted. He dragged her soul to hell—she'll never know peace. Sam was beaten— whipped—because of that scroll, and you stand there and shrug?!"

"I told you not to trust me."

I laughed. I laughed so hard. And then I doubled over in agony and cried out. The beast inside me liked all my rage and pain. I was too worked up and now it wanted to play. It wanted out. I felt the fresh searing pain of a claw mark on my back and another on the back of my arm. I cried out, reaching out to steady myself against the wall. The beast surged forward and I fell onto my knees, gagging, trying not to throw up. I tasted something metallic in the back of my throat and gagged some more. Riley knelt beside me and reached out a hand.

"Don't you dare touch me."

"Calm down," he said, his voice actually holding a hint of concern.

I laughed. It was a bubbly sound, and then I coughed, blood coming out onto my hand. "What do you care? You got what you wanted."

Riley said nothing.

I looked up. "But you didn't, did you?" He looked away and I knew I was right. "Beelzebub told you he would break the curse and when you delivered the scroll to him, he laughed, didn't he? You're still bound to him."

Anger lit his eyes… but there was also pain.

"How does it feel, Riley? You betrayed me, someone who actually cared about you, for nothing." I coughed again and more blood splattered my hand.

"Come on." Riley put his arm around my waist and lifted me off the ground. I stifled the cry of pain as another claw mark seared my insides.

The door opened and Logan came running into the room behind us. "Heven? What's he doing here? What's wrong?"

He caught sight of the blood on my hands and cheek and he launched himself at Riley, leaping on his back and punching him in the head. "Logan! No!" I cried.

He was so fragile. One strong hit from Riley would break him… and he might never recover.

Riley's eyes flared silver as he reached around to pull Logan off his back. I went forward, inserting myself between them as Riley pushed out to shove Logan away. Thankfully, Logan landed on the bed.

I hit the wall and slid to the floor.

It was that moment that Sam came through the window.

I was on the ground, against the wall, with blood on my hands and cheek and Logan was on the bed while Riley stood, heaving, in the center of the room with eyes of pure silver.

Sam flew across the room and grabbed Riley by the throat and dragged him to the window, tossing him out into the night. Then he leaped out after him.

The angry sounds of snarling and snapping teeth filled my ears. I looked at Logan. Logan looked at me.

Gran drove up the driveway as two very large, black hellhounds disappeared into the night.

Chapter Twenty-Three

Sam

I found it ironic that I had been out trying to make up for a death and now here I was about to kill someone.

Vivid pictures of Heven lying on the floor with blood on her skin and Logan's frail body lying across the bed while Riley stood there, his eyes sparking with silver flame, enraged me further and further. He was worse than I thought.

I didn't have to be told that he stole that scroll from Heven. I didn't need to be reminded of the curse that made him act inhuman, because it was no excuse. I let this guy go before; I settled for running him out of town once.

No. More.

He charged at me and I threw him off again, this time sending him flying out of my sight. I knew he was still in the orchard because I heard the tree break so I followed the sound. He was still lying on the ground, changed into his human form. Blood was on his face, but that gave me no satisfaction; it only served to anger me more.

I reached down and grabbed a handful of his hair and pulled him up, about to deliver yet another blow when his words stopped me.

"She still has something he wants."

"What?" I twisted the hand that was in his hair. I hoped it hurt.

"He wants the name. He thinks she knows it."

"What name?" I was interested now because I had heard Beelzebub demand a name from Heven. I pulled Riley up to his feet, but kept hold of his arm. He wasn't running off. If he had info, I was getting it. Now.

"A piece of the scroll was missing. He wants the name of the Soul Reaper. He thinks she knows it." I didn't want to believe him—but I had to. Snippets of the conversation I heard between Beelzebub and Hecate came back to me. Hecate telling him that "the girl" looked at it before it was destroyed. Then I remembered Beelzebub demanding a name from Heven, a name she couldn't give him… It was the reason he put that damn beast inside of her.

"What's a Soul Reaper?"

"I don't know."

"If you think this information will buy you your life…"

Riley laughed. "Kill me, go ahead. I welcome death—the freedom. Any death you give me will be far easier than what he gives me."

I pushed him away, sickened.

"What's the matter? Don't want to kill me now because I want you to? Did I take away your fun?"

"You stayed around," I said, measuring him. "After you took the Map, you stayed around. Why?"

"Because I promised Heven I would get you out of hell."

"You had the scroll before I was set free?"

He nodded.

"It was you I heard talking with Beelzebub that day. He threatened you."

"That was one of his nicer threats," Riley said and smirked.

"So why stick around? Why go to hell with Heven?"

"Because I told her I would."

I scrutinized him for long moments. I knew this guy was a good liar, but hell if I didn't believe what he was saying. "You like Heven."

Riley said nothing; he gave no reaction at all.

That was answer enough for me. "What I just saw back there..."

"Was what it looked like. I was attacked. I was defending myself."

I punched him in the face.

"If you ever touch her again, I will kill you."

I walked away, every muscle in my body screaming for me to go back and hit him just one more time.

"He won't stop until he gets a name!" Riley yelled behind me.

Once again, I believed him.

Heven

I was getting very good at looking like everything was normal when in actuality, everything around me was in chaos. Logan was good at pretending he hadn't just watched his brother throw Riley out the window and then rush off into the night. I cleaned the blood off my face and hands and changed into some loose pajamas that covered all the claw marks on my skin. When Gran came up the stairs, we were sitting in his room, watching a movie. She went back downstairs for some chamomile tea and cookies, and we both let out a collective breath.

"Do you think Sam is okay?" Logan asked, looking at his window.

"I really do. He'll be back in a few minutes, I'm sure."

"He's been through a lot."

"Yeah, he has. He's a strong person."

"I want to be like him."

I smiled. "You're on your way. I think you're a lot like Sam."

He widened his eyes, but then he looked away.

"Is something bothering you, Logan? I mean, besides the fact Sam and Riley are out there probably fighting?" I glanced at the window and hoped Sam would return soon. I wasn't worried about him getting hurt. Riley was strong and mean, but he was no match for Sam—especially as angry as Sam probably was right now. Inside I cringed because it really hadn't been what it looked like—Riley wasn't trying to hurt us, physically anyway. I still couldn't believe he took the scroll. That he used me like that. I had trusted him. The betrayal had a heavy sting.

"I have to tell you something," Logan whispered

"Sure."

Logan took a deep breath. "I'm the one who hit your mother. I'm the reason she went to the hospital. I'm the reason she's dead." He hunched his shoulders, shame and sorrow radiating off him.

"You… I thought you found her after she hit her head?" My head was spinning.

Logan shook his head and swiped at his face, looking up. "The demon in me took over. He made me do it… When I came to, I was standing over her body with the pitcher in my hands." His face fell with his admission.

"Oh." I sat there for a second and then I reached out and took Logan's hand. "You know it really wasn't you. It was the demon inside you."

"But it was using my body, using me, and now your mother is dead. Maybe if I had been stronger I wouldn't have done what it wanted."

"I don't think you're the reason my mother is dead, Logan. You did hit her, send her to the hospital, but all the doctors thought she would wake up. It wasn't an injury that should have caused her to die. You weren't responsible for her death. Beelzebub was."

"What do you mean?"

I told him about the letter and how Beelzebub probably manipulated her.

"I hate him!" Logan said when I finished.

"I pretty much feel the same way." I half smiled. "I wish you would've come to me sooner with this. You've been feeling guilty all this time for no reason. I don't blame you."

"But I hit her."

I grabbed his wrists and he looked up. "And I forgive you. We all do things we don't mean."

I was shocked when Logan hugged me. It was a tight, quick hug, but it was real. I hugged him back, grimacing at how thin he was and at the pain of being hugged where there were fresh claw marks.

"How about some of those cookies Gran went downstairs for? I'm starving."

He glanced back at the window. "What about Sam?"

"He's probably starving too. We can make a plate for him."

Logan laughed. "Okay." He got up from the bed and we made our way into the hall.

When we passed my bedroom, the door opened a crack and Sam's eye peaked out. Logan was already on the stairs and I called down to him, "I'll be right there. I'm going to grab a sweater."

I hurried into my room and closed the door. "Sam, are you okay? That wasn't what it looked like."

"Are you okay?" He demanded, his breathing fast as his eyes swept over me, looking for blood and injury.

"I'm fine. I promise."

Sam was still pretty keyed up and he paced back and forth by the window. "Riley took the scroll, Hev." He pushed a hand through his hair.

"I know." Sam paused to look at me. "I passed out after… after I killed Colin. That's when he took it."

Sam shook his head. "He was after that scroll back when China was looking for it."

"That long?" I gasped. "Why did he even leave town, then?"

Sam shrugged. "I guess he figured it wasn't here. He didn't know we found it…"

"Then Beelzebub told him," I murmured, remembering what I saw in Riley's mind. I looked up at Sam. "Did you hurt him?"

"I wanted to," Sam began. Then he came to stand directly in front of me. "Beelzebub thinks you have a name,

Heven, a name from the piece of the scroll that was destroyed."

"But why would he think that?" I remembered when he demanded I tell him the name of the Soul Reaper. I shuddered. That person sounded creepy.

"Because Hecate told him you read it before it was destroyed."

I had. My photographic memory stored that information in my brain automatically. But my photographic memory didn't work that way. Sure, the information was there, but I didn't know it. I would have to call the list up in my head and then look at it. "I might have seen that list, but I didn't really *see* it." I tried to explain to Sam.

"Could you recall the list, Heven? Could you see who is listed as this Soul Reaper?"

"Yes," I said, my voice hoarse. Then I looked up at Sam. "Beelzebub will not rest until I give him that name."

"Then give it to him."

"What?" I said, shocked. I looked up into his whiskey-colored eyes and noted he was quite serious. "I can't do that! I'll pretty much be sealing that person's death."

"If you don't, you'll be sealing *your* death," Sam said quietly.

"Maybe not," I said.

Sam let out a frustrated breath. "He put a beast inside you, Heven. If we don't get it out…" His words faded away until there was only silence between us.

"Airis told me every person on the Map was being protected now that Beelzebub read it. Maybe this Soul Reaper is safe."

"She told you that?"

I nodded. "Right before she told me I wouldn't see her again."

"What if we find the Soul Reaper, tell him Beelzebub is looking for him? The person assigned to protect him can get him somewhere safe where Beelzebub can't hurt him."

"That's a good idea," I said as a wave of dizziness swept over me. I felt a sudden longing for hell.

"But first we have to get that thing out of you."

"How?"

"Give Beelzebub a name. Make one up. Tell him something to get that thing out of you. Then he can go looking for someone who doesn't exist."

"But when he figures out I lied…" He would kill me. We were trying to avoid that.

"There has to be a way to take him out of the equation," Sam reasoned. "We can't kill him, but there has to be a way to stop him, to keep him away."

"What if we trapped him like he did you?"

Sam looked up. "It would have to be a strong trap."

I nodded. "We could find my mother and all the other stolen souls and set them free. Gemma says if we do that then a lot of the princes' power will be lost."

"So it would weaken Beelzebub?" Sam asked hopefully.

I smiled, real hope blooming in me. It was a good feeling. "I think this is what I was meant to do all along, Sam. We can't destroy hell, but we can take away a lot of its power."

"And then you would be safe." There was genuine relief and longing in his voice.

"We would all be safe," I corrected.

"Now all we need is a way to trap Beelzebub."

From the bottom of the stairs, Logan called my name. "We're supposed to have cookies."

Sam smiled. "I heard. Thank you for understanding, for forgiving him." He reached out and cupped my face in his palms. "You feel warm." He frowned.

"Logan is my family. Of course I would forgive him. I'm warm because I'm happy." I leaned up and kissed him.

I hoped the feeling lasted.

Chapter Twenty-Four

Heven

My feeling of happiness didn't last very long at all. I felt like death. And because I had already died once and come close to dying several other times, I could say this with absolute knowledge. If I didn't get this thing out of me soon, it was going to tear me apart from the inside out until I was nothing but a damaged shell.

Last night was so wonderful. We watched movies, ate cookies and drank soda. Sam and I held hands beneath the blanket and butterflies danced in my belly when he kissed me. It was everything we never got to have, and for the first time in forever I relaxed. I forgot about everything swirling around us and just focused on the present.

When I lay down to sleep, I wasn't feeling as great physically as I was mentally. Every time I closed my eyes visions of hell overwhelmed me. The back of my head began to squeeze and I was terribly afraid that meant Beelzebub was planning on terrifying me in my sleep. I thought that maybe since he unleashed this thing inside me, he would leave me alone.

I should have known better.

If I had been scared to sleep before (for fear that whatever was inside me would drag me back to its lair), I was downright terrified now. Because of our Mindbond, I couldn't fool Sam. He could feel my fear so I told him what was going on. He spent the rest of the night sitting vigilant, hunched over me while I lay huddled beneath the blankets, shaking in pain and forcing myself to stay awake.

Just before the sun started to rise, I began throwing up. I felt like the beast was using my stomach as a punching bag, and unfortunately, all the cookies and soda weren't welcome. After the fourth time of running into the bathroom, I didn't have the energy to walk back into my bedroom so instead, I lay on the cold tile floor and prayed it would stop. To make things worse, Sam couldn't be in the bathroom with me because Gran kept coming in to make sure I was okay.

I had to keep a blanket wrapped around me even though I was burning up because I was positive I had new claw marks on my skin. I hadn't yet looked, but I could feel them burning and stinging every time I moved. I was so exhausted from puking and lack of sleep that the hard floor began to feel comfortable and before I knew it, my eyes closed in surrender.

Hell was there waiting, calling out to me. It promised me relief from the pain. I found myself reaching out to it, wanting to be there. Then Beelzebub appeared, laughing.

"Give me the name."

I told myself to wake up. I tried to get away.

"Does it hurt much? How anxious is that beast to get out? I promise you that this is nothing yet; your torment will get worse."

I gasped as my eyes opened. The nightlight on the wall was bright and I squinted my eyes against it. I woke up. I got away. Then Sam was there, lifting me off the floor and carrying me back into my bedroom.

Gran will see you.

I don't care. I couldn't wait in your room anymore.

I fell asleep.

He looked at me sharply as he laid me gently on the bed. I gritted my teeth against the fresh stinging pain that stabbed through me. *Did you see him?*

Yes. He said the pain would only get worse.

Sam's mouth flattened as he tucked the blanket around me.

I'm so hot. I pushed the blanket away. Sam made an anguished sound and I followed his stare. Welts covered my arms and chest. Before I could say anything, Sam lifted the tank top I was wearing and looked at my stomach. I could tell by the look on his face there were marks there too.

You have bruises all over your body.

It wants out.

I'm going to get it out, sweetheart. I promise.

When the sun came up, I made him leave to do the barn chores. Just because I was sick didn't mean the horses had to starve. Besides, it was the perfect opportunity for him to 'arrive' and find out I was sick. Maybe Gran would finally allow him to come to my room.

I wasn't sure what time it was when he finally came through the bedroom door, but the sun was high in the sky. He showered and changed because he was dirty from the barn work and the ends of his hair were damp. I smiled when he brushed the hair back from my face and softly kissed my temple.

"How is she?" Gran fretted from behind.

Sam's eyes locked on mine. *I'm going to move you, sweetheart. It's the only way she'll let me in here.*

"I think I'm feeling a little better, Gran." I lied, trying to make my voice sound strong.

Sam lifted me up, holding me against his chest, and carried me downstairs to the couch. I held back the grimace when the fresh claw marks burned. *I'm so sorry, baby. I had to bring you down here. I have to be able to stay with you.*

It's okay. I'm fine and I want you to be here. Gran was very generous with the time she allowed Sam to spend here and all the meals he shared with us, but her rule about no boys (except for Cole because he's my brother) in my room was firm, and I guess not even me being sick was enough to sway her.

Sam was quick to pull the blanket up when it fell off my shoulder and exposed the ugly looking welts. I could see that he had brought some DVDs over to make Gran think we were going to watch movies until I was better.

Unfortunately, I wasn't going to get better. I was only getting worse.

I started coughing then, a wet kind of cough that shook my chest and brought something warm up past my throat. I put the blanket up to my mouth just as the blood came out.

Sam hunched over me, blocking me from sight and shaking like he might change. Quickly, I wiped the blood away and tucked the red stain beneath my chin. *I'm all right. Calm down.*

His eyes were wild and his pupils were dilated. His size seemed to swell before my eyes. A fleeting thought went through my mind, but then it was gone.

Sam will you get me some water?

The simple task seemed to center him, give him something he could do, and he nodded and went off to get the drink. It hurt to move, but I reached out with a trembling hand and grabbed Sam's cell phone that was lying on the coffee table. I quickly dialed Cole.

He picked up on the first ring. His hello was gruff.

"Cole, it's me." I stopped to cough again. "I'm not feeling so good and Sam is really freaking out. Could you—"

"I'll be right there."

"Bring Gemma," I told him and then the line went dead. I dropped the phone in my lap and willed the pain to stop.

Sam came back in carrying a large water bottle and a bottle of pain reliever. Gran came bustling in behind him so I forced myself to sit up and smile.

"How is your stomach feeling?" Gran asked, concerned.

I took the water Sam offered and forced myself to take a sip. It seemed to scrape down my throat. "I think it's getting better. I haven't thrown up in a few hours." Coughing up blood didn't count as throwing up, did it?

"Must just be some twenty-four hour bug," Gran nodded.

"I was thinking about some of that homemade chicken soup that you used to make me when I was little."

Gran's eyes lit up. Like Sam, giving her something to do made her feel better. "What a wonderful idea! It will fix you right up."

"It always did."

She frowned. "I don't have all the ingredients I need, though." She looked at Sam. "Will you sit with her while I go to the store to get what I need?"

"Of course," Sam said, picking up a DVD. "We'll watch a movie."

Gran kissed me on the cheek and I heard her moving around in the kitchen before calling out a good-bye and closing the door behind her. I let out a hard sigh and let myself rest back into the pillows. My whole body was shaking from the effort of sitting up.

"You're not as good as you let on," Sam said, looking at me.

"She's been coughing all morning," Logan said, coming down the stairs with a sullen look on his face.

I was saved from answering because Gemma came through the door. She came over to the couch and looked down, her gray eyes apprising me. She came around the couch and held out her hands above me. I knew she was going to try to heal me. I also knew it wouldn't work. But I let her do it anyway because even if I got only a little relief, it would be welcome.

I didn't get any relief and after several minutes, I told Gemma to stop trying. It was only making her tired. Cole arrived and stood over me, looking like he was waiting for me to die.

Gemma pulled out the books from her leather bag and dropped them on the table. "There has to be an answer in one of these," she said and began flipping pages. She knew the books like the back of her hand and she turned the pages with confidence, like she knew exactly where to find the answer.

Everyone began reading. Silence fell over the room. Another coughing spasm burned my lungs and blood filled my mouth. I ran to the bathroom and vomited more blood than I cared to see. Intense pain seared down my back and I collapsed on the floor. Then everything went dark.

* * *

I woke to the sound of arguing. Sam was holding me—clutching me—against his chest as he stared down Riley. They both looked down when I groaned.

"What's going on?" What was Riley doing here?

"Heven?" Cole said from somewhere off to the side. "Let me see her." I felt a tug against Sam and he turned so I could see Cole.

"Hey." He reached out to touch me and Sam jerked me away. Cole scowled at him but returned his attention to me. "You're in some rough shape, huh?"

"I'll be fine." I don't know why I even bothered to say that anymore.

"Can we go already?" Riley said.

"Meet us there," Sam told him. "If you make it through the portal, we'll ride with you then."

"I'm telling you it will work."

"Yeah, well, I'm not willing to risk her life on it! She's already half dead!" Sam roared. Everyone gasped in shock that he would say such a thing. Even he paused and looked down, shame in his eyes.

Don't worry about it, Sam. I know what's happening to me.

"We're going," Sam told everyone and took off running. I turned my head to see the fountain. We were in Portland and he was taking me through the portal into hell.

The knowledge actually relieved some part of me and I felt a small burst of energy. Maybe now the beast would stop pummeling my insides for a few moments. He went right through and landed smoothly on his feet, absorbing all of the impact. I looked up and saw his eyes were pure melted gold and I knew he was holding back the hellhound within.

"You can put me down," I offered.

He smiled. "Are you kidding? Did you see what Riley wanted to do? Who knows what's going to happen."

Sam turned as the portal opened up once more, looking like a large swirling black hole. Then I heard the sound of a revving engine and squealing tires. The portal seemed to widen and then all of a sudden a Jeep Wrangler burst through and came skidding over in front of us. Sam dashed backward as the Jeep jerked to a stop. Riley leaned out the window, which was unzipped, and grinned. "I told you it would work."

"You *drove* a Jeep into hell?" I asked, more alert than I had been the entire day.

"Walking around is boring," he quipped smartly, but when he met my gaze, his eyes were serious.

He came to help me. After everything, he still came. He could have left by now, should have, but he was here. That didn't make everything he had done right. I was still beyond mad, but I had to admit any help we got was better than none. Hopefully, he wouldn't betray us. Again. "Well, it definitely looks like something you would drive."

It was army green and had a scuffed-up tan soft top. The tires were huge and I knew if I wanted to ride in it, I would have to climb in. There were huge fog lights on the roll bar at the top and written across the windshield in green letters was: Eat My Dirt. It also had a very long antenna with one of those yellow smiley face balls at the top.

He gunned the engine. "Get in."

Sam seemed to have no trouble climbing into the Jeep while holding me. I didn't expect to see Gemma, Cole and Logan sitting in the back. Sam seemed surprised to see them too. In fact, he scowled.

"I'm not staying behind," Cole said tightly. "She's my sister."

"Fine," Sam spat coldly. "But I don't have time to watch your back. Heven comes first."

"Sam." I gasped. He didn't apologize; he barley even glanced at me.

"I can take care of myself," Cole snapped.

"Logan, you gotta go home," Sam said, seriously.

"I want to help. Sitting around isn't going to make me any better."

Sam scowled and was about to argue. "The kid stays," Riley burst out from the driver's seat. "We don't have time to get a Lucent Marble."

Sam swore, looked down at me and realized he was right. Riley hit the gas and tore off across the barren gray landscape.

"Where are we going?" I asked.

"I'm taking you to Ana. Hopefully, she'll know what to do. Maybe that flower will heal you."

"The flower may heal my injuries, but it won't get rid of the beast. It'll just tear up my body again."

"It'll at least buy us some time," Sam said, avoiding my gaze.

Or prolong my death. Did I really want to be healed just to go through this over and over again?

Depression seemed to settle over us and we rode in silence. I didn't know what to do, short of finding Hecate and begging her to get this thing out, but I knew it wouldn't do any good. Beelzebub wanted that name and he wanted me to suffer. I wondered how much more of his tirade we would have to bear before I succumbed.

I began to feel restless. The beast in me no longer seemed satisfied to be back in hell. It wanted something more. It seemed to take control of my weak body and I sat up to look out the window. "Stop the car," I told Riley. My voice didn't sound like my own.

"Are you crazy? We aren't anywhere near the island."

"I don't care."

He kept driving, ignoring my pleas to let me out.

"Heven, hold on. We're almost there," Sam said and tried to wrap his arms around my waist. I howled in pain and then grappled for the door handle, throwing open the door.

"Shit!" Riley yelled and slammed on the brakes. I jumped out, falling onto the ground, and lay there stunned for a few moments before the beast picked up my body and forced me to walk.

Sam was there, Riley too, and they both stared at me like I'd lost my mind. But I barely noticed because I had to get there. I had somewhere to be. Sam grabbed my arm and that horrible sound ripped from my throat, the sound that I recognized from when the beast had taken me to its lair. He didn't let go, only swung me to face him and grabbed my face in his hands.

"Heven," he implored, his molten eyes staring into mine. It was like a lightning storm of gold in his gaze. I knew he could sense the beast. It was so close to the surface. I wondered how he held himself back from attacking, from letting the hellhound in him out. His arms were shaking and his breathing was shallow, but he stood firm and never once dropped my gaze.

"You have to fight, sweetheart. Don't let this thing take over."

I nodded, the color of his eyes bringing a little bit of myself back to me. But that only angered the beast and he began an internal assault. I cried out and fell to my knees, blood pouring from my mouth.

Sam picked me up, supporting my weight alongside him.

"Please, let me go." I begged. "It's going to keep punishing me if you make me stay here."

Riley was there, pulling Sam back, telling me to go. Sam let him pull him back, but he kept his arms out to catch me if I fell. His jaw was locked and his eyes were hard.

"I'm so sorry," I whispered before turning and limping away.

I barely thought about the fact that I was walking toward my death.

Chapter Twenty-Five

Heven

I walked for what seemed like hours. They followed me, of course. Cole was in the driver's seat of the Jeep, at a nonthreatening distance away, while Sam and Riley walked just steps behind me, flanking me like two bodyguards.

I paid them no attention. I only knew that I had to walk, that I had to go home. When the huge free-standing caves came into view, that horrid sound ripped from my throat again, over and over until my throat went hoarse. When I got to the entrance of the biggest cave, my legs gave out and I sank to the ground.

Dark shadows surrounded me and I looked up to see the deformed bodies of the hellhounds coming out of their caves. I heard the sound of ripping fabric and I knew Sam and Riley were morphing. I could hear the idle of the Jeep's engine and was glad Logan, Cole and Gemma stayed in the car. The largest of the beasts put its nose down to smell me and then it made the same sound that I had made before.

So this was it. This was how I was going to die. I didn't have any strength left in me to fight. Frankly, death seemed like a relief. It wouldn't be for whom I was leaving behind, but I would welcome it. One of the beasts lunged and I covered my head with my hands, but it never made contact.

Sam intercepted the blow and an all-out war began raging around me. Sam and Riley were outnumbered by the things that lived in the caves. How long could they fight before they were taken down? I couldn't let them die for me. They weren't really saving me anyway because my death was sealed.

Sam, please stop. You can't save me.

He roared. It was ten times the sounds the other beasts made. I forced myself to sit up and watched in horror as Sam took down two of the beasts in one blow. He didn't even pause when he tore out their throats.

He had never looked so big. In fact, his size matched the overgrown size of the things he was fighting. I realized then that the anger and frustration he had been living with since being trapped was affecting his size. He was so enraged and distraught that he was swollen with it.

Riley was fighting with equal vigor. Violence came natural to him. He didn't have to be angry to fight like Sam; it's just the way he was. Although, not even his natural meanness matched what Sam was doing right now.

Suddenly, from out of the smallest cave darted another beast. It came right at me, its jaws open wide. I didn't have time to scream, but just as it lunged it fell out of the air, dropping at my feet.

Cole appeared over it and yanked the jewel-handled dagger out of the back of its neck. Then he lifted me in his arms and took me farther away from the fight, from the carnage. I knew Sam was okay because I could feel the adrenaline surging through his body and hear his roars that cut through the darkness. But what about Riley?

"Riley?" I said to Cole as he sat me on the ground. I shouldn't worry about him, but I did.

"He's fine."

Before I could say anything else, he ran off into the mix and began fighting. Gemma was in the mix too, having pulled out a bow and arrow. Tears filled my eyes. I didn't want to die. These people were fighting for me to live; they were risking their lives on the slim chance I survived.

I pushed myself to my feet, looking for the strength to do something, anything that would end the fighting, but then another one of those howls ripped out of me and I knew the strength I used wasn't mine. It was the beast's. A lone beast broke away and came rushing at me. Sam landed in front of me. All the midnight hair on his back rose as he made sounds that terrified even me.

The beast didn't back down, which only incensed the thing inside me. It began fighting and clawing, trying to rip through my skin to get out. I felt a warm trickle of something on my chest and I looked down. It had finally done it. It had pierced my skin, really gashed it open. Folds of skin lay against me as I bled what little blood I had left. It was only seconds away from tearing me open.

I love you, Sam.

Sam roared and took out the beast threatening me and then turned just as I fell onto the ground, unable to do anything but hurt. Dimly, I heard a new sound, a familiar sound, but I couldn't place it. Sam, still in hellhound form, stood over me, whining and licking my face.

Hold on, Heven. Please don't leave me like this.

I'll try.

Something loomed over us and I opened my eyes and tried to focus. It was The Devourer. He must have heard the fighting and come to help. Or maybe he sensed my death. At least I knew my friends, my love, would all be safe now. The Devourer came close, sniffing me. The hot breath that blew out of its nostrils brushed over me as my life slipped away.

Then something happened. It opened its mouth and started to suck…

NO! Sam roared and launched himself at the dragon, but Riley threw himself at Sam and knocked him away.

The dragon thought I was dead and he wanted what was left of my soul. I heard snarling and fighting beside me as everything began to fade and I felt an intense pulling on my chest like I never felt before. Before I knew it, something dark and cloudy flew out of my chest, right out of the huge gash that the beast made, and then everything felt better. I felt so much lighter. Relief washed over me and I saw a wonderful light, warm and welcoming.

Somewhere in the distance I heard yelling, begging, fighting. "Heven! Please, baby, no." *Don't do this to me again.*

The light looked so welcoming. Behind me there was so much pain and fear. The air was whirling around me, tugging me fast, inviting me closer, and for a moment I wanted to go there.

Then I turned my back.

The sucking stopped and everything fell still.

I lay on the hard, dirty ground and looked up into the eyes of The Devourer. His brightly colored feathers were a happy sight. "Thank you," I told him.

The Devourer had sucked that beast right out of me. It was gone. I was free. For one brief moment, I felt hope.

Then the pain started, the pain that I had been blissfully free of for such short moments. Blood covered my body, and I couldn't find the strength to move. Sam fell to his knees beside me. Bruises covered his face and chest. His eyes were wild, but when he touched me, it was gentle.

Heven?

I'm still alive.

A single tear fell from his eye and trailed down his ash-streaked face. *I thought The Devourer wanted to eat your soul.*

He ate the beast inside me.

Can I touch you? His hands hovered over me, unsure.

Please.

He gathered me close then buried his face into my neck and hair. It hurt to be touched, but the look on his face when he thought I was dead was far worse.

Behind us, everyone let out a sigh and the dragon made a sound.

"Let me by," Gemma said. "The beast may be out, but she's still dying. Let me help her."

Sam moved away as Gemma began trying to heal me. The wound in my chest closed and I began to feel better, but I was still in a lot of pain and feeling very weak when she collapsed at my side.

"Just give me a second," she said. "You're in really bad shape."

"Gemma," Cole said, cautiously.

"You've healed her enough. She'll make it to Ana. She'll be able to heal her completely," Sam said, laying his hand on Gemma's shoulder.

Gemma nodded as Cole helped her to her feet.

Sam lifted me and climbed onto the back of The Devourer. I heard him talking to Cole and Gemma, but I was too out of it to make out their words. Before I knew it The Devourer was taking off and I did what I could to hold on to my life.

* * *

I was hot, so incredibly hot. I felt like I was in the center of a burning flame with no way out. But then Sam was there. He was so close I could feel him breathe. He whispered words of love through my mind and held me as closely as he dared until I began to cool and come out of the pain.

When I opened my eyes, I saw that I was lying in a bed, a huge white bed with a breezy white canopy draped overhead. Sam was with me, lying far enough away so we didn't touch. I knew then what I had felt earlier was the Mindbond. He managed to get in so close without any help from me and he held it there, soothing me and bringing me back.

I sat up, shocked that I felt great. All my limbs bent and moved without effort and the pain in my chest was gone. I held out my arms and was surprised to see only thin, silvery lines from where the beast had clawed me.

They must have fed me the flower tea. The heat I felt had been it healing me. I was alive. I had made it.

I looked over at Sam, the huge smile on my face falling away. He looked horrible. Bruises covered his face and body and deep circles ringed his eyes. When was the last time he slept? He sat over me most nights, vigilant, ready to chase away whoever came to torture me. He took down a family of rabid, deformed hellhounds to give me a chance to live and then he exhausted himself further by using our Mindbond to draw as close to me as he could while I healed.

A tear fell from my eye and I wiped it away. "Oh, Sam."

I brushed the golden hair from his face and leaned down to kiss his cheek. His eyes flashed open and his body tightened. When he saw me there, he relaxed.

"Heven?"

I nodded and smiled. "I'm better now. The tea worked."

He launched himself at me, pinning my body to the mattress. *Don't ever do that to me again,* he said as he peppered my face and neck with kisses.

I giggled and he groaned. *I didn't think I'd ever hear that sound again.*

Everything is fine now. We're fine.

He kissed me then, a kiss of epic proportions. A kiss that would linger on my lips and in my soul for months after it was over. He kissed me like he might never again and then he kissed me like he couldn't get enough. When he was done, he laid his forehead against mine and sighed.

"I need to shower."

"You need to stay in this bed."

I laughed even as desire filled me. "I'm covered in blood and dirt and I smell."

"I don't care."

"I do." And I cared that he obviously hadn't drank any of that tea to heal his injuries. "Come on." I slid out from under him and stood, thrilled that all my strength was back. I tugged his hand so he would follow and grabbed the white silk robe at the foot of the bed.

"Where's Ana? You need some of that tea."

"Uh-uh," he said, pulling me back into his chest. "I'm fine and we're not going out there."

"Why not?"

"Because I have to be alone with you for a while. I…"

I put my hands up to his lips. "I know. Me too." Then I frowned. "You're hurt."

"I feel so much better now." He kissed the pads of my fingers.

I eyed the spa-like bathroom attached to the room. "Let's shower. But later, you'll have some tea?"

He went over to the nightstand and picked up a half-empty mug. "How about I just finish this one."

"We've had that all along and you haven't drank it?"

He looked appalled. "I was saving it in case you needed more. This is your second cup."

It took almost two mugs of that tea to keep me from dying? The horror must have shown on my face because Sam's face darkened too. "It's over. Don't think about it."

I nodded and pushed the thought away. I held out my hand and he took it. "I'll wash your back if you wash mine," I said and smiled.

* * *

A long time later we left the bedroom, fully dressed in new clothes that we found in the huge closet just off the bathroom. I felt amazing, better than I had in a long time. My hair was down and shining and I was dressed nicely but comfortably in jeans and a lightweight lilac-colored sweater. Before entering the great room, Sam pulled me back and pressed me up against the wall to kiss me as he had a thousand times since we got here. Every time it left me breathless.

He grinned and pulled me away from the wall and I couldn't help but think how gorgeous he was in his black polo and jeans. The bruises on his face had healed from the tea and the hardness in his eyes was gone, leaving only the warm honey color I loved.

Ana was in the great room, sitting on one of the large couches that flanked the fireplace. I was about to call out to her when I saw Riley. He was inhaling something out of a bowl while Ana watched him, fascinated. Riley sensed us before Ana did and he stopped to look up. His eyes went to

Sam first, then flicked away to settle on me. "She lives," he quipped.

"Yes. I want to thank you all for everything you did to save me."

"We're very glad that you are all right," Ana said, unfolding her legs and standing. "I made soup if you would like some."

"What is he doing here?" I said as she walked through the room and into the kitchen.

"The Devourer went back for your friends. This is the most company I have ever had!" Ana said with delight.

"Everyone is here?" I said as the French doors opened and Logan, Gemma and Cole came inside. "Is that allowed? Will you get in trouble?" I worried us being here was breaking some kind of unspoken code.

"This place is amazing!" Gemma said, a joyous smile on her face. She had never looked so much like an angel as she did right now.

Ana began ladling soup into bowls for everyone. "Yes, this is just fine. They are all here to help you, just like me."

Logan ran over and hugged me. "So glad you're okay now."

"Me too. The Devourer knew exactly what to do," I said.

"The Devourer is a very special creature," Ana said, handing out the soup. Everyone took a seat on the couches and on the rug by the coffee table.

"I thought The Devourer was about to eat her soul," Sam admitted.

"Do you know why The Devourer eats souls?" Ana asked.

"I've always wondered about that," I said, tasting the soup. It was really good.

"That way the princes of hell cannot take them and use them for power."

I felt my mouth drop open. It was brilliant. In hell, The Devourer was the most feared creature. When it appeared, even Beelzebub took cover. They let him eat what he wanted because they thought it would keep the beast calm. Little did they know The Devourer was only trying to diminish some of hell's power.

The Devourer wasn't a creature to be feared, after all. It was to be celebrated.

"He's amazing," I murmured.

"You two have a special bond." Ana agreed.

I wasn't sure about that, but I did like The Devourer and was grateful that it got that beast out of me.

Riley made a rude noise. "Dragon," he muttered.

"How did you get that dragon to give you a ride anyway?" I asked him. The last time, The Devourer wouldn't let him near him.

Riley shrugged.

"The Devourer can sense darkness within anyone. He will not allow anyone of that nature onto this island. Perhaps he sensed that in you. Perhaps something within you has changed?"

"Riley hasn't changed," Sam said flat.

"Maybe he wants to," Ana said, looking at Riley, who finished off his soup, then burped.

No one said anything else as we finished off our soup. Once the bowls were put away, I turned to Ana.

"I think I know my purpose."

Ana smiled.

"But I need your help."

"Of course I will help you. What do you need?"

"I was hoping you could tell me."

Ana inclined her head and long wisps of blond hair fell over her shoulder to frame her angelic face. She waited for me to explain, but something stopped me. I looked over at Riley. I wasn't sure he needed to know what we were up to. He betrayed us. He betrayed me. Who's to say he wouldn't do it again?

"What are you doing here, Riley?" I said point-blank.

His very dark eyes that were really blue looked at me. It was a level stare, but I couldn't read what was behind his eyes. "I think it's obvious."

"Is it?" I lifted an eyebrow. Beside me, Sam leaned forward. "He was at the farm, Hev. When you passed out. He saw me rush out of the house with you and drive away. He got Cole and Gemma and found me at the fountain."

I, of course, didn't remember any of this, but Sam seemed to give him the benefit of the doubt. I looked at Sam. "I'm surprised you let him near any of us."

"You were dying. I was going into hell alone, where I thought I would most likely be attacked by Beelzebub. Riley is a hellhound. He knows Beelzebub's tricks. He offered to help. I was in no position to turn him down."

"Do you trust him?" I asked Sam in a low voice.

Sam looked at Riley, then at me. "Nope." But then sighed. "But he did help get you here."

I looked at Riley. "Whose side are you on?"

"Mine."

Well, he certainly never tried to convince me he was a good guy. That actually worked in his favor. Maybe that's why he acted that way.

I looked at Gemma who looked back and nodded. I know she was telling me to trust my gut, to do what I thought was right.

"You still want that curse broken, the one Beelzebub put on you, right?"

Riley nodded, all trace of sarcasm gone.

"What if my plan could help with that? Could we trust you not to betray us again?"

"Yeah," he replied, his voice low.

I glanced at Sam. He seemed as wary as I. The truth was, having another hellhound on our side would help us. It was going to be hard to take down Beelzebub, to lock him up. Riley would be a good ally to have.

"Fine, you're in," I said.

Then Sam pinned Riley with a look. "And if you betray us, I won't kill you. I'll let Beelzebub do it."

I looked at Sam, confusion on my face. But Riley seemed to know what he was saying and he nodded, grim.

"Here's what we're going to do…"

* * *

Everyone was on board with mine and Sam's plan to trap Beelzebub and then set my mother and the other stolen souls free. Now we just needed to figure out a way to trap him.

Riley, who had been fairly quiet up until this point, spoke up. "I fail to see how this plan helps me get rid of the curse that binds me to Beelzebub."

"It probably won't get rid of the curse," I said honestly. "But if Beelzebub is trapped and his power is greatly diminished, then he won't be able to order you around. Your life will be your own."

Riley thought about that for a minute. Then he shook his head. "It's not enough."

"Why?"

"Because he thinks breaking the curse is the only way to get rid of his anger, his rage." Gemma spoke up quietly. "Even if Beelzebub is leaving him alone, the curse will still be there."

"That's a bunch of crap." I looked at Riley. "I've seen the good in you. It's there. It's your choice whether you let the good out over the bad. You can turn away from the anger and rage inside you. You choose not to and you use the curse as an excuse."

Riley's eyes lit with anger and he sat forward. Beside me, Sam stiffened. "You think it's easy to walk around with a curse?" He growled.

"No. I don't." I glanced at Gemma. "I also don't think it's easy to be a fallen angel, to be stripped of what you were meant to be and sent to earth and live alone because the man you love died." I glanced at Logan. "I don't think it's easy to have to live with the things you did when someone else was in complete control of your body." I glanced at Sam. "Or to be tossed out of the only home you had ever known because the devil twisted part of your soul before you were born. To fight against that part of yourself every day, yet accept it at the same time."

I looked back at Riley who was looking at me with no emotion in his eyes. "And I certainly don't think it's easy to walk around disfigured, to be murdered, brought back to life and then basically have a target placed on my back because I'm trying to do the right thing." I lifted my chin. "If you think any of us are going to excuse the bad choices you've made or feel sorry for you because your life has been so hard, think again. Look around. Every single one of us has problems. Only you choose to let that corrupt you."

No one said anything for long moments and then Riley got up and went out the French doors, going to the end of the patio to stare out at the sea.

"If we're going to trap Beelzebub, I think we should trap Hecate with him," Sam said, his arm sliding around my waist and pulling me into his side. *I'm proud of you.*

I'm proud of all of us. "It's a good idea. She'll try to stop us too. She probably gets her power from those souls too."

"Is there a way to bind her powers, Ana?" Gemma asked. "I've looked in my books and haven't found anything."

"I can help you with that," Ana replied.

"How?" I asked eagerly.

"The dried petals from the flower can be ground down into a fine powder and when blown on Hecate, her powers will be bound."

"Do you have any dried flower petals?" I asked.

"Yes. I will get them." She went from the room.

"How are we going to trap them?" Cole asked.

I frowned. "I don't know. It would need to be somewhere that Beelzebub couldn't break free." An idea began to form in my mind when Riley came back into the room.

"In or out?" Sam asked him.

"In." He sat back down on the couch and glanced at me. I nodded.

Ana came in the room carrying a small fabric bag and one of those mortar set things to grind down the dried petals. She set everything out on the wooden coffee table and sat down on her knees in front of it all.

"The reason this works is because the flower petals harvest the light and energy from the sun. The sun is the single most important thing on this planet that gives life to everything. Hecate uses her powers to seek and destroy life, to taint it. The flowers are dried, which concentrates the sun's powers. When it comes in contact with the kind of energy Hecate gives off, it automatically reacts to replenish itself, the life she tries to steal, and binds whatever it is that she harnesses."

We all watched in quiet fascination as she took out four dried petals from the bag and placed them in the stone dish and ground them down into a fine, sparkling golden dust.

When she was satisfied, she poured the dust into the fabric pouch and some of it danced in the air around her. She laughed.

I caught Riley staring at her when she handed the pouch to me. "Here you are, Heven. I give you the power of the sun, a power you also harness inside you."

I took the pouch. "What do you mean?"

She smiled. "I think you know."

I didn't, but we had to go.

"Thank you, Ana," I said sincerely. "For healing me and giving us a place to rest, for this." I held up the pouch.

"It is what I am here for," she said kindly.

"How long have you been here?" I asked.

"This island has been hidden here since the creation of hell."

"How old are you?" Riley asked, making a face.

Ana smiled. "Not that old. My mother was once the keeper here. When she died, I took over."

"You were born here?" Sam asked.

Ana nodded. "Yes. I was raised here too."

Had she ever been out of hell? Did she even know what lay beyond this island?

"You must be really bored," Riley said.

I rolled my eyes. "Riley can't stand to be bored."

"I like it here," Ana said simply.

"I like it here too. We all do." I stood and hugged her. She seemed surprised, but then she returned the hug.

"We should be going," Sam said from behind us. I pulled back and reached for his hand.

"Can we come back to visit you?"

"I would like that."
"Assuming we live long enough," Riley intoned.
"I have faith in you," Ana said. "In all of you."
I only hoped that our plan was strong enough to work.

Chapter Twenty-Six

Heven

The Jeep was exactly where Cole left it. The Devourer delivered us right to it and I was shocked it was still in one piece. Everyone climbed in as the dragon watched.

"I wish I had some candy bars," I muttered, trying to think of a way to keep The Devourer from leaving.

"Here you go, sis." Cole tossed me a bag from the back seat. It was filled with Snickers bars.

"Awesome." I unwrapped the candy and dangled it out the window. The Devourer rumbled closer and snatched the candy from my fingers. "Good boy," I told him and unwrapped another.

Riley drove slowly and I kept holding candy bars out the window so the dragon would follow. When we started to run low, I began to worry, but then I saw the looming shape of Beelzebub's ominous castle in the distance and I knew we would make it.

All of a sudden a terrible ripping sound filled the Jeep and the canvas top was torn away and went flying with great force into the air.

"Shit!" Riley yelled as he slammed on the brakes. Dust and ash from the ground whipped up into the air and wrapped around us all like a heavy fog. The Jeep fishtailed before coming to a stop and we all sat there in menacing silence. Logan began coughing from all the ash and his thin shoulders shuddered as he tried to stop. Sam wrapped an arm around his brother as I strained my eyes, trying to see through the ash, but it was too thick and we were forced to wait until it settled.

I prayed that The Devourer didn't fly away in the chaos. Then the laughing began. It was sick and sinister, dark and mean. It could only belong to one person. To the Prince of Demons.

Sam wrapped his hand around mine and held my fingers tight, as if he were afraid I might be snatched away.

"Can anyone see where he is?" I whispered.

The ash was settling and I knew in just mere seconds he would be revealed to us.

He laughed once more and we all turned our heads in the direction of his voice. I could make out the looming shape standing just yards away. Doubt and fear crept into my mind. Could we really pull this off? The Prince of Demons was no joke. He was the most powerful man in the underworld. He'd been torturing me for months. He killed my mother. Was I really sure this plan could work? Was I just putting everyone I cared about in even greater danger?

Then the ash was gone and we could all fully see him.

"There you are," he said, reaching out a hand to me. I felt the familiar squeeze in the back of my skull. It was his way of reminding me he was still in my head, that he still had control over me. "I thought you'd be dead by now."

His new body was just as good-looking as the last, but his soul ruined it. It didn't matter how beautiful the person he found to live in because he was ugly inside and it always showed through. He was larger than before, with broad muscled shoulders and arms. He had sandy brown hair that was pulled back into a ponytail at the base of his neck and a square jaw covered with stubble. He was dressed in black slacks and a white button-up shirt with the sleeves rolled to the elbows. I took a moment to feel sorry for whomever he took this body from. What a sad waste of a human life.

I decided to meet this challenge head on and I opened the Jeep door and climbed out. Sam followed, keeping one hand tucked into the back waistband of my jeans. "It turns out that thing and I didn't get along very well so I got rid of it."

His eyes widened, then narrowed as he took in my well appearance and began screaming for Hecate. In that moment he reminded me of a spoiled child screaming at his mother for something he wanted but couldn't have. She appeared beside him, wearing a long, dark cloak.

My friends all gathered around me and the five of us stood in a line to face these two villains together. I looked off to the side and was incredibly relieved to see that The Devourer was still nearby.

"How did you get that beast out of you?" Hecate asked, coming closer, as if to study me. "What have you been up to?"

She was far more astute than Beelzebub. She could sense that we had found a source of power and she wanted it. She knew that we were more resourceful than he gave us credit for. After all, why else did she follow us the first time we went to the island? She, too, must be searching for the 'life' of hell, for the power it would give her. Thank God she didn't know what we did. It was all the more reason she had to go down with Beelzebub. She would only get closer until one day she stumbled upon the secret.

As she drew closer, Sam shifted his stance so he was half in front of me, using himself as a shield. Hecate cackled and threw her hand out, sending Sam flying backward through the air.

"Don't you have any new tricks?" I asked wearily. "That one is so old."

She smiled and used her invisible power on me too, yanking me closer. She grabbed my face between her fingers and squeezed, looking into my eyes.

I stared back, refusing to back down, praying Sam wasn't hurt.

"She's mine," Beelzebub said from just behind the witch.

She threw me on the ground away from her and I scrambled to my feet to go after Sam.

"Where do you think you are going?" Beelzebub grabbed my arm and yanked it hard. I felt something in my shoulder pop and give way, but I didn't cry out. This pain was nothing compared to what I suffered before.

"I always knew you were tough. You do belong here," Beelzebub said the words in appreciation and ran a finger down my cheek. I resisted the urge to spit on him.

"But first, I must have the name."

"I'm not giving you the name."

"So you do have it?" He lifted an eyebrow. "What will it take to get it from that pretty little head of yours?"

He glared at me, a sadistic grin splitting his face. I braced for the blow, but it never came. Instead, he raised a hand and I heard a roar behind me. I turned to see Sam's body, now a hellhound, suspended in the air. He didn't appear hurt, but as he hung there Beelzebub pulled out a dagger and tossed it into the air. The dagger buried into the dark fur of Sam's side.

"No!" I screamed and threw myself at Beelzebub. I caught him off balance and we fell. Out of the corner of my eye I saw Sam fall to the ground and launch himself at us.

Riley was there, knocking me out of the way and creating a clear path for Sam to pounce on Beelzebub. Hecate went after Cole, using her magic to send him flying backward into a rock. He got up instantly and charged at her, daggers appearing in both his hands.

I didn't know where to look. Sam and Riley were fighting Beelzebub and Cole was fighting Hecate. I saw Gemma take out her bow and take aim at Hecate so I launched myself into the fight with Sam.

Beelzebub threw Riley back and away, then did the same to Sam. Instead of doing the same to me, he grabbed me by the throat. I kicked and fought as fiercely as I could, but he just stood there, holding me, laughing. Then he looked into my eyes and pain burst through my head. I tried to look away, but I was suspended by his stare. I couldn't hear anything and my eyesight began to dim. I felt as though my head might fall off my shoulders.

Sam knocked into him from the side with an enraged roar and took a huge chunk of flesh out of Beelzebub's face. I fell back, stunned.

Sam pinned him to the ground and tore into his flesh like he was an excited kid on Christmas opening a gift. Beelzebub screamed and fought, but Sam wouldn't back down. Riley stood off to the side, pacing, waiting to pounce.

"Heven, hurry!" Gemma called and I turned. She shot Hecate through both shoulders with two arrows, pinning her to a large rock. The witch closed her eyes and began chanting, my brother stood nearby, bleeding from his mouth.

I dug the pouch out of my pocket and rushed forward, stopping just in front of the chanting witch. I hurried to pour the dust into my palm and then I held it up.

She opened her eyes and paused in her chant. Her eyes focused on the golden dust I was poised to blow and she gasped. "No."

I blew the dust, emptying my lungs of air, and prayed it would do what we hoped. The dust floated out of my palm and danced around the witch. It looked like millions of golden lightning bugs playing on a warm summer night. She began to scream and cry as the dust clung to her clothing and skin. It shimmered around her and I imagined it was heating against her skin and causing some sort of burning sensation.

"What have you done?" Hecate screamed, and I knew then it would work. Before my eyes she seemed to shrivel. She didn't get smaller, but the air around her did. I wasn't sure how old she was, but suddenly she looked far older than she had before, her skin becoming paper thin and taking on a translucent cast.

Once she stopped screaming and had slouched against the rock, I knew her powers were bound and we were safe from her evil.

I heard a cry behind me and I turned. Riley was lying unconscious a few feet from where Sam and Beelzebub were fighting. Sam had yet another dagger sticking out of his side and I could tell he was beginning to feel the pain. Beelzebub tossed him away and came toward me.

"What would it do to your soul if I killed him?"

Sam lunged, baring his teeth and sinking them into the flesh of Beelzebub's shoulder. Sam fell back, making some sort of choking sound, and Beelzebub chortled. He looked vulgar and disgusting standing over Sam. He was bleeding from so many places I had no idea where he was injured. His arm hung from his body, barely attached, and his face was completely destroyed. Yet he was still standing. Sam made another gagging sound and blood poured from his mouth. Then something covered in gore fell out of his mouth and he collapsed.

Beelzebub made a tsking sound. "You should have been paying attention." He picked up the glob that fell from Sam's throat and wiped it on his pants. "You never know where I might hide a razor blade." He laughed. "I bet those really hurt going down."

Oh. My. God.

Beelzebub tossed the blade onto the ground and stalked toward me.

Run, Heven, Sam said.

I wasn't going to run. I'd had enough.

Beelzebub looked at me and smiled. Then he pulled a dagger out of his bootleg and turned to face Sam. "Give me the name."

From out of nowhere, Logan launched himself at Beelzebub. He leaped onto his back and used a dagger that was in his hand to stab him in the shoulder. Beelzebub screamed in agony and rage. He reached around and grabbed Logan, slamming him down onto the unforgiving ground. Sam got up on wobbly legs, but fell back down, coughing up more blood. Beelzebub laughed and raised the dagger over Logan's body and I threw myself at him. We rolled across the granite floor. Beelzebub landed on top. "The name!" he screamed, holding the dagger high.

"Heven!" Logan cried fiercely and charged Beelzebub, who turned and buried the dagger into Logan's chest.

"No!" I screamed. "No!"

Beelzebub twisted the dagger and laughed. "Give. Me. The. Name."

Logan looked at me with wide, unblinking eyes. Shock registered on his face.

"Okay, I'll tell you."

Beelzebub turned to me, still holding the dagger and Logan in the air. I closed my eyes, asking my memory to call up the picture of the Map. It came easily as Logan began to cough. Warm droplets of blood splattered my face. I began to cry.

Then I saw it. The name.

It was scrawled right next to the words Soul Reaper.

I opened my eyes.

"Let him go," I demanded, proud of the even tone of my voice.

Beelzebub viciously yanked the dagger out of Logan and dropped him onto the ground. He lay there, unmoving. I scrambled to his side and took his face in my hands.

"Logan!" I said as his eyes fluttered open and he looked at me.

"Are you all right?"

A sob ripped from my throat. "Yes, thanks to you."

Beelzebub grabbed me from behind, but then an arrow shot into his back and a dagger buried itself in his side. I looked behind him to see my friends advancing.

"Tell me the name or I will kill you all," he said as Sam raised himself up to loom behind him. His eyes were wild.

"It's me," I said, looking him straight in the eye. "I am the Soul Reaper."

And then Sam took him down. He did not get back up. Sam collapsed beside us and Gemma ran over and shoved her hand down his throat and grimaced. When she pulled it back out, she had two razor blades in her hand.

Sam shifted and crawled over to where his brother lay gasping and took his shoulders in his hands. "Logan."

Logan smiled.

"Gemma," Sam said, hoarse. "Get over here!"

"No," Logan said. "Let me go, Sam."

"What? No!" Sam cried, his voice hoarse. "We will take you to Ana. The tea, it will heal you."

Logan was shaking his head. "No. There's not enough time. And even if there was... I don't want to live, Sam. That stuff would only help someone who truly wanted to heal."

"You do want to live! Don't say that! *I* want you to live!" Sam looked up, his eyes were completely desperate. "Heven!"

I crawled closer and yanked out the pouch that held the dried flower dust I used on Hecate. Maybe this would work like the tea, or at least buy us some time to get back to Ana. I dumped what was left of it onto my palm and prayed it would be enough. Logan was shaking his head when I lowered my hand and gently blew the dust over him.

We all stood there silently waiting, watching to see if it would work.

The dust glittered and danced over Logan, bringing life into the air and then it floated down onto his chest, making him sparkle.

And then the sparkles faded and the dust turned gray.

Sam made a sobbing sound and grabbed at his brother's arm.

"I told you. I'm too broken." Logan smiled. "I was dying anyway. This is faster; it's easier. You have to let me go."

"No, I won't," Sam said. A single tear fell from his eye, making a track through the ash and dirt on his face.

"I made amends for everything I did. I was strong, like you."

I started to cry. He was such a good person, a strong person. He deserved better than this. Than death. I crouched down on his other side and took his hand in mine. "You're the strongest of us all."

Logan coughed, but then he smiled. "I learned it all from Sam."

"Gemma," Sam cried. "Please."

"Let me go," Logan said softly. "It's peaceful there. It doesn't hurt. I can already see the light… It's welcoming me."

Sam put his head down and began to cry. Logan grabbed his hand. "Don't cry for me. I'm going to be just fine. I love you."

"I love you too, Logan," Sam said, wiping his face with the back of his hand.

And then all the light, the life, went out of Logan's eyes. His body released the pain it held and his muscles relaxed.

He died.

We all cried. We all stood there looking down on the boy whose life was cut too short. We would never see him smile again, or watch his eyes light up at the sight of a new comic book. We would never again hear him laugh at his video game or find stashed candy wrappers all over the house.

We would never be touched by his love again.

Gemma was the first to move away. She went to Riley, who still lay gagging from the razors that Beelzebub stashed on his clothing and body. She must have healed him because he appeared, dressed and in his human form, beside us and looked down at Logan with sadness on his face.

Sam was broken. He sat clutching his brother, not saying a word, not looking at anyone. He simply sat with silent tears dripping off his chin. It wasn't the time for me to try to comfort him because there was no comfort I could give. Some pain just couldn't be taken away.

Behind us, Hecate made a sound and I looked up to see Beelzebub rise up off the ground where he had fallen.

The sight of him ignited intense anger within me. It swelled up so strong that my body turned hot. Sweat broke out across my brow and I took a deep breath. Beelzebub looked at me and grinned.

Heat rushed to the surface of my skin. I wanted him to suffer. I wanted him to know pain. I was so intent on destroying him that it took a moment to realize what was happening.

His screams are what brought me out of my trance.

His whole body was on fire. Flames engulfed him, angry white-hot fire melted the flesh off his bones, and he screamed once more. It was a scream I would never forget: blood curdling but angry at the same time.

He collapsed in a fiery puddle as we all watched in horror as he burned to death.

Slowly, everyone's gazes shifted to me.

I knew I was responsible. That I somehow lit our enemy on fire, but I had no explanation.

You have been blessed with the power of the sun. It is awakened in you. Use it with care.

Ana's words clicked into place. I knew exactly what the power of the sun meant now. Drinking that tea had awakened a new ability within me. An affinity for fire. The power of the sun.

Movement caught my eye and I looked up. The Devourer was positioned over Beelzebub's smoking remains and I watched as Beelzebub's immortal soul drifted up over his ruined body and into the air.

It was the moment we had been waiting for.

"Help us," I asked the dragon. "Please. All you have to do is what you do best."

I swear he understood me because when The Devourer looked up I saw it in his eyes. I nodded then said, "You can do this."

The dragon opened his massive jaws and everything around us began to tug forward, the force of his pull was so strong I stumbled even as I dug my feet into the ground. Dust and ash whipped around us, my shirt and hair were yanked forward trying to follow The Devourer's call. I pushed back the hair from my face and watched as Beelzebub's soul began to waver. Even he with all his power was no match for a mighty dragon.

Then, with great triumph swelled within me as the Prince of Demon's soul was sucked into the dragon and disappeared from sight.

Chapter Twenty-Seven

Sam

Death. I don't think dying hurts. My brother seemed to be at peace. Death is hardest for those the dying leave behind. The finality of death is what hurts, the absence that will be in your life until you die too. In my brother's case, it's also the horrible injustice of a life cut far too short. Of a boy who was so good, yet ended in such a terrible, tragic way.

I tried to protect him. I tried to give him what he deserved.

I failed.

All I could do now was honor his life—his sacrifice—by not wasting the life I still had.

But it hurt. The loss cut deep.

"Sam," Heven whispered, crouching down beside me. She didn't try to touch me and I could sense her wariness. She didn't know if I would be angry, if I would need to yell.

I didn't feel anything but sad.

I looked up into her blue eyes and felt some comfort. "I know it's hard, baby, but we have to go."

Our job wasn't finished down here and I'd be damned if I let that old witch and that psycho Beelzebub get away with anything else. Heven was holding some clothes, and for the first time I realized I wasn't wearing any. I looked down at the blood streaking my body. I had no idea whose it was.

"Will you stay with him?" I asked. My throat felt raw.

"Of course."

I lowered my brother's body to the ground and went to change at the Jeep. I wanted to mourn, but mourning would have to wait.

Once I was dressed, I had Riley pull the Jeep close to Logan's body and everyone climbed in. I held my brother with great care as I settled in the passenger seat and Riley began to drive.

"Go to the castle," Heven said as she coaxed The Devourer into following us.

"How do you know that oversized bird isn't digesting Beelzebub right this second?" Riley said, tossing the words sarcastically over his shoulder as he drove.

Heven turned her attention away from coaxing the "oversized bird" and hushed Riley. "You'll hurt his feelings!" she said.

He snorted.

"Beelzebub is immortal remember? I'm guessing that makes him indigestible."

"Wouldn't want that heart burn." Riley cracked.

No one else laughed. It might have been funny in a different situation but nothing about what was happening was funny to me. My baby brother was dead, we were in hell, and I just wanted this one plan to work. Heven went back to luring the dragon with candy bars and I went back to staring down at the body in my lap.

We stopped at the drawbridge and I stared up at the castle. Heven leaned into the front. "I can handle this. You stay here, with Logan."

I shook my head. I needed to stay with her. My brother died helping to protect her and me and I wasn't going to do anything to jeopardize her safety.

Gemma and Cole stayed with Logan's body in the Jeep while Heven, Riley and I climbed out. Riley went around to the back, where Hecate was basically half in, half out, and grabbed her lifeless frame.

"What happened to her?" I asked.

"I bound her powers, but when Riley tried to put her in the car she was struggling so he knocked her out."

"I think we should throw them in Kimber's cell," Heven announced.

"Do you think that'll work?" I asked.

"It's enchanted by Hecate herself to keep a soul in. Beelzebub is a soul. And Hecate is so weak and without power she won't be able to get out or break the spell that holds them."

"Let's do this," Riley said, walking toward the castle.

I looked at The Devourer. "He won't fit down in the dungeon. We need something to put his soul in until we get down there."

"Here," Gemma called. She reached into the pouch at her side and pulled out the box that held the amulet. Riley and I both stiffened when she took the amulet out and stuffed it into her pocket. She tossed Heven the box.

Heven caught the box and opened it, standing in front of The Devourer. "Sneeze," she told it.

I didn't think it would work. But the dragon seemed to understand and he did exactly what she said. He sneezed. The blackened soul of Beelzebub shot out and landed in the box. Heven slammed the lid shut and gripped it in her hands. "Good boy," she told the dragon and patted it on the nose.

The Devourer made a sound and then flew away.

"Let's go," Heven said and we all made our way to the dungeon.

"Kimber," I called when we approached her cell. "We're here to break you out."

Kimber appeared in the door and stared at Hecate, who was wrinkled and weak in Riley's arms. "What happened to her? And who are you?" Kimber said, looking at Riley.

"We need your cell," Riley said by way of greeting.

Kimber crossed her arms.

Heven stepped forward. "We found a way to bind Hecate's power's and trap Beelzebub in your cell. You need to put your soul back in your body so you can come out."

"I can't come out." She protested.

"Yes, you can." I reminded her. "Beelzebub said you were free. You just have to get your soul."

"How?"

Heven grabbed an unlit torch from the wall and stared at it until it roared to life with flames. I stared at her until she turned to me. "Power of the sun," she said. I nodded, remembering what Ana said. The sun was essentially a giant ball of flames so it made sense that an affinity for fire would be the power of the sun.

Heven held the torch up to the cell entrance so we could see farther into the chamber. Her soul was suspended against the far wall. I watched as Heven unlatched the door and stepped inside. "Hev," I said, reaching out to her.

"It's okay," she said softly and brushed her fingertips against mine.

She walked toward Kimber's soul slowly and then stopped in front of it. I watched her as she took a deep breath and then exhaled. She stared right at the soul, and I could hear the thoughts circle through her mind.

You are safe. You are calm. Go back into your host.

She repeated the mantra in her head slowly as she stared at the soul. I wasn't sure what she was doing and I didn't think it would work, but then something happened. The soul seemed to shudder and then began to move. Heven held up the hand that wasn't gripping the torch and moved it toward Kimber who was standing there watching in awe.

We all watched as the soul went toward Kimber and then absorbed into her body. Kimber stumbled back as her soul reentered her body. She gasped and fell to her knees.

Heven lowered her hand and smiled.

Several moments went by and then she looked up. "Well, that feels better." Then she looked up at Heven and said, "*Who* are you?"

Heven looked at me, then back at Kimber. "I'm the Soul Reaper."

Riley was the first to break the silence. He walked right into the cell and dumped Hecate onto the hard floor. She moaned. Heven took the box that held Beelzebub and sat it in the corner and then walked away, returning to my side.

We all watched as Kimber took a tentative step outside the cell and then she smiled.

I slammed the door shut, the metal making a loud clattering sound. Hecate aroused and saw what we were doing. "You can't keep us in here forever!" she cried as she got to her feet.

I pulled Heven back away from the cell door when Hecate came forward and lifted her hands trying to use her magic to open the door.

Nothing happened.

"Think it will hold Beelzebub?" Heven worried. "I didn't feel anything when I walked in and out of it."

As she spoke, the box burst open and Beelzebub's soul flung up toward the ceiling and bounced off. Then it shot toward the cell door and we all held our breath. I felt sick satisfaction when the soul bounced back into the room when it hit the cell doors.

"I'd say it works," Riley said.

"Stand back," Heven said and we all moved back. I watched in awe once again as the girl I loved seemed to center herself as a wall of flames burst up around the cell. Then she turned and looked at the three of us as we stared. She shrugged. "Just a little added security."

Gone was the insecure girl that would hide and cringe at the slightest of noise. Gone was the girl who didn't think she was strong enough to face her fears. This girl had strength that matched our greatest of enemies. This girl was no longer shy and timid, but powerful and confident. My chest swelled with love for everything she had been and everything she had become.

This girl was mine.

Heven

It didn't seem right that Earth looked the same as we left it only hours before. Because everything was changed.

Nothing would be the same again.

We had all suffered. Pain, betrayal and loss were emotions that cut deep and changed a person irrevocably. Death left a nasty stain on a person's soul. And I would know… being that I was the Soul Reaper.

I wasn't exactly sure what it meant, other than making me even more wanted by Beelzebub and probably every single prince of hell down there. But I also knew that I was meant for this. This might not have been the exact path I was to take, but this was the path I *chose*. I could do this.

We could do this.

I looked over at Sam, who was holding his brother's lifeless body in his lap. The sorrow that he wore cloaked him and I understood his pain. He deserved to mourn his brother. His brother deserved the respect of a funeral and I was going to make sure he got it. He looked up at me and I gave him a small smile, reaching out my hand and entwining it with his.

Riley pulled the Jeep onto the road that lead to Gran's and stopped. He looked in the rearview mirror at me and I shook my head. "Keep driving. Right up to the house."

"But Gran," Cole protested from the front seat and Gemma turned in his lap to look at me.

"I'm done lying," I said as Riley drove toward the house.

"Heven?" Sam said, his voice questioning.

"It'll be okay. Bring Logan," I said as I climbed out of the Jeep. Gran met us at the door as I was walking up the steps, my friends, my allies, behind me.

"Heven?" Gran said, taking in my horrible appearance, the people she didn't know and finally Sam, who was cradling his brother in his arms. She looked up at me with tears in her eyes.

"We have to talk, Gran. There are things you need to know."

Gran stood there a moment and then slowly opened the door. "And there are things I need to tell you."

Epilogue

Riley

I burst through the castle door with enthusiasm. "Honey, I'm home!"

The place was dark and smelled of stale death. I blinked my eyes, trying to hurry their adjustment to the dark. Every time I had been in this place, it was so dark I didn't really even know what it looked like.

There was a torch hanging on the wall and I grabbed it, setting it on fire with a lighter I pulled out of my pocket. The foyer around me illuminated and for once, I got to see what this place looked like. The walls were black unpolished granite and sconces filled with oil lined them. I lit those too, and the room actually looked bright.

I turned and looked back at the massive front door. It was black iron. Embedded in silver on the back was a large skull and crossbones. The door was flanked with black urns. Probably filled with dead people.

There was a black wooden console table against the wall coated in thick dust. It sat atop a floor made up of granite tiles in alternating colors of black and white.

I was a little disappointed there weren't bodies everywhere. "You'd think a guy would be greeted at the door," I muttered.

As if on cue, a demon shorter than Heven stepped into the room. He was wearing a little suit with a black bowtie and carried an empty silver tray. He seemed startled to see me standing in the foyer.

"The master is not at home," he said, looking pointedly at the door. He was bald, his skin was unnaturally white and his ears were too large for his head.

I pounced and threw the demon up against the wall, sending the silver tray clattering to the floor. "The master is standing right here." I growled.

"W-what happened to the old master?"

"I disposed of him," I said, getting into the demon's face, clutching at his shirt and pinning him against the wall.

"He can't die," the demon retorted. I held the flaming torch right up to the demon's face and its white skin seemed to melt away. The demon struggled, trying to get away, but I held him firm.

"I put him somewhere and he isn't coming back. Maybe you can hear the witch's screams in the basement?" I dropped the torch and ignored the flames as they licked up the demon's leg.
"Any more questions?"

"No, sir," the demon murmured, watching the flames reach out and burn up my leg. It didn't hurt and my skin was not melting as his was. When he looked up, there was real fear in his eyes.

I smiled. "Good, now go clean something. This place looks like shit." I shoved him away from me and picked up the tray to throw it at him. The demon cowered and scurried away, only for me to yank him back.

I got down into his face, let my eyes flash silver and growled.

"And spread the word there's a new ruler in town."

Cambria Hebert grew up in a small town in rural Maryland. She is married to a United States Marine and has lived in South Carolina, Pennsylvania, North Carolina and back to Pennsylvania again. She is the mother of two young children with big personalities, is in love with Starbucks (give the girl a latte!) and she is obsessed with werewolves. Cambria also has an irrational fear of chickens (Ewww! Gross) and she loves to watch Vampire Diaries and Teen Wolf. Her favorite book genre is YA paranormal, and she can be found stalking that section at her local bookstore. You can find her never doing math. It makes her head hurt.

Cambria is the author of the Heven and Hell series, a young adult paranormal book series. The series begins with *Before*, a short story prequel and is followed by the first novel in the series *Masquerade* and is followed by *Between* (A Heven and Hell novella), *Charade* (Heven and Hell #2), *Bewitched* (A Heven and Hell novella) and *Tirade* (Heven and Hell #3). The final titles in the series will be released in 2013.

You can find Cambria on Facebook, Good Reads, Twitter, Pinterest and her website http://www.cambriahebert.com for her latest crazy antics and the scoop on all things Heven and Hell.

To further your reading enjoyment,
please turn the page for an excerpt of
Dark Summer, a young adult paranormal novel
by bestselling author Lizzy Ford.

Excerpt from *Dark Summer*
by Lizzy Ford

Chapter One

Summer stepped off the stuffy bus, at once struck by the smog-free air and towering pine trees of the northern Idaho town. The sun shone gentler here than in her native Los Angeles, and the heat of noon was pleasant.

The bus driver pulled her bags from the storage compartment under the bus and left them beside her. She didn't meet his eyes, not wanting to tell him she had no tip money. The orphanage had paid for her trip via Greyhound and given her a meager ten dollars a day for food.

"My sister lives up here. She tells everyone to avoid the forest after dark," the bus driver said cheerfully.

Summer sneaked a look at him. He didn't look upset at her for not tipping, and he said nothing else about his odd warning. He boarded the bus with a smile, and the lumbering vehicle merged back onto the single, two lane road hedged by pine trees running through Priest Lake, Idaho. She looked at the run down school in whose parking lot she stood. It was closed down for the summer, the cement of the parking lot cracked and the field behind overgrown with grass.

A warm breeze swept by her. It smelled of trees and burning wood. Something else was in the air, something that tickled her body from the inside out. The breeze seemed to return and swirl around her, lifting the hem of her shirt and jeans. She pushed her top down self-consciously.

"Ignore that."

She looked up into the most beautiful eyes she'd ever seen. The teen walking towards her from the street was around seventeen with breeze-ruffled brown hair and eyes as clear and teal as footage of the Caribbean she'd seen on TV. His smile was bright and friendly, his skin and facial features indicating he was of Native American heritage. Around six feet tall, he'd begun to fill out, and his arms were muscular in the snug T-shirt he wore.

"You'll understand in a few days. This isn't a normal town."

She couldn't find her voice. Aware of how hard she was staring at him, she looked away as heat spread across her face.

"I'm Beck, the good half of the Turner twins. You'll hear about us, I'm sure. You have a name?" he asked.

She nodded.

"Well, what is it?" he asked with another of his infectious smiles.

"Summer," she whispered.

"Welcome, Summer." He extended his hand.

She hesitated then shook her head, withdrawing.

"No worries," he said. "But, just so you know, whatever your gift is, it's okay here. We all have them."

Summer looked up at him again, surprised.

"Come on. I was supposed to get my driver's license last spring, but, well, stuff happens. If I had known I'd be stuck walking to and from here picking up new people *all* summer long, I would've gotten it," he said with a sigh. He reached forward to take her suitcase and began walking towards the road.

She followed, curious about his statement about a town of gifted people.

"We all live at the boarding school," Beck continued. He grunted as he lifted her suitcase from the parking lot onto the road. "Do you play any sports?"

"No."

"Cheerleader?"

"No."

"Band?"

"No."

"What do you do?"

"Nothing really." *Except get ridiculed and kicked out of school after school for being different.* She hadn't had time to learn a sport, not when she switched schools every other month. The orphanage had run out of schools to send her to in Los Angeles and Orange County and banished her here. Beck wouldn't call her magick a *gift* when he saw what it did and how little she could control it. It acted out everywhere she went, sometimes knocking over full rooms of people as if they were shoved by an invisible hand and sometimes doing much more damage, like the fire two schools ago.

Summer looked straight up at the sky, marveling at the tall trees lining the road. The road itself looked worn and run down like the school, with faded lane lines and potholes filled with grass. The forest seemed to be trying to reclaim the human invasion. It had swallowed what might've one time been a sidewalk alongside the road and replaced it with orange, waist high tiger lilies and white daisies. Birds were loud without the constant drone of LA traffic.

She liked the feel of nature. Its subtle magick hummed in the air around her. Her eyes went to the forest again. She caught the movement of grasses and branches as someone with bright auburn hair darted from the gutter into the forest. Summer squinted, trying to see into the woods. She sensed someone there but saw no one.

Beck's soft laughter drew her attention. He was a good twenty feet ahead of her. She'd stopped in place and gotten lost in her head.

"Come on!" he said and began walking again.

Summer hurried to catch up, embarrassed at what the handsome boy might think of her after just five minutes with her. She always made the worst impressions. Staring at the ground, she focused on ignoring the woody magick and just walking. Like a normal person. Like someone who wasn't cursed with magick in her blood.

They walked farther than she expected, past a small string of ranch style houses, driveways to hidden homes, and a tiny strip mall with a convenience market, gas station and realtor's office. They kept walking until the road forked and the forest closed in on either side once again.

At last, they reached a dirt road leading off the paved street into the forest. Beck said a few curse words that made her blush as he struggled to roll her suitcase on the dirt road. Summer watched, amused, before her eyes went to the trees. They were so tall, their tops almost met in the middle of the sky above her.

Beck's loudest curse yet drew her eyes to him again. He shoved the suitcase onto its side, his earlier good humor turned into frustration.

"I'll bring one of the guys back to help me," he said. "I'll take you there first."

Summer drew near her suitcase, not wanting to leave the few things she did have. Mementos from her mother and father were in there, along with the pictures of the very few friends she'd made over the past sixteen years. Clothing, trinkets, an amulet from the only teacher who didn't turn on her …

"I'll help you," she said and bent to grab the bar at the bottom of the suitcase.

"This isn't LA. No one will take your stuff," he said.

"I don't want to leave it."

"Are you sure?" He looked her over. "You're kinda small."

She flushed as his eyes lingered on her breasts. She was small – in every way but *that* one.

"I can do it," she said.

"Well, it's my fault anyway for not getting a driver's license," he said with a frown. "Fine. I'll use my ESP to call my brother."

She waited to see him reach for a cell phone. He closed his eyes, held out his arms and went perfectly still for a few seconds.

"Just kidding. I don't have ESP," he said with another grin. "He was supposed to meet me at the school. He should be here soon. Don't be surprised. Decker's a little –"

"A little what, Beck?"

Summer turned to see the second Turner twin stepping out of the forest. Decker looked identical to Beck, except his eyes were as black as his clothing. Forest shadows seemed to cling to him, and she stepped back as he approached. Decker didn't smile like Beck did.

"I knew you'd be prowling the forests. A little help," Beck said, indicating the suitcase.

"This wouldn't keep happening if you'd gotten your driver's license."

"You don't have yours either."

The twins glared at each other before Decker strode forward. He and Beck reached for the suitcase and lifted it.

"Her name is Summer, by the way," Beck said.

"Has she – " Decker started to ask.

"No, Decker. Obviously, she just got here. She's from an orphanage in LA, and I think this is the first time she's ever been anywhere with trees. She's sixteen."

"Let the girl tell her own story, Beck," Decker snapped.

Uncertain what to do with the tension between them, Summer said nothing.

"*Do* you talk?" Decker asked, turning his attention to her for the first time. Though he was as handsome as his brother, his abrasive manner reminded her too much of the bullies she'd dealt with her whole life.

"Leave her alone," Beck replied.

Thank you! she cried silently to the nicer of the twins. Beck was hot and sweet. She'd never met someone quite like him.

They walked in silence down the winding road. The rocks made her twist her ankle more than once. She'd worn sandals, not expecting to hike to get where they were going, and blisters were forming on her heels. She tried not to limp, not wanting to cause even more trouble to them.

A sprawling log building came into view finally and she sighed. It grew larger the closer they got, until they stood on the front porch. Feet aching, Summer sat on the stairs of the porch and pulled off the sandals. The back of her heels were bloodied. She grimaced at the stinging pain.

"Why didn't you tell her to change shoes before dragging her three miles?" Decker demanded of his brother as they placed her suitcase down.

"I don't know what she's wearing."

The two stood over her. Summer shifted away and stood.

"I'm okay," she said, holding her sandals in her hand.

"I'll show you where the bathroom is," Decker said and swung open the screen door.

"I'm sorry, Summer," Beck said as she passed. "I'll get you checked in. The girls stay in the main house, so you don't have to walk anymore."

She smiled up at him, caught by his teal gaze. He held the screen door open for her, and she paused in the doorway, letting her eyes adjust. The door opened into a tall foyer flanked by an open living area on one side and a formal dining room with a table that stretched thirty feet on the other side. The house was log on the inside, too, making it feel warm and welcoming.

It was nothing like the orphanage, with its cement floors and walls and yard sale furniture. She took in the comfortable, worn leather furniture in the living area featuring a stone hearth and a huge flat screen television mounted on a wall. There were chairs everywhere, as if a group of people had been gathered around to watch a show.

Decker was standing in front of a door down a hall ahead of her, waiting impatiently. She moved into the house. The floors were wooden, covered in thick rugs that quieted her steps.

"Thank you," she murmured to the darker twin. The bathroom was huge with a small sofa on one wall, several stalls and a row of polished bronzed sinks on top of dark cabinets.

"Sit down," Decker said with abruptness. He followed her in and opened one cabinet after the other until he found what he sought.

Summer sat down on the couch. He filled a plastic bowl with warm water and a wash cloth and brought it to her.

"Oh, seriously?" Beck demanded, standing in the doorway. "Starting a little early, aren't you?"

"You want me to let her bleed to death?" Decker shot back.

"This won't change anything."

"Then why are you complaining?"

The Turner twins glared at each other, bristling. Summer stared at them, not understanding what the issue was. They looked ready to fight.

"I can do it," she said and took the bowl. "Thank you both."

"You heard her," Beck said and stepped aside, motioning to the door.

"After you, brother."

They left. Summer waited for the door to close then shook her head. Whatever sibling rivalry was between the two, they had it bad. She dipped a foot in the warm water and tried to work the blood off without touching her raw heel with the washcloth.

"I told the Turners to get their licenses," a woman said with a sigh.

Summer looked up as a pretty woman in a flowing dress entered. She was barefoot, and her ankle bracelets jingled with each step. She wore a dazzling turquoise necklace that matched her eyes.

"I'm Amber, one of those who will be overseeing your education. You must be Summer."

Summer nodded.

"I hope the Turner twins didn't scare you off already." Amber laughed.

Summer shook her head. She liked Amber. The blond woman had a large smile and sparkling eyes. Amber brought her a towel and sat cross-legged on the floor a few feet away.

"Our school is for children with special gifts that keep them from integrating into normal schools. A lot of behavioral issues are simply a lack of understanding by mainstream teachers about how unique some of you are."

"What do you mean?" Summer asked. "I don't have behavioral issues."

"We'll talk about it more later," Amber promised. "For now, just know this is a safe environment. We operate classes year round. The summer schedule is very relaxed, more like a college environment than the typical high school schedule. I think you'll enjoy it."

Summer looked down at her feet. She dried them without speaking. She'd never lasted more than two months in any one school. It was not a matter of her enjoying it; it was a matter of her and everyone around her surviving it.

So far, she really, really liked this place. It was beautiful and peaceful. Beck was the best-looking guy she'd ever seen, and Amber was far friendlier than any teacher Summer had ever had. With a heavy heart, she realized she couldn't get attached. In a month or two, people would realize what she was. They'd turn against her, as usual, and this wonderful place with the magickal breeze would be gone from her life.

"I'll show you to your room," Amber said.

Summer trailed her through the house and up a set of stairs that led to a second floor lined with doors. She heard the sounds of giggling from behind some of the doors and at least one television as she passed. Amber led her to the end of the hall and opened a door. Summer expected to see the sparse, prison-like sagging metal bunks of the orphanage and was surprised to see two twin beds separated by a nightstand. There was carpet in the bedroom, dressers on either wall, and closets. One dresser was littered with makeup and perfume. The windows above the beds were open, the blue-edged, white curtains matching the fluffy comforters on the bed.

She'd never seen a bed that looked so comfortable!

"Your roommate's name is Trinity," Amber said. "She's on vacation with her family right now. She'll be back before school starts in about a month."

Summer's suitcase was already beside her dresser. She set her purse on the bed and pressed her hand into the comforter.

"Dinner is at six downstairs. We have a few basic rules," Amber continued. "Dinner is mandatory during weekdays. After dark fall, no one leaves the house without an adult escort. Breakfast hours are from seven to nine and lunch from eleven to one. We keep chefs on staff, so you can order whatever you want. No smoking, no drugs, no candles, no pets, no food in the rooms. The television downstairs goes off every night at ten, but you can stay up as late as you want in your room. There's also a shuttle that leaves hourly to the store, resort, and a few other small stops around town."

Summer listened. She walked to the window beside her bed and pushed aside the curtains, gazing into the backyard hedged by two long rows of dorms. In the center were several fire pits, barbecues and picnic tables. As she watched, she saw the Turner twins appear. Beck went to the table with kids wearing jeans and shorts while Decker went to the table where everyone wore black. Two barbecues were going, and the kids at both tables were eating and laughing.

Where the property ended, the forest was thick and the trees swaying. She saw it again, the movement of someone darting into the forest.

"You can go down, if you'd like."

Summer jumped at the nearness of Amber's voice.

"No, thank you," she said.

"Go down and meet people," Amber insisted. "The Turner twins will introduce you around."

Summer's gaze went to the forest again. Someone was following her, had been since the bus left her. She nodded.

Satisfied, Amber smiled, saying, "Change shoes and go. Don't be shy!"

She left. Summer opened her suitcase and pulled out another pair of sandals, these sliding between her toes so as not to hurt her heels. She left the room and trotted down the stairs, exiting the front door.

Her new world amazed her. She found herself waiting to feel the magick she'd sensed at the school and gazing at the trees. The dirt road continued past the long dorms towards the forest. She walked to the end of the dorms then looked into the forest where she'd seen the dark figure disappear.

Summer stepped into the forest, at once intrigued by the sense of magick in the swaying trees. Sunlight splashed through the pine canopy onto bright purple bluebells that layered the forest floor. Small bushes hunched against trees and one another, and Summer stopped to try a few tart berries.

Continuing into the forest, she watched startled birds flit away above her. The brilliant color of a blue jay made her forget whoever it was following her. She followed the bird through the forest and into a small meadow filled with wildflowers.

She'd ever been anywhere as beautiful or magickal. Grinning, she ran across the meadow then twirled around in the middle of it, spinning amidst the wildflowers as she stared up at the blue sky. The breeze joined her, throwing her hair around her while filling her again with the warm, tickling sensation.

A dark figure crossed her vision. She stumbled and fell, seeking out the shape she'd seen. No one was there. She pushed herself up. A deep growl made her turn. Staring at her through golden eyes, a sand colored cougar crouched on the other side of the meadow. Its tail twitched.

Summer froze. The animal raised itself and took a step closer. Her heart hammered in her breast. She looked beyond it to the trees then recalled how foolish it would be to try to climb a tree to escape. A beast like this lived in trees.

The growl came again. The great cat lowered itself, bunching its body in a sign it was preparing to pounce.

Summer whirled and ran. The auburn-haired figure ahead of her disappeared into the forest. The growling and sound of pursuit stopped suddenly. She glanced over her shoulder and slowed. The cougar was gone. She pressed her shaking hands to her face.

It was early for hallucinations. She'd only just arrived.

"What're you doing here?"

She looked up, dismayed to see Decker there. He lingered at the edge of the forest, as if sunlight would disable the shadows guarding him. His piercing gaze was on her.

"I was just exploring," she managed at last.

"Do you know the way back?"

The way he said it made her want to tell him she did, so he'd leave her alone. Summer gazed around her. The forest looked the same in each direction of the meadow. She'd been too absorbed in the forest magick to consider where she went.

"I'm guessing no," Decker said. "I've had to rescue you twice today."

"I'm fine," she replied. "It can't be that hard."

"Until a cougar corners you."

She stared at him.

"They're usually nocturnal. The wildfires are driving them out during daylight. You should probably come back with me."

She shivered, sensing danger from him, the same danger she'd felt from the cougar. Only instead of pouncing on her, Decker wanted to lure her somewhere. The idea made no sense. Just because he dressed all in black didn't mean he was any more of a threat than his more cheerful brother.

"C'mon." He turned and walked into the forest.

With another look around, Summer trailed.

"You're rooming with Trinity?" he asked.

"Yes."

"When's your birthday?"

"Next month."

"So is mine." He stopped to look at her curiously. "What date?"

"Twentieth."

"I'm on the nineteenth. I'll be eighteen. I assume you'll be seventeen. Turning seventeen is a big deal here," he told her and continued walking.

"Seventeen? I thought most people considered sixteen the big year."

"Not here."

They reached the edge of the forest and the school property. He headed for the picnic tables, but she stopped.

"There's food," he said over his shoulder.

"No thanks."

"You're on your own. Stay out of the forest."

Irritated at his rebuke, she trudged to the road that wrapped around the dorms, not wanting to meet anyone just yet. Chances were, she'd be gone soon anyway. No use making friends. She went back to her room, and her spirits brightened. She'd never had her own room, even if this one was hers alone for a month.

Summer flung herself across the bed, sinking into it with a deep sigh. She'd never had such comfortable bedding, such a peaceful place to sleep. She eyed the dresser. While she'd had dressers, she'd never unpacked.

She unzipped her suitcase and pulled out the old wooden jewelry box holding her treasures. Her eyes went to the pile of jewelry and makeup on Trinity's dresser. Summer tentatively set her box on her own dresser and sat down, staring at it. It looked lonely and small.

Her sense of anxiety grew again, and she took it down. She didn't know how long she'd stay; it was easier to keep everything packed up. Picking out her least worn clothing, she set it on the bed for dinner then set her alarm and lay down for a nap.

Hungry for more? You can purchase *Dark Summer* in paperback and Ebook where all books are sold. Visit LizzyLand for more information on all things Lizzy Ford at http://www.guerrillawordfare.com.

Tirade